The Lake

Deborah Rine

D1372785

This book is a work of fiction. The characters, incidents, and dialogue are drawn from the author's imagination and are not to be construed as real. Any resemblance to actual events or persons, living or dead, is entirely coincidental.

ISBN-13: 978-1482642452 (CreateSpace-Assigned)
ISBN-10: 148264245X

Deborah Rine can be contacted at:

www.deborah-rine-author.com

http://dcrine.blogspot.com/

Face book and Twitter

For
Mary Lorraine
My mother

Acknowledgements

This is a book of pure fiction. It is loosely based on the lovely town of Lake Bluff, Illinois, but the characters and happenings come from my imagination. However, I would like to acknowledge the people who helped me in my research although I sometimes wavered from appropriate police procedure.

First of all, I would like to thank Diane Piron-Gelman, my editor, who took my manuscript to a higher level and kindly instructed me in the art of writing.

Thanks to Adrienne Fawcett, Founder and Editor of the *GazeboNews* who shared her story which was the basis for my character "Francesca Antonelli."

I would like to thank Deputy Chief Karl Walldorf of the Lake Forest, Illinois Police Department who spent several hours with me talking about the inner workings of a police department.

Thank you to Detective David Kowalski, of the Chicago Police Department who met me for a discussion of detective work.

Thank you to Steven Genyk, Chicago realtor, who gave me some key ideas to my plot.

Thanks to Rebecca Milos who did an initial reading of the manuscript.

Thanks to Daphne Dennehy for reading the manuscript and sharing her advice. And thanks for the encouragement of the girls in the CHS writing club.

Last of all, thank you to my husband Larry, the techy genius, who was helpful in a myriad of ways.

Loom large, sweet lake.
Dangerous and deceitful
You caress our souls and bodies,
Hiding secrets in your depths,
Willful winds disturb your surface
And in pain we must obey.

Prologue
Sunday morning, May 16th

The young woman and her dogs creep silently out of the house in the darkness. She is dressed in her running gear and casts a slim, black silhouette. The dogs are dancing on their leashes as they turn onto Banner Boulevard. No one is up yet and they own the streets.

There are no lights in the houses they pass. The morning papers are strewn on the dewy grass. The world is still—black and grey and colorless in the soft light. As they trot down the center of the street, the dogs pull on their leashes and her heart beats rhythmically.

When they arrive on the bluff, she removes the dogs' leashes and they plunge down the hill, sniffing and rollicking for joy. She walks down the steep stairs, holding on to the railing. At the bottom, she takes the path down to Lake Michigan.

The lake is grey and glistening. The water barely moves and she feels as though she could walk across its silent surface. The horizon is clean cut with a slender white line between the lake and the grey-pink sky. The water takes on a rosy glow and the dogs ruffle the surface as they plunge into the lake. They swim back and forth, like large-headed otters disturbing the mirrored stillness.

She turns south and walks along the water's edge. The spring air smells fresh and sweet. As she walks, the sky takes on a riotous explosion of colors. Shades of magenta, orange and fuchsia radiate from the east across the lake. She is going to witness a wonderful sunrise.

She calls to the two yellow Labs and continues down the beach. Here's the stone picnic shelter with its tables and rustic fireplace. Further along is the playground equipment. In a few weeks, when school is out, this beach will be filled with happy voices and splashing water.

At the south end of the beach there is a boat yard for small craft and then another stretch of beach shaped like a small bay.

"Bailey, Benjy, come on! Over here! Bailey, Benjy, come!"

They have found a ball and are tossing it in the air and chasing each other across the sand. When they finally do come, they are highly agitated. Both dogs sniff the air nervously. Benjy shakes and water sprays everywhere. Then they dash down to the water's edge, racing back and forth, barking furiously.

She can see something in the water, floating a short distance from the shore. It looks like a pale pink blanket. Benjy is whining and his tail is between his legs as he runs back towards her. Bailey has her ears back as she continues to bark frantically, racing along the shore.

What are they so upset about? She walks down the gentle incline to the water's edge. Now she can see more clearly. With horror, she realizes that she is looking at the body of a small child floating face down in the water. The blond hair is fanned out in the gentle ripples and the pink fabric moves rhythmically. A dress. It's a little girl.

She wills her body forward and staggers into the water. Part of her knows this child is dead and part of her wants to believe she can save her. The small, wet body is heavy and she can barely pick it up. She nestles the cold, white face under her chin and stumbles to the shore.

She sobs uncontrollably and then begins to scream. "Someone, help me! Help me! Oh please dear God, help me!"

Behind her, a golden sun appears on the horizon. A blood-red path streams across the water to the beach.

Snap that picture! Snap it fast!
Embalm the present! Make it last!
Capture time, imprison in gel
Use your iPhone, pad or cell.
Clip its wings! Nail it fast!
Yikes, you've solidified the past!

Chapter 1
Friday morning, May 14th

Rosie opened the screen door and found her pink Crocs by the front mat. They were still pretty muddy from yesterday's adventure in the ravine with Daddy and Jack. Jack scratched at the screen door and Rosie let him out. Together they went down the steps. Jack was a large golden retriever that often served as Rosie's self-appointed body guard.

At the bottom of the steps, she turned left towards Emma Boucher's house. Jack padded along behind her sniffing at all the wonderful new morning smells along the sidewalk. She looked at the little army of red tulips marching beside her. She remembered when Mrs. Boucher planted those tulips last fall. She had put down a pillow to kneel on so that her "poor old knees won't be the worse for wear." Mrs. Boucher always wore a house dress and an apron and they always smelled fresh and starchy. She even wore the dress when she was out planting tulips, when everyone else wore jeans.

Last night, Mrs. Boucher had called and asked Daddy if he could run up to Walgreen's to get her some cough drops and some cold medicine in a bottle. She was feeling just terrible. So Rosie and Daddy had got into the car and driven to Walgreen's. Since she had eaten all her dinner, including the yucky zucchini, Daddy bought her a chocolate ice cream cone at the Cool Cow shop on the way home. She had dripped ice cream down her dress and onto her car seat, but Daddy hadn't scolded her.

When they got home, he gave her the Walgreen's bag and told her to run next door. When Mrs. Boucher opened the door, she was coughing and her nose was red. She grabbed the bag and shooed Rosie away. "I don't want you to get this spring cold, honey. "No one should ever get sick when warm weather finally arrives in the Midwest. It's just not right! You run along home and tell your Daddy he's a dear."

Rosie was thinking about how bad Mrs. Boucher must feel. What could she do to make her feel better? She stopped and looked at the tulips. Poor Mrs. Boucher was stuck inside on this beautiful morning and she couldn't enjoy her tulips. Rosie decided to pick a big bunch. She leaned over and began to pick all the tulips along the sidewalk. When she had her arms full, she went and knocked on Mrs. Boucher's door. She knocked three times but she knew Mrs. Boucher couldn't hear so well, so she just left the tulips on the front mat.

Martin didn't realize that Rosie had slipped out of the house still wearing her baby blue Dora nightgown. He was puttering in the kitchen, getting ready to make some French toast and sipping his first cup of coffee. Tall and skinny with glasses perched on his nose, he embodied the classic absent-minded professor. He was dressed in old khaki shorts and a purple tee-shirt emblazoned with the logo "Banner Bluff College". He gazed out at the back yard, thinking that he should mow the grass on Saturday before he took Rosie over to St. Luke's Spring Fair.

He heard Rosie shout from the front door, "Guess what Daddy?" Lately, she had been asking "guess what" at an exhausting level. As she and Jack raced into the kitchen, Martin looked down at his five year-old daughter. Her blue eyes were shining and blonde curls framed her glowing face.

"I give up, Rosie," he said. "You just tell me."

"Daddy, I made Mrs. Boucher so happy. I picked all her tulips so that she can have them in the house since she's too sick to go outside."

"You did *what*?"

"I picked all the red tulips and put them on her mat because she wouldn't answer the door."

"Oh my God, Rose Marie; what have you done?" Martin went to the front window and groaned. Emma Boucher was going to have a conniption! All of those carefully planted tulips had been decimated by his darling daughter in ten swift minutes. He hadn't even heard her go outside. What kind of father was he? He decided he would wait until eight-thirty and give Emma a buzz. Meanwhile, he would run over and get the tulips and put them in a couple of vases. He decided to text his wife, who was in Paris at an international convention. She would probably think he wasn't keeping a close enough watch on Rosie.

He picked up his phone and quickly tapped out a message to Kate: Rosie has done it again—picked ALL Emma's tulips please advise love M

Susan Simpson stood at the kitchen counter sipping Earl Grey tea and mentally going through her day. Susan was the newly hired manager of Oak Hills, a golf and tennis club. Her college friend, Francesca Antonelli, had emailed her about the job opening. A week later she had flown in from California where she'd been assistant manager of the Rancho Cucamonga Park District. The interview had gone well and a month later she'd moved to Banner Bluff on the shores of Lake Michigan.

Today, there was a meeting with the Board at eight o'clock and after that she had asked the persnickety new chef to come in for a chat. He was not happy with some of the kitchen staff. That afternoon there was a meeting with a disgruntled club member displeased with changes in the tee-time registration policy. Keeping everyone happy was turning out to be a major part of her job description.

She put her cup in the sink and took a peek in the fridge. It held a lonely container of vanilla yogurt and a bunch of tired-looking green grapes. If she could leave Oak Hills early this afternoon, she hoped to make a trip to Appleby's Grocery store for the basics and a stop at Home Depot for some blinds.

She went upstairs and dressed, choosing a perfectly cut deep blue suit and crisp white shirt. Back downstairs, she applied lipstick in the hallway mirror and then checked her appearance. Slim and small-boned, her blonde hair swept into a chignon with tendrils framing her face, she looked every inch the attractive professional woman.

She picked up her purse and went into the living room. Unopened boxes stood in the corner and the sun was streaming in through the unadorned windows. Hopefully, this weekend she could finish unpacking and hang the blinds so she didn't feel like she was living in a fish bowl.

Friday morning! Francesca pulled herself out of bed with a groan. She had stayed up way too late researching an article about the Smithfield Conference Center for the *Banner Bee* and would pay the price today. She'd also had a glass of wine during dinner and another while she was working. Not a good idea when she had to get up and run this morning.

Wasn't that what life was really about, making decisions each day? Couldn't you parse out someone's life by the decisions they made: coffee or tea, brown shoes or black, Cheddar or Swiss, Fox or CNN? Maybe that was why people were often so dependable. If you did the same things in the same way every day, you could relieve yourself of a lot of decision-making and just float through life.

She reached over and turned off the bedside lamp that had bathed the room in a rosy glow all night.

In truth, Francesca felt the weight of all her decisions and she was pretty sure that they weren't always the best. Like her decision to marry Dan. Was that really a decision or just an inevitable happening? They'd been together during high school, college and Dan's law school years. Their marriage had seemed inevitable, and when she woke up one day and realized that they had very little in common, it was too late. The glue that had held them together was their shared upbringing, their families' close relationship and their mutual friends.

She reached down under the bed, feeling for her slippers. The wood floor was chilly in the early morning. She looked over at the wall above the antique maple bureau where a nondescript floral print hung on an angle. In that spot, there used to be framed photographs of their enormous wedding with umpteen bridesmaids and groomsmen. Soon after the honeymoon, they'd moved from California to Chicago. Dan was offered a job in a prestigious law firm. Francesca had studied journalism in college and ran the school newspaper. After settling into their new home, she was fortunate to find a job as the features editor for *The News Source*, a small suburban paper north of Chicago. Dan worked long hours and was rarely home. Meanwhile Francesca was chasing down charity fashion shows, local theatre productions and the latest Thai restaurant.

As the months went by, they grew apart. It seemed as though they lived on different planets. When they did find themselves together, be it a quick cup of coffee in the kitchen at 6 AM or a glass of wine at midnight, they were both too tired to think straight. Even sex became a chore and then something to avoid. Little by little their marriage evaporated. To Francesca, Dan no longer seemed a visible, concrete person. He floated in the periphery of her life.

Francesca slipped out of bed and went into the hall, turning off the bathroom and the hall lights as she went by. She padded downstairs in her old UCLA tee-shirt, her favorite nightgown these days, definitely not sexy but superbly comfortable. Dan had always wanted her in a skimpy, silky nighty.

The dogs greeted her as though she had just returned from a year-long trip to Antarctica. After a good-morning pat, she let them out to her postage-stamp back yard.

Why was Dan occupying her thoughts this morning? She remembered those colorless days. They'd stayed together for four years in limbo until Dan met the beautiful Jessica. Francesca had agreed to an uncontested divorce and a few months later Jessica and Dan were married. Now they lived in the western suburbs and had two children. Francesca knew these details because her parents insisted on keeping her informed. They could not understand what had happened. Dan had been part of their family for so long and they blamed her for the breakup.

She'd had the same conversation with her mother so often, she had it memorized. "We just didn't have anything in common anymore, Mom."

"What do you mean? You and Dan went to dances and football games all through high school. You talked on the phone every night even when he was away at law school. How could you not have anything in common?"

"We just grew apart. I can't explain it."

"Well, your dad and I had our problems, but we're still together after forty years. You have to work at marriage, Francesca. Maybe it's our fault, maybe we didn't teach you proper values."

"No, Mom. You and Dad did a great job." Francesca always sighed at this point, feeling helpless. "Dan and I never should have gotten married. We discovered we were two very different people."

Whenever she talked to her mom, she felt insufficient and irresponsible. How was it that she went through her day feeling very much a grown-up woman, but became a four year-old when she talked to her mother?

In the kitchen, Francesca fed the dogs and then made a small pot of strong coffee and heated some milk in the microwave. She carried a frothy cup into the living room. The sun was streaming in the windows and she could see the morning light glinting off the pond. There was a noisy family of geese swimming across the surface and the sky was a clear blue.

The living and dining room faced south and contained three French doors that opened to a patio. Along the windows were large pots of red and pink geraniums in bloom. They had spent the winter in this sunny room and soon it would be time to move them outside.

Dan and Francesca had bought this two-bedroom condo in Banner Bluff and agreed that Francesca would keep it at the time of the divorce. When Dan moved out, she encouraged him to take the beige sofa and his dark brown leather chair as well as the black and beige minimalist artwork. Slowly she had redecorated, buying her sofa and armchairs at Carson's and finding used lamps and side tables on Craigslist.

The living room was cozy and sunny and Francesca had filled it with bright colors. A large floral print by Monet hung on one wall and a couple of Georgia O'Keeffe flower prints on another. The sofa and chairs were a warm yellow, enhanced by orange, yellow and red-striped pillows.

The ideal thing about this condo was that she could walk to the village green and to her office, which was located above Hero's Market. Francesca was the Editor-in-Chief of the *Banner Bee*, an on-line newspaper that reported the news of Banner Bluff, Illinois. After Dan left she'd decided to try something new and different. The development of the *Bee* had been slow and tedious but she now managed a lively local website that received thousands of hits each day. Since its inception Francesca had realized little by little that she could do something on her own. She could be a success in her own right and not just someone's wife. It was a heady and self-fulfilling process.

Thinking about the office brought her back to the present and her need to get going on her day. She picked up her iPhone to check her text messages and email.

The first text was from Susan: run at liberty grove saturday 6am? She texted back: okay coffee after?

The next was from Marcus: How about Saturday dinner at Sorrel's - 7:30?

What should she answer? Marcus was nice, but so reserved and boringly dependable. They would have a pleasant time; but no fireworks. On the other hand, what else did she have to do Saturday night? She didn't want to think about work or how she was going to pay her bills. She did need a night off. She texted back: with pleasure—7:30—chez moi?

Marcus would probably bring her flowers. He knew she loved them and he would be the perfect gentleman throughout the evening. Why couldn't she just fall in love with him? He *was* tall, dark blond and handsome.

There was an email message from Frank Penfield, her helpmate and associate ever since she'd started the *Banner Bee* five years earlier:

> Hello Francesca,
>
> It looks like the city council is going to discuss the various options regarding the Smithfield Conference Center at the meeting on Monday night. If you like, I will attend and get all the info. I'll be coming into the office this afternoon and we can talk! Frank

> She wrote back, Deal- see you at 4 tea/cookies!

With no other text messages or emails to address this morning, Francesca ran upstairs to get into her running clothes.

Yahaira Gonzales pushed back the covers and slipped from the bed. Luis was still sleeping, his arms flung out and his mouth slightly open. He was gently snoring. He slept with the innocence of a child, his face free from worry.

Goodness knows they had plenty to worry about during the day. They both worked several jobs to make ends meet. It was rare that they were home at the same time. Yari worked as a cashier at Appleby's grocery store, but Andy, the manager, would never schedule her enough hours in the week, so she also worked at Hero's Market on the Green. Today, she was up early to get her tamales ready for the farmer's market. They had been popular last summer, as was her salsa that she sold in pretty flowered jars. This was the first market of the spring and she was hoping to make enough cash over the summer to cover the three-week baseball camp for Roberto and Raul.

Yari was 35 years old and she felt as though she'd been working all her life at one job or another. Her dream was to have her own Mexican restaurant. She loved to cook and she thought she would be a good manager, but where would she ever get money for that? It was hard enough just keeping the wolf from the door.

Mr. Smith would want the rent tomorrow and there was the payment for the Ford Fiesta due next week. She felt caged in, like a hamster on its running wheel, running and running but getting nowhere.

She stepped into the shower as her mind raced through everything she had to do that day. Every day was a juggling act between children and her two jobs.

She toweled off quickly and took a look at herself in the mirror. She still looked pretty good. Her figure was trim and her face had few lines, just some smile wrinkles around her deep brown eyes. Luis said she was still a beautiful woman; but he was prejudiced.

Yari dressed quickly in a denim skirt and a rosy-red V-necked tee-shirt. She swept her hair off of her neck in a tortoise-shell barrette and went down the hall to find her red flip flops.

It was kind of amazing, she thought, the difference between her morning and evening persona. Right now she felt super, as though she could conquer the world; but by ten at night everything seemed like too much. How great it would be if she could have this level of energy all day.

She peeked into the boys' room. It was a mess; tee-shirts, shorts and toys were strewn across the floor. The boys were bathed in the pale morning light. Roberto, like his father, slept with total abandon, his arms over his head and his legs splayed across the covers. Raul was curled into a tight ball, his little hands in fists. How different they were, yet such good friends.

In the kitchen, she switched on the light. As she started a pot of coffee, she wondered what had been bothering Luis last night. He had been there watching a Cubs game when she got home from her shift at Appleby's. The boys were already in bed and Luis had cleaned up the kitchen. She'd walked over and dropped a kiss on his head.

"Hola, mi amor. How was your day?" she'd asked.

Luis had looked up and given her a tired smile. "Same old, same old.

"Mine was exhausting. There was this problem with the bar codes and some of this week's specials were not entered into the system. What a nightmare! People are so impatient and downright rude." She'd stretched and groaned. "I've got to get to bed."

He'd smiled sympathetically and then looked back at the T.V. "We've got to talk tomorrow night, when I get home."

She'd been instantly alert. "Why don't we talk right now? Is there something wrong?"

"You're too tired now, Yari, and so am I. Don't worry. Tomorrow will be time enough."

She knew she couldn't budge him when he didn't want to talk. So she'd kissed him again and gotten ready for bed. This morning she had a vague sense of doom. What could be bothering Luis?

Kate Marshall was sitting at the Café du Jardin in the garden of the Musée Rodin when she received Martin's text message. This was her favorite place in Paris. Although it was in the heart of the busy city, the gardens provided a quiet respite. At the entrance, tourists stopped to take pictures of the statue of *The Thinker*. Inside they were mesmerized and slightly uncomfortable at the passion exhibited in the statue *The Kiss*. Kate found the sculpture highly erotic.

Today, she had the afternoon off from the conference on the Francophone World. She'd decided that what she most wanted to do was come here, stroll the gardens and relax with a cup of tea. She needed some quiet time to unwind.

The conference included educators of the French language from around the world as well as businessmen and government officials. Kate had been honored to be chosen to attend through her involvement with the Association of American Teachers of French.

Although the school year was not yet over, her principal, Harry Sanders, had urged her to go.

She had agreed to prepare a PowerPoint presentation for her students when she returned with pictures taken during her trip. She'd started with a photo of the departure gate: "Flight 2140—Paris, France—Departure time: 4:05." She'd also taken pictures of some of her fellow passengers waiting at the gate. There was the iconic Frenchman, complete with beret. Unbelievable! Who wore a beret nowadays? Then there was a picture of a gorgeous skinny girl who could well be a Parisian model and another of a handsome dark-haired French teenager. The girls would swoon over him. She even had a picture of the pilot. He was tall and stern with a no-nonsense way about him. During the last few days in Paris, she'd snapped pictures of monuments as well as people, cafés and pastries. She should have plenty of material by the time she got home.

She'd just finished a pot of tea and a piece of apple tart when she heard the beep of her cell phone. When she read Martin's text message, she couldn't stop laughing. Oh, her dear little Rose Marie, what would she do next? Kate could envision Rosie's little face beaming with pleasure and her arms filled with red tulips. She could also envision Martin, worried and perplexed. The conference would be over on Saturday and she would be leaving Sunday morning. She realized how much she truly missed her husband and her daughter. They were the heart and soul of her life.

She tapped out a reply: hang in there, home soon; maybe we need a leash for rosie, miss u love u

Chapter 2
Friday morning, May 14th

Emma Boucher was not asleep at seven AM when Rosie knocked on her door. She was upstairs in bed, doing the *New York Times* crossword puzzle and drinking a soothing mint tisane. She had the TV on with no sound. It was tuned to the Weather Channel and from time to time she would glance up and watch the meteorologists pointing and gesturing about the day's forecast. They managed to make every cloudy day seem like a major event. She liked looking at those attractive young women and she imagined that their skimpy dresses represented the latest in fashion. Tina, the little blonde with the sweet smile, had recently had a baby. She had been gone for six weeks and now she was back looking as though she had never given birth! She'd probably started on a workout schedule immediately so that she would be back in shape for her job. The brunette, Lisa, had perfect make-up. She didn't even have a wrinkle when she smiled. How did they manage that?

Emma sneezed and grabbed another tissue from the box beside her. Lord, she felt terrible but she was going to have to get up soon. She needed to make a batch of Snickerdoodles and a pan of her special mint brownies for the church spring fair. She had to do it this afternoon, because there would be no time tomorrow morning. Reverend Barnaby had asked her to be in charge of the bake sale and she planned on getting to St. Luke's at 8 AM to set up her sweet table. Her friend Louisa Gorton would be there too. Louisa was a terrible gossip and had something to say about nearly everyone. Emma was never sure how she learned all the juicy tidbits, but Louisa delighted in being the bearer of good news and bad. Tomorrow might be a very long day indeed.

When she had coffee made and the cereal boxes on the table, Yari went in to wake up Luis and the boys. She needed to be at the village green at six-thirty to set up her booth at the farmer's market and to lay out her wares. She had washed and ironed the red and green tablecloth last week. The cartons of tamales were ready to go in their coolers and she had packed the jars of salsa. Luis always helped her set up her booth before he went off to his job with the Banner Bluff Park District. Roberto and Raul would sit with her or play at the nearby park until it was time for school. Just a few more weeks, and they would be on vacation.

Roberto rifled through a dresser drawer. "Mom, where's my Mario shirt? I want to wear my red Mario shirt and I can't find it."

"Roberto, you wore that shirt yesterday and the day before. You can't wear it today! Wear the Star Wars shirt."

Raul spoke up next. "Mom, what did you do with my Nikes? I know they were in the hallway."

"Raul, you dropped your shoes by the front door and I nearly tripped over them last night!"

She heard the shower running and a few minutes later, Luis came into the kitchen in his dark green park district work pants and shirt. He was a short, powerfully built man with a ready smile and intelligent, warm eyes. People liked Luis and trusted him. He and Yari had met in Chicago in the Pilsen neighborhood ten years ago and had moved up to the North Shore soon after Roberto was born. They wanted good schools and a safe environment to raise their children. After much searching, they had found this apartment on the second floor of a small Victorian house. Mr. Smith, their landlord, lived downstairs and he was not averse to renting to Hispanics. His wife spoke excellent Spanish; she had been a Peace Corps volunteer in the 60's. The Smiths were friendly and loved the boys. Sometimes they would babysit in a pinch. But Yari didn't like to bother them.

After a rushed breakfast, the Gonzales family drove over to the village green, which was a hotbed of action. Brightly colored canopy tents were lined up under large shade trees. This was a small farmer's market, but it included a nice variety of fresh fruits and vegetables. There were several vendors of fresh flowers, and a man selling mushrooms both fresh and prepared in garlic oil. Several bakery stands offered blueberry scones, apple-cinnamon bread, chocolate chip cookies and fresh berry pies. A cheese man from Wisconsin displayed classic American cheeses as well as artisan goat cheese and domestic Brie. The Banner Bank and Trust provided free lemonade and today a Peruvian musical group was tuning up their wooden pan flutes.

Luis helped Yari with the table and the red and green canvas canopy while the boys ran to get some lemonade.

"Luis, I'm worried about what you said last night, that we needed to talk? Are you sure everything is all right?" Yari stacked the colorful jars of salsa on a tiered stand without looking up at her husband.

"Don't worry." He gently touched her arm. "I just need your advice. We'll talk tonight."

Luis kissed Yari goodbye and went off to work. Across the grass Yari could see her friend Francesca out on her run with her dogs. Francesca raced by dressed in royal blue running shorts and top, her dark curly hair pulled into a ponytail through the back of a Cubs baseball cap. She waved and rolled her eyes. She was sweating profusely and wouldn't stop to talk. Yari wondered if she could advertise her tamales and salsa in the *Banner Bee*. What would Francesca charge for a small ad?

Royce Canfield was not doing so well this morning. Usually great weather, manicured greens and rolling fairways were a recipe for happiness. But this morning he was feeling irritated at his partners. His swing was off and he was trailing the others. They were playing a skins game and he was losing. He did not like to lose. Royce was glad when the nine holes were over and he could escape the course.

After a shower, Royce, Harry and Bradley met in a quiet corner table in the Acorn Room for a short meeting and one of Chef Jeremy's delicious breakfasts. Tom Barnett didn't join them. He had to get over to the police station for a weekly meeting; he grabbed a cup of coffee and left.

Royce was served oatmeal with fresh berries and chilled guava juice. He didn't have to order it. The waiters knew exactly what he wanted. Royce was a control freak and he still weighed the same 190 pounds he had weighed in college. He was extremely careful with what he ate and drank. Moderation in all things was his motto. He was a tall man who carried himself with military bearing. Sharp, calculating eyes and an aquiline nose gave strength to his handsome face. He was a modern day Caesar who thrived on acclamation and praise, and his demanding demeanor was part of his success as a lawyer.

He expected the same level of self-control in his son Colman and his daughter Samantha, but rarely got it. This morning when he had looked into Colman's room on the way downstairs, the mess made him furious. Dirty clothes were strewn across the floor. Books and notebooks lay haphazardly in the corner by a book bag. Coke cans and empty Dorito bags cluttered the desk and bureau. His son was a slob and Amanda was not doing her job keeping after him. Royce had spent a fortune buying this house in east Banner Bluff and his son treated it like a pig sty.

He shook Colman awake and pulled off the covers. "Colman, do you hear me? Are you awake?" No response. Royce shook him again. "Get up and clean this room! Now! If it isn't in order when I come home tonight you'll be without wheels this weekend and maybe all month. Do you hear me?"

Colman mumbled, "Yeah, old man. I'm not deaf. Stop shaking me and get the hell out of my room."

Royce had trembled with rage, one hand rising to strike his son. Then he'd let it drop, horrified by his own action. These frequent confrontations with Colman were exhausting. Where had the curious and alert ten year-old boy gone? Colman used to be a good student and a great athlete. Now, he trailed around in a grey hooded sweatshirt and faded jeans, his mood alternating between sleepy disinterest and a belligerent glare. He had no ambition. He wasn't filling out college applications like the other high school seniors and he no longer participated in school activities. Royce didn't know who Colman's friends were anymore except for his girlfriend Carrie. He had seen the two of them in the kitchen last week. She could just as well be Colman's twin; dressed in a matching grey hooded sweat shirt and jeans. She came from a good family. Why didn't she dress like a girl should?

When he went downstairs, he found his wife Amanda sitting in the kitchen, drinking tea and watching *Good Morning America*. As he went out the door, he yelled, "Amanda, I want Colman to clean his room before he leaves for school and I want you to check it before he leaves. I told him I would take away his car keys if he didn't get the job done." He banged the door to the garage shut and then opened it again. "Amanda, you're responsible for him. What else do you have to do, anyway?"

She raised her hand in a mock salute. "Aye aye, sir!"

Royce frowned. "Just make sure he gets it done."

Amanda sighed and sipped her tea, not honoring him with so much as a glance.

Text message from Colman to Carrie: can't pick u up this am, no time, my dad is real asshole

Bradley Harrison eyed Royce's oatmeal and grinned. "Never anything different, huh? I know, I know. Why mess with what works?"

Royce looked annoyed, but Bradley ignored him. He'd been a friend of Royce's since they entered kindergarten. In grammar school, they were the bullies who controlled the playground. In high school, they both played three varsity sports and had their pick of the cheerleaders. Blessed with good looks, quick minds and well-off families, life had been smooth sailing for both of them. Royce had attended the University of Illinois and law school at Northwestern. Bradley had gone out east to Princeton and had come back to Chicago to join his dad's firm, Harrison Financials.

Brad's father had retired a couple of years ago and now suffered from advanced Alzheimer's. Brad kept telling his mother to put his father in the nursing home in Evanston, but she insisted on caring for him at home. She would call at odd hours and plead for Brad to come over and visit. Brad couldn't stand to see his father drooling and staring blindly out the window. It was visceral; he couldn't stand to go over there. He had offered to pay for a part-time nurse, but his mother didn't want anyone else in the house.

When he took over the helm of Harrison Financials, a couple of people had resigned. On the whole, they were employees that lacked vision and couldn't see the necessary changes he proposed. He wanted staff that was loyal and unquestioning. He was sorry to lose his father's administrative assistant because she knew intimately the day-to-day workings of the firm. But her barely concealed disapproval was something he didn't need. He hired a competent, unattractive widow who needed the job and whose desire to please caused her unquestioning allegiance. Now, there were elements of the business to which he alone was privy. This morning, Brad, Royce and Harry needed to discuss the latest developments of their little arrangement.

The waiter placed an order of eggs Benedict and home fries in front of Brad and a plate of bagels, cream cheese and lox in front of Harry. He refilled their coffee cups and then left them alone.

Brad asked Royce what was bugging him that morning. His game was off and he had been a bear to play with. Looking with distaste at his companions' choice of breakfast, Royce said, "I've just about had it with Colman. He's a slob, moody and disrespectful. I just about can't stand to be around him. My own son! I haven't had a civil conversation with him in months. Anyway, this morning we had another confrontation." He put down his spoon, clearly too agitated to eat.

"I'm glad Katherine and I didn't have kids. I wouldn't have the patience to deal with them," Brad said. He'd been married for five long years, but found it difficult to fulfill Katherine's demands and remain a faithful spouse. He needed his freedom. There were too many beautiful girls and he couldn't resist. After years of arguments and recriminations, they finally decided to call it quits. Katherine had moved back East, and he was totally free.

Harry didn't have kids either. He'd often said he and Sally didn't want children. Brad knew they were all about business and their marriage was one of convenience.

"So," Harry asked, "what are the latest developments? Who have you been talking to recently?"

Royce named two older women from St. Luke's who he thought were good prospects: Louisa Gorton and Emma Boucher. "Neither of them has any family nearby who could give us a hard time. Gorton is the only daughter of Alvin Rumour, the meat-packing giant. She lives alone in that big house a block from Lake Michigan. She doesn't live a life of luxury, but she's got to be rich. I took her out for lunch last Thursday. You know her, Brad; she's the busybody always hanging around the church office, playing Barnaby's handmaiden."

"What does she look like?" Brad asked.

"White hair in a bun, stylish clothes, lots of scarves and red-rimmed glasses. I did tell her that you were involved in this 'exclusive' business. She seems smitten with the idea of working with you. I think you should give her a call and clinch the deal."

"Oh yeah, I know her. I'll give her a call later today. How did you present things?"

"I gave her the facts and figures, told her she could make a lot of money with a reasonable investment. I said the company would take care of purchasing properties in foreclosure in exchange for a small fee or percentage of the purchase price. Then I mentioned I was working with you." He sipped his guava juice with a cynical smile. "She loved the idea of doing business with a member of St. Luke's and the owner and CEO of Harrison Financials; made her feel nice and secure, knowing she'd be dealing with fellow parishioners. I told her we'd manage her money in an escrow account, gave her a bunch of brochures with pictures of the homes we've bought. The whole works."

Louisa Gorton loved gossiping. Brad felt almost sorry for Royce, forced to listen to stories about church members they both knew. The luncheon must have been a tedious experience, but would undoubtedly be a lucrative one.

"Did she ask about our other clients?"

"I kept it a little vague. I don't think we want everyone talking with each other. I told her that we owed our clients confidentiality. We've got a great deal going here and we have to keep it moving."

"The American United Investment Club," Brad said, raising his coffee cup. "Here's to it, and to its continued profits."

Harry mostly listened as Brad and Royce continued their discussion. Harry's firm, Trustworthy Real Estate and Escrow, worked closely with the AUIC. How far he'd come, he thought, for a working-class from Skokie. He spent most of his miserable childhood working in his immigrant parents' deli and getting bullied by high school jocks. These days he was a man to be reckoned with.

Short and overweight all his life, Harry had earned the hated nickname Bubbles. "Hey, Bubbles, why don't you roll over here?" "Hey Bubbles, do you want to finish my lunch?" He'd spent a lot of time on his own, working on the computer his Uncle Joel had given him when he wasn't slicing pastrami or serving up blintzes in the shop. He mastered the intricacies of programming and became a hack, good enough to break into his high school's computer system and sneak a look at the grades of the jocks that he hated. The experience had made him feel powerful and superior. No one knew what Bubbles could do.

He'd put his geek expertise to work for his Uncle Joel, a real estate broker with three offices on the North Shore. Uncle Joel took Harry on in the hope that Harry could relieve some of his workload. Harry was a genius with the company finances and after a few years he took over the back office. He leveraged the company investments so that his uncle was making a nice profit… and if Harry didn't tell him all the details about the shadier deals, who did it hurt? Uncle Joel trusted Harry and gave him free rein. After all, Harry was family.

Thoughts of Uncle Joel brought up more pleasant ones of Sally, Harry's wife. She was an ace saleswoman, the company's top earner the year they got involved. Back then, Harry found her slightly frightening. She came on with a big, sincere-looking smile; but she was ice and nails underneath. One night while he was working late she'd knocked on the door of his office. He got up to unlock it and there she was, wearing a tight, low-cut black dress with a slim gold necklace and gold dangling earrings. Her black hair was pulled back in a chignon and her nails and lips were a wet red. Out of the blue, she asked him out for a drink. Feeling flustered, he had blurted, "Yeah, uh, sure. That would be great."

Until that night, Harry had never gone on a date, let alone been asked out by a woman. Sally didn't seem to notice his discomfort or the perspiration gathering on his forehead. As they headed out of the office, he realized Sally was about 5'7" just like he was. He wished he didn't have this bulky body. He wished he'd worn a clean shirt and pressed khakis instead of a Bulls t-shirt and jeans. He wished he could schmooze like his Uncle Joel.

They drove to O'Brien's on Dempster. The lights were low and jazz music was playing in the background. Sally suggested a booth. She sat down and patted the seat next to her. "Sit next to me, Harry, so we can talk. What would you like to drink?"

Harry swallowed hard. "I don't usually drink." He tried to think of something to order. "Maybe I'll just have a gin and tonic."

When the blonde waitress came over to take their order, she greeted Sally. They obviously knew each other. Sally must have invited other guys for a drink. Harry was probably part of a long parade of Sally's conquests.

"How did last Saturday go?" the waitress asked. "Did you close the deal with that couple from New York? They sure had a lot to drink; you could have sold them the Sears Tower by the time they left."

Sally laughed and said the closing would be in a month. She introduced Harry as her boss's nephew. Then the women laughed again, likely at some inside joke about Harry. *Whatever*, he thought.

Sally ordered gin and tonics for both of them. She was definitely in charge. When the waitress left, Sally leaned toward him and said, "Tell me a little about yourself, Harry."

Harry played with a cardboard coaster. "There isn't much to say." He couldn't help looking down at her round, smooth breasts cupped in the bodice of her dress. He quickly looked back at her face.

She had a slight, knowing smile. "What are your ambitions? Do you want to work for your uncle forever, or do you want to make some real money? Maybe if you went out on your own, you could do the things that you've always wanted to do."

"I don't know. I've never thought about it." He felt foolish. She knew he'd been checking her out. He felt like he'd been caught with his hand in the cookie jar.

The waitress brought their drinks and added some more nuts to the dish Harry had emptied. Sally raised her glass in a toast. "Here's to a fabulous new friendship."

Harry smiled, raised his own glass and took a long drink. He didn't know what was going on here. He felt out of his depth.

Sally moved closer. Her warm arm pressed against his. "Come on, Harry, you're a financial genius. We all see what you've done for your uncle. The numbers look great; but I was looking at the April statement…"

Suddenly alert, Harry took another swallow of his drink and felt the unfamiliar warmth spread through his body. Why was she talking about the statements? Where had she seen a copy?

"Harry," she said, "who or what is the WIC Company? Why do you pay them every month? What service do they provide?" She looked directly at him and he felt her hand on his thigh.

"They deal in office supplies," he lied. Sally was dangerous. What had he been thinking, going out with her? She'd either been nosing around on his computer or had seen the report he put on his uncle's desk. No, she couldn't get into his computer with all the firewalls he'd installed. How had she gotten into Uncle Joel's office?

She was still looking at him with that sardonic smile. "Harry, you're up to something. What about Gloss Ltd.? I can't see where they fit into a real estate company, but you're paying them a tidy sum each month."

Before he could respond, she leaned over and whispered in his ear. "You're cheating your uncle, aren't you, Harry?" He could feel

31

her warm breath on his cheek and those red lips tickling his ear. He was highly aroused and scared as shit. This woman must have broken through his elaborate passcode system. How else would she know he had set up those bogus companies and was making a nice little profit off them every month? Uncle Joel had so much money and wasn't paying Harry what he was worth. Harry was entitled to a little something on the side.

After Luis left Yari at the market, he drove over to the Banner Bluff Town Hall. He parked his car and went in to get the keys for one of the village trucks. Gloria Jimenez was there and asked how Yari and the kids were doing.

"I just dropped Yari off at the farmer's market. Roberto and Raul are great. They both want to go to baseball camp this summer. Let's hope we can swing it."

"They're both so cute. You're lucky to have such good boys. I'll have to run over to the market and buy some tamales during my coffee break."

He laughed. "Don't wait too long. They might all be gone. Hey, is Chief Barnett in his office?"

"He's at his golf game, but he does have a meeting with the Fourth of July parade organizers, so he should be along soon. I can tell him you're looking for him, if you'd like?"

"No, no. Don't bother. Maybe I'll drop by later. Have a good day." He went down the hall to get the keys off the rack.

Luis drove down the streets he knew so well. He was headed for the beach. Now that the weather had improved, part of his job was to clean up the beach and empty the garbage cans. The village owned a tractor outfitted with a giant rake that he drove back and forth across the sand to remove debris about twice a week. Sometimes, when a family had rented the picnic shelter, he had to clean up and do multiple garbage hauls.

When he arrived at the top of the bluff, he unlocked the gate and swung it back, then drove slowly down the driveway to the beach. He always had to be careful in case there were runners or dogs off their leashes. Since this access road represented the only steep incline in this flat part of the state, many runners liked to run up and down the hill to build stamina.

In the cement parking area, he stopped for a minute and gazed out across Lake Michigan. Small waves lapped against the breakwater and seagulls cried out as they swooped across the sparkling blue-grey surface. He loved living near this mini-ocean and delighted in the changes the weather and seasons brought to its appearance. Working down here in the early morning seemed like a gift.

He turned left and drove across the sand to the dog swimming area. An early morning walker was standing at the shore, his hands in the air, probably performing yoga or Tai Chi. Slowly he swung his arms up and then reached out towards the lake. His movements were smooth and rhythmic and his stance was one of supplication.

Luis got out of the truck and walked over to the garbage can. He removed the lid and pulled out the smelly bag containing baggies of dog poop, and then slung the bag into the back of the truck. He put in another plastic liner and then checked the supply of baggies for dog walkers.

He drove across the sand to the stone picnic shelter and checked it carefully. Someone had lit a fire in the fireplace last night; a few embers still smoldered at the back. The same person or persons were down here often. Periodically, he found roaches from pot smokers thrown behind the low stone wall at the back of the shelter. Two days ago, though, he had found some needles. This was definitely a different situation.

He was of two minds about what to do. He was pretty sure it was Colman Canfield and his girlfriend and that other kid, Craig Thompson. Those kids were up to no good. He had had run-ins with them since they were twelve years old and he didn't relish talking to them now. Should he go to Chief Barnett and involve the police? Barnett was a friend of Royce Canfield. Luis knew he would have Mr. Canfield on his case as well as Craig Thompson's dad, who was president of Banner Bank and Trust. Luis needed this job and was apprehensive about angering the powers that be. He wondered if he should try and talk to the kids first. Maybe he could talk some sense into them. He should have discussed all this with Yari last night. She always gave him good advice.

Luis looked around carefully and found an empty fifth of White Horse behind the woodpile to the left of the fireplace. Those kids had been here last night. He knew it.

They said he had been a puny, sniveling baby. For the first six months of his life he had screamed most of the day and night, suffering from colic. More than once his father had shaken him to get him to stop. Then his mother would scream and his father would toss him on to the shabby sofa and leave the house, slamming the door. For hours she would pace up and down the small living room cradling him in her arms and crooning sweet lullabies.

Chapter 3
Friday morning, May 14th

Martin dropped Rosie off at school. He watched her as she ran up to her friend Lilly and gave her a hug. The two of them looked like twins. They had the same curly blonde hair and sturdy little bodies. Holding hands, they ran into the kindergarten playground. He saw Rosie's teacher and waved hello. Then he left.

He had put three canvas shopping bags in the car. He grabbed them and headed into the farmer's market. He saw Louisa Gorton from church and waved, but decided to avoid talking to her. Unfortunately, that wasn't possible.

"Yoo-hoo, Martin, yoo-hoo. Is that dear wife of yours home from her trip?" Louisa yelled as she strode across the green. "It does seem as though she's been gone an awfully long time. How are you and Rose Marie doing? Didn't I see you at Walgreen's last night? Is Rose Marie sick? Maybe she's missing her mother."

Martin didn't know which question to answer first. He knew that whatever he said would be blasted around town within the hour. He tried his best to be cordial. "Hello, Louisa. What a beautiful bouquet of daisies. They do have great flowers here."

"When is Kate coming home?" she inquired.

"On Sunday afternoon." He paused. "I think I'll get a bunch of flowers too. Rosie can give them to her mommy when we pick her up! It's been nice seeing you. I'm in a hurry…"

"Martin, what is that Spanish lady selling over there? What are those things…food wrapped in corn husks? I can't believe anybody would eat them. They can't possibly be clean."

Suppressing his anger, Martin found himself crushing the handles of the shopping bags in his fist. In carefully measured tones, he responded, "Those are tamales. They're delicious. I think I'll buy some for supper tonight for Rosie and me. You should try them."

Louisa Gorton sniffed. "I have a tender constitution and I have to be careful what I eat."

"Well, I'll probably see you at the church fair tomorrow. Take care." He turned away, feeling proud to have escaped some of the usual interrogation. He could hear Louisa's piercing voice accosting someone else as he moved off.

After buying carrots, fresh peapods, and new potatoes, he headed over to Yari's stand. "Hello, Mrs. Gonzales. How are you?" He picked up a jar of salsa.

"I'm doing fine, Mr. Marshall. Would you like some tamales? I know Rose Marie likes them."

"Yes, please give me a half dozen. They make for an easy meal. Right now my wife is out of town, so I need all the help I can get."

Yari handed him his purchases. He added them to his sack and handed her a twenty-dollar bill. "When will Mrs. Marshall be home?" she asked as she handed him his change.

"Sunday! And it won't be soon enough! Thanks so much." Martin liked and admired this hardworking woman and her family. Here was someone fulfilling the American Dream.

Continuing his shopping, Martin bought a triangle of Wisconsin Brie and a chunk of white cheddar. He and Kate could have cheese and crackers Sunday night when she got home, along with a good bottle of cabernet. Across the aisle were some quart boxes of perfect strawberries, probably not local, but they perfumed the air. He knew Rosie and Kate both loved strawberries, so he bought a box. As Martin headed back to the car, he was almost run over by Colman Canfield. He jumped back on the curb as the red BMW raced around the corner, and got a brief look at Colman's petulant, angry face.

That kid was a disaster. Kate had to deal with him in French class, and he was often belligerent and rude. Kate always looked for the best in her students, and had told him she thought Colman's aggressive behavior masked a very unhappy young man.

Francesca came back from her run completely drenched. She took a long hot shower, enjoying the water running down her back. After toweling off, she put on a fresh pair of jeans and a peach-colored scoop-necked tee. In the drawer she found a filmy apricot and beige scarf that she wrapped around her neck. She would grab her beige linen jacket from the hall closet.

She debated on breakfast on the way downstairs. She should have some whole grain cereal and a banana, but she remembered the blueberry scones she'd seen as she ran by the farmer's market. She would walk over for a scone and take it up to the office. She could get coffee at Hero's.

It was a fifteen minute walk over to the office past Banner Bluff Elementary and through the village green. As she approached the school, the traffic was intense. She stopped at the crosswalk. A dark blue van was parked across the yellow lines, making it impossible to cross. The man in the van was staring avidly at the school entrance. Obviously a devoted parent making sure his little darling got into school safely. Francesca looked up at the driver, raising her eyebrows and gesturing with both hands. He looked down at her and yelled, "Sorry." Then he flashed her a dazzling smile and drove off.

Francesca shook her head and laughed. Another helicopter parent, she thought, hovering over his child.

When Colman arrived at the high school, he couldn't find a parking space in the student lot. After circling twice, he decided to park in the faculty lot. This was against the rules. *Screw it*, he thought. *Does anyone really come out to check? That fat security guy never gets off his ass to do anything.* It was almost the end of the year and he was a senior. *So what the fuck...* Colman pulled into a spot and locked the car.

He was still raging inside. After his dad left this morning, he had lain in bed feeling anger well up. When he finally got out of bed, he threw his pillow on the floor, and then swept the books and trash off his bureau. "There, Dad, are you happy?" he'd said as he kicked the clothes on the floor. He'd looked at his reflection in the full-length mirror on the back of the door. He saw his skinny body dressed in underpants; his hair hanging limp and the beginnings of a beard darkening his face. He looked like a maniac, he thought, a fucking maniac. He grabbed the golf trophy he'd won when he was twelve and threw it at that hated reflection. Glass came crashing down in a million pieces. Tears of anger and pain welled in his eyes.

First period was beginning and Colman walked into French class just as the bell rang. They still had the substitute teacher, Madame Berger. She'd sent him down to the dean yesterday. He'd been trying to get his friend Brian's attention by whistling softly, and she had stopped the class. "Monsieur Canfield, s'il vous plaît, would you stop disturbing theez class. I cannot teach."

She was actually from somewhere in France, which was why she talked funny. He had responded, "Madame Burger, that's because 'theez' class is fucking boring."

She had started to sputter, and then reached in the desk and pulled out a dean's referral. She'd scribbled his name on the form, her face red and her body trembling. "Theez is the last straw, Monsieur Canfield. Pleeze go down to the dean now."

He had grabbed his books and left the room amid a swarm of titters.

The dean, Mr. Johnson, had called his mom, who came in to school to discuss his behavior. Colman sat there looking at the floor while the dean berated him. He couldn't stand the pain and exasperation in his mother's eyes. He mumbled that he was sorry.

The dean continued. "There are only two more weeks of school for seniors; you're going to have to shape up or you won't be allowed to participate in the graduation ceremonies."

Colman couldn't have cared less, but his mom got all upset. "Come on, honey. You've only got two more weeks."

He'd agreed to apologize to Madame Berger and keep out of trouble for the rest of the school year. When they left Mr. Johnson's office, Colman had pleaded with his mom not to tell his dad. "He doesn't need to know. I'll shut up for the rest of the year. You can count on me. I'll be good."

Today, Colman had decided not to rub Madame the wrong way. He handed her the re-entry form and mumbled an apology before heading for his seat. He looked over at Brian and gave him a thumbs-up. Brian turned away and didn't smile back.

After class, he looked for Brian, but his friend had disappeared. Colman headed down the hall toward the Science wing where Carrie had her locker. They usually met there between classes. He saw her standing in the hall looking at herself in the mirror on the inside of her locker door. He moved over quickly and put his face next to hers so she could see his reflection as well as her own. "Hey!" He smiled at their reflection. The two of them looked like siblings with their sun-streaked, light brown hair and blue eyes. He whispered in her ear. "Hey, hot pants."

She didn't smile at him, but turned away and started rummaging in her locker.

"Hey, Carrie, like I'm sorry about this morning. My dad woke me up yelling about my room. I got so angry that I broke the fucking mirror on my door. God, what a mess. My mom had a cow."

"You're a jerk, Colman. I'm way tired of your crazy temper. You should learn to chill. After last night, I want to call it quits."

"What do you mean, last night?"

"You know, down at the beach. You were all over Craig and me. We were just joking around and you like went nuts. You like knocked me down and you almost strangled Craig."

"Come on, Carrie, I just don't want you guys making fun of me."

"Well, we weren't making fun of you. We were talking about someone else when you went ballistic. Listen, Colman, it's like, I'm," her voice wavered. "I'm afraid of you when you get high. You turn into some kind of monster."

"Carrie, that won't happen again. I'm sorry, really."

"Maybe you are, but I want out. Don't text or call me anymore."

Carrie slammed her locker door. Colman grabbed her arm as she walked away. She shook it off and hissed, "Don't you dare touch me, Colman Canfield." He watched her walk down the hall. Then he realized a group of kids was watching him. He gave them the finger and headed for physics class.

He nestled his head in her soft bosom. His sobs were muffled in her warmth. The smell of talcum powder filled his nostrils. She crooned to him, a wordless song, and stroked his head with soft, gentle hands. "You are Mommy's darling boy. Yes, you are the light of my life." She kissed the top of his head. He felt drowsy and warm.

Then big hands grabbed him. "What are you doing, Claire? Stop babying this kid! Damn it! I'm tired of his sniveling...always running to Mommy."

Big, rough hands yanked him to his feet.

Chapter 4
Friday afternoon, May 14th

It was two forty-five and Martin had been at his desk all day, grading term papers for his European History class. He felt brain-dead. They had been studying Europe in the 1830's, a time of revolution and change. They'd discussed the seeds of revolution scattered throughout Europe and compared it to the Arab Spring that was occurring right now in the Middle East. Some of the kids could take the readings and the lectures from the semester and put together a cogent argument. These well-written papers were a breeze to grade. Other students couldn't present a clear hypothesis. Their papers were impossible because Martin couldn't follow their train of thought. He found himself rereading the same paragraph over and over.

He stretched his arms over his head and yawned. It was time to pick up Rosie. He gathered his coffee mug and a plate with the remains of his lunchtime roast beef sandwich and chips. In the kitchen, he put the plate on the floor. Jack licked up the small corner of bread crust and the miniscule chip crumbs. Martin put the plate in the sink.

He decided to walk over to the elementary school with Jack. They had just enough time. As he passed Emma Boucher's house, he smiled. That morning he had taken over the vases stuffed with red tulips and rung the doorbell. Emma had come to the door, sneezing with a hanky in her hand. She had stared at him, dumbfounded, then peered around him at her front yard.

"My gracious, what happened?" she gasped.

He explained Rosie's logic; that she had wanted Emma to enjoy her tulips *inside*. He apologized profusely. It was really his fault. He should have been watching his daughter.

Emma had laughed until tears ran down her cheeks. "Please thank Rosie for thinking of me," she said as she sneezed into her handkerchief. "She is one of a kind!"

41

Martin walked along the sunny street. He looked up at the fresh, spring green leaves that had just appeared on the trees. One day the trees were barren and the next they were adorned with new foliage. Chicago didn't have much of a spring, so these few days had to be relished.

He arrived just in time to see Rosie come outside. She ran to him and he bent down to give her a big hug. Lilly Lawrence's mom had just arrived as well. Jan Lawrence was a pretty, nervous woman. Her pale blonde hair was cut in a perfect swinging bob and she was dressed in slim cropped pants and a creamy silk shirt. Her tentative personality and uncertain smile made Martin wonder what made her tick. She was the antithesis of Kate.

"Daddy, can Lilly come over to play today?" Rosie asked.

"Of course she can. That would be fine." Martin turned to Jan. "How are you, Jan? Are you guys going to the fair tomorrow?"

"Yes, we are! Will Kate be home in time?"

"No. She's arriving on Sunday afternoon. Rosie and I can't wait!"

"Are you sure you want these two wild ones this afternoon?" Jan asked. "They can be a handful."

"They'll be fine. You know, it's actually easier if Rosie has someone to play with."

Jan smiled and asked if it would it be convenient for her to pick Lilly up at five-thirty. Martin assured her five-thirty would be fine. Jan grabbed Lilly's purple Barney backpack to take home and told her daughter to be a good girl and remember to say her "thank yous" and "pleases." Then Martin, the girls and Jack made their way to the village green.

"Daddy, could we get a popsicle to eat on the way home?" Rosie begged. "Please, Daddy, please?"

"Okay, but I'll stay out here with Jack. We'll be across the street in the park." Martin gave Rosie five dollars and reminded her to ask for change, then watched as the two girls crossed the street, clambered up the stairs and disappeared inside Hero's Market.

Lilly liked Hero's Market. Mr. Hero always smiled at her when she came in. Today he joked with her and Rosie, saying they looked like sisters. That made them giggle as Rosie gave him the five dollars. "Don't forget to come back for your change," Mr. Hero said as they walked toward the back of the store where the Popsicles were.

They took their time getting there; they had to look at the candy shelves first. Hershey bars, M&M's and Skittles were lined up in irresistible rows next to pink candy bracelets and hard candy whistles. Lilly liked the bracelets best. She picked one up and tried it on.

She heard the door bang open as someone came in, then Mr. Hero asking, "What can I do for you." He didn't sound so friendly now. When Lilly heard who answered him, she knew why. It was that big boy, Colman Canfield. He wanted a piece of pizza and a Coke. Lilly felt glad that the tall racks of cards and magazines hid her and Rosie from view.

Lilly heard Mr. Hero walk away. "Let's go," she told Rosie. She didn't want to be here as long as Colman was. She led the way around the racks, hoping they could sneak out, and then stopped in surprise. Colman was grabbing money from the cash register; handfuls of it. He didn't even count it, just stuffed it into the back pocket of his jeans.

He looked up and caught Lilly staring at him. He came over and grabbed her shoulders. "If you tell anyone, I'll kill you. Do you understand? I'll find you and you'll be in big trouble," he hissed as he shook her.

Lilly started to tremble and then burst into tears. She was afraid of this big boy with the mean face, and she knew he was doing something wrong. Just then, Mr. Hero came back.

"What happened?" He sounded mad. "What are you doing to that little girl?"

Colman said, "This kid was going to steal a candy bar. I told her to put it back and now she's crying. You have to watch these little brats."

Mr. Hero handed Colman his pizza slice and took his money, then gave him change. Lilly didn't know what to say. Colman was staring at her, daring her to tell what had really happened. She felt too scared to say anything. She just stood there with tears running down her cheeks.

Mr. Hero came over and patted her shoulder. "Don't cry, honey. I'm sure you didn't mean to take anything. Let's forget all about it."

Rosie came up then, with two orange popsicles. "What happened, Lilly? Are you okay?" Lilly couldn't answer. She just stood there crying and looking at the floor. "Here, take your popsicle, Lilly," Rosie said. Behind them, Colman Canfield slipped out of the store. "Let's go outside with Daddy."

Martin watched the girls come out. He could see Lilly was upset. "What happened, Rosie? You were in there a long time."

Rosie frowned. "Daddy, that big boy was being mean to Lilly."

"What big boy"?

"The one with the red car!" Rosie said, peeling the paper wrapper off her Popsicle.

Martin had seen Colman peel away in his BMW, the usual scowl on his face. Second time today he'd seen that kid. Martin looked at Lilly, who was opening her Popsicle and avoiding his gaze. "Do you want to tell me what happened, Lilly?"

She shook her head "no" and began to lick her Popsicle. Martin gave her a hug and decided to let the matter drop. "Let's go over to the park and you guys can run around."

"Daddy, we're not guys, we're gals."

He laughed. "Okay. How about if I call you 'young ladies'?"

Francesca was working in her office above Hero's Market. It had been a long morning. Chief Barnett of the Banner Bluff police had called at ten o'clock to ream her out. "Let me get to the point, Ms.

Antonelli," he'd said, after giving his name and rank. As if she didn't know which Chief Barnett might be calling the *Banner Bee*. "Your police blotter yesterday contained several errors. This little blog of yours needs to get things straight if it's going to be a reliable source of information. You need to stick to the facts."

Francesca flushed with anger as she clutched the phone. "I have never overstepped the boundaries of my role as reporter. I do not fabricate information, as you're insinuating. And I don't have a blog, but a respectable online newspaper." She was fuming. "The names, dates and crimes were verbatim what I received from your office."

There was silence on the other end of the line.

"Why don't you check it out with Officer Kathy Hanson, with whom I spoke Wednesday? Then you can call me back and apologize." She'd slammed down the phone. Ten minutes later she'd received a brief email:

Apparently, incorrect information was passed on to you. It will not happen in the future.

No apology. *What a jerk*, Francesca thought.

Around noon, she'd gone down for a crispy square of spanakopita followed by a cup of Hero's homemade Greek yogurt sprinkled with fresh berries. They had a brief chat and then she'd gone back upstairs.

When Francesca had asked to take over this office space, she hadn't realized how much work was needed to make it livable. There was one big room, a closet and a very small bathroom. In the main room three large windows faced south onto the green and the park beyond. In the winter she could watch children and people walking in the park. In the late spring and summer, her view was blocked by all the green leaves on the trees.

Before moving in, Francesca had scraped off layers and layers of flowery wallpaper. As she worked, she had thought about all the people each layer represented. Probably, like her, they had felt excitement at redecorating this room. She loved older buildings like this one that had a history. She'd discovered a natural oak wood floor underneath the tattered carpeting. So she'd asked Luis Gonzales and a buddy of his to refinish the floor for her.   Then she'd painted the walls a fresh spring green and the baseboards and moldings sparkling white.

Now, it was a lovely room whose shiny floors reflected the dappled light that streamed in through the windows. On the walls were colorful prints of Capri and Venice. She had refinished an old wooden desk, which stood under the windows. There was a round wooden table in the center of the room and a small work table on the east wall, with two additional computers. Sometimes Frank Penfield worked here, as did Hero's granddaughter Vicki.

She used the closet to store materials, some file cabinets and her server. Behind a Chinese screen in the main room, she had put a small refrigerator and an electric kettle. On the shelves above the fridge were coffee mugs, a tea pot, teacups, sugar and her grandmother's blue and white cookie jar.

She heard heavy footsteps on the stairs and turned as Frank Penfield opened the office door. Frank was a large man in his late sixties. He had a full head of white hair and merry blue eyes, just like Santa Claus. His voice was low and gruff, but his manner was gently cheerful. "Hello there, beautiful," he said. "Now, when is my tea going to be ready?"

Francesca laughed, "Boy, you're demanding. Two teas coming up."

Frank Penfield had been a godsend. When she started the *Banner Bee* she had desperately needed someone to advise her about the newspaper business. He was a retired *Chicago Tribune* writer and just showed up one day. He didn't want to be paid; he just wanted to keep his finger in the news business. He became her business associate and she paid him in morning scones and afternoon cookies. He had become a very dear friend as well as an advisor.

She went over behind the screen and turned on the teakettle. She put some loose tea in an infuser and placed it in the teapot, then reached up for the cookie jar. Yesterday afternoon when she got home, she'd made molasses spice cookies. She knew Frank loved them. So did Hero and Vicki. She put six cookies on an antique rose-patterned plate and took down two bone china teacups and saucers.

She and Frank liked having tea in proper cups. She filled the pot with boiling water and placed it on the round wooden table to steep.

With their tea and cookies, they sat down to talk. They discussed the article Frank had written on the renovation of Sunnyside Park, and Francesca told Frank about the article Vicki wrote on high school Honors Night. "When you think that four years ago, I was tutoring Vicki in English; it is truly amazing how well she can write. I'm so proud of her."

"Well, I think it's great you're giving her a chance to be part of the *Banner Bee* staff. I'm sure Hero is as pleased as punch. You know, this is forcing him to become computer literate so he can read Vicki online."

Offering Frank another cookie, Francesca said, "I got an email today from Gloria Jimenez, the receptionist over at City Hall. She told me the Well-wisher struck again! Who could it possibly be?"

Over the last six months, someone in town had been handing out sums of money to needy people. Somehow, this anonymous person learned where there was a need and sent a cashier's check to the lucky recipient. A note was always included, signed: "Wishing you well." Francesca and Frank had reported on these happy occurrences in the *Banner Bee*. Once it was a fourteen year-old boy whose bike had been stolen at the train station. The bike was one he'd bought himself with money he earned doing lawns and gardening around town. The Well-wisher found out about it and sent enough money to buy an expensive Trek bike and a sturdy kryptonite lock.

Another time, it was an elderly couple living carefully on Social Security in a second-floor apartment with no elevator. They were finding the stairs impossible to manage until they received a check to pay for an Acorn stair lift and its installation. Now the Well-wisher had worked his magic again.

"Gloria said a girl who works at Appleby's Grocery store got money to buy a car! Can you imagine? This girl's car was totaled; she needs transportation to get to work and to drive her grandfather to his chemotherapy sessions down in Evanston. What a wonderful story!"

"Maybe you could ask Vicki to cover this? I know she normally only reports on high school events; but I bet she could handle this story." Frank reached over to stack the teacups and plate.

"That's a good idea," Francesca agreed. "Hey Frank, leave the teacups alone. I'll wash them up later." She trusted Frank with a lot, but not with her delicate china.

"Hello. Ms. Gorton's residence." Louisa's maid, Alma, answered the phone.

"Good afternoon. May I please speak to Ms. Gorton? This is Bradley Harrison."

"Good afternoon, Mr. Harrison. I will call Miss Gorton to the phone."

Louisa was actually standing a foot away from the phone; but she liked having Alma answer it. The old black wall phone had been there for years. She waited a minute to take the receiver that Alma was extending towards her.

"Who is it, Alma?" she said, stalling for time.

"Mr. Harrison, the investment man. You know." Alma shook her head in exasperation as she handed the phone over and went towards the kitchen.

"Good afternoon, Mr. Harrison, how nice of you to call." It was hard for Louisa to keep the smile out of her voice.

"Hello, Louisa. Please call me Brad, especially now that we are going to be business associates."

Louisa felt flattered. "Well, hello, Brad."

"This morning I had a meeting with Royce Canfield, who told me you were coming on board and joining the American United Investment Club. We would love to work with you."

"Well, I'm still thinking about this proposal. Royce is my lawyer so I do trust him, and I knew your father, but it is a lot of money to invest."

"Louisa, I would love to go over the figures with you and show you some of the real steals we've made this past year. All these foreclosures are a boon for people who have the money and are in the know. Rest assured, you're safe investing in the Club."

"Well, I guess I'll consider the investment. I just need to be careful."

"I understand. You're wise to be cautious. How about if we meet this evening at Sorrel's for a drink? Say, at five o'clock? If you feel that you don't want to invest, that's perfectly fine. On the other hand, if you want to join our exclusive little group, we can go over the details."

"That would be very nice, Brad, and five o'clock would be fine. I think I need to hear more about the actual houses that the Club has invested in recently."

They made their plans, and Louisa rang off. She was glowing with anticipation.

Brad hung up the phone and stared out his office window. He hated groveling to this silly, insipid woman. This was the worst part of these sales. But when he thought of the money they would make, he smiled. God, he was clever!

Emma Boucher was baking when the phone rang. "Hello," she said, picking up the phone with sticky fingers.

"Emma, it's Louisa. You will never guess who called me."

"I can't imagine who. The mayor or the President?"

"No, Emma. Bradley Harrison, that's who! He and I are having a drink at Sorrel's this evening. He is so...so debonair."

Emma was thinking of other terms: arrogant, shrewd and cunning. "That's nice, Louisa. Are you two good friends?"

"We're becoming close friends. Actually, we're business associates. I have been invited to be part of an investment club. Brad and I are going to go over some facts and figures tonight."

"What investment club is this?" Emma asked, worry and suspicion creeping into her voice.

"Oh, Emma, I don't feel comfortable talking about my private affairs. You understand, don't you?"

"I'm not prying." Emma said. "I just hope you're making a wise decision."

Louisa wasn't really listening. She started talking about what she was going to wear. "I think my blue linen dress. It makes my blue eyes just shine, don't you think?"

Emma rolled her eyes. Thank goodness Louisa couldn't see her. "I'm sure you'll look lovely. You'll have to tell me all about your big date tomorrow. Now, have fun! I have to get back to my baking."

"Goodbye, Emma, I'll see you tomorrow at the fair, I'll be there with bells on."

Emma hung up and thought about women. Were they all putty in the hands of handsome men? Here was Louisa at sixty-five, all aflutter at the thought of a drink with a much younger man. She wasn't acting that different from a fifteen year-old girl who had just been invited to the homecoming dance. "What should I wear?"; the timeless battle cry of women of all ages.

She did wonder if having drinks with Bradley Harrison was such a great idea; but she wasn't in a position to advise Louisa. Even though Louisa wanted to know about everyone else, she was amazingly secretive about her own life.

Mommy put the ice cream cone in his hands. She wrapped it with a napkin so it wouldn't drip on his clothes. It was a double chocolate ice cream cone and he took small licks so it would last. The ice cream began to run down the cone and Mommy said to lick around the sides; but he wasn't licking fast enough. Mommy was upset. He could tell.

Then one big hand grabbed the cone and another big hand slapped his head, hard. "Idiot, stupid idiot! You can't even eat a fucking ice cream cone! Claire, get him out of this car and wipe off his face. He's disgusting! And wipe off the car seat. God damn it!"

His father picked him up like a rag doll and tossed him onto the grass beside the car. His head hit the sidewalk.

"Please Stan, don't hurt him. He's just a little boy!" His mother was crying.

Chapter 5
Saturday morning, May 15th

Francesca met Susan in the parking lot of Liberty Grove. This enormous park, which had recently opened, held two man-made lakes contiguous to each other, surrounded by a figure eight of bike paths. In the summer, there were paddle boats and canoes to rent. A wide sandy beach curved at the end of one lake next to a fantastic playground complete with caves and climbing walls. On the hill above the lakes was an outdoor café with attractive wooden tables and chairs.

The young women ran along the bike paths at a comfortable rate. They discussed their jobs, yoga workouts, the latest *American Idol* competition and the men in their lives. "I'm going out for dinner with Marcus tonight," Francesca said. "I imagine we'll be going to Sorrel's or Trattoria Verona. Marcus is on call, so we can't go down to the city."

"Lucky you! He *is* a nice guy. He was in the club this past week when some woman slipped on the marble floor and went crashing down. She was wearing those high platform shoes, you know what I mean? Anyway, she fell with all her weight on one foot. She was crying and limping. I was going to call 911 when Marcus showed up. He settled her on the sofa and felt for broken bones. He calmed her right down and told her it was just a sprain. Later, he and I helped her out to her car. Of course, you know what I was thinking?"

"I know, lawsuit! Hopefully, Royce Canfield wasn't around. He'd be sniffing the air like a hound dog, smelling dollar signs," Francesca said with a laugh.

"Marcus wasn't just doing his job, though. He was truly kind to this hysterical woman. I don't know if all doctors are as caring."

"Well, I know all those things about him, but he doesn't set my heart racing. I think he might have a thing for me and I feel guilty about not reciprocating."

"No zing-zing?" Susan asked.

"No zing-zing, just lots of warm feelings."

They had reached the top of an incline and stopped talking to catch their breath. Below them was a rich panorama of sparkling water, green leafy trees and a perfect deep blue sky. They trotted down the slope.

"Well, Francesca, maybe this is the better way to go. Sometimes I think true friendship might make a better marriage than passion that lasts six months."

Francesca shrugged. "I'm not sure if marriage is on the horizon, but we do have lots to talk about. Marcus seems honestly interested in the *Banner Bee* and its workings and he's given me some great ideas for stories. He has a whole different perspective on life, which I do value." She paused, thinking. "I just don't want to lead him on."

"Just let yourself go. Enjoy Marcus and don't worry about where things are going. You're not responsible for his feelings."

"Yeah, I guess you're right. What about you? Haven't you met Prince Charming at Oak Hills yet? My goodness, that place is crawling with men!"

"You know what, Francesca? I don't want to mix work and play. It would be bad news if I dated someone and it didn't turn out. I would have to deal with them on a regular basis when it was all over."

The women rounded a curve and almost ran into Bradley Harrison. They kept running, but gave him a friendly smile. "Now, that guy is a hunk," Susan said when they were out of earshot. "I think he comes to the club, but I haven't been officially introduced."

Francesca grimaced. "Maybe that's just as well. He can be a real jerk!"

As they ran past, Brad was thinking Susan Simpson was hot; beautiful face and great long legs. He hadn't met her yet, but Royce had seemed almost in awe of her. She was running with Francesca Antonelli, the newspaper chick. What a pair! He turned around and watched them jog. They were like two matched fillies, their legs moving in unison and their ponytails swinging rhythmically. That Susan Simpson had one sweet ass.

Rose Marie watched her daddy mow the lawn. She knew he wanted everything to be just right because Mommy was coming home. She couldn't remember if it was today or tomorrow. This morning he had cleaned the bathroom and vacuumed the living room. He had gone up to her room and helped her put away all her toys and clothes, so that her room looked spiffy. She didn't know that word, but it must mean nice and clean. Last night, he had spent a long time cleaning the kitchen after supper. He had put away all the dishes that had piled up this past week and had washed the floor. "Now the kitchen is spic and span," he'd said. Rosie was thinking that the whole house would be spiffy and spic and span!

She was tired of waiting for Daddy to be ready. She had put on her yellow sun dress and her pink jellies and she was ready for the fair. She shouted to Daddy, asking if she could go over to St. Luke's by herself right now. He smiled and waved, but she couldn't hear what he said over the racket of the lawnmower. She decided he would know where she was, so she went through the side gate and walked up the street. She got distracted by an ant family living between the sidewalk slabs. She squatted and watched all the little ants coming in and out of their house. They were so busy. Everybody had a job. Maybe they were getting ready for a mommy coming home or a visit from their grandma.

At the corner, she looked both ways like Mommy said, and when no cars were in sight she crossed the street. Two blocks further, she skipped into the church parking lot. It was so exciting! At the entrance there was a giant slide to go down in burlap sacks. Set up in the parking lot was a Ferris wheel and lots of game booths with cool prizes. In the far corner was a face-painting booth and she could smell charcoal burning. There would be hamburgers and hotdogs and cotton candy. Under a giant oak tree there was a circular fence and inside the enclosure were five ponies to ride. Rosie loved the pony ride best of all.

On the wide lawn, was a big canopy. Under the yellow and white striped canvas, Rosie spotted Mrs. Boucher behind two long tables loaded with boxes of cookies and cakes and pies. Everything looked yummy.

"Hi, Mrs. Boucher," Rosie said when she walked over. "I don't have any money to buy cookies yet. I have to wait for Daddy. Are you still sick?"

Mrs. Boucher smiled at Rosie. "I'm feeling a little better today. Thank you for asking. But Rose Marie, does your Daddy know you're here?"

Rosie avoided Mrs. Boucher's gaze. "I got tired of waiting. He's mowing the lawn." She fidgeted, hopping from one foot to the other. "He'll know where I am."

"Rosie, I think we should call your Daddy and make sure he knows you're here. Okay?" She lifted Rosie's chin with the palm of her hand and looked into her eyes. "Your Daddy might worry about you."

Martin felt his phone vibrating in his shirt pocket. He looked down and was surprised to see Emma Boucher's name. He turned off the lawnmower to answer. "Hi Emma, what's up? How are you feeling today?"

"Hello, Martin. I'm all drugged up with cold medicine, so at least I'm not coughing and my nose isn't running. But Martin, I called because I'm over at St. Luke's and I have Rose Marie here with me. I didn't want you to worry."

"What? I thought she was in the house. You mean she walked over by herself? Oh, my gosh! Every time I turn around, she's wandered off. We had a big talk yesterday morning about always telling me where she was going and she obviously forgot all about it! You must think I'm a terrible parent!"

Emma laughed. "I don't think any such thing. You just have a very independent little girl! I'll keep her in my sights until you get here, okay?"

"Thanks so much, Emma. You're a gem. I'll hurry up here and get cleaned up. I should be there in thirty minutes."

"No problem, Martin. Rose Marie can help me set up my sweet tables."

Rosie hadn't wanted to be a naughty girl; she just didn't want to have to wait forever to come to the fair. "Can I help you, Mrs. Boucher?" she asked.

"You certainly can. I need lots of help because Mrs. Gorton isn't here. I wonder where she is? She was going to come early and help me set up."

Rosie helped put the individually wrapped brownies and cookies on platters. They decided to put all the pies together at one end and the cakes at the other end, and the bars and cookies in the middle. Then they put little price tag signs in front of each item. Mrs. Boucher had made them in beautiful squiggly writing that she called calligraphy. She had drawn a miniature flower on each one. Rosie thought they were *so* pretty.

When they finally finished placing everything just right, Louisa Gorton arrived, out of breath. "I'm so sorry, Emma. I overslept this morning. Remember, I had a big night last night."

"Not to worry, Louisa. I have a super helper. Do you know Rose Marie Marshall? She's Martin and Kate's little girl. They live next door."

"I certainly do. Isn't she precious with those big blue eyes and blond curls?" Louisa turned to Rosie. "Rose Marie, are you missing your mother? I don't think your mother should go away and leave you for such a long time."

Rosie's face clouded over. She looked down at her hands, twisting them together.

"This young generation of mothers has no sense of responsibility," Mrs. Gorton went on. "Kate shouldn't be gallivanting all over Europe when she has a young child at home."

Mrs. Boucher grabbed her friend's arm. "I think you should mind your own business, Louisa, and not upset this child. Use a little common sense!" she snapped. "You handle the cake sale while I take Rosie to the ticket booth." She took Rosie's hand and led her away from the table. "Come on, honeybun. Let's buy some tickets for you so you can go on a pony ride."

Rosie's face shone with pleasure. "Will you watch me, Mrs. Boucher?"

"I certainly will. Which pony do you want to ride; the shiny black one or the snowy white one?"

"Which one would a princess ride?" Rosie asked.

Martin: going to fair. rosie with emma. we miss u can't wait to see u tomorrow. LOVE M

Kate: flight arrives 4pm. I miss u both so much LOVE K

He looked at the baby who was sucking Mommy's breast. It frightened and disgusted him. Maybe Mommy would disappear? Maybe the baby would suck her away. He wanted to get in bed beside her and cuddle like he used to.

"Be careful, honey, don't bump the baby. Why don't you go downstairs and play in your room? I'm busy feeding Julie. Go on! You can play by yourself. You're a big boy."

Daddy said this was a good baby. "She's not a screaming brat like you were. We don't have to shut her up." Daddy liked to cuddle the tiny girl and even kissed her gently on the head. He hated Daddy.

He went downstairs. He hated his new room off the kitchen. It was small and dark. The baby was in his old room, upstairs with Mommy and Daddy. When Mommy came home from the hospital, she'd said that the baby needed to be near her upstairs. He hated the baby.

He was feeling very angry. He hated everyone. He even hated Mommy. He went into the kitchen and got the big knife. Then he went back into his room and grabbed the new teddy bear Grandma had sent. He put it on his bed and then he took the knife in both hands and stabbed the teddy bear in the face again and again. Then he stabbed it in the tummy and on the neck. He stabbed it over and over until the stuffing came out all over the bed. He knew he would be sent to the basement tonight, but he didn't care.

Chapter 6
Saturday afternoon, May 14th

Father Barnaby was feeling very happy. Here was a perfect spring day and the church grounds were bustling. The proceeds from the annual church fair went entirely to Missions and Outreach in the Chicago area. This year's fair promised to be a very successful event. These days, churches reflected the financial difficulties of society at large. Fewer people had pledged this year and there was less money coming in on the collection plates each Sunday. St. Luke's had promised to provide funds to many area food kitchens, homeless shelters and a myriad of other needy causes. But even the church was strapped for funds. Some parishioners had told him the church needed to cut back in its charitable contributions, but no one could agree on which charity should be cut.

Even here in Banner Bluff, there were people without food. Every day senior citizens and young families showed up at the church's food pantry asking for a bag of groceries. Father Barnaby's heart went out to each and every one of them. What kind of country was this that could not provide jobs and food for all of its citizens? Sometimes he felt angry, sometimes he fought back and sometimes he was overcome with sadness.

In his mind, this fair provided the best of both worlds. Families of Banner Bluff and the surrounding communities were enjoying a wonderful day together and the money would be there for the charities St. Luke's supported. He smiled at the sight of Rosie Marshall with her little friend Lilly Lawrence. They were racing across the lawn, their faces painted like miniature clowns. In their hands were paper cones of sticky pink cotton candy. They beamed at him and shouted, "Hi Father Barnaby! We're going to ride the ponies again!"

Martin had gone on the Ferris wheel three times with them. Lilly's daddy had been in the carriage behind them. They had all gone down the slide lots of times, and then the grown-ups watched while Rosie and Lilly went around and around on the miniature train. They had gobbled hotdogs and chips with cans of pop and an hour later got blueberry Slurpees that turned their tongues bright blue.

Lilly had brought her friend Bunny, a pink and grey stuffed rabbit. Bunny had to go on every ride with them. He sat between them on the train and he rode along with Lilly on the ponies. Lilly even gave him a taste of her Slurpee, and her daddy said Bunny looked like he would need a trip to the washing machine when they got home.

At four o'clock, Martin went to man the ticket booth. Rosie and Lilly were going to a puppet show put on by the high school students in the activities room of the church. Lilly's parents took them to the show and got them settled. "We'll be waiting at the picnic tables when the show is over," Lilly's mommy said as they walked off. Her father said nothing. They hadn't talked to each other very much for most of the afternoon.

Soon after the show began, Lilly looked around for Bunny. She poked Rosie, and they both looked under the folding chairs, but Bunny wasn't there.

"I have to find him," Lilly whispered. They got up and quietly walked out of the room. When they reached the hallway, Lilly was in tears. Rosie gave her a hug and said, "We'll find Bunny, don't worry." She looked down the hall and saw Mr. Gonzales, Roberto's daddy. "Mr. Gonzales," she called. "Lilly can't find Bunny."

He bent down to their level. "Are you sure you brought him to the fair?"

Lilly nodded as tears rolled down her face.

"We had Bunny with us on all the rides," Rosie said. "Maybe we left him by the ponies, or maybe at the cotton candy stand?"

"Where were you last?" Mr. Gonzales asked.

"We were in the puppet show when we figured out he was lost."

"Where were you before that?"

Rosie frowned, thinking hard. "I think we were making bracelets."

"O.K. Let's go there and look. I'm sure we'll find him." He took their hands and led them outside.

From her seat behind the sweets table, Louisa looked up and saw Luis Gonzales walking along with Rosie Marshall and Lilly Lawrence in tow. She frowned, wondering why he was holding their hands and where he was leading them.

Francesca had decided to spend an hour at St. Luke's Fair so she could write it up in the *Banner Bee*. She had asked David, her photographer, to attend as well. They met at the hamburger stand and ate lunch together. David was a freelance photographer who'd helped her out for a couple of years. He was a keen observer and his deep-set hazel eyes constantly swept the crowd, envisioning a shot as they talked. He wore his shoulder-length hair in a ponytail. Dressed in jeans and a jean jacket, he seemed like a throwback to the 70's. Francesca didn't know much about his background, but he was a great photographer.

"Don't you just wish you were a kid again," he said, taking a bite of his cheeseburger, "where happiness could be a ride on a carousel, or a big cloud of cotton candy. Sometimes we adults are way too complicated."

"You're right." Francesca munched on a potato chip. "We want too much and we're rarely satisfied. There are always other hopes, other wants and past regrets overshadowing a perfect moment."

He picked up his camera and snapped a picture of a grinning boy who had just whizzed down the giant slide. "There's a perfect moment. I love capturing these smiles on film!"

After lunch, they walked around and David took some candid photos while she soaked up the vibes of the event. Francesca interviewed parents and children and David took pictures that they could post on the webpage of Monday's issue of the *Banner Bee*.

Bradley Harrison strode over, calling her name. "Francesca, no wonder you're in such great shape. I saw you running this morning. Great legs!"

Francesca flushed. "Hello, Brad, nice to see you too. Gosh, two times in one day. I'm doubly blessed." She started to turn away.

"By the way," he continued, "I haven't met that friend of yours, the one you were running with this morning. How about you introduce me to her? I think she's a babe."

"Babe or not, you don't need me for an introduction. You know where she works and you're all grown up. I'm not a dating service."

Brad gripped her arm. "Hey, that would be a great idea. Why don't you add a dating service to the *Banner Bee*? Think how popular it could be!"

She shook him off. Nearby, she could hear David snapping pictures of them as they sparred. "I'll think that over. See you around!"

"I'll want my share of the royalties," he shouted after her as she and David walked away.

Francesca turned to David and held up her hand. "Better not put those pictures up on the website. Brad'll want royalties on them, too."

Sally and Harry were in their shared office at the back of the Trustworthy Real Estate Company. It was elegantly appointed, with deep oak paneling and gleaming mahogany desks. An imported Aubusson carpet in deep blues and reds covered the dark wood floor. Under the window were a rich red leather sofa and two matching armchairs. The walls were extra thick with special soundproofing. This place was their shared haven. There were no secrets between them as they led their lives in tandem. They had been married twelve years and had built a successful real estate business and escrow service.

Sally shut the door and went to sit on the leather sofa, crossing her slim legs. She picked a bit of lint from her dress and looked up at Harry. "So tell me exactly what happened at your breakfast yesterday? What are those clowns up to?" She patted the sofa beside her. "Have we added some new members to our little club?"

Harry flopped in an armchair, his stomach falling over his belt and his legs splayed. "They've got some old babe on the line and she should be handing over a check for $750,000 any day now. I'll be safely depositing it."

Sally groaned. "It takes them so long to close these deals. We're hurting, Harry. You know that? Karen Hobbs quit today. I keep losing salespeople. They just can't sell anything in this economy. House prices keep going down and nothing is moving. I've got to have more money to keep afloat."

"These deals take time, Sal. It sounds like they have to coddle each prospect to convince them to invest their savings in our worthy cause."

"I just wish we were on our own in all this. I don't like sharing and I don't trust Brad. He's a snake in the grass."

"Well, they probably don't trust us. But we need them and they need us. If we're going to keep this little scheme going, we're going to have to work together." He reached over and squeezed her hand. He reflected on their relationship; they both lived for work and the accumulation of wealth. They were perfectly suited to each other.

It was five o'clock. The fair was winding down and church members were beginning to take down the booths. Martin went into the church office to hand in the cashbox from ticket sales and then went looking for Rosie. He went down the hall to the activity room, but saw only a few teenagers putting away the puppets and dismantling the puppet stage. They told him the puppet show had been over for a while.

He went out through the side door to look for Lilly's parents and the girls. He could see a commotion across the lawn and he heard Father Barnaby's voice resonating over the loudspeaker. Earlier, they had used the sound system to project a variety of music: Frank Sinatra, The Beach Boys, U2 and Lady Gaga.

As he approached, Father Barnaby's words became clearer: "Would you all stop putting things away for a minute and help us out? Lilly Lawrence's parents can't find their daughter. Would you all take the time to look around for her? Lilly is five years old and has blonde hair and blue eyes. She was wearing light blue shorts and a striped pink and blue t-shirt. She might be with Rose Marie Martin, who looks a lot like her. Thank you all."

Martin rushed up to Lilly's parents. "Where are the girls? Why aren't they with you?"

Lilly's mother looked distraught and her husband seemed annoyed. "We left them together at the puppet show and went out to sit at the picnic tables and have a Coke," Jan said. "I told the girls to come and find us there when the show was over. Bob and I have looked all over, but we can't find them."

"They must be here somewhere." Martin felt uneasy, considering Rosie's propensity to wander off. He went over toward the ponies, which were being led away into their trailers. The owner remembered the two little girls. They had been his best customers, but he hadn't seen them during the last hour or so.

Martin looked behind the giant slide and the Ferris wheel, which were being dismantled. Nobody had seen the girls. "Sorry, man, but I seen so many little kids today. I don't know who you're talkin' about," the ride operator told him. "After a couple of hours, the kids all start to look alike."

He went inside the community building and looked upstairs in the meeting rooms, in the basement and even in the church sanctuary, calling for Rosie over and over. The entire clean-up crew was searching every inch of the church and its grounds. Nobody was having any luck. Martin went back outside and found Father Barnaby, who was talking to the Lawrences.

"Nobody has seen them! I wonder if they went home, or to the park? Why don't you go home and check before we call the police?" Father Barnaby suggested.

"Lilly would never leave without us," Jan said. "She's never done that before! She always does what she's told." She looked accusingly at Martin. "Maybe Rosie convinced her to go somewhere."

Martin felt uncomfortable. He knew Rosie wasn't always dependable, but he didn't like Jan's tone. She was probably as nervous as he was, so he let it pass. "That's a good idea," he said. "I could run home and check to see if the girls are there. Maybe you could check out the park?"

Worried and angry, he nearly ran the three blocks to his house. He saw Emma on her porch swing, rocking slowly back and forth and resting her legs on a hassock. "Emma, have you seen Rosie? She seems to have disappeared with her friend Lilly. Do you know if they're here?"

"I've only been back a little while. I haven't seen any action over at your house," she replied.

He nodded and ran up his front steps. He burst through the front door, calling, "Rose Marie, where are you? Rosie, are you here?"

He went through the rooms on the ground floor and then rushed upstairs. He looked in Rosie's room, the guest room, his and Kate's bedroom, behind the shower curtain, in the closets, everywhere. Then he raced back downstairs to the basement playroom. He even looked behind the furnace, even though he knew Rosie was afraid of the dark furnace room. His heart was beating fast and his breathing was uneven. "Oh, my God, where could she be?" he whispered. "Would she go down to the lake by herself, or over to the train tracks?" Suddenly, the whole town of Banner Bluff seemed dangerous and sinister.

He ran back up the basement stairs, calling in fright and in anger, "Rose Marie, answer me right now!"

He heard a rustling from upstairs and then a little voice. "Daddy, Daddy, I'm here."

He raced up to the second floor and went into his bedroom. He heard some sniffling. There was Rosie under the comforter that he had piled on Kate's side of the bed that morning. She was curled up hugging Kate's pillow. He hadn't seen her when he had rushed through earlier. "What are you doing here? You are *never* supposed to go off without telling me!" He was trembling all over with anger and relief. Then he bent down and picked her up to hug her and kiss her and just feel her little warm body in his arms. "Oh, Rosie, I was so worried about you." He took a ragged breath. "Daddy loves you so much but you scared me to death!"

Rosie was crying. "I miss Mommy. I thought maybe she would be home now, but when I got home, she wasn't here and I felt so sad. When is Mommy coming home?"

"Mommy will be here tomorrow, just one more night." He hugged her tight and felt his body relax with exhaustion and relief. This had been one hell of a day.

He carried Rosie downstairs and grabbed his cell phone to call the church. Father Barnaby sounded greatly relieved to hear that Rosie was home. He hadn't heard from the Lawrences yet. He said he would keep Martin informed.

Rosie was hungry in spite of all the junk food she'd consumed at the fair. Looking in the fridge, Martin decided on scrambled eggs, toast and some strawberries. After a bath, he would pop Rosie in bed and lock all the downstairs windows and doors. He did not want to worry about his wayward daughter creeping out that night.

Daddy was drinking beer. Daddy put down the empty bottle and told him to get another one out of the fridge. This was the fourth beer. The bottles were lined up by the bread box. Mommy was holding Julie on her lap and humming to her. Mommy looked nervous and wouldn't look at Daddy. Daddy leaned back against the kitchen counter, looking at the receipt from the grocery store. He was wearing his muddy work boots and dirty work pants. There were little chunks of mud around his feet. Later, he would make Mommy clean them up.

"Claire, look how much you spent at the grocery store! What in the hell did you buy?"

"Just the basics: milk, eggs, applesauce, potatoes, hamburger, and oatmeal. I didn't splurge on anything. Don't be angry, Stan."

"'Don't be angry, Stan. Don't be angry, Stan.'" Daddy mimicked her in a high voice. "This is my hard-earned money, Claire, that you fritter away every week. I want to see the change from my fifty-dollar bill. I don't want you stealing from me."

Daddy lurched towards the kitchen table and stumbled over the red fire engine. He'd been playing with it before Daddy got home. "How many times have I told you not to leave your fucking toys on the floor, idiot? Come over here and pick it up! Now!"

He sidled away towards the hall. He would run. He would get away from Daddy. But Daddy was fast, even when he was drunk. Daddy grabbed him by the shoulder, the sore one, and pushed him down, shoving his face against the linoleum floor. "What did I tell you to do, idiot?"

Then it happened. He couldn't stop it.

"You filthy little pig! You're peeing all over the floor. God damn it! You're coming downstairs with me, now." Daddy dragged him towards the basement steps.

Chapter 7
Saturday night, May 15th

Chief Tom Barnett felt the day had gone well. The department had effectively managed the traffic and parking during St. Luke's Church Fair. There had only been one incident when two competitive fathers nearly came to blows over a parking spot within easy walking distance of the church. Now it was six-thirty and he had just poured himself a healthy measure of fifteen year-old McCallan single malt scotch. This was a rare occurrence since the damn stuff cost a fortune. His sister and her husband had brought him a bottle when they came for Thanksgiving that year. It was a tradition for them to spend Thanksgiving with him and do some Christmas shopping downtown on Michigan Avenue. They lived in Iowa on a small farm and relished a trip to the big city.

He knew that Jenny, his sister, worried about him being alone for the holidays and she usually tried to pressure him to come to the farm for Christmas. He would always beg off, citing police business. He actually didn't mind working on Christmas Day and he liked giving the time off to the family men. Things were quiet and there was truly a sense of "peace and good will toward men" until late in the day, when somebody's Christmas dinner inevitably turned into a family brawl.

Most women found him handsome with his strong-boned face, blue eyes and dark wavy hair. "The strong, silent type," Jenny liked to joke. It was true that he kept his counsel and assessed situations before acting. Like many quiet people, he saw and heard a great deal: the raised eyebrow, the shrug of the shoulders, a mumbled aside. He watched and remembered. Some people found him aloof and taciturn. But he knew his silent observation made him an astute policeman.

He carried his scotch into the den and turned on the TV, looking for the Cubs game that should be on about now. As usual, the

Cubs weren't doing so well; but he was addicted to the game and to his team. Just as he settled his tall, lean frame into his favorite chair, the phone rang.

He picked up. "Barnett here," he said.

"Chief? This is Father Barnaby. We've got a problem here at the church."

He was instantly alert. "What's up?"

"We can't find Lilly Lawrence. Her parents, some parishioners and the neighbors have all been looking for her. No one took it too seriously at first. We thought she couldn't have wandered off too far. Earlier, she was with Rose Marie Marshall, but Rosie's father found her at home. We've combed the church, the parks and the neighborhood. No one's found any trace of Lilly."

Tom thought the rector should have called him much earlier, but he didn't let his irritation creep into his voice. "I'll get over to the station right now and we'll start an organized search. Could you please bring the parents over there so we can interview them? They should bring a recent picture of their little girl. How old is she?"

"Five or six. She's in kindergarten."

"Who did you say she was with before she went missing?"

"Rosie Marshall. They're friends and they look like two peas in a pod, blonde and blue-eyed. You must have seen them around."

"Yes, I think I have. Well, we'll have to talk to Rosie. Is she over at the church?"

"No, she's at home with her dad."

"We've got to get moving on this, Father. I'll see you in a few minutes."

Tom put down the phone and carried his beloved scotch to the kitchen. He poured the liquid back into the bottle and screwed it tight. This was not going to be a night to kick back and relax.

Luis came home about eight o'clock. He had helped with the cleanup at the church and had done a final sweeping and washing of the hallways after everyone left. Although the Gonzales family didn't attend St. Luke's, Luis was always pleased to take on an extra job for

Father Barnaby. He respected the priest as a man of the cloth; but also because he was an honest and kindly person and welcomed everyone in the community.

Yahaira had brought the boys to the fair for a few hours in the afternoon. Now, they had finished supper and baths, and were watching *Star Wars* for the hundredth time. "You must be exhausted, *mi amor*," Yari said. "You were gone for fourteen hours today. Would you like some dinner? I've got a chicken and rice casserole."

He gave her a tired smile and sat down at the kitchen table. "I really don't want anything except a cold beer. I ate a hamburger for lunch and had a couple of hot dogs in the late afternoon."

Yari reached in the fridge and brought him a Corona and a hunk of cheddar. In the cupboard, she found some crackers and put them on a plate with the cheese. "Maybe you'd like a snack?"

She sat down at the table and watched him eat. He smiled up at her as he cut a slice of cheese and put it on a Ritz cracker. "We had a scare at the end of the fair. Rosie Marshall and her little friend, Lilly Lawrence, went missing. Earlier I helped them look for Lilly's stuffed rabbit. It got kicked under a table at the bead and bracelet stand. But when the fair ended at five o'clock, their parents couldn't find either one of them. We were all looking everywhere. Rosie's dad found her at home, but they're still looking for Lilly."

Yari looked dismayed. "The parents must be frantic."

He nodded and took a drink of beer. "Anyway, the police are organizing a search party. I decided to come on home. I'm sure they'll find her sooner or later. I'll bet she went over to the Cool Cow or to Gilmore playground."

"Or she's over at a friend's house and the parents didn't bother to call her mom." Yari sighed.

Luis pushed away his plate and leaned on the table, his arms folded. "Yari, I need to tell you about what's been going on at the beach. I've been wondering what to do. You know that Canfield kid, Colman, and his friend Craig Thompson?"

She nodded.

"Well, they've been going down to the beach to drink late at night and I know they smoke pot. But these last few weeks, I found some needles. They must be shooting up."

Yari breathed in sharply. "I can believe that! Colman's probably high half the time. Some days he just looks like he's not all there, like he's wandering around in a daze. Other days he looks like he's angry about something. He's one unhappy kid."

"I haven't told Chief Barnett. I'm kind of worried about Royce Canfield's reaction. Chief Barnett plays golf with him every Friday. I wonder if they would prefer that I not know anything. You know what I mean?"

Yari nodded, her eyes worried.

"And Craig Thompson's dad is a big deal around here, too. I'm worried about what he might do if I say anything. It doesn't look good for the head of a bank and leader of the City Council to have a son on drugs. On the other hand, if I don't say something, I could be in trouble. What if some little kids find those needles? I just don't know."

He paused, then continued. "I was thinking about driving down there tonight and talking to those boys. Maybe I could reason with them."

Yari looked hesitant. After a moment, she said, "I think you should talk to Chief Barnett on Monday morning. You could just tell him what you've found and avoid saying who the culprits might be. That would be up to the police to figure out. As for trying to reason with those kids, if they're high on something, they're not going to listen to you." She picked up the plate and empty bottle and said, "Let's go to bed. We've had a long, long day."

Tom Barnett decided to go over to the Marshalls' house to interview Rose Marie. They had organized a task force and divided up the town into quadrants to be searched, starting in the general area of St. Luke's and Lilly Lawrence's house. The officers had all received a copy of her school picture and were out going door to door. Surrounding communities had sent officers to assist in the search.

He'd enacted the Code Red system, an emergency communications network designed to help local government officials record, send and track personalized messages to thousands of citizens in minutes. Tom had recorded an emergency message notifying everyone in Banner Bluff and nearby villages that Lilly Lawrence was lost. He'd described the little girl, what she was wearing and where she was last seen. Citizens were asked to contact Banner Bluff Police Headquarters with any information.

Officer Johnson was fielding the calls and two other officers were in charge of following up on tips. An Amber alert was in effect and staff was researching the names and addresses of known sex offenders in the area. At the elementary school, Officer Conroy was organizing local people into a volunteer search party.

Detective Sergeant Puchalski had interviewed the missing girl's parents at length. The first place to start was always the family and the home. Children often went missing after a domestic altercation, or hid from their parents if they were in trouble. It took a great deal of finesse to get parents to admit to family problems or actual abuse. Puchalski's natural charm, though, often disarmed his subjects and prompted them to tell the truth.

The Lawrences weren't a happy couple, Puchalski had reported, though there didn't seem to be any major issues in the family. The father was a pushy guy who wouldn't be easy to live with, and the wife seemed nervous and lacked self-confidence. They both claimed there was no trouble that would have precipitated Lilly's disappearance, and Puchalski hadn't found anything to suggest otherwise.

Tom knocked on the Marshalls' door and then looked down the street at the setting sun. The sky was glowing orange, the tree branches etched in black. He wished they could have found this little girl before the sun went down.

Martin Marshall opened the door. "Chief," he said, looking bewildered. "What's up?"

"I'm here about Lilly Lawrence. We still haven't found her. I've just been talking with the parents and Father Barnaby. I'm told

Rose Marie was the last person to see her. Could I come in and talk to Rosie?"

"They still haven't found her? This is turning into a nightmare." Martin ran his hands through his hair. "You want to talk to Rosie? I just finished reading her a bedtime story. " He looked up the stairs. Tom peered past him and saw Rosie staring down. "Rosie, can you come down and talk to Chief Barnett about this afternoon?" Martin said. "They're looking for Lilly and they can't find her."

Rosie padded down the stairs in her white cotton nightgown, looking worried. "I don't know where she is, Daddy."

"I know you don't, but maybe you can help out. How about that?" He led her to the sofa and settled her in his arms. Tom sat in an armchair across from them, leaning back so Rosie would feel less threatened.

Rosie told Tom that they'd been on all the rides and then Lilly's mommy had taken them to the puppet show. But Lilly couldn't find Bunny, so they'd gone to look for him and found him under the bracelet table.

"What did you do then?" Tom asked, smiling.

"We went to see St. Francis," she said, her eyes aglow.

Tom looked at Martin. "Where is St. Francis?"

"There's a garden behind the church in a little courtyard. In the middle, there's a St. Francis statue surrounded by sculpted animals."

Tom looked back at Rosie. "Why did you go there?"

"We wanted to thank St. Francis for finding Bunny. St. Francis is the saint for all the animals. He loves rabbits and he helped us find Bunny. We put Bunny in his arms and we made the sign of the Cross." Rosie jumped down and demonstrated, crossing herself with her chubby little hand.

"What did you do then?" Tom asked gently.

Rosie climbed back into her father's arms. She looked up at Martin. "I came home. I know I wasn't supposed to come home by myself. I'm sorry, Daddy. I thought Mommy would be here. I really did." She had tears in her eyes now, and looked down at her hands laced together in her lap.

Martin hugged her to him. "Don't worry honey, it's all right. I'm glad you're safe."

Tom paused and then asked Rosie, "Where do you think Lilly is?" The question hung in the air.

"I don't know," she whispered. "I just started thinking about Mommy and I wanted to come home. Lilly wanted to stay with St. Francis and play with Bunny. So I just said bye and left." She looked up. "Besides, she wouldn't let me hold Bunny. She didn't want to share."

Francesca and Marcus Reynolds smiled at each other as they each settled back with a glass of wine. They were in a cozy booth at the back of Sorrel's restaurant. The lights were low, and on their table a candle flickered beside a small bunch of miniature roses. This was the ideal spot for a quiet, leisurely dinner. Marcus wore an immaculate blue dress shirt and dark slacks. His dark blond hair was carefully combed and his deep-set grey eyes met Francesca's appraising glance with a quizzical look. "So? Do I meet with your approval?"

"Marcus, you look great! You always look sharp."

"Well, you look ravishing, yourself." He admired her deep-red wrap sweater smoothed over sleek black sateen pants. Tonight, she wore her shiny dark hair in burnished waves around her face.

The waiter handed them menus and placed a basket of warm, crusty rolls on the table. Francesca was hungry, and everything on the menu looked enticing.

"What are you going to have?" Marcus asked.

"I think I might try the soft-shelled crab appetizer. That's a seasonal treat."

"Hmm." Marcus looked up. "I think I'll have the crab cakes and the veal medallions with mushroom sauce. What do you want for a main course?"

"I'll have the veal, too."

The waiter arrived and they gave their orders. Marcus picked up his wine glass and smiled into her eyes. "Here's to us!" he said.

Francesca felt a twinge of panic, but she smiled in return. They clinked glasses. Now, they could settle down and talk. "So what have you been up to?" Marcus asked. "I try to check out the *Bee* every day, just to see what's happening in town."

"It looks as though the vote on the Smithfield Conference Center is imminent. The people against the sale are getting rabid. The last meeting was a zoo. The Board President couldn't get everyone to calm down. People were yelling and shouting. One side wants the building to be used as a community art center. And they want the surrounding meadow and gardens to become part of the village land trust. Other people feel the village would benefit financially if this developer came in and built townhomes and a small shopping area. It would be more tax money in the village coffers." She took a small sip of wine. "What do you think about it, Marcus?"

"I've heard both sides. My concerns are about the main entrance on Charles Street. I really don't think we need any more traffic on that road. There will be years of snarl-ups because of construction, and then once the project is complete, I envision double the traffic. Charles Street is only two lanes, and it's already overly congested during rush hour when everyone is heading to the highway on their way to Chicago."

"So you're basically against bringing in the developer, right?" Francesca sighed. "I think I am, too. I just wish everyone could conduct themselves in a rational manner. I get frightened when people let their emotions drive their actions."

"Yeah, mob rule is not a pretty scene and it can happen so easily. We're about this far from being wild beasts." Marcus held his thumb and forefinger a quarter of an inch apart.

When their first course arrived, they stopped talking to enjoy their selections. "This is fabulous," Francesca said. "The crabs are so crispy and delicious, and the sauce is to die for. How about those crab cakes?"

"Wonderful," Marcus said. "You can't beat Sorrel's for dependable fare."

The waiter cleared away their first course and set down two plates of golden polenta topped with the tender veal. The meat was covered with a rich sauce and a sprinkling of gremolata. "Voilà," the waiter said, "bon appétit."

When the waiter left, they looked at each other and burst out laughing. "Bon appétit," Francesca mimicked. It was nice to see Marcus laugh, she thought. Usually, he was more careful in his manner. Nice enough, but too cautious. Not like her. Sometimes, she thought she was too expressive. She knew Marcus found her fascinating, which was flattering and uncomfortable at the same time.

Over coffee, Francesca told Marcus about the latest Well-wisher occurrence. He didn't know who it could be, either. "It's nice to have good news to share," Francesca said. "There's too much gloom and doom in the world today."

After dinner they ambled back to Francesca's condo where Marcus had left his car. The spring air was soft and warm. It was a perfect night. There was a slight breeze and they could smell the lilac blooms from the bushes in the park. As they turned onto Hennessey Street, a patrol car slowly approached. It pulled up next to them and the front window rolled down. A policeman poked his head out, and Francesca recognized Lieutenant Lewis. "Hey there, folks!" he said.

"Lieutenant, I'm glad to see you out protecting the citizens of our fair city," Francesca said in jest. "It isn't as though there's much crime in Banner Bluff."

"Actually, we do have a crisis. A little girl is missing. Lilly Lawrence. She's five years old. Here's her picture." He held out Lilly's picture, then grabbed his flashlight and shone it on the photo. "Have you seen her? She disappeared from St. Luke's fair this afternoon."

"I was at the fair myself," Francesca said. "There was a big crowd. I don't remember seeing her. But it would be hard to remember with all those kids and their parents."

"We just walked here from Sorrel's," Marcus said. "We didn't see anything along the way. You've already checked the hospital?"

"I think we've checked about everywhere, but no luck yet. Call the station if you see anything. Thanks, folks," Lewis said as he drove away.

"She's got to be hiding somewhere," Francesca said. "That's what I used to do as a kid, especially when I got in trouble."

Marcus nodded. "But she's pretty little to be out this late. It's almost ten-thirty."

Francesca's house was lit up like a Christmas tree, lights on in every room.

"What's going on?" Marcus asked.

"I don't like to come home to a dark house." Francesca lowered her head and searched in her purse for the key. She didn't want to tell him she was petrified of the dark and had timers set for all the lights. She didn't want him to know she had to sleep with the lights on. She didn't want him to know that when this fear gripped her; she shivered uncontrollably and sweat poured down her body. No, she didn't want to share her demons.

She invited him in for a glass of wine, figuring that would distract him. As she unlocked the door, she looked down the row of townhouses. She could see a van turning into a garage at the end of the street. "You know what's weird?" she said. "I've lived here for over five years and I barely know half the people on this street. I just don't see them. They open their garage doors with a remote and drive in and shut the door behind them. I never see who they are. That guy down there has tinted windows; he could be Tom Cruise or Matt Damon or Jack the Ripper. I don't have a clue."

"Maybe he's Warren Buffet or Bill Gates or an oil magnate. Maybe he'd like to invest in the *Banner Bee*," Marcus said, laughing.

Both dogs were there to welcome them home. Bailey madly wagged her tail while Benjy whimpered with joy. Francesca shooed them into the kitchen since Marcus was not fond of dogs. "Make yourself at home while I get a bottle of wine," she called.

He found her CD selection and put on some light jazz. When she came in with the wine, Marcus opened it and poured them each a glass. Then they settled on the sofa. Marcus took her hand and they sat comfortably together, sipping wine and listening to the music. Francesca looked down at their hands lying entwined on the sofa cushions. At that moment, it felt right to be there together.

Marcus leaned over and kissed her gently on the lips. He looked into her eyes and kissed her again, longer and deeper. She reached up and pulled him to her. They melted into one another; lips to lips, searching hands and melding bodies. Francesca felt a tender pull deep inside, a timid flowering. Could she open her heart once again? She felt tremulous and uncertain.

Susan Simpson stretched her arms over her head and yawned. This had been a really long day. The morning included a ladies' golf clinic, followed by an elegant brunch. In the afternoon, Wallace Industries had used the club for a company golf outing, followed by a sumptuous dinner and an award ceremony. Susan had been working since 8 AM organizing the details and ensuring that everything went like clockwork. She felt good about her day, but she was glad it was almost over.

During the cocktail hour, she'd noticed Bradley Harrison mingling with the Wallace golfing party. She didn't think he was part of the group. When she checked her log of attendees, he wasn't on the list; but he seemed to know many men in the group. He was a real schmoozer; working the crowd, talking and laughing with just about everyone. Susan wondered what he did for a living. Just then, he came up behind her.

"Hello, Ms. Simpson. I'd like to introduce myself." Susan turned to face him. "My name is Bradley Harrison and I'm a member here at the club," he went on, smiling warmly as they shook hands. "I saw you running this morning with Francesca Antonelli and I thought I'd say hello. Is she a close friend?"

"Yes, Francesca is an old friend." She gave him her most professional smile. "Tell me, do you work at Wallace Industries? I'm not familiar with the firm, since I moved here recently."

"Actually, I'm not part of the Wallace group. I just have a couple of buddies here and I wanted to say hi. I'm a pretty social type of guy." He laughed. "And I like a smooth martini and the club has the best. Can I interest you in a drink?"

"I don't drink when I'm on the job, Mr. Harrison. I've got to keep all my wits about me!"

"Please, call me Brad. How about after work? Let's go over to Hobson's when you're finished here. That's the new microbrewery that opened downtown, near Hero's Market."

"Oh, I don't know." Susan wavered. She pushed back a wayward strand of hair. "I'll be wiped out and no fun!"

"Come on. It will be a great chance for us to get to know one another. Just one beer and then you can go home and crash. And," he added, "I think you'll be a lot of fun!"

Francesca had warned her off this man, but in person he was charming and seemed truly interested in getting to know her. Why not have one beer with him? She hadn't dated anyone since she'd landed in Banner Bluff. "All right. One beer. And thanks."

Brad turned out to be the perfect gentleman, entertaining her with stories about the foibles of Oak Hills Club members on and off the golf course. He was a gold mine of information about Banner Bluff. He covered everything, from where to find the best chocolate chip cookies to the name of the most expert dry cleaners. It was an enjoyable evening, but by eleven-thirty, Susan said she had to get going. Sunday was another big day at the club and she needed her beauty rest.

"Night-night, sleeping beauty," Brad said, offering his hand. "Let's have dinner together soon."

"That would be lovely," Susan said, feeling his firm, warm handshake.

Luis lay awake after Yari was deep asleep. He could hear her regular breathing and he smiled at the speed with which she was able to drop off. Once her head hit the pillow, she was out. What a blessing. He, on the other hand, would lay awake for hours while random thoughts swirled through his brain. He had tried getting up and reading for a while and had even taken a sleep remedy once, but he didn't like the way he felt when he got up in the morning.

Most of his thoughts tonight involved the kids at the beach. Should he go down there and try to talk some sense into them? Should he talk to Tom Barnett in the morning? Or should he just let it go? He looked over at the clock on the nightstand. It was one AM. He couldn't stand it any longer. He slipped out of bed without making a sound. His pants and shirt were on the chair and his shoes were by the door. In just a few minutes, he was dressed and outside. He got into the car and drove down the street towards Longview Road and then down to the lake.

When he arrived at the beach, there were no cars parked along the street. He drove to the north end of the bluff and saw the little red BMW parked in the shadows under a tree. Nearby was the construction site of an enormous mansion right on the bluff with fabulous views of Lake Michigan. No one had been here for over a year. The unfinished house stood vacant with boarded-up windows and doors. Luis figured it was another foreclosure disaster. Apparently, there was no money to finish up the construction.

He decided to park on the street along the bluff and walk down to the beach. He listened intently, but heard no sound of talking or laughter. He wondered how many kids were down there. He didn't want to walk in on Colman and his girlfriend "in the act," so to speak.

He took the steep stairs and then the path down towards the covered picnic shelter. From this angle he could see the light of a cigarette or a joint. He smelled smoke and heard the crackle of a log fire. The park district kept wood down here so people could light a fire in the large stone fireplace.

Luis walked around behind the shelter and then stepped into the light. He saw Colman leaning back against a picnic table, one leg crossed over the other, gazing into the fire. In one hand he held a joint to his lips. In his other hand was a fifth of some dark liquid, maybe scotch or bourbon. At first, he seemed oblivious to Luis's arrival. Then he turned his head and took a minute to focus.

Luis broke the silence. "Good evening, Colman. Where are your friends? I thought you would be having a party on Saturday night."

At first, Colman said nothing. He still seemed to be processing Luis's presence inside the shelter. "What the fuck are you doing here? Is it time to pick up the garbage already? Hey, dude, you must work all night long. That's what we've got spics for; to clean up our shit."

Luis didn't respond. Then he said, "I'm here, Colman, because, in fact, I do clean up after you many mornings. I know that you and Craig and that girlfriend of yours are down here smoking pot and drinking many nights. I also know you are underage and could get in big trouble."

"Big trouble, big trouble, you scare me to death, Señor. What I do down here is my business and I could give a shit what you think."

"It's not so much what I think, but what the police and your parents will think. I haven't talked to anyone else. I'm coming to you and suggesting that you clean up your act. I didn't come down here to discuss the pot smoking. I'm more concerned about the needles I found and the fact that they could get into the hands of some little kids."

"Why don't you get lost, Señor? Why don't you go back to Mexico where you belong? All you spics come here and take our jobs and use our health care. You're probably an illegal alien." Colman dragged out the words and stared up at Luis. "Don't you like that term? It sounds like a goddamned Martian from outer space. Maybe I should check your papers, huh?" Colman took a swig of scotch. "And by the way, there won't be any more needles. I'm into OxyContin and Vicodin. Heroin is Craig's drug of choice and I'm not hanging with him anymore. He won't be coming down to the beach."

Colman threw his roach into the fire and struggled to keep his balance as he grabbed onto the picnic table and turned to sit down on the wooden bench. He was visibly too drunk to stand, let alone walk back up the hill. "I am here on my own and you can go tell whoever you want. I don't give a fuck. Go tell my dad. Bring him down. Yeah, bring him down. Emperor Royce, let's bring him down."

"How about I help you up the hill?" Luis suggested. "I think you could use some help. Then I'll drive you home."

"Will you get the fuck out of here and leave me alone? I don't want to go home and my parents could care less. I want to hang out here," Colman said petulantly.

Luis realized that reasoning with this screwed-up kid was a waste of time. Here was someone so disturbed that his difficulties went way beyond his addictions. Yari was right. He couldn't talk sense to a drugged-up, alcoholic teenager. Tomorrow, he would call Tom Barnett.

He left the picnic shelter and slowly started back up the path. As he neared the stairs, he heard a car approaching from the southern parking lot. Strange, he thought, that its headlights weren't on.

Louisa couldn't sleep. She hadn't eaten much dinner since she'd snacked on cookies, brownies and a big piece of coconut cake late in the day. She practically never ate sweets, but yesterday she hadn't been able to resist all the fresh baked goods spread before her. One bite led to another while she was gossiping with Emma or one of her church friends.

When she got home, she asked Alma to bring a bowl of her special chicken noodle soup and an apple carefully cut into thin slices. After this meager repast, she had read for a little while and then gone right to bed.

Now, at two AM, she felt wide awake. Was she hungry or just having one of those nights when she couldn't sleep? She decided to go downstairs and pour herself a glass of sherry. That should do the trick. As she made her way down, she looked out the long window near the wide staircase. Earlier, while getting ready for bed, she had seen several police cars combing the neighborhood, probably looking for that little Lawrence girl. Now she heard a car coming along the street. She glanced out the window and saw a dark van, going down the street with its headlights off. Probably some irresponsible teenager.

She poured herself a nice glass of sherry and made her way back upstairs, stopping to gaze out the window again. The moon had come out from behind a cloud and the street was eerily illuminated.

She could hear another car coming. Wasn't that the noisy little car belonging to that Spanish family? What were they doing out at night? Maybe they were hunting for the lost child as well. There was entirely too much traffic at this hour of the night, she thought.

"Come on, honey, play with her. She's your little sister and she wants to play Sleeping Beauty."

He had just come home from school and was hanging up his jacket on the coat tree. Julie was lying on the couch, her baby blue blanket spread out under her. She was wearing her pink princess dress.

The game was always the same. Mommy would put on a record of Tchaikovsky's ballet music and Julie would dance around the living room. Mommy was the wicked witch and she would cast a spell on Julie at the ball. Then Julie would prick her finger on a knitting needle in Mommy's knitting basket and fall into a swoon on the couch. He was the Prince. He had to kiss her. He had to kiss her on the lips. He hated kissing her. He hated the game. He hated doing it over and over. If he didn't do it, she would start to cry, sobbing quietly. Mommy would come out from the kitchen, her hands on her hips, pleading with him. "Is it too much to ask? Can't you spend a little time with your sister? Just kiss her so she'll stop crying. I've got to get dinner started."

He balled his hands up in tight fists. He bent over and kissed his four year-old sister's small, wet, pink lips. He hated her.

Chapter 8
Sunday morning, May 16th

Francesca awoke slowly. It was very early. Still in that delicious state of semi-consciousness, she stretched and smiled to herself. Last night had been a pleasant surprise. She and Marcus really had a good time and they seemed to have clicked. The conversation had gone smoothly and those kisses on the sofa had been, well, quite delightful. Then Marcus's pager had gone off. He had grabbed it from his pocket, checked the screen and then reached down for his shoes. "I've got to go, Francesca. A patient of mine in the ER had a heart attack. It doesn't look good. I know the family well." He had stood abruptly. "I better get over there. I'm sorry about the quick exit."

Francesca had understood. He was a doctor; this kind of thing happened. At the door, they'd had another quick kiss and he'd left. She'd watched him drive away and then closed and locked the door. Somehow, the house had felt especially empty. She'd gone into the living room and gazed at the yellow tulips he'd brought her. They'd closed their petals for the night. *Thank you, Marcus,* she'd thought.

Then, gazing out the windows into the darkness, she'd felt the familiar irrational fear roll over her. Who was out there? Who was watching her? She'd felt the familiar symptoms: cold sweat trickling down her spine, clammy hands, heavy breathing. She'd rushed over to check the locks and close the blinds. Then she'd typed in the security code on the alarm system. Only after that did she begin to relax.

She didn't like remembering the source of her fear. Even in the morning light, the memory filled her with terror. She had been about six. Her parents were outside in the back yard, talking after dinner. Francesca had been in bed in her room near the front of their little ranch house, already asleep when an intruder came in through her window. He'd cut the screen and climbed into her room. She'd awakened to see a shadowy figure outlined by the dim porch light. Paralyzed by fear, she'd been unable to scream. For what seemed like hours she'd lain frozen in bed, her eyes squeezed shut while the invader prowled around in her room. Then he'd come and stood over her, exuding a fetid smell.

Only when he opened her door to go down the hall had she started to scream. The intruder—most likely a robber, her parents said later—had taken off through the house and out the front door as her parents rushed in from the back deck. He had not taken anything of value, except the happy insouciance of Francesca's childhood.

For years afterwards, she'd insisted her parents look in the closet and under the bed to assure her that there were no monsters. Then they would double-check the lock on the window and turn on her bedside lamp. When everything was safe and secure, her dad would lay down with her as she fell asleep. Often he would be snoring beside her while she stared up at the sparkling paper stars and silver moon glued to the ceiling, her hand clutching his.

Francesca was wide awake now. It was no longer dark outside. There was a soft light coming from the east. If she hurried, she could make it down to the beach for the sunrise. She rummaged around for her running clothes and got dressed quickly. Downstairs, the dogs were excited. They loved going to the beach.

They left the house jogging. She thought about her plans for the day. When they got back she would make some blueberry pancakes. Her dad used to make pancakes on the weekends, and eating anything else would have been a sacrilege. After a little laziness, she would do a few loads of laundry and push the vacuum around. She didn't relish these household chores, but they needed to get done. Then she would sit down and write her article about the church fair. She could upload it this evening and it would be ready for Monday morning. David would have sent her some pictures already and she could make a selection for the story. Everyone in Banner Bluff loved photos of local events…and especially of themselves.

She could see the water as they drew near the lakeshore, gleaming silver in the first light of dawn. Eagerly, she and the dogs headed toward it.

Tom Barnett got the call from the station at six AM. He had been in the midst of a sinister dream. He was flying while black-hooded monsters chased him through dark streets. Then he came to a tall chain-link fence at the back of a dark alley. The hooded monsters were gaining on him. Terrified, he stepped back and pushed off the ground, spreading his arms and sailing up into the air. Down below, the hooded creatures grabbed at his feet, but he kicked free and zoomed into the sky. A fabulous sense of freedom filled him as he soared over buildings and bridges. He felt weightless and all-powerful, a superior being. In the distance, a medieval bell tower with spiked crenellations loomed large and the bells boomed into the air. They rang and rang in his ears and he could feel himself losing momentum. He was being pulled back to earth. He awoke to the ringing of his phone beside the bed.

"Tom Barnett, here." The caller ID told him it was Lieutenant Lewis. He thought instantly of Lilly Lawrence. "Did you find her?"

"We think so, sir. Down at the beach. She, uh..." Lewis's voice caught and he swallowed. "She's dead, sir. A woman found her floating in the lake down at the south end of the beach."

God, why didn't we find her earlier? Where was she all night? Tom felt personally responsible. He balled up his right hand into a tight fist and smashed it into his left hand over and over. He'd been up for hours coordinating the search and only came home for a couple of hours of sleep at 4 AM. All night, the entire police staff and eighty volunteers had covered each street and visited each house. They'd even gone into the three deep ravines that dug their way down to Lake Michigan. By midnight, they'd turned up nothing. Yet now, six hours later, Lilly Lawrence was dead.

He cleared his throat. "Lewis, I'll be down there in ten minutes. Cordon off the scene and make sure no one comes down the access road to the beach."

As he put the receiver back, he saw the picture of Candace on the bedside table. She gazed back at him, her eyes looking deeply into his, her knowing smile for him alone. Candace was his girl and she was gone. Cancer had taken her five years ago just when they learned she was pregnant with their first child. Routine blood tests had discovered acute lymphocytic leukemia. Rare in adults, it had raced through her body. She was gone in only a few weeks. Every morning, he woke up with the irrational hope that she would be there beside him. It was a game he still played each day.

He shook off the memory as best he could and got out of bed. He shaved quickly and put on his summer uniform, short-sleeved white shirt and dark blue pants. He strapped on his bullet-proof vest and slipped his gun into its holster. On the way out the back door, he glanced at Candace's overgrown garden. It looked thirsty and unloved. He would have to find time tonight or tomorrow to water the roses. They were determined to bloom again this year, as they had every year since their mistress died.

Lake Avenue was already filled with police cars, ambulances and fire trucks. Families living along the avenue were peering out of their windows or sipping coffee on their porches. Before long, the news that the police were investigating the south beach would be popping up on cellphones and computer screens.

Tom checked in with the officers on the headland and then proceeded down the access road to the beach. The entire area had been roped off and it was a busy crime scene. Deputy Chief Bob Conroy had the investigation in hand. Tom was eternally grateful to Conroy, who handled his job with efficiency and aplomb.

"That's Francesca Antonelli over there; she's the one who found the body," Conroy said, pointing across the tarmac to a park bench under the trees.

Tom felt foolish and inept. Francesca Antonelli. What was he going to say to this woman he had been sparring with as recently as last Friday?

"She's in a bad way right now," Conroy continued. "Lewis went to find her a cup of hot coffee and a blanket."

Tom looked across the sand at her hunched figure. She was seated on a wooden bench near the tree line, protected by two large yellow Labrador retrievers. The S-curve of her body and the sense of abject despair she radiated made him think back to the long days he had spent in the hospital with Candy. For a moment, he saw Candy hunched on a bench waiting for another useless chemo session. As he approached Francesca, the dogs eyed him guardedly.

"Hello, Ms. Antonelli. It's Chief Barnett."

She barely nodded, her face drawn as she looked away. This pain was not something she wanted to share with him.

"May I talk to you a moment about what happened here this morning?" He sounded hesitant and—he hoped—empathetic. "We'll want to take a statement later at the police station; but I wonder if you could just fill me in right now?"

She looked out at the water. Tears welled up in her eyes. "I came down here to walk the dogs. I walked along the beach like I always do." She wiped tears from her cheeks with her palms. "When we came to the south end of the beach, the dogs went nuts, running around and whining." She swallowed hard. "I thought it was a blanket or a tablecloth in the water. How stupid is that? Why would a tablecloth be in the water?" She looked up, her eyes searching his.

"And then when I got close, I realized the pink cloth was a little child. I waded into the water. I couldn't think straight. I thought I could save her even though she was floating face down." She began to sob, wrapping her arms around the two dogs and smothering her face in the larger one's ruff.

Tom stood rigidly. Perhaps he should offer comfort. He felt out of his depth. He patted her shoulder tentatively and then asked if there was someone he could call to come and be with her.

"Susan Simpson, she's an old friend. She works at Oak Hills."

"I'll get her down here," Tom said gruffly. "I'll give her a call."

"Would you, please? Thank you, thank you so much." Francesca gave him a wobbly smile through a veil of tears.

Tom was relieved to see Puchalski on the cement walkway and he beckoned him over. The detective was as tall as Tom and dressed impeccably. His shoes shone like mirrors. Though he looked like an inflexible neat-freak, his manner was friendly and warm, his eyes perceptive and disarming. "Detective Sergeant Puchalski, this is

Francesca Antonelli. She discovered the body this morning. Would you take down her story?"

Puchalski bent and shook hands with Francesca, and gave her dogs a pat. Then he sat down beside her on the bench. He took out his notebook and began to ask her basic questions: her name, her address, and so on. He was patient and encouraging. She began to relax and repeated the story she had already told Chief Barnett.

Tom turned away and called into the station for Susan Simpson's number. Above on the headland were police cruisers from Banner Bluff as well as vehicles from the county sheriff's office. An ambulance waited, escorted by a cruiser with flashing blue and red lights. Already trucks had arrived from local TV stations. He frowned and groaned inwardly. Dealing with the media was one of the drawbacks in his job, especially on a day like this.

Edmond Hollister, the Medical Examiner, had come down from Waukegan. Tom walked over to hear what he had to say. Hollister was a small, energetic man with quick hands and a wry sense of humor. He accomplished his job with vigor, no matter how gruesome the task. He had a round, bald head with a ring of grey hair reminiscent of a fifteenth-century monk's tonsure. He had just completed an inspection of the body as Tom came up. "Hello, Hollister. What have you found?"

"Good morning, Chief. Well, maybe not a good morning. What a tragedy. I believe this little girl drowned approximately five or six hours ago. Rigor mortis has barely set in, but with the cold lake water it'll be difficult to estimate a precise time of death. I don't see any signs of violence. When I get the body into the morgue, we'll check for puncture wounds or broken bones. We'll do blood tests, a spinal tap and vaginal swabs. However, I'm thinking that the water will have washed away considerable evidence."

"Right. Unfortunately, the woman who found her pulled the body out of the water and on to the beach. Between that and her dogs racing around, we don't have any obvious footprints."

"So was she in a play or playing dress-up when she disappeared?" Hollister asked. "The dress looks like a Halloween costume, one of those princess dresses my granddaughter runs around in all the time."

"When she disappeared, she was wearing shorts and a tee-shirt according to the parents. Maybe she went home and changed."

"She's pretty young to have been wandering around by herself," Hollister said.

"You're right. She would have had to walk eight blocks to get here. All evening there were searches in town, on the beach and the bluff. Yet nobody saw her. It doesn't make sense. And why would she go into the water at 3 AM?" Tom paused and looked up at Hollister. "We're going to treat this as a homicide."

He heard a commotion on the access road and looked over. Lewis and another officer were trying to hold back Bob Lawrence, who had broken through the yellow caution tape and dashed down the road.

"What are you doing, you assholes? Let me go! That's my little girl down there. I've got to get to her," Lawrence screamed.

"You can't go down there, sir." Lewis tried to grab his arm.

"Let me go, God damn it. Lilly needs me. I'm her daddy."

"No one can disturb the crime scene, sir," Lewis shouted.

The other officer caught hold of Lawrence's arm just as he aimed a punch at Lewis. Tom rushed up and grabbed the man around the waist as he broke loose from the officers. They went down together on the hard cement. Bob Lawrence cried in pain and tried to fight Tom off.

Tom felt for him. This was a policeman's worst nightmare. But the law stood. Even the father of this little girl could not touch or hold his daughter until the ME had completed his examination of the body and the crime scene had been gone over with a fine-toothed comb.

Bob Lawrence began to sob. All the fight went out of him. He covered his face with his hands and mumbled over and over, "My little girl, my little girl."

Chapter 9
Sunday morning, May 16th

Here was another perfect morning with sun streaming in the windows and the birds chirping. After checking that Rosie was still safe asleep in her bed, Martin came down to the kitchen. He thought he would look into rigging up a bell or buzzer to be triggered by the opening of the front or back doors. He had seen such a gadget at a neighbor's house. At the time he'd thought it would be annoying to hear that buzzer fifty times a day. But now it seemed like a great idea. He would have to check out the possibilities at Home Depot.

He filled the coffee grinder with coffee beans. The whir of the blades and the sweet aroma filled the kitchen. There was nothing like that smell, he thought as he filled the paper filter with ground coffee and switched on the pot. He leaned against the counter and gazed out the window over the kitchen sink, feeling again that awful fear of yesterday when Rosie was lost. Thank God she was all right. And thank God Kate hadn't been here to go through that anguish.

Raising children was a crapshoot. As a parent, your heart trembled with every illness, every scraped knee and every injustice your child experienced. Parenting was a harrowing ride, he mused as he reached for his favorite mug decorated with a picture of his two favorite girls. Today, he would call the Lawrences and find out where they had finally found Lilly.

Just then, there was a gentle knock on the back door. Martin went over and opened it. Emma stood there, her face strained and haggard, wringing her hands. "Martin, something terrible has happened," she whispered.

He stared down at her as though frozen in time.

"They found Lilly. She was floating in Lake Michigan, down at the south beach. The police won't say it's her, but who else could it be?" Tears welled in her eyes.

Martin couldn't move. All he could think was, thank God it wasn't Rosie. He felt relief and guilt at the same time. What kind of person was he? He stared at Emma and then moved forward, opening his arms to comfort her.

When Tom Barnett turned into the police station parking lot, he felt drained even though it was only ten AM. This was going to be a very long day. Lilly Lawrence might simply have drowned, but there were too many unanswered questions. How did she get to the beach? When? Where did she get that dress? The number one question was, with whom did she go down to the beach? Because Tom didn't believe she wandered down there by herself.

Once the task force completed their investigation of the crime scene, he would meet with Officer Johnson, Chief Deputy Conroy and Detective Sergeant Puchalski. He wondered if Officer Johnson had received any useful tips. Usually, they got a slew of worthless calls, but buried among the useless information could be the golden nugget that would provide a valuable clue.

He grabbed a cup of tired coffee probably made at four AM and went down the hall towards his office. He nodded to the dispatcher, who looked at him, eyes clouded with anxiety. She handed him three phone messages and then looked down, unable even to say hello as she clicked the security door open into police headquarters.

As he entered his office, the phone rang. Against his better judgment, he picked up the receiver. "Chief Barnett, Banner Bluff Police."

"Good morning, Chief Barnett. This is Louisa Gorton. I got a phone call earlier this morning telling me you found that Lawrence girl drowned in the lake. I think you ought to press charges against those parents. They weren't watching that little girl. She was running wild at the church fair along with the Marshall girl."

Tom could barely contain his anger. "We appreciate your call, Mrs. Gorton, but we have not yet verified the identity of the body and..."

"Well, who else could it be? Weren't your officers looking for her all over town yesterday? There were police cruisers driving around all night long. I couldn't sleep."

"We were trying to locate this child and the hunt didn't stop when the sun went down," he retorted. He looked up at the ceiling fan and silently pleaded for patience.

"Besides the police cars," she continued, "that Spanish man was driving around, and the Canfield boy. I'll bet he was up to no good."

"What Spanish man are you talking about?" Tom's interest was piqued.

"The one who works for the city, with the wife who works at Appleby's," she said, with unmasked disapproval in her voice.

"You mean Luis Gonzales. He's a fine, conscientious city employee." Tom decided not to point out that Luis was Mexican by ancestry but as American as Louisa herself. "What time did you see these cars, Ms. Gorton?"

"Well, I couldn't sleep and I went downstairs to get a little something to help. I think it's probably the full moon. Anyway, that's when I saw the cars. Let me see, I think it was about one AM. When I went downstairs, I saw the Spanish man's noisy car. And I saw the Canfield boy's racy little car earlier on. Or wait a minute, maybe I saw his car the day before. Well, he goes down there a lot. You know, to the beach."

Tom could barely contain his impatience. He tapped a pencil on his desk and frowned at his phone messages. "I will talk to Mr. Gonzales. He might have some useful insights. Thank you for alerting the police…"

"Maybe he kidnapped that little girl! I saw him holding her hand at the fair. I certainly would talk to him if I were you."

"Yes, yes, we'll follow up on this. Thank you again. Goodbye." Tom replaced the receiver with quiet determination. That woman was a piece of work.

In spite of last night's fruitless adventure, Luis managed to sleep until nine. The kids were already up watching cartoons and Yari was quietly preparing breakfast in the kitchen. He smelled coffee and frying bacon. She would be making huevos rancheros with eggs, refried black beans, pepper jack cheese and her special salsa. The kids were probably having Cinnamon Toast Crunch cereal. They had yet to figure out what a great cook their mother was.

Luis took a quick shower and pulled on a comfortable pair of jeans and a Bears tee-shirt. He padded barefoot into the kitchen where Yari was at the stove. He went over and encircled her with his arms and nuzzled her neck. She had a fresh citrusy smell. She turned and they shared a close hug and a good morning kiss. "Love you!" she said.

"Love you too," he answered. He poured a cup of coffee and sat down. The kitchen table was already set with silverware for the adults and cereal bowls and spoons for the kids. Even for a simple family meal, Yari always used colorful placemats and matching napkins. Sitting down together was an important event. She called the boys for breakfast and told them to turn off the TV. They came running in with shining faces, jostling each other and giggling.

"Okay, you boys settle down," Luis said, rumpling their hair as they sat. Yari poured them each a glass of orange juice and filled their cereal bowls. She went to the stove, filled the large tortillas with eggs and placed them on the table. She added a bottle of hot sauce for Luis. Then she poured herself a fresh cup of coffee and sat down.

"What are we going to do today, Mommy?" Roberto asked. "Are we going to the park or down to the lake?"

Luis responded too quickly. "No, not to the lake!"

Yari looked up at his abrupt tone of voice. She eyed him questioningly. Then she said, "I talked to Gloria and Jose yesterday and we thought it would be fun to have a picnic at Liberty Grove. Gloria has some cousins visiting from Ecuador and she would like them to meet us. So how about that?"

The boys were ecstatic. They loved playing with the three Jiménez boys. "Can we bring the soccer ball and our scooters?" they clamored.

"Sure you can," Yari said, "and the bocce game too." She turned to her husband. "What do you think, Luis?"

"Sounds great! Now, let's eat. I'm starving." Just as he picked up his fork, there was a knock at the front door.

Father Barnaby had received the terrible news from various sources. He was standing in the sacristy staring blindly out the small, stained-glass window. He looked at the distorted landscape that he could glimpse through the colored glass. The world became unintelligible through this tinted prism. It made him think of the mysterious ways of God. Perhaps mankind could only comprehend God's truth in a similar distorted manner. The Lord's reality seemed murky and amorphous to a lonely Christian.

As he dressed in his white alb and deep green chasuble, he quietly mourned the darling child that the Lord had called home. His heart was heavy and he would need all of his emotional strength to lead the congregation through this morning's service.

In the adjacent room, he could hear the ladies of the Altar Guild dressing the chalices, and pouring wine and water into the cruets. Their voices were low murmurs, not the usual chattering and laughing. When he had completed his preparations, he knelt down on the antique prie-dieu and asked God to give him strength. He asked for help in finding the comforting words to console his suffering congregation. He asked God to be with Jan and Bob Lawrence in their anguish.

When Royce Canfield arrived at church, he was surprised to find the parking lot almost full. It made him think of Christmas or Easter when all the wayward parishioners showed up in force. He wondered what was going on today. He wasn't an expert on the liturgical calendar, but he was pretty sure today was nothing special. He turned to Amanda to ask her what was up, but she seemed as baffled as he was.

As usual, it was just the two of them attending St. Luke's. Royce could not convince Colman and his sister to come to church anymore and they were too big to drag here by force. The children claimed that all religions were "opiates for the masses." Apparently, all those years of Sunday school and Bible camps had not turned them into believers.

In the narthex, people were patting and hugging each other, talking quietly about what had happened to the Lawrence girl. Of course, that must be why the place was so full. Royce couldn't remember what she looked like; but Amanda had helped out in the nursery for years and had known Lilly since she was a toddler. She had tears in her eyes as they moved into the church with the subdued crowd.

As the service began, Royce's eyes roved over the parishioners. He saw his latest catch down in the fifth row. Louisa Gorton had asked to meet him at his office yesterday and had brought her check for the American United Investment Club as well as the $5,000, one-time-only enrollment charge. He always smiled at that. The five thousand was the tidy little sum that he moved over to his private account. He thought of it as his "tip" for a job well done.

Next to Louisa was Emma Boucher. She seemed like a possible candidate; although he had a feeling she was less malleable than Louisa. Louisa was vain and pompous. Flattery would get you everywhere with her. But Emma had always struck him as a sharp lady. It would be hard to pull the wool over her eyes. *Nothing ventured, nothing gained*, he thought. He was willing to "venture."

Detective Sergeant Ron Puchalski and a Banner Bluff officer were at the door when Luis opened it. He knew them both well. The Department of Public Works was located in the same building as the Police Department. They all shared the same lunch room and coffee pot. Luis was puzzled at first to see them, then uneasy. What would bring Puchalski to his door on a Sunday?

"Hey there, guys. What are you doing here? It's Sunday morning!"

Puchalski gave his slow grin and said, "We're wondering if you could come down to the station and give us some information. It'll just take a few minutes."

"Could we talk here? We've got a big day planned with the boys."

Puchalski lowered his voice. "I think it would be better down at the station. I don't think you want your kids listening in." Luis looked down the hall and saw Roberto and Raul peering around the corner with eyes big as saucers. "Hi there, kids," Puchalski said. "We need your dad to help us out. Is it all right if he comes down to the station?"

Both boys nodded slowly. Yahaira came out of the kitchen, looking bewildered. "Hello, officers. We're just having breakfast. Would you like some coffee?"

"Thank you, Mrs. Gonzales, but we've reached our quota," Puchalski said, smiling. "We're just here to pick up your husband. We need to talk to him. We'll bring him back in a little while."

"Luis, what about your breakfast; you haven't even started?" Her eyes were wide with apprehension.

"Just cover it up and I'll eat it later. I'd rather get this over with. I'll be back for the picnic." He slipped on his sandals. "Let's go," he said to Puchalski.

Luis said nothing on the short ride over to the town hall. Ron Puchalski was on the phone and the officer said nothing to him. He knew he hadn't done anything wrong, but that didn't make him feel any less nervous. He was perspiring and his palms itched. He imagined it had to do with the beach and Colman Canfield. When they arrived at the town hall, they went directly in the side door to the Police Department. Puchalski was still on the phone. The dispatcher waved hello to Luis, and he smiled uncomfortably. What was she thinking; that he was some criminal? She clicked open the security door and they went through, forming a little parade: the officer, Luis, and Puchalski behind him.

"Can we get you some coffee?" the officer asked as they headed for one of the two interview rooms.

"No, thanks," Luis said. His mouth felt dry and his voice was hoarse. They entered a small room with grey carpeting, grey walls, a small round table and padded grey chairs.

Puchalski turned off his phone and removed the headset. "Sit down, Mr. Gonzales. Make yourself comfortable. I'm just going to get Chief Barnett; he'd like to be in on this."

"Mr. Gonzales" instead of "Luis." Luis had sat around the lunch table talking with the detective, but he guessed Puchalski wanted things to be more formal today. He still wondered why he was there. A minute later, Barnett appeared. He greeted Luis with a smile and inquired how Yari and the kids were doing. Luis mumbled that everyone was fine. He felt increasingly frightened. He could barely look the policemen in the eyes.

Puchalski turned on a small tape recorder and explained that they would record this conversation in case they needed to go back and remember what he said. Then the detective said, "You have the right to remain silent. Anything you say can and will be used against you in a court of law. You have the right to speak to an attorney, and to have an attorney present during any questioning. If you cannot afford a lawyer, one will be provided for you at government expense." He handed Luis a paper and a pen to sign it.

At hearing his Miranda rights, Luis almost shot from his chair. "What's going on? Why am I here? Am I being arrested? I haven't done anything wrong."

"Calm down," Puchalski said. "You're not being arrested. But we need to precede our questions with your Miranda rights. It's the law." He smiled at Luis. So did the chief. "We're hoping you can be helpful in our investigation into the drowning death of Lilly Lawrence."

"Ay, *Dios mio!*" Shock made Luis revert to Spanish. "Dead? I thought they had found her at the park or at home." He looked from one officer to another. "I just saw her yesterday! I was holding her hand at the fair." He stared at the two policemen in disbelief.

"That's why you're here, Luis. We thought you might have been one of the last persons to see her alive. Can you please go through your day yesterday? Maybe you saw or heard something," Barnett said.

Luis's eyes were moist. "I will be glad to help you, my friends." He gave them a description of his day at St. Luke's fair: setting up in the early morning, keeping things swept up during the fair, stocking the food stands and emptying garbage cans. He sat rigidly on the chair, his back straight and his hands in his lap.

Then he told them about seeing Lilly and Rosie in the hallway when he was inside the church building getting a load of supplies for the hamburger stand. "The little girl, Lilly, she was crying and her friend Rosie did most of the talking. You know, they could be sisters. They look so much alike," he said.

"What time was this, Luis?" Puchalski asked.

"I'm not sure. They'd been at the puppet show and it was still going on." He thought for a moment. "Probably about four, four-fifteen, something like that."

"What did you do then?" Tom prodded.

"Well, Rosie, she's the talkative one, she told me Lilly had lost her stuffed rabbit. She called it 'Bunny.' So, I told the girls I would help them find it."

"Where did you go with them?" Puchalski asked.

"I said we would look together, just like I would with my two boys. We went out the side door and across the lawn to the driveway where they had set up all the booths."

"Did you talk to anyone as you went over there?"

"No." He paused, thinking. "We went right over to the booth where they made these little bracelets with beads and string. The little girls love that stuff. There was a long tablecloth around the display table. I looked under the cloth and there was Bunny…probably kicked under there by somebody."

"Did anyone see you there?" Puchalski asked.

"I don't know. I remember everyone being so busy with all the kids sitting at these little tables. I don't think anyone noticed us at all!" He looked up at them searchingly. "Is that a problem?"

Puchalski nodded. "What happened then?"

"The girls were all happy and smiling. They said thank you, thank you a bunch of times. Then they ran off together. That's the last time I saw them."

"What did you do after that?" Barnett asked.

"Let me see, I helped clean up over by the Tilt-a-Whirl. Someone had gotten sick."

"Then what?"

"The fair was winding down by then." He paused. "I did help search the church after the fair was over, you know, with the cleanup crew. We looked everywhere. We didn't find Lilly. But I was sure she had just gone home or gone to play somewhere. Anyway, I went home about eight o'clock. I was bushed." He felt relieved as he finished his story. They had him go through it again and then they left him alone.

A few minutes later, they came back into the interrogation room. Puchalski brought in three bottles of water and asked Luis if he wanted to use the washroom. "No, thanks," Luis said. "I'm fine. Can I go home now?"

"We have a few more questions," the chief said. "We'd like to know what you were doing last night around midnight."

Tension shot through Luis. He sat up straight and rubbed his knees with his hands. "Why are you asking that? I told you I went home after the fair. You can ask my wife."

"I believe you," Barnett said, "but someone reported seeing you driving from the beach sometime after midnight."

Puchalski leaned forward and jabbed his finger at Luis. His usual friendly manner had vanished. "You were at the beach. Lilly Lawrence drowned at the beach. Don't bullshit us."

Luis shrank into himself. He hunched his shoulders and looked away.

"Luis, we know you. We know you're a responsible guy, but if you saw something, you had better tell us…now." Barnett said.

Luis sat silently looking at his hands in his lap. Then he looked up and addressed Chief Barnett directly in a quiet voice. "I went down there to talk to Colman Canfield and Craig Thompson. I thought I could reason with them. Yari told me it was a bad idea, but I went there anyway."

The chief and the detective looked at each other, as if mystified, and then back at Luis. "Why did you want to talk to them?" Barnett asked.

Luis explained about his job cleaning up the picnic shelters and garbage receptacles. "I went down there one night and saw those kids smoking pot and drinking. Lots of times I saw Colman's car parked in the driveway of the abandoned construction site near there. Some mornings I'd find cigarette butts, marijuana roaches and empty bottles, but recently I found some used needles. I was worried about those needles getting into the wrong hands. What if a little child started playing with them?"

"So that's why you went there last night?" Puchalski asked. "Gonzales, that's police business. You should have notified us immediately. Why didn't you?"

"I thought I could talk some sense into them. It was a dumb idea, I know." He glanced down at his clenched hands. "Last night, only Colman was there. He was high on drugs and drinking. He couldn't even stand up. I wanted to drive him home; but he wouldn't let me."

"You should have called the police right then," Barnett said, his blue eyes boring into Luis's. "Why didn't you?"

Luis flushed. "Mr. Canfield is your good friend," he muttered. "And Craig Thompson's father doesn't like to hear bad things about his son, and he's on the City Council." He swallowed and paused. "And I need my job."

"Oh, man." Chief Barnett leaned back in his chair and scratched his head. "You think we'll hold it against you if you report something about those kids? Luis, we're on the same side here. We want to help those kids, too. But they are breaking the law and they're underage!"

Luis nodded. He felt pretty stupid. What had he been thinking?

After Luis left, Tom got a call from Edmond Hollister. The ME had done an initial examination of Lilly Lawrence's body. The cause of death was drowning. Her lungs were filled with water. There were no bruises, lacerations, or scratches. A vaginal swab showed no genital trauma. "However, I did find a puncture wound on her left arm. I'm thinking a drug was administered. We drew blood, but those results will take at least a week."

"Right," Tom said. "Anything else?"

"After measuring the water temperature and considering the victim's temperature, I'd guess she died about three AM. We analyzed the contents of her stomach and determined that she had not eaten for at least ten hours."

"Thanks for getting back to me so quickly," Tom said. "I'll be waiting for those blood results. The County Homicide Task Force will be meeting this afternoon. We're treating it as a kidnapping and murder."

Mom dropped them off at the beach. It was really hot in the house. The fans moved the air around, but they didn't make you feel cool. She said they would be better off at the beach playing in the water. At the curb, they unloaded the towels, beach chairs and picnic hamper.

"Watch Julie while I park the car. Hold her hand!" Mom said.

When the car pulled away, Julie pulled her hand out of his grasp. "I don't want you to touch me. You've got cooties," she sneered.

He tried to grab her hand as he was told; but she ran away towards the water. He didn't know whether he should stay with the beach stuff or run after Julie. He looked down at the pile of towels and the picnic cooler, and when he looked up again she had scampered off. Mom would be furious. He felt dark anger swelling up inside. She would tell Dad that he hadn't minded. He would be in trouble, not Julie. She never did anything wrong. Dad would go after him. But it was Julie's fault. She was a stupid brat. He hated her.

Chapter 10
Sunday afternoon, May 16th

Susan drove Francesca home. They put the two big dogs in the small back seat of her blue Mini. The dogs were sandy and damp. When they got to Francesca's condo, Susan went inside as well. They toweled down the yellow Labs, who trotted over to their doggy beds for a day-long nap.

"Why don't you take a hot shower," Susan suggested. "I'll make us some coffee and something to eat? Remember I'm not a great cook like you."

"There isn't much in the fridge," Francesca replied. "But there might be some eggs and sliced bread in the freezer." She stood there indecisively, pale and wan.

"Go on, take a shower. I'll handle it!" Susan wondered how long it would take her friend to get over this frightening experience. Hopefully, she wouldn't have nightmares for months.

Susan found just what she needed in the fridge. She whipped up some scrambled eggs with cream cheese and chives and popped some multigrain bread in the toaster. There was just enough pink grapefruit juice for two small glasses. She set the table with two cherry red placemats and matching napkins that she found in the pantry, and added a pot of clover honey.

When Francesca came into the kitchen, she was wearing grey sweatpants and a tee-shirt. Her face was scrubbed clean and she looked much younger than her thirty-odd years. Susan wondered if Francesca would be hungry, but she gobbled up the eggs and had three pieces of toast.

"Do you want to talk about what happened? Or would you prefer to just forget it?" Susan asked after she had poured a second mug of coffee.

"I do want to tell you about it. I guess what shocked me was seeing death up close. I've never seen an actual dead person and I certainly have never touched a dead child." Tears welled up in Francesca's eyes. "She was so cold, and so wet. Her parents must be miserable. I'll have to call them, or maybe go over there and talk to them. Do you think I should?" She looked up at Susan, pain in her eyes." Or maybe they won't want to see me because I was too close to her, to Lilly, too close to her death."

After Luis Gonzales left, Puchalski and Barnett headed over to Churchill's. The cozy sandwich shop was decorated in a British theme, with pictures of well-known London landmarks and photos of British royalty. They stood in line to order their sandwiches. As they waited, Tom eyed the counter display of pictures taken in Banner Bluff. Part of the charm of the restaurant, the slowly revolving digital collection was a favorite of amateur photographers. While you waited to place your order, you could spot your neighbor shoveling out his driveway after a blizzard or your daughter dressed as a wood nymph in the school play.

Tom ordered his usual, hot pastrami on rye with spicy mustard. They took their sandwiches to a nearby empty table and sat. "Here's what I'm thinking," Tom said after swallowing his first bite. "There's no way that little girl walked down to that beach by herself last night. Someone would have seen her. There was no reason for her to run away or hide from her parents. Maybe she saw something at the fair or in that garden with the St. Francis statue that scared her. But this is a five year-old! She isn't going to drown herself at three AM. Someone brought her down there."

Puchalski nodded. "I think we need to talk to the Canfield kid and see what he has to say. We're going to have to go at him about this drug and alcohol business as well. I'd like to know who his supplier is."

"Right." Tom took a sip of iced tea.

"We know the shelter Gonzales mentioned is on the north beach so I doubt either one of them would've heard or seen anything…assuming Gonzales told us the truth about not seeing anybody."

"I'll go pick up Colman after lunch and bring him in. I may play golf with his father, but I *am* going to do my job." He gave Puchalski a meaningful glance. "I suppose if I was a Hispanic living in this WASP town, I'd feel insecure about risking my job with the powers that be."

Puchalski nodded, eyeing the wedge of dill pickle on Tom's plate. "Are you going to eat that?"

Tom passed his plate. "Help yourself. I think we should talk to Rosie Marshall again, find out if there was anyone else they talked to at the fair. Anything she might remember. Anyone she might remember. Could you go over there after you finish your pickles?"

"Sure thing, boss," Puchalski said, smiling.

Puchalski knocked at the Marshalls' house. He could hear an animated conversation going on through the screen door. "I won't wear that dress to the ball, it's way too flashy." Pause. "But that color is perfect on you."

A minute later, Rosie appeared holding a Barbie in each hand. "Officer Friendly," she squealed. "What are you doing here?" The Marshalls' dog, Jack, started barking and wagging his tail vigorously.

"I came to see you," Puchalski said. "Is your daddy here?"

"Daddy," she yelled. "Officer Friendly's here."

Martin came hurriedly down the stairs. He looked less than thrilled to see Detective Puchalski at his front door. He didn't want Rosie to know what had happened to Lilly just yet. He wanted to wait until the right moment to tell her. "What can I do for you, Detective?" he asked, somewhat grudgingly. "We're leaving for the airport in a little while. My wife is coming home from Paris."

"I'd like to have a little talk with Rosie." Puchalski smiled down at her. "It'll just take a few minutes." Rosie was jumping up and down with excitement, probably wondering if Officer Friendly had lollypops in his pockets. Sometimes he carried them when he went to the school to talk with the kids.

Martin opened the door and led him into the living room. As soon as Puchalski sat down in the armchair, Rosie climbed onto his lap and smiled up at him

"So, Rosie," he asked, "what is Barbie going to wear to the ball?"

Rosie giggled. "She's going to wear the sparkly blue dress, because she's a Cinderella doll."

"What about Snow White?"

"Her dress is blue and yellow and red. Do you want me to show you?" She jumped down and ran upstairs. While she was gone, Puchalski took his chance to tell Martin he wanted to ask a few more questions about anyone she might have seen at the fair. He assured Martin he wouldn't discuss the drowning.

Rosie came down with a Snow White dress for Puchalski to admire. Then she climbed back into his lap, her arms full of dolls and doll dresses.

"So Rosie, I wanted to ask you some more questions about the fair, yesterday. Okay?"

"Okay." She nodded as she twirled a Barbie in her hand.

"Did anyone come and talk to you and Lilly at the fair? Did anyone help you out or ask you questions?"

The little girl dropped the dolls on the floor and bent over to pick them up. She shook her head.

"Are you sure?" he prodded.

She paused a minute. "Well, Roberto's daddy helped us find Bunny. He talked to us."

"Yes, he's a nice man. How about anyone else? Was someone unkind to you?"

"What's unkind?"

"Was anyone mean or nasty?"

"Well, there was the mean boy when we got Popsicles. He made Lilly cry. But that wasn't at the fair."

Puchalski looked up at Martin.

"On Friday, Lilly came over to play after school," Martin said. "We stopped at Hero's and the girls ran in for Popsicles. I stayed outside with the dog. When they came out, Lilly was upset but she didn't want to talk about it."

"Do you know what happened, Rosie?" Puchalski asked.

"Uh-huh, that mean boy said Lilly was stealing candy, but I know she wasn't. He whispered mean things to her. I didn't hear what, though."

"Was Hero there? What did he say?"

"Hero said he knew Lilly didn't mean to take any candy, but she was upset anyway."

Puchalski looked at Martin. "Who is this mean boy she's talking about?"

Martin frowned. "It's that Canfield kid, Colman Canfield. He's a piece of work."

Amanda had checked on Colman before they left for church. He'd been curled in a ball, turned towards the bedroom door. In sleep his face was young and defenseless. Gone was the glowering expression he wore each day. Gone was the anger and arrogance. She wanted to wrap him in her arms and soothe away the pain that seemed to throb within him when he was awake. But he was eighteen and he didn't want her gentle arms. What did he want? She was at a loss to know.

She'd been horrified to learn of Lilly Lawrence's death. Here was a little five year-old who had been vibrantly alive yesterday and was tragically dead today. It was difficult to conceive of the anguish her parents must be suffering. Amanda had spent most of the church service trying to comprehend death, an impossible exercise. Father Barnaby had given an eloquent sermon, which was all the more poignant as his voice shook with emotion.

During the coffee hour, small groups of parishioners huddled together in quiet conversation. In muted tones they gossiped about Lilly's death. Amanda witnessed with distaste the avid pleasure some people displayed in discussing each juicy detail. She wanted to drag Royce away; but he was deep in conversation with Emma Boucher and another older lady. She didn't really want to know what they were discussing. He told her that he had to take advantage of the coffee hour to "make connections." It was some new angle of his law practice.

When they got home, Colman's car was not in the driveway. As usual, they didn't have a clue where he'd gone. As Royce opened the garage door, a police car pulled up in front of the house. Chief Barnett and an officer got out of the car and walked up the driveway. Royce turned off the engine and he and Amanda got out of the car.

"Hi, Tom," Royce said. "What can we do for you? I'd invite you in for a beer; but it looks like you're on duty!"

"Royce, Amanda. We would like to talk to your son, Colman. Is he around?" Barnett was all business.

Royce frowned. "What's this about, Tom? Why do you want to talk to Colman?"

"We just have some questions about what he was doing last night. We heard he was down at the beach around midnight."

"Who told you he was down at the beach?" Royce's eyes blazed. "Is someone accusing my son of something? I would like to know who it is."

Patiently, Barnett responded. "Listen, Royce, at this point, we would just like to talk with him. Is he here?"

Wanting to defuse the situation, Amanda chimed in. "We don't know where he went, Chief Barnett. He was sleeping when we left for church. We just got home and his car is gone. Let me try calling his cell phone." She rummaged around in her voluminous purse, pulled out her iPhone and pushed a speed dial number. It rang and rang. She smiled at the officers apologetically and dialed again. Colman was not going to answer the phone.

"Damn that kid. I pay a fortune for that phone and he won't answer. Where in the hell is he?" Royce glared at Amanda and then turned to Barnett in frustration. "You know what, Tom? I don't have a clue where he goes or what he does. I am so damn fed up with that kid." He threw up his hands. "You know what? I don't care what you do with him. When you find him, you can lock him up. Maybe he would be better off in jail. I'm ready to wash my hands of him!" He walked around to the driver's side door; climbed in, slammed it shut and drove into the garage.

Amanda mumbled a quiet goodbye and hurried under the garage door before it shut.

After Susan left, Francesca stood at the window watching her drive away. She was emotionally drained but she couldn't relax. Knowing herself, she decided it would be better to find some way to get her mind off of what had happened. Work was the best antidote. She went upstairs and got dressed in clean black jeans and a burgundy long-sleeved V-necked tee-shirt. She slipped on a pair of sling back sandals and grabbed her gold hoop earrings. She looked longingly at the bed. A sleeping pill and oblivion would be the easy way out, but she would never get through this if she didn't find a purpose. She needed to write that article about the fair. First, she would check out David's photos. People would still want to see pictures of themselves and their children. Later she would need to compose an announcement of Lilly's death. At some point she would have to talk to Chief Barnett. He had seemed almost kind this morning when he approached her.

As she drove over to the village green, she thought about Susan's date last night. She couldn't believe Susan had actually gone out with that jerk Brad Harrison. How could she find him appealing? But Susan said she'd had a good time, learned a lot about Banner Bluff and Brad had remained the perfect gentleman. *You never know*, she thought. She probably had a tendency to make rash judgments about people; but she *did* trust her intuition.

When she arrived at Hero's, she found Vicki sitting at a table in the shop. Vicki's granddad had gone up to their apartment above the store for a Sunday nap. She had her math book, a notebook and a calculator spread out on the round table by the window. Her long black hair hung in a loose ponytail down her back and she was dressed in the teenage uniform of low-cut jeans and a dark blue hoodie. Francesca remembered when Vicki arrived in Banner Bluff, wearing a little flowered dress with a white collar, sturdy shoes, white knee socks and a bow in her hair. Now, she was transformed from a little Greek schoolgirl to an American teenager.

Francesca bent down and gave Vicki a hug. Vicki looked up and frowned, "Gosh, Francesca you look wiped out. Are you all right?"

"Yeah, I'm just tired today." She didn't want to reveal what had happened that morning; not now when it was still so fresh. "How about you? We thought that article you wrote about the Honors Night was great. Frank commented on how well you put the story together. Maybe you should quit the *Banner Bee* and move on to the *Chicago Tribune*!" They gave each other a high five.

"Thanks, Francesca that makes me feel really good!" Vicki had mostly shed her accent, but still had very precise pronunciation.

"Frank also suggested that maybe you would like to play reporter and do an interview for us and write it up. What do you think?"

"Who do you want me to interview?" Vicki asked.

"Do you know Gloria Jiménez, the receptionist over at City Hall?"

Vicki nodded.

"Well, she said the Well-wisher has struck again. A girl who works at Appleby's Grocery got money to buy a car! Can you imagine?"

"Do you really think I could do it? That would be like being a real reporter."

"Of course, you can do it. See if you can get the name of the woman from Gloria and maybe talk to Frank about some good interview techniques. He would be glad to help. And you know what? I'll pay you!"

This time Vicki initiated the high five. At that moment, Ron Puchalski walked into the store. He looked at Vicki and Francesca's beaming faces and their outstretched hands.

"What are we celebrating here?" he asked.

"Hello, Detective Puchalski. We're celebrating Vicki's formal entrance into the world of journalism. She's going to do an interview and write an article for the *Banner Bee*!"

Vicki asked the detective what she could get for him, a Coke or something to eat.

"I came to talk to your grandfather," he said. "Is he around?"

"He went up to take a nap, but he's probably ready to get up now. I'll run up and get him."

When Vicki had left, Puchalski turned to Francesca. "Don't you think you should be at home resting after what you went through this morning?"

"Listen," she said. "If I stayed home I'd go crazy. I would be going over and over that walk on the beach. I'm actually better off busy at work."

He nodded. "I hear you." He looked tired himself. He probably had been up most of the night in the search for Lilly.

"You look exhausted! Are you going to be able to go home now and get some sleep?"

"Hopefully later on, after we clear up some details. This is an ongoing investigation. We don't know where Lilly was for nine hours and we don't know how she got down to that beach. Parents are panicking about their children. We've had a lot of calls and right now we have no answers."

"Detective, I think I should report the drowning in the *Banner Bee*. I don't want to overstep any boundaries. Could I send you a copy of my article, to go over before I post it? Or should I send it to Chief Barnett?"

"I think you better email it to the Chief. He's pretty sensitive about that kind of thing."

Hero's heavy steps sounded on the stairs. He came into the shop yawning, his grey hair disheveled and his eyes sleepy.

"Hello, Francesca. Good afternoon, Detective Puchalski." He made a slight bow and turned to Ron. "What can I do for you? Vasiliki said you wanted to talk to me."

"How about if we sit down," the detective suggested as he pulled out a notebook. "This should only take a few minutes."

"See you later; I'm going up to work." Francesca made her way up the stairs.

110

Puchalski watched as Vicki went back to her calculus. He beckoned Hero over to the back table, a little out of earshot. "As you might have learned, we found Lilly Lawrence drowned in Lake Michigan this morning. Your friend Ms. Antonelli found the body. She was pretty shook up."

Hero turned to look up the stairs and then back at Ron. He was visibly shocked. "Oh my God!" He clasped his hands together on the table. "How did this happen?"

"We don't know yet but we're treating Lilly's death as a homicide. I'm here to ask you about last Friday. Apparently, she was in here with her friend Rose Marie Marshall and left in tears. We learned this from Mr. Marshall and his daughter."

"Oh, you're talking about that business with the young man, Colman Canfield. You know what, Detective, I think he robbed me on Friday and that little girl saw it."

"What happened exactly?" Puchalski asked.

"First the girls came in and were looking at the candy shelves. They were on their way back to the Popsicles, but they were taking their time. Then Colman came in and asked for a slice of pizza and a Coke. The girls had given me five dollars and I rang it up. The drawer was still open when Colman came in, or maybe I left it open when he paid me? No, I don't think so." He scratched his head, as if trying to remember.

"Anyway, while I was in the back room for the pizza, I think Colman took about $160 out of my cash drawer. I had a large lunchtime crowd. The kids from the high school can go off campus for lunch and on Fridays I make extra pizzas and Italian sandwiches. So there's a lot of cash in the register." He paused again. "When I came back in the room with the slice of pizza, the little girl, Lilly, was crying. Colman said she had tried to steal some candy. She didn't have anything in her hands. I told her not to worry…that it was all right. But I think she saw Colman stealing the cash."

"When did you realize the money was gone?"

"Not till after eight, when I closed up the shop and bagged the money for a deposit. I always take it right over to the night box at the bank. It's only a block away."

111

"You should have alerted the police on Friday."

"Detective, I felt stupid to have left that kid alone with an open cash drawer." He shrugged. "Maybe it was a good lesson for an old man who is too trusting."

Puchalski looked at his phone. There was a message from the Chief. They had brought Colman Canfield in for questioning.

Colman woke up about noon. His head was spinning and his mouth was dry. He went into the bathroom, drank a big glass of water and took three aspirin. Then he lay back down for a few minutes, waiting for the aspirin to kick in. He couldn't remember what happened last night. It was all a fog in his head. He'd bought some Vicodin from a guy in Lindenville who also sold him a fifth of scotch. This guy was the big brother of a kid at school. He had moved out of Banner Bluff and lived in a cruddy apartment west of town. Colman didn't know if he had a real job, but he was definitely the Man when you wanted to buy.

Then he had driven down to the beach road and sat in his car, hidden in the unfinished garage at the construction site above North Beach. There had been a lot of action on the streets and cars driving up and down the access road. He didn't know what was going on. He'd taken a couple of pills and gulped the scotch. It had taken a few moments for the edges to smooth out and pretty soon he was feeling good, very good. He'd listened to the Black-Eyed Peas blasting in his earphones and let the drugs do their trick.

After a while, the beach traffic died down and he'd made his way to the beach shelter; his home away from home. He remembered putting a few logs in the fireplace and lighting a fire. When it was crackling he had sat down on the low wall and watched the moon rise over the lake. Then that Mexican had come down there. What an asshole! He couldn't remember what that spic wanted. When did he go home? He didn't remember shit. Thank God he hadn't been stopped, because they would have slammed him with a DUI for sure.

He looked at the clock. His parents would be coming home from church soon. He didn't want to have to deal with them today.

Quickly he picked up his jeans and sweatshirt from the floor and pulled them on. After slipping on his Reef sandals, he made sure his wallet was in his pocket. He would make a fast getaway.

Once he was out of the house and safely on the road, he could hear his stomach growl. He was trying to remember what he ate for dinner last night. His parents had gone out and he and Samantha had ordered in Thai; but that was a long time ago. He decided to head over to Denny's on the highway. After one of their Grand Slam breakfasts, his head would clear up and he would feel a hell of a lot better.

The waitress named Sherri had just put down his Grand Slam with sausage and bacon when the cops showed up. Sherri was a big-assed girl and he figured she ate a lot of these Grand Slams. Not like Carrie, who lived on yogurt and bean sprouts. He had been looking at his iPhone for messages. Carrie hadn't answered his texts or calls for two days. He didn't deserve her attitude. What a bitch! He looked up when Sherri plopped the plate down and saw Big Chief Barnett and one of his Indians coming towards him. He thought about getting up and heading for the side door, but what the hell for? What did they want? Then, his mind cleared and he remembered the Mexican coming down to the beach. Oh, shit!

Martin and Rosie arrived at the airport a little early. Rosie was bubbling with excitement and skipped back and forth in front of the doors that Kate would be coming through when she finished with Customs. The doors opened every few minutes and crowds of people poured out. There was an onslaught of Indians or Pakistanis looking tired and disheveled after a very long flight.

A bunch of Spanish speakers came through the door, probably from somewhere in South America. At last, a trickle of people appeared speaking French and carrying plastic Duty Free bags with PARIS marked on the side.

"It's going to be any minute now, peanut, keep your eyes peeled!" Martin said.

Just then Kate appeared, pulling her suitcase and carrying a big doll dressed in a sixteenth-century costume. Rosie jumped up and down, and before Martin could grab her she had scooted under the rope of the cordoned-off area and was in her mommy's arms. They hugged each other with the doll squeezed in between. The crowd walked around them, smiling at their shared embrace. Finally, Kate put Rosie down and grabbed the handle of her suitcase with one hand and her darling daughter with the other. They walked past the guard and over to Martin. Martin and Kate shared a long, sweet kiss while Rosie studied her magnificent doll. She was beautiful; dressed like a miniature Marie-Antoinette.

"Do you love her? Kate asked. "She's dressed like a real French princess."

"She's beautiful, Mommy. She's so fancy."

"I'm glad, sweetie. Now let's go home! I can't wait to be in my own house, with my own bed and my own shower!" She bent down and kissed Rosie again on the cheek and then reached for Martin's hand and kissed him softly on the lips. "I love you guys!"

"No Mommy, guy and gal!"

Chief Barnett said Colman could finish his breakfast, but they asked him to hand over his iPhone. He figured they didn't want him to contact anybody. Who did they think he would call? Certainly not his effing parents. Barnett and the officer moved over to the next table and ordered coffee. Colman took his time chewing each bite. What was the hurry? Hell, this might be his last meal in freedom. Sherri came over shyly and gave him his check. He had just enough to cover the bill and a nice tip.

"I'm ready to go," He told the cops.

They got up and followed him out of the restaurant.

This wasn't the first time Colman had been arrested. He knew the drill. After settling into the interview room, they started quizzing him about last night, about the alcohol and drugs he'd obtained. Where did he get them? Where were his buddies? What about his girlfriend? They seemed to know all about who he hung with and what they'd been up to. He figured that little spic rat had been watching him for a while. He didn't really deny or admit to anything.

What could they prove? He didn't have any drugs on him and he knew his car was clean. He figured he could just sit tight and they would have to let him go.

After an hour, there was a knock on the door and the Big Chief got up and went out to talk to Detective Puchalski. Colman stretched in his chair and yawned. This was going to be a very long and very boring afternoon.

A few minutes later, Barnett and Puchalski came back in. They told the officer who'd been babysitting Colman that he could go. Somehow, the tone had changed. He could sense the tension in the air. He sat up a little straighter and eyed the two policemen.

"Tell us about last Friday afternoon, Mr. Canfield," the detective said.

"Whaddaya mean?"

"What did you do after school?"

Colman was trying to remember. What had he done after school? Oh yeah! He'd gone to the Greek's grocery for pizza. Oh, fuck! They'd found out about the money. "I can't remember," he mumbled, looking at the circular pattern of coffee-cup stains on the table.

"We think you do. Think a little harder," the detective spat, leaning towards him over the table.

"I dunno, just drove around."

"Come on, Colman, let's hear the truth," Barnett snapped. "Stop screwing with us. We do know where you were and we have witnesses."

"Well, then why ask me? Ask them where I was," he shot back.

"You better get talking. We'll keep you here all day and all night." They kept after him a while longer. Then they left him alone. He was getting scared. Maybe he should just tell them about the money. He could pay the old Greek man back. His dad would be good for it.

They came back in and started questioning him again. Finally, he mumbled, "Okay, I bought some pizza and a Coke at Hero's."

"What else happened? Tell us about the money. You needed cash for the drugs and the booze, didn't you?"

"Yeah, okay, yeah, I stole the money; but I can pay it back. I'll ask my dad for the money. I'll give it back to Hero." He felt relief now. He had told them. They could call his dad and he could go home. But they didn't seem satisfied.

"Who saw you steal the cash, Colman?" Barnett asked his eyes like steel.

"This little blonde kid, she was watching me. I wanted to scare her. I didn't want her to tell Hero, so I got down and yelled at her. Not really yelling, though. I didn't want the old man to hear, so I whispered loud."

"What did you whisper to her?"

"I said, 'Don't tell anyone what you saw or I'll kill you.' You know, just to scare her."

"Did you?" Chief Barnett asked.

"What?" He looked up blankly.

"Did you kill her?"

It was hot at the beach, too hot to sit in the sun. So they played in the water. Mom sat in a beach chair close to the lake with her feet dangling in the water. The sky was cloudless and the sun beat straight down. The light reflected off the water in glittering shards.

Julie wanted him to carry her on his back and then dive under like a big shark. He did it over and over. He sang the "Jaws" music and then whoosh, he dove down into the water and she would scream. He wanted to really drown her. He wanted her gone.

"Don't be too rough. That's your little sister on your back," Mom shouted as she got up. "I'm going to go get the lemonade from the car. I'll be right back."

Julie pulled his hair and kicked his back. He pushed her off and she began punching him. She hit him on his bad shoulder.

"Get off of me, Julie! Leave me alone." He shook her off.

He looked back at the shore. Mom was heading up to their beach towels. No one was looking. He jumped on Julie and pushed

116

her down with his whole body. She was only five and he was much bigger. She was wiggling, but he held her head down and straddled her. Mom was talking to a neighbor. She didn't look towards the beach. Julie tried to wriggle free, but he kept pushing. He held her until she stopped moving. Then he dove underwater and swam out, away from shore. He only came up for short gulps of air, and then he went back under, down into the deep, dark water.

Chapter 11
Sunday night, May 16ᵗʰ

Banner Bee, May 17, 20__

There is incredible sadness in the community of Banner Bluff over the death of Lilly Lorraine Lawrence, aged five. Lilly's body was found floating in Lake Michigan at the Banner Bluff South Beach early yesterday morning. Chief Thomas Barnett asks that anyone who has knowledge of Lilly's whereabouts between Saturday afternoon and Sunday morning, please contact the Banner Bluff Police Department.

Francesca had written the short article about Lilly Lawrence's death and emailed it to Chief Barnett. She thought it was better to email it than walk over to the station, although it was just a short block from her office. He had sent a terse reply saying the announcement seemed appropriate at this time. Then he emailed a little later thanking her for her 'lucid and coherent statement that morning in spite of the shock you experienced.' That gave her pause. She really didn't know what made him tick.

For whatever reason, David hadn't sent her his pictures from the fair. He was usually on the ball. So she posted the death announcement and also the cute article Vicky wrote about the Well-wisher. Some good news and some bad news; that's the world of journalism, she thought. She would hold off on the spring fair story until Tuesday.

She yawned and put her computer to sleep. Then she walked downstairs to the kitchen to make a tomato, mozzarella and pesto sandwich. She had some great rustic Italian bread. She would make a panini and pour a glass of Pinot Grigio.

As she was letting the dogs outside, the phone rang. She looked at the caller ID. It was her mother. She stood there staring at the phone. She really didn't feel like dealing with Mom tonight. Oh, well, better answer it and get it over with.

"Hi Mom, great to hear your voice."

"Hi, sweetie. What have you been up to this week?"

"Well…"

"Your sister just left. She was here to pick up the kids. They're so cute. Libby helped me fix supper and Robby played video games with your dad. We just love having them over and giving Sandra and Henry a break. Well, you didn't tell me about your week?"

That's because you didn't give me a chance, Francesca thought. "I've been very busy, Mom. There's a lot going on in town and lots to write about. This morning I had a frightening experience, a little girl…"

"Oh, yes, your little writing activity."

Francesca bristled. "Mom, please don't call my online newspaper a 'little writing activity'. I've increased readership and I even won an award recently from the Media Association of Chicago. Please give me a little credit here."

"Whatever," she answered. "What about your social life? Did you go on any dates? You know, Francesca, you need to get yourself out there."

She hated having to justify herself, but her mother brought that out in her. "I did go out for dinner with the doctor I told you about, Marcus Reynolds."

"Did you have a good time?"

"Yes, we had a lot to talk about and a wonderful dinner. We had this delicious veal…"

"Francesca, I don't care about the dinner. Do you think he might propose soon?"

Francesca groaned inwardly. "Mom, I don't have a clue. Right now we just enjoy each other's company."

"Well, my dear girl, you are not getting any younger. If you don't grab someone soon, you'll be all wrinkled and no one will want you." There was a pause, and then she softened her tone. "That was unkind. I'm sorry, Francesca, I just want you to be married and happy like your sister…and have children."

Unbidden, the image of Lilly floating dead in the lake filled Francesca's mind.

"Well, guess what, Mom? I am happy! I am very happy! Say hello to Dad, I've got another call coming in. Bye!" She punched the red bar on her iPhone and collapsed onto a kitchen chair. She felt tears well up in her eyes. She never should have answered the phone, not tonight, not when she needed to hear a comforting voice.

She was used to comparisons with her older sister. Sandra was just like their mother: petite, blonde and green-eyed. Francesca resembled their father, being five foot nine with dark brown hair and deep brown eyes. Her mother could never quite accept her younger daughter. In her mother's eyes, Francesca seemed gawky and enormous. At the shoe store, Sandra tried on size five and a half while Francesca was into a size eight by age twelve. Her mother would wring her hands: "What are we going to do with you? You're going to be massive; not a cute little lady like your sister." The words "cute little lady" had stuck. Francesca went through years of hunched shoulders and bad posture trying to appear shorter than she was.

But the differences between the sisters were more than physical, Francesca thought as she took out a tomato and sliced it neatly. Sandra was bubbly and fluffy. She giggled her way through life, wearing pretty feminine pastels. In high school she was a cheerleader and flitted from boyfriend to boyfriend. Her social circle included the popular girls who twittered and gossiped like sparrows on a telephone wire. Sandra's grades were not the best, but to her mother that didn't matter as much as social success.

Francesca was different. She'd spent hours in her room, reading and writing. As a preteen, she'd been like a caterpillar enclosed in its chrysalis. She was awkward and clumsy, her face spotted with acne. When she emerged at sixteen as a tall, willowy, attractive young woman, neither she nor her mother had quite known how to deal with it. Men turned to look at her when she walked by; she'd been approached several times by photographers who saw her as a potential fashion model. It had made her susceptible to a charm offensive from Dan, who knew her well enough to know just what would work on her.

She laid the tomato slices on the bread and covered them with the mozzarella. Back in high school, Dan had shown up one day at a meeting of the Progressive Anarchy Society she had founded. Good-looking and intense amid the geeks and nerds who made up the club, he'd suggested they march downtown to protest the inhumane treatment of illegal immigrants. No one had ever proposed such direct action before. Subsequently, they had spent hours sprawled on the sofa in her basement planning chaos and rebellion to change the injustices of the world. What happened to that Dan, she wondered as she slathered pesto mayonnaise on her sandwich. The one who went to law school to strike a blow against discrimination and inequality, but got sucked in by the power and monetary success of corporate law.

She shook herself, finished putting her sandwich together and then picked up her phone again and scrolled through her text messages. There was one from Marcus: Hello Francesca, I heard about what happened? Is there anything I can do for you? I'm stuck at the hospital tonight.

Susan had texted her as well: I'm covering a reception at the club. I wish I could keep you company tonight. Talk tomorrow. Get some sleep.

She placed the phone on the table and sighed. She was overcome by a wave of loneliness. Her mother was infiltrating her psyche. She decided she wasn't all that hungry after all. She would skip the sandwich and have that glass of wine.

As she carried the glass into the living room, she stopped to look at herself in the hallway mirror. She could see tiny smile lines around her mouth and eyes. Weren't they a good thing to have? She would remember to put on that moisturizer every night, starting tonight!

Kate and Martin were in bed. Kate wore the long silk nightgown she had bought in Paris and smelled of a new floral scent. He was holding her close, their bodies entwined. Earlier, Kate had put Rosie to bed after reading her three Pinkalicious books. Meanwhile, Martin had prepared cheese and crackers on a tray along with a bottle of cabernet and two glasses. He had arranged a ring of strawberries on two plates with a small mound of sugar in the middle. When Kate came downstairs they had curled up on the living room sofa and enjoyed their simple repast while Kate told him all about her trip.

Martin hadn't wanted to ruin the homecoming, so he hadn't talked about Lilly Lawrence. He'd heard Rosie mention in passing that Lilly had gone away, but luckily Kate hadn't paid much attention. Now, as he held her close in their bed, he decided to tell her.

Kate was horrified. "She drowned in Lake Michigan? How did she get down there by herself at night? How terrible." She clung to Martin then, as if the worst had abruptly occurred to her. "It could have been Rosie; dear God!"

That idea still haunted Martin as well. "I think somebody must have lured her away at the fair. Maybe it was a prank gone bad."

Kate sat up. "We've got to watch Rosie all the time. We can't let her go anywhere by herself!" She looked at Martin, her eyes wide and frightened. "Have you told Rosie anything? What does she know?"

"She knows Lilly disappeared after the fair. Chief Barnett was here Saturday evening to question her. Then Officer Friendly—you know, Ron Puchalski—was here again just before we left to get you at the airport."

"I guess we have to tell her that her friend died. She'll probably hear about the drowning, so we'll have to tell her Lilly drowned and went to heaven."

"Let's tell her together tomorrow morning. Maybe she should stay home from school if she's too upset," Martin said.

Kate nodded, her face damp with tears. "Poor Jan and Bob, I'll have to call them in the morning. What shall I say?" She fell back onto the bed and reached for Martin. He clutched her to him, feeling relief at sharing his sorrow with his darling Kate.

Brad was stretched out on his dark brown leather sofa in his "man cave." The room exuded wealth and machismo. The walls were covered with walnut tongue-and-groove wainscot paneling, and were painted a rich burnished spicy paprika. There were shelves lined with books about baseball, basketball and football as well as sports bibelots he had accumulated. A large flat-screen TV hung on the opposite wall, flanked by posters of Michael Jordan and Walter Payton. A bar nearby included a wine cooler, a small fridge, wine glasses and tumblers and a well-stocked liquor cabinet. Tonight he was sipping a glass of Courvoisier Hors d'âge, which cost a fortune. He saved it for special moments like this when he was alone and had had a successful weekend.

He'd sent Susan Simpson a bouquet of roses after their date. Red seemed too garish, so he'd gone for a delicate pink. She would get them tomorrow along with his note: I enjoyed our rendezvous Saturday night. Let's do it again soon.

He liked Susan. She was bright and articulate and had the kind of slim-hipped body he enjoyed. Full-breasted and long-legged, she was a living Barbie doll. He'd like to get into her pants, but it might take a little wining and dining first.

He'd learned from a golf buddy that Francesca Antonelli had discovered the dead body of that little girl. The guy had probably texted everybody he knew. Everyone wanted to be the first one to spread the news, be it good or bad.

He didn't like Francesca. She was a pushy bitch. But he had less empathy for the irresponsible parents. They had the whole town searching attics and basements when this kid had just wandered off. He wondered how she'd gotten all the way down to the beach. That was a long way for a little kid. Maybe she went down through the ravine?

He picked up the remote and switched on the baseball game. The Cubs were ahead by two runs. Could that be? If they stayed ahead, it would definitely make his day, along with the call from Terrence. He'd run into Terrence Tifton yesterday afternoon at the Wallace golf outing. Crashing the company party had totally been worth it. Terrence came over to talk to him about their years at BB

123

High. After joking about the good old days and Brad's prowess on the football field, Brad had brought him around to investments and what looked good right now.

Today, Terrence had called him and asked about joining the AUIC. Terrence Tifton III, with all the money a name like that implied. God, he was good! Here he'd been out trolling the waters and this big tuna had jumped right into his net. He would call Larry and Royce tomorrow; right now he was going to mellow out, watch the game and sip his well-deserved brandy.

Colman was lying on his bed staring up at the ceiling. This had been the worst day of his life. He'd had to tell his story to the police fifty thousand times. He'd finally admitted where he bought his drugs, and by now that guy west of town was probably busted; and would probably want to get back at him.

After the interrogation was over, they called his dad. His parents came to pick him up and then they drove over to Denny's to get his car. Dad wouldn't talk to him and his mom sat in the back seat crying. At Denny's she'd gotten out of the car and asked for his keys so she could drive the BMW home.

When he and his dad were alone, his dad looked at him and said, "Tomorrow you'll be admitted into the West Haven Behavioral Clinic. You will be there for the rest of the school year, Colman. You will deal with your drug and alcohol addiction. I called them this afternoon, but they couldn't take you today."

Colman didn't say anything.

"You are a thief and an addict. We'll take care of your addictions and then we'll see what reparations you can make to the Greek."

Again, Colman didn't say anything.

"You have embarrassed your mother and me."

Colman didn't say anything. What was there to say?

When they got home he went up to his room and shut the door. They'd removed the lock a few years back—one more way to control him. He lay on the bed and thought about his life. He had no friends. Carrie and Craig didn't want anything to do with him. School was basically over and there was a long, meaningless summer ahead. Then what? He hadn't applied to colleges. Who would want him? He didn't have the grades and he hated classrooms and teachers. His parents hated him and he hated them. His dad was an asshole and his mother was a wimp. And he was a loser. Maybe he should kill himself. Everyone would be happy that way. He wouldn't embarrass his parents anymore and he would be "outa here."

He felt his eyes stinging. He hadn't cried for years. What was happening? He just lay there while tears streamed down his cheeks onto the pillow.

In town the air was thick and still. The leaves on the trees were sullen, hanging low and full. He heard the mournful cooing of doves perched among the branches. The moon was just rising when he came to the headland. Below, he could hear Her. She was moaning and thrashing. He walked down the path into the wind. She was smashing Herself into the rocks, spewing mountains of spray into the air. Along the beach, She reached long tentacles up towards the tree line. With each wave She lunged on to the shore, trying to possess it as She possessed him.

Chapter 12
Monday, May 24th

Tom Barnett had been working with the Homicide Task Force this past week. This morning, Edmund Hollister had called with the lab results on Lilly Lawrence. Now Tom faced the team and delivered the bad news. "Her blood showed intoxication from the combined effects of cyclobenzaprine, a muscle relaxant commonly sold as Flexeril or Fexmid, and hydrocodone, commonly sold as Vicodin. Hollister also found a residual quantity of Propofol and a small puncture wound on Lilly's upper left arm. He thinks she was injected with Propofol to subdue her, and then the perpetrator forced her to swallow the other drugs. Apart from the puncture wound, there was no sign of physical trauma." He looked up at the men around the table, measuring his words. "An adult could easily have held her under water and she would have been too intoxicated to resist. The only good thing is she probably was unaware of what was happening to her."

"I guess that cinches what we figured all along. She was kidnapped, drugged and kept for about eight or nine hours and then brought down to the beach and drowned. What kind of psycho are we talking about?" Detective Jose Ramirez said from his place at the conference table. Jose had joined the task force on leave from the Lindenville PD for the duration of the investigation. He was a specialized evidence technician and would be doing a closer analysis of evidence brought in. Detective Puchalski and Officer Lewis rounded out the investigative team.

"We've got someone who planned carefully, and was brazen enough to kidnap her in a relatively public place and then go down to the beach when everyone in town was out looking for her. Why would he chance being caught?" Puchalski said.

Lewis spoke up. "Maybe something went wrong with his plans. Maybe he wanted to get rid of her."

126

"Yeah, but he didn't try to hide the body. He wanted it to be found. It's like he's showing off," Puchalski said.

"I don't get what he wanted her for. I mean, if he didn't rape or molest her, why take her?" Jose asked.

Tom listened to them and said, "I think we should go back and talk to everyone again. I mean the Lawrences, Rose Marie Marshall, Luis Gonzales and the Canfield kid. We also need to encourage anyone who was at the fair to come forward with anything they can remember about Lilly's movements that day."

Tom took Puchalski with him when he went to talk again with Lilly's parents. The Lawrences lived in an attractive yellow house with white trim. A large front porch was surrounded by newly planted flower beds. On each side of the front steps, graceful urns contained bright pink geraniums. On the right side of the porch a polished wooden swing hung from the beams. To the left was a set of white rattan porch furniture covered with plump flowery cushions. Two large ferns stood on pedestals to each side of the front door.

Tom knocked on the screen door and looked into the darkened front hall. He saw Bob Lawrence appear from a room to the left. Bob wore rumpled khaki shorts and a dark blue polo shirt.

"Why are you here again? Have you got news?" he asked, without opening the door.

Tom ignored his hostile tone. "We've received information from the Medical Examiner that we would like to share with you. May we please come in and talk?"

Bob nodded. He opened the door and led them to the darkened living room. He didn't invite them to sit, so they stayed near the doorway. Jan Lawrence was stretched out on the sofa with one arm bent over her head, covering her eyes. She clutched a handkerchief in her other hand.

"Who is it, Bob?" she asked without moving.

Tom spoke before Bob could. "Hello, Mrs. Lawrence. It's Chief Barnett and Detective Puchalski. We're here because we received the Medical Examiner's report." He waited for her to sit up and look at him, but she remained supine.

"Let's hear it," Bob said, clenching his jaw, his hands in tight fists.

Tom took a deep breath, steeling himself. "Lilly was drugged with muscle relaxants and Vicodin. The ME said she didn't suffer when she drowned because of the level of drugs in her body."

"Oh, my God, my poor baby, my poor baby. Who did this to my little girl?" Jan covered her face with both hands and broke into racking sobs.

Bob Lawrence looked at his wife coldly. "See what I have to deal with? She's a basket case." He left the room and returned a moment later with a glass of water and a couple of tablets. Jan was sobbing, curled into a fetal position. "Sit up, Jan, and take your pills. You won't be able to get through the day without them."

Slowly, she sat up. She took the pills he held out to her and swallowed them with the water. Then she lay back down and turned to face the back of the sofa, as if willing them all away.

"You told us this guy didn't rape her, so why did he get her high on drugs? What did he want with her? She was just a little girl." Lawrence's aggressive tone wavered on the final words.

"We won't know that until we find the person or persons that abducted her," Puchalski replied. He looked at Jan, who was sobbing more quietly now. "Have you thought any more about the pink dress she was wearing? It looked like a costume, like a Halloween princess dress."

"It couldn't have been Lilly's dress. She didn't do the princess thing. She liked Dora the Explorer. And she played with Legos." Bob paused, his face crumpling "Hell, I don't know what she did all day. I was at work in Chicago." Arms wrapped protectively around his body and tears in his eyes, he looked at his wife. "Jan, where would Lilly get a princess dress? You can answer that."

"I don't know. Maybe Rosie gave it to her?" Jan mumbled.

"We'll check with the Martins," Tom said. "Another thing, you told me your brother was here for the weekend and then left abruptly on Saturday morning before the fair. Why was that?"

Bob glared at them. "He just felt like going home. What does that have to do with Lilly?"

"Did you have an argument? I'm asking because sometimes children run off when they've overheard adults quarrelling. They'll go and hide when things aren't copasetic at home."

Bob avoided his gaze. "He just wanted to go home. Call him. Charles Lawrence! He lives in Wisconsin in some trailer. You want his number?" He looked Tom in the eye. "Do you think he's the one? That's nuts! He loved Lilly and she adored him."

"I would like his number," Tom said. "We'll give him a call and see if he remembers anything useful."

"I'll get it for you. Then I would like you to leave. You've upset my wife and you've upset me." Lawrence strode out of the room.

After they were back in the car, Puchalski shook his head. "Man, that guy is hard to take. I know he's suffering, but..."

Tom nodded. "Yeah. I know they're in pain; but they're trying to hide something. It's just a feeling I've got."

They decided Puchalski should go to the Marshalls' house. He had the best rapport with Rose Marie. He called them and made an appointment for that afternoon, when Mrs. Marshall and Rosie would be home from school.

When Puchalski arrived, Kate and Rosie were sitting on the screened-in porch waiting for him. Kate was reading a story and Rosie was cuddled in her lap. Puchalski figured the Martins had not told Rosie the truth about what happened to her friend. If it were he, he'd put off telling her as long as he could. He knocked on the door.

"Please come in. We were waiting for you." Kate smiled as she reached up to shake his hand. "May I get you a glass of iced tea? I made it this morning." In her blue-sprigged linen dress and white sandals, her blonde hair pulled back in a low ponytail, Kate exuded a sweet brand of femininity. Puchalski was entranced by her warmth and smile.

"That'd be great," he answered. He sat down on one of the gently used arm chairs. The porch furniture had that comfortable feeling that made him feel right at home.

"Rosie, will you please entertain our guest while I get the tea?" The little girl climbed down, and Kate went into the house. The door banged shut behind her.

Rosie seated herself in her mother's chair. She seemed unnaturally subdued.

Puchalski smiled at her encouragingly. "Hi, Rosie. How are you?"

Silence.

"I bet you're happy that school is almost over for the summer."

She ignored his question. "Officer Friendly, do you want to talk to me about Lilly again?" She looked at him with big thoughtful eyes. "Lilly's gone, you know. She went to heaven and now she's with Jesus."

He nodded. "Do you miss her? She was a good friend."

"Do you think there are little girls for her to play with in heaven? She probably doesn't even miss me." She looked at him questioningly and then said, "Maybe Lilly can have ice cream whenever she wants."

"Rosie, can you tell me again about when you went to play with Lilly at the Saint Francis statue after the fair?"

"No, I don't remember."

"Did anyone come and talk to you two girls, maybe a friend of your mommy? Maybe someone Lilly knew?"

"I don't remember." She looked at the floor. "Sometimes Lilly wasn't a good friend. She never wanted to play princess with me."

Kate came back, carrying a tray. "Rose Marie, will you please open the door for me?"

Rosie clambered out of the chair and opened the screen door. Puchalski saw that the tray contained two tall glasses of iced tea with sprigs of mint, a smaller plastic tumbler of apple juice and a plate of sugar cookies with sprinkles.

"I helped Mommy make the cookies. Didn't I, Mommy?"

"Yes, you did. Now pass the plate to Officer Friendly." Kate smiled at him.

"They look great," Puchalski said. Rosie glowed with pleasure.

Once they all had their drinks and a cookie, he tried another tack. "How do you play princess, Rosie?"

She thought about this. "Well, you can play with Barbie princess dolls. Or you can play dress-up."

He helped himself to another cookie. "Did you let Lilly borrow a princess dress?"

Rosie looked at him incredulously. "Hell-o-oh!"

"Rose Marie, don't be rude," Kate said sharply.

"I told you she didn't play princess with me! She didn't like to play dress up," Rosie said indignantly.

"You're right, Rosie," Puchalski said, "but someone saw her in a pink princess dress."

"That's Aurora's dress," Rosie said.

"Who's Aurora?"

Kate explained. "Aurora is the Disney name for Sleeping Beauty."

The meeting was held in the large interview room at police headquarters. Hero Papadopoulos was first to arrive. He wore a well-worn black suit, a carefully ironed white shirt and a thin black tie. His worn black shoes had been highly polished and his hair was slicked back from his deeply lined face. He shook Tom's outstretched hand and was about to sit down when the others arrived.

Royce Canfield walked into the room, his son in tow. His manner was cautious and he greeted Hero and Tom courteously. He was dressed in a grey wool crepe suit—Armani, Tom guessed—and a pink dress shirt with French cuffs. His striped silk tie and Ferragamo loafers were in sharp contrast to Papadopoulos's well-worn attire.

The big surprise was Colman. His long, scraggly hair had been neatly cut. He wore charcoal grey dress pants and a French blue dress shirt. *What a handsome kid,* Tom thought. *You never know what's hiding behind those hooded sweatshirts and baggy jeans.* Colman was looking down at the floor, his arms dangling at his sides.

Hero stepped forward and shook Royce's hand, and then turned to Colman and held out his hand. Royce said sharply, "Colman, look at Mr.—how do you pronounce it?" He looked from Hero to Tom.

"Pa-pa –do-pou-los!" Hero said.

Royce repeated the name as best he could. Colman smirked.

"Perhaps you could do better, yes?" Hero said to Colman. "May we please hear you repeat it? It's Mr. Papadopoulos."

Colman stood there tongue-tied, looking embarrassed. Hero waited for Colman to repeat his name. When he finally did, Hero shook his hand.

At that point, Tom asked them all to sit down. He placed a sheaf of papers on the table and began to read. It was the police report describing Colman's arrest, his robbery of $160 and his reported addiction to alcohol and drugs. After Tom finished, he addressed Colman. "Does that sound correct to you? Is there anything I need to add?"

Colman shook his head, looking down at his clenched hands.

"Is there anything you would like to say, Colman?"

Again, Colman shook his head.

Royce Canfield was itching to talk. "We've got Colman in a drug program, Tom, I mean, Chief Barnett. He spent two full weeks there and he's going to attend an out-patient program every afternoon for the rest of the summer. He's clean now, right, Colman?" Colman nodded, and Royce frowned. "Speak up, Colman; stop nodding your head like some idiot. You have a voice, use it!"

"Yes, sir." Colman flushed and looked up briefly, then back at his hands.

Royce continued. "I, uh, I would like to give Mr. Papy-dopus the money Colman stole." He paused. "I'll even double it so we can all move on."

132

"Mr. Papadopoulos has some thoughts about that." Tom nodded to Hero. "Would you please tell Mr. Canfield and his son what you have in mind?"

Hero looked at Colman, then at Royce. Colman fidgeted and clutched his hands tighter. Royce looked slightly irritated. "You know, they say, money doesn't buy happiness. I think this is right," Hero said. "I do not think your money, Mr. Canfield, will buy Colman's happiness." His keen black eyes bored into Colman's frightened ones. "I think true happiness comes from a sense of self-worth and, how do you say, accomplishment." He looked at Royce. "You cannot do that for him with all your money; but maybe I can."

"Tell them your plan, Hero," Tom said. "You should both know that Mr. Papadopoulos has not yet pressed charges against Colman. However... "

Colman looked at his father, a relieved smile on his lips.

"Here is my plan," Hero said. "Colman will come and work for me this summer. I need extra help because we have more business. The kids don't have school so they come in and out all day long. The mothers bring the little ones in for lunch and we have the tables out on the sidewalk that have to be cleaned. There is much to do, stocking shelves, cleaning, preparing sandwiches, many things. Colman is eighteen, he can help."

Colman leaned forward, his shyness forgotten. "Wait a minute. You want me to work there all summer? That's *more* than a hundred and sixty dollars' worth of labor. That's like slave labor. That's like twenty cents an hour. That's not fair." His eyes flashed with anger.

"Ah, my friend, life is not fair," Hero said calmly. "I press charges, people find out and you have a criminal record, *or* you come and work for me." He gazed at Colman steadily. "You must make a decision. That is life. Every day you must make decisions."

Royce was watching this interchange. Tom could almost read his mind. He probably thought this little Greek grocer was kind of nervy, but Colman would be busy every day and couldn't get into trouble—or at least, not as easily. That had to be a relief.

"I'm thinking this might work," Royce said. "In lieu of community service, Colman could work with you. I approve."

"Ah," Hero said. "But it is not your decision to make, Mr. Canfield. It is your son's." He turned to Colman.

Colman tapped the table with his fingers, making a little drum roll. "When would I have to start?"

"I would expect you there at six AM tomorrow," Hero said.

"Six AM! You have got to be kidding! I could never get up by then in the summer." Colman fell back in his chair.

"Well, that is part of the deal. Six AM until two PM. You will have to go to bed earlier. I need you there to help with coffee preparation for the commuters. They want coffee and fresh pastry before they take the train."

Colman turned to his father. "Dad, help me. I can't do this. It'll suck! The whole summer'll suck! At three o'clock, I have to go to drug therapy sessions. I'll have no time to do anything. It's way not fair."

Royce eyed his son coldly. "Maybe you should have thought about all this before you stuck your hand in the cash register!"

Francesca had been reliving the moment she'd found Lilly Lawrence floating in Lake Michigan. She couldn't get the image out of her mind. She was obsessed. She had gone back down to the beach several times, looking along the access road for who knows what. At the bottom, the road opened up onto a wide cement parking area between the north and south beaches. Yellow caution tape barred her access to the south beach. Each time she made her pilgrimage she relived the scene. The only way she would ever find closure was when this monster was arrested. She was on her own personal vendetta.

Today in her office, she had spent a couple of hours going over the pictures David had taken at St. Luke's fair. It took a long time because she wanted to look at each one carefully. She was amazed at how many people she recognized, but plenty of others were total strangers. She looked for pictures with Lilly and Rosie Marshall, hoping to see someone lurking in the background. No one stood out. After going through them a couple of times, everyone began to seem familiar.

She considered the pink princess dress that Lilly had been wearing. Francesca knew Disney had made a fortune on the whole princess thing. Little girls wanted the dresses for themselves and for their dolls. She'd read that Disney's Cinderella was even printed on diapers. She went online to learn a little more. The Disney Princess website had pictures of all the princesses. Some, she had never heard of before. The current line-up was Snow White, Pocahontas, Aurora, Ariel, Tiana, Cinderella, Jasmine, Belle, and Mulan. Each one had her own story book and activities on the site. The two princesses with pink dresses were Aurora and Ariel. Did that have any significance? Ariel was wearing a pink dress in the line-up, but she was actually a mermaid and had her fishtail for most of her story. Aurora was Sleeping Beauty. Francesca clicked on the storybook and renewed her knowledge of the fairy tale. It was a little different from the one she had learned as a child, with some twists and turns, but basically the same. The wicked fairy put a curse on Aurora, who pricked her finger on a spindle and went to sleep. Then the Prince kissed her and she woke up, and they lived happily ever after. If only life were so easy! Love conquers all and evil is destroyed!

Francesca felt depressed. Maybe the dress meant nothing. Maybe the color of the dress was insignificant. She made a list of the facts she knew about the drowning and saved it in a folder entitled *Lilly Lawrence*.

After the day he'd had, Royce didn't know why he'd agreed to this meeting down at Trustworthy Realty. His life had been a nightmare these last few weeks. How was it that in spite of the success of his law firm and the money coming in from the AUIC, he was still in arrears? The second mortgage on the house, the payments on the two Mercedes and on Colman's BMW... no matter how much money he earned, it was never enough.

He never should have bought the Thunderbird PC Cruiser. At the time, it had seemed like something he needed. Needed? Right! He'd gone down to the marina with a buddy. The whole boat thing had seemed so exciting, so cool! That day people were out buzzing around on the lake. In the late afternoon and evening they came back to the marina. Everyone was partying on their boats. You could hear music and people laughing and talking. He imagined a whole summer of water skiing, fishing and socializing. Without even consulting Amanda, he had bought the boat. It was used but in perfect shape. It slept eight and had a luxurious interior and a full galley. He had taken out a loan to pay for it, which was another drain on his bank account.

But the 37-foot cruiser was a disaster. Amanda and Samantha had both been seasick when they went out the first time and had to be cajoled to go out with him the next week. Colman didn't think it was "cool" to go boating with his dad.

The first summer, it had rained just about every weekend and they had barely used it. Then they were given a mooring next to an annoying couple that played rock music loud enough to reverberate in their boat. But the real truth, which he had never revealed to anyone, was that he was afraid. He was afraid of Lake Michigan. He was afraid of the deep, black water. When they were far out from shore, he would sweat and feel his stomach churning. He didn't want to look down into the water's depths. It made him feel powerless and light-headed. He knew the winds across Lake Michigan could change direction in a minute. Storms were dangerous and there were seiches—tsunami-like waves that could occur. If you fell into the water in early spring, you could die in minutes from hypothermia. These real dangers were bad enough, but he also felt as though a malevolent spirit lurked in the rolling swells.

Last summer he had put the boat up for sale, but with this economy, no one would buy it. Then there were the credit card bills. Amanda had spent a fortune at Bloomingdale's and Neiman Marcus this last month. What did she need all those summer clothes for? It wasn't as though they were going to be hosting parties or going out for dinner every night. No, he was planning on lying low this summer. He wasn't going anywhere if he could help it. And at night he would stay home and make sure Colman was home, too.

He was ashamed of how Colman had acted at the police department that day. Well, he'd do one thing for sure. He was going to sell the BMW. He didn't want to pay for it and Colman could just ride his bike or walk. It wasn't as though Banner Bluff was a big town. Amanda could drive Colman to the West Haven Behavioral Hospital in the afternoon. And what about this mental hospital for wackos and druggies; his insurance wasn't going to pay for all these weeks of therapy. Money seemed to disappear like water down a drain.

When he arrived at the Trustworthy offices, he saw Brad's silver-grey Bentley Continental parked at the far end of the lot, away from other cars. Brad did that at Oak Hills too. He lived in fear of someone scratching the gleaming exterior. Brad was lucky. He didn't have children or a wife. All he had to worry about was that damn car.

Royce got out of his Mercedes, went to the sleek building and pushed the side-door buzzer. Once buzzed in, he went down the carpeted hallway and knocked on the locked office door. Sally opened it. She was decked out in an emerald green, low-cut dress, her hair loose around her face. She wore four-inch heels and a subtle, earthy perfume. She shook his hand and ushered him into the room.

"Why all the double-O-seven security? Is there anyone lurking in the hallway?" Royce asked.

"Better safe than sorry. Harry and I never want anyone listening to our conversations. Our office is our sanctuary."

Brad was lounging on one of the armchairs, looking irritated. "Better late than never, I'd say. Where in the hell have you been? You're half an hour late."

"Sorry, Mother," Royce said sarcastically. "I don't need you giving me a hard time. I've got plenty of others on my case."

Sally sat down close to Harry on the sofa. She crossed her legs and cuddled under Harry's arm. The two of them were a mystery to Royce. Here was Harry, a dumpy guy, with this sexy knock-out wife. The two of them had this touchy-feely relationship that was uncomfortable to watch. Royce felt like telling them to sit on opposite sides of the sofa.

They were both sharks, though. Harry could manipulate numbers and Sally could manipulate people. They were a formidable duo.

"Let's get started," Brad said. "Robert Lanhart has been calling lately. He is not happy with the return on his investment."

"We sent him a check last week. What does he expect?" Sally drummed her manicured nails on the arm of the sofa. "How did you deal with him?"

"I pointed out that the economy had not turned around as everyone hoped after the stimulus money. I told him even though we've made some great purchases; we're feeling the pinch like the rest of America. He grumbled some more and then finally calmed down."

"We need to bring in more investors if we're going to make this work. Who have you been talking to lately, Royce?" Sally asked.

Royce sighed. "I'm just like Lanhart. I need more money coming in." He looked pointedly around the room. "I agree we need more investors. I've put feelers out at church and at the club. I'm talking to two guys currently that I met at a legal technology conference. Then I'm going to approach Emma Boucher from church." He paused. "But I need more cash coming in. I would like a bigger check this month."

Harry sat up. "You're going to have to wait. I've done some money managing." He made quotation marks with his fingers. "Next month we should all be able to take a bigger cut." He turned to Royce. "You're going to have to sit tight."

"What 'money managing' are you talking about?" Royce asked nervously.

Sally looked at him intently. "You probably wouldn't understand. As I remember, your computer skills and mathematics acumen leave something to be desired. Just let Harry perform his magic." She put her hand on Harry's thigh and gave it a squeeze.

Brad rolled his eyes at Royce. Royce shared the feeling. How had they ever gotten mixed up with these two? Mercifully, Brad changed the subject. "Last week, I went to a private cocktail party put on by Wallace industries at the club. I kind of slipped in, talked to a bunch of people. Two of them called me back. I'm planning on meeting with them this week." He turned to Sally. "I think we need to update some of the materials we hand out."

"As a matter of fact, I actually bought a couple of properties last week. I've got Ivan, the Russian contractor, signed up. He's dying for work. I kind of dangled him along and he came way down in price. He's going to do a quickie fix-up of both properties. Then we can put them up for sale. These are great houses and we got them at killer prices." Sally paused. "They'll look good in the brochure. I'll revamp the cover and print out some new, flashy copies and Harry can screw around with the price sheets." She looked at Harry. He nodded, placing his hand over hers where it rested on his thigh. "We'll get all this done in the next few days, so you'll have fresh materials." Sally's smile and eyes didn't match up; the former was broad and toothy, the latter cool and calculating.

She was all powerful; the Goddess of the deep. He went down to Her at sunrise. She was beckoning him. Today, She was soft and serene. Her waters moved in lethargic swells. Her silky, rosy surface glowed with post-coital pleasure. She caressed his bare feet, luring him into Her depths.

Chapter 13
Monday morning, June 14th

It was Flag Day. The streets downtown were festooned with American flags every twenty feet. Each household had hung a flag on the front porch or garage. Several years ago, the Village Board had issued flags and flag holders for a nominal fee to encourage pride of country. Today, on the village green, the Boy Scouts had bivouacked at daybreak and proudly raised the flag as a high-school trumpeter played reveille. Afterwards they headed to Dunkin' Donuts for a nutritious breakfast.

Colman still hated getting up so early. It was torture, but getting a little easier. He'd heard the trumpet vaguely, but had turned over to sleep a few more minutes. Now, at five-forty, he was in a rush. He showered and dressed quickly and put on a forest green shirt and khaki shorts. Hero had told him to wear this uniform every day, so people would know he was an employee. He felt like he was in the army doing six AM boot camp. He was out of the house and speeding away on his bike in ten short minutes.

The first week at Hero's Market had been a marathon learning experience. He hadn't realized how much there was to do in this small store. Hero had taught him how to run the coffee machine and by Friday he had become adept at making cappuccinos and lattes. While he worked the machine, Hero and Vicki were busy toasting bagels, warming sweet rolls and popping doughnuts in bags. Some customers wanted to take a sandwich to work and the store provided little carrying boxes with a sandwich, an apple and a cookie. The bakery truck arrived at five AM, and by the time Colman got there, the pastries were attractively displayed and some sandwiches were made.

Colman had never really noticed Vicki at school. She seemed nice enough and she was actually kind of pretty. He would look at her surreptitiously when she was moving around the store. She smiled and was friendly to all the customers and they all had something nice to say to her. In contrast, he felt shy and uncomfortable. He took orders and handed out the prepared cups of coffee without saying much. One morning, he nearly died when Craig came into the store. Craig was with a friend and they both were cracking up. Colman knew they were saying something about him and he felt himself blushing.

When Colman came in this morning, Vicky and Hero were bustling. Hero said good morning and waited for Colman to respond. This was part of the morning ritual. They had to go through these niceties. He greeted them both formally. "Good morning, Mr. Papadopoulos. Good morning, Vasiliki." He had learned how to say their names after a little practice.

"Please go down to the basement and bring up some more twelve-ounce cups, a large bag of coffee and some of those plastic stirrers," Hero said. "We're going to need them during the morning rush. Vasiliki will show you where everything is."

The two of them tromped downstairs to the storage room. Colman didn't know what to say to Vicki and she seemed to feel the same. They had been working together for more than a week, but had never really talked to each other. She handed him some boxes and picked up a few cartons herself, and then they went back upstairs. He couldn't help checking her out as he followed her up. She had a cute butt, though he felt guilty even thinking such a thing. Hero could probably read his thoughts.

They were in high gear by seven o'clock. At seven-ten, Mr. Reinhardt came in right on schedule. He was a tall, thin man with a pinched mouth, a pointy nose and a perpetual scowl on his face. His order was the same every day. He wanted a latte made just right and a lightly toasted bagel with a minimal amount of cream cheese. Vicky had toasted the bagel too much yesterday and had to toast another one. Today, Colman got the latte wrong. It was too frothy. Mr. Reinhardt asked Colman to make another one to his specifications. Once he had his coffee and bagel, he headed for the door, angrily mumbling about being late for the train. On the sidewalk, he was busy balancing his briefcase and his breakfast when he walked right into another commuter. She was looking down at a train schedule and didn't see him approach. Reinhardt's coffee cup sailed into the air and then splatted on the sidewalk. The coffee went everywhere and the cup bounced into the gutter.

Colman looked at Vicky. Vicky looked at Colman. Together they burst out laughing. They laughed so hard they couldn't stop, even when Hero came in and told them to calm down. Vicky explained what had happened and pretty soon her grandfather was chuckling along with them. At that moment, Colman realized he was happy for the first time in months.

Things were not good for the Gonzales family. Yahaira's hours at Appleby's had been cut back in the beginning of June. She had arranged to work on the weekend and evening shifts when Luis was home, but she wasn't bringing in the money she had been. In addition to the Banner Bluff farmer's market, she had signed up to sell her tamales and salsa at two additional farmer's markets, but she had to pay a fee and so far she hadn't made the money they'd hoped. Whenever she was home, she made tamales and salsa in preparation for the next market day. Luis felt like they never had time to talk, which relieved and troubled him at the same time.

Yari still worked a couple of hours in the afternoon at Hero's Market. The Smiths, luckily, were delighted to babysit the boys. Many afternoons, Roberto and Raul helped Mr. Smith with the many projects he had going on in his garage. He was an accomplished carpenter and he made beautiful carved chairs and tables. He had infinite patience and let the boys help out. Other days Mrs. Smith would bake cookies with the kids or play Uno for hours. Luis knew he and Yari could never repay them for all their kindness.

Times were tough. The current economy had cost Banner Bluff considerable revenue from sales and income tax, and the Village Board had moved to privatize garbage collection as well as snow removal. At a recent meeting they had voted to consolidate jobs within the village, which meant Luis's hours were cut as well.

Luis hoped he could pick up a few jobs helping out at St. Luke's or maybe the high school. This summer they were painting the classrooms and redoing the landscaping around the track. He thought he might be able to get a few hours there. But nothing was for sure.

The day he received the bad news about the cutbacks he felt depressed, but he hadn't said anything to Yari. When he arrived home that evening, she was on her way out to Appleby's. "Luis, the boys had their dinner and yours is on the counter. Could you make sure they take their baths before they go to bed? And they both need to do their summer reading. The books are beside their beds. Sorry, I'm late, I've got to run."

That was it. That was the extent of their marriage. Two ships that pass in the night... and all that.

Tom Barnett washed out his coffee cup and cereal bowl and put them in the drainer. He never used the dishwasher. Living alone, he used the same few dishes every day. The pleasure of a shared meal at home was a thing of the past. He ate almost all of his meals at the station. He would eat a sandwich at his desk or grab a pizza or a salad for dinner. He missed cozy dinners with Candace when they would linger over a glass of wine. They had never run out of things to talk about. But those days were long gone.

Work had become Tom's God. It filled his time and kept him from thinking. Initially after Candy's death, the few friends they had made in Banner Bluff had called often and invited him over for dinner. But he always refused. After a while, they stopped calling. Candy had been the key to those relationships. She could talk to anybody and make fast friends in ten minutes. Tom was the quiet one, Candy's sidekick. People tolerated him so they could enjoy his cheerful, affable wife. Now he enjoyed his solitude. He even craved his time alone in the quiet house.

He went into the den to retrieve his gun. He kept his Glock 21 in a safe when he was at home. Even though he lived alone, he didn't believe in leaving it out where an intruder could get it. He took the

143

gun out and holstered it, then briefly checked his email. His sister Jenny had sent a message:

Hey big brother. Summer is almost upon us. When are you coming down to the farm for some good old-fashioned fun? We can go on a hay ride and eat corn on the cob and homegrown tomatoes. Come whenever you can! We miss you!
Your lovin' sister, Jenny.

With this murder investigation hanging over him, he didn't see when he could get away. Maybe today would give them a lead. So far, they had nothing. Absolutely nothing. Jose Ramirez and Officer Lewis had fine-combed the beach again and had come up empty. They had gone back to Luis Gonzales and Colman Canfield. Neither one remembered seeing or hearing anything. The only clue, if you could call it that, came out of another session with Louisa Gorton.

Tom had not noted everything she'd said the first time or maybe she'd forgotten to tell him. Anyway, she now claimed that not only had she seen Luis's and Colman's cars in the early morning of May fifteenth, but also a dark van driving away from the beach with its headlights off. Of course, there were hundreds of vans in and around Banner Bluff. They would just have to keep that bit of information in the file for now.

He was supposed to pick up Ron Puchalski in a few minutes. They were on their way to Wisconsin to talk with Bob Lawrence's brother, Charles. He lived about ten miles north of Sheboygan. It would take about two and half hours to drive up there. He had called Charles multiple times, but gotten no answer. Something about the Lawrence family dynamics bothered Tom, so he'd decided to drive up with Puchalski and talk to the guy. After some thought, he decided not to contact the local police. He didn't want anyone to give Lawrence a heads-up that they were coming.

Tom locked his front door, tossed the paper on the porch and got into the car. He backed out of the driveway and headed over to Puchalski's.

The detective sergeant lived a few blocks away on the south side of town, in a small Victorian house painted a muted blue with white shutters. The front lawn was littered with tricycles, pink doll strollers and yellow TONKA dump trucks. On the sidewalk was a red ceramic water bowl labeled BARNEY. An assortment of stained glass decorations and happy face stickers adorned the windows.

He sat in the car for a few minutes, gazing at the house and yard. Part of him yearned for a family like Puchalski's, with a pretty wife and three rambunctious children. But it didn't seem to be in the cards. He was getting older and he'd forgotten how to relax and flirt with a woman. At the station he was consistently respectful of the female officers and staff. But he couldn't seem to lapse into a comfortable camaraderie when it came to women.

He got out and went to the door. He rang the bell and listened to the racket emanating from inside. After a minute, Bonnie Puchalski opened the door with a big smile. She had the youngest little girl on her hip and was dressed in jeans and one of her husband's old shirts. She wasn't exactly chubby, but she wasn't skinny either. With her clear, fair skin and big blue eyes, she looked like a model for a Renoir painting. She was the perfect foil for Puchalski. Where he was a strict perfectionist, Bonnie was laid back. Tom didn't know how Puchalski put up with the happy chaos of his home. But he and Bonnie seemed to have a good marriage.

"Hello, Tom," Bonnie said. "Do you believe this weather? Fabulous! We're going to go on a picnic today at the Nature Center."

"It'll be a perfect picnic day. Too bad Ron has to come with me."

Just then Puchalski came down the hall, followed by two little boys and a big, furry dog.

"Hi, Chief," the boys said in unison. Puchalski held onto Barney's collar so he wouldn't jump on Tom and then he leaned down to kiss everybody goodbye.

"See you guys tonight! Be good and help Mommy!"

Bonnie kissed her husband, and a moment later Puchalski and Tom were out in the quiet morning street.

They decided to stop at Hero's for coffee to take on the road. When they went into the store, Colman Canfield was manning the coffee machine. He looked up at the two officers, then blushed and looked down.

Tom smiled to put him at ease. "Good morning. How's the job going?"

Colman looked over at Vicki, who was wiping the counter. "Fine... fine, sir," he stammered.

"Good to hear it. Could we have two large coffees to go?" Tom turned to Puchalski. "Do you want anything to eat?"

"No, I'm fine. Hot, strong coffee would be great."

Colman poured the coffees and pushed the plastic tops down. "Here you go," he murmured as he put them on the counter. He took the five-dollar bill Tom held out and rang up the two coffees.

"Keep the change," Tom said.

"Thanks," Colman said as he dropped the coins into the tips jar in front of the cash register. He didn't look up as they exited the store.

"I think Hero is taking a big chance hiring that kid," Puchalski said. "He's running the cash register he stole from a month ago!"

"Well, he didn't hire him exactly. He's giving him a chance to redeem himself. I think maybe Hero did the right thing. That kid has been in all sorts of trouble and needs some guidance. Hero is willing to take a chance on him. That fact alone must give Colman a positive feeling."

"Hmm, maybe. But I would be counting every penny that comes in if I were Hero." Puchalski sipped his coffee. "This should wake me up! We were up with the baby last night. She was coughing like mad. Bonnie thinks she's got allergies. Anyway, I didn't get my beauty sleep." He looked over at Tom. "So how are we going to handle this visit?"

They'd reached the car by now. Tom opened the driver's-side door. "Chuck Lawrence lives on a small road off of Route 43, ten miles north of Sheboygan. We'll take the Tollway up there towards Milwaukee."

"What does this guy do for a living?" Puchalski asked as he climbed into the passenger seat.

"I don't know. We'll have to get him to tell us. I want to get a feel for his relationship with his brother and a clearer idea why he left Banner Bluff so quickly. Something weird is going on there; I'm not sure what, but I want to find out."

"He a suspect?" Puchalski asked.

"Not yet."

They drove on, discussing the great season the White Sox were having and Tom's recent meeting with the Fourth of July committee. After a few minutes of comfortable silence, Puchalski said, "So, are you seeing anyone these days?"

Tom looked over at him, frowning. "No. Why did you ask me that? You know how I feel."

Puchalski shrugged. "I'm asking you because Bonnie has a cousin that lives in the city and she was thinking maybe you two could get together. You know, maybe come over to our house for dinner some night."

"God, Ron, are you trying to fix me up? Forget it!"

"Listen, you might actually like this woman. She's a buyer for Mason's Department Store and has a lot of pizzazz. Why not give her a try?"

"Bonnie put you up to this, didn't she? Tell her thanks, but no thanks. When and if I want to date, I'll do it myself." He was gripping the steering wheel tightly and didn't look at Puchalski, who was leaning back in his seat with a big grin on his face.

A while later they turned off Route 43 onto a tiny dirt road that didn't seem to lead anywhere. Tom drove slowly until they came to two hand-painted signs on the right-hand side of the road that said: KEEP OUT! NO TRESPASSING! Beyond the signs, a dirt driveway wove back between the trees. A dilapidated wooden fence barred their way, so they got out of their cruiser and continued on foot.

Puchalski kept his hand near his service revolver and looked carefully to the right and left as they walked. The woods were silent. They came out into a small clearing and saw a ramshackle trailer, surrounded by broken-down machinery: a grimy dishwasher on its side, a bicycle missing a wheel, a rusted lawn mower, a refrigerator missing a door, and a snowplow attachment leaning against the trailer's wall, as well as rusting garden equipment. To the right, under the trees, was a battered Ford truck with a vanity license plate that read POWER8.

Tom made his way through the junk to the door and knocked. Puchalski stood off to the side at the ready. They heard a groan from inside the trailer and then a loud thud. A few moments later, the trailer's rickety metal door banged open, revealing a pumped-up version of Bob Lawrence. Chuck was somewhat taller and twenty pounds heavier, with broader shoulders. His face was fuller and his lips fleshier. He was handsome in an Elvis Presley sort of way, though he looked like he had been run hard and put away wet. His blue eyes were bloodshot and he reeked of Jim Beam and pepperoni pizza.

"Whadda ya want?" he said, looking from one officer to the other. "Whadda ya doin' on my property. Didn't you see the signs? 'Keep out' means you!"

Nonplussed, Tom said, "Good morning, Mr. Lawrence. I'm Chief Barnett of the Banner Bluff police and this is Detective Sergeant Puchalski. We'd like to ask you a couple of questions. We called you multiple times but couldn't get through."

"Whadda ya want to talk to me about?" His eyes began to fill with tears. "It's about Lilly, isn't it? She was just the sweetest thing. I loved her." He sat down on the rickety step. Through the open door, Tom could see inside the trailer. He spied an overturned chair, near a table covered with pizza boxes, frozen food cartons and empty beer bottles. The floor was littered with newspapers and magazines.

Chuck covered his face with his hands. "Who would take Lilly away and do that to her? She was so innocent." His shoulders shook and his grief seemed genuine. They waited for him to get control of himself. He rubbed his eyes with his hands, snuffled loudly and finally looked up. "Did you find out who did it?"

Tom said, "We're still investigating. We hoped you could tell us what happened the Friday night and Saturday morning before you left. Maybe you saw someone around the house? Maybe Lilly told you something?" Chuck must not talk much to his brother, Tom thought. He obviously hadn't heard the latest about the case.

Chuck seemed to sober up and looked from one officer to the other. "Do you want to come inside?" He turned and eyed the interior of the trailer. "My place is a mess. Maybe I could bring some chairs out here." He stood and hitched up his pants, then went inside and retrieved two aluminum kitchen chairs. They were covered with junk, which he swept onto the floor. He brought them outside and then sat back down on the stoop.

Tom took a chair. Puchalski looked at the other one dubiously. He took out a handkerchief and wiped it off.

When they were settled, Tom asked, "So, why did you come down to Chicago that weekend?"

"I was down for a Guns'N'Roses concert at the Allstate Arena. It was on Thursday night."

"When did you arrive at your brother's house?"

"Oh, sometime Friday afternoon." He didn't look up at them. He was studying his large hands, which were spread out on his knees.

"Did you see Lilly then?" Puchalski asked.

"No, she was at school."

"When did she come home?"

"I don't know... after school... no, wait, she went over to a friend's house."

"What were you doing?" Tom asked.

"Wait, what are you asking me all these questions for? I didn't do anything." He looked belligerent now.

"We're trying to get a picture of what happened that day. You're helping us get a better understanding." Tom spoke softly to calm him. "What happened that afternoon while you were waiting for Lilly and your brother to come home?"

"I don't know. I took a shower and a little nap. I hadn't slept much the night before..." His voice trailed off. Still no eye contact, Tom noted. *And you were probably wasted*, he thought. "What happened Friday night after Lilly came home?"

"Well, she wanted me to play with her, so we built stuff with Legos and I pushed her on the swing in the backyard." He paused, his voice wavering.

"Did you all have dinner together?" Puchalski asked.

Chuck took a deep breath. "Yeah, after Bob got home. We sat down for a jolly family dinner. We all put on a good show for Lilly's sake. Bob and I didn't get into it until after dinner."

"You don't get along?"

"Let's just say that after five minutes together he starts picking at me." In a whiny voice, he mimicked his brother: "Why don't you get a real job. What future do you have? Why do you live like a pig...yadda, yadda, yadda."

"So you spent Friday night there," Puchalski said. "Why did you leave in the morning? Jan Lawrence said you were going to spend the weekend but changed your mind."

"That's none of your business. My brother and I don't get along. I left because I couldn't stand to be around him all weekend. Okay? I left long before Lilly disappeared."

Did you? Tom thought. "Where did you go Saturday morning?"

Chuck stood up abruptly. His hands were balled into fists. "I don't have to talk to you guys. I don't have to defend myself. I came home Saturday morning. Okay? Now get lost." He jabbed his finger towards the driveway. Then he turned around and stomped into the trailer, slamming the door behind him.

Francesca sat at her computer, gazing out at her leafy bower. It was a fabulous day. She could see puffs of white clouds floating in a blue, blue sky. She was dressed in a lime green cami and black cargo pants. Her hair was twisted up onto her head in a lazy bun secured with lime green chopsticks. She was thinking about her morning. She'd gone running with Susan and the dogs. They had gone to Liberty Grove really early when it was still cool.

She didn't want to go down to the beach these days, so she had been running at the Grove or in the woods. Some days Susan accompanied her. Today they were discussing their current social lives. Susan had gone out again with Bradley Harrison. They'd had dinner at Trattoria Verona last Saturday.

"He was the perfect gentleman. I sort of like him." Susan glanced at Francesca. "I know what you think, but we had a lot to talk about and he didn't put any moves on me."

Francesca rolled her eyes. "So he didn't attack you? Great! But I just don't think he's entirely on the up and up."

"Well, there *is* something that bothers me. He often shows up at the club when we're having a private golf outing. He's not part of the guest list. I've checked. He just walks in during the cocktail hour and starts talking to people. He's a member of the club, so I guess he has a right to be there and no one complains. But I don't know…"

Francesca nodded. "He's a financial planner and investment advisor, so he's probably trying to inveigle some new clients." Her eyes gleamed with mischief. "Maybe you should sneak around and see what he's talking to people about."

"Oh, I know what he's pushing. I did listen in! Something called the AUIC. Whatever that stands for? I don't have a clue, do you?"

"No. Let's see… maybe it's the Affluent Ultrafashionable Inclusive Club… or the American Unisex Independent Counsel? Could be anything, but probably it has to do with money!"

Now, sitting in her office, Francesca looked down and saw Brad crossing the street headed for the post office. *Speak of the Devil,* she thought. It would be nice to know what Brad was involved in. She had seen him having lunch at Churchill's with Royce Canfield and Harry Silverman. They were literally as thick as thieves, leaning in around the small table, almost whispering to each other. It would be nice to know what they were talking about.

Downstairs, she heard the murmur of voices. When she arrived that morning, Vicky had smiled and said a happy "hello." Even Colman had said "hi." That was a first. Somehow, the tension that had reigned since Colman began working had dissipated. A few weeks ago, he had worn a smug, angry expression and had hardly acknowledged her presence. What a change! Maybe this crazy idea of Hero's was a good one after all.

Emma, Kate, Martin and Rosie were walking down to the lake for a picnic. Rosie had on her new summer swimsuit, a turquoise and green bikini. She was skipping ahead of Kate and Emma swinging her mini beach bag. Martin was pulling Rosie's red wagon piled high with a cooler, towels and beach toys.

Emma had taken out her ancient swimsuit that morning. To her dismay, it had lost all of its elasticity. It looked like a droopy bag on her, so she had decided to just wear shorts and a tee-shirt. Kate was wearing a large pink sun hat and matching cover-up. They walked along the sun-dappled sidewalk in the morning quiet.

"I love these first few weeks when school is out for the summer, "Kate said. "I feel totally liberated. No papers to grade, no lessons to plan. I can devote myself to Rosie and Martin."

"Ah-ha," Martin said. "I am ready to be spoiled rotten. Tomorrow morning I want breakfast in bed."

"Right," said Kate. "You might just starve."

Kate looked down the street to the corner. "Rosie, stop at the curb! Don't cross the street. Wait for us," she called.

A dark blue van came slowly down the street with its right turn signal flashing. It stopped a few feet from the corner. Rosie was hopping from one foot to the other. The driver waited. When the adults arrived, he waved them all across the street before turning.

They reached the headland and went down the access road. At the bottom, they turned left towards the North Beach. Rosie liked to split her time between splashing in the water, making sand castles and climbing on the playground equipment. Lake Michigan was still very cold this early in the season, so they didn't plan on going all the way in. The lake sparkled in the sunlight, a welcome sight.

Rosie pointed to the right towards the South Beach. "Is that where Lilly died?"

Martin looked at Kate over Rosie's head as the little girl continued. "Somebody at school said she drowned over there. Can we go see?"

"No, Rose Marie. Can you see the yellow tape? That means it's off limits. No one can walk over there," Kate answered sternly.

His schedule was irregular and he was gone a lot. When he was home, he prowled the streets looking for the proper Gift. He was the avenging Angel, the equalizing Prince. She was his Redeemer. No one had understood before. No one would understand now. He played their game; lived the proper life; hid the Truth.

Chapter 14
Friday afternoon, June 18th

Jesse Lewis was a young cop who had joined the force a couple of years ago. He had a fresh-faced grin and an open manner that endeared him to the local matrons. He got plenty of ragging from his fellow cops, who called him "baby face." But they'd soon learned that he was a dependable member of the team.

Lewis couldn't wait for this day to end. He was off tomorrow and he had a date tonight. He was meeting this girl he had been chatting with online for about two months. This was their first face-to-face and he was pumped. They were meeting at Hobson's for a beer at eight-thirty. He only had a couple of hours to go.

He went into the control room where Bernice, the dispatcher, was perched on her stool wearing headphones. She nodded to him and he nodded back. He went over to the video security tapes and pulled down the one for the last four weeks. Someone had to check through them periodically.

Longview Street ran from Lake Michigan west through Banner Bluff and towards the town of Lindenville. It started out as a two-lane street but became a four-lane road half a mile before hitting the North-South Highway. People would speed up when they hit the four-lane section and there had been multiple accidents at the intersection of Longview and the highway. Drivers would try to make it through the intersection on a yellow light, or they would enter into a turn on a yellow arrow. Because of the number of accidents and a couple of fatalities, security cameras had been installed on two corners to photograph cars going through red lights. Tickets were issued by mail, containing a picture of the guilty party's license plate.

Lewis's job was to go through the tapes and verify the pictures, license plates, addresses and names of the offenders. It was tedious and the last thing he wanted to do for a couple of hours on Friday. Still, the sooner he got started, the sooner he'd be done.

He'd reached the early morning hours of Sunday, May 16th when he spotted a Ford truck zipping through the intersection. It came from the east on Longview and turned north onto the North-South Highway. The truck bore a Wisconsin license plate: POWER8. The time stamp in the upper right-hand corner of the tape read three-fifteen AM.

Lewis ran the tag. The Wisconsin plate was registered to a Charles Lawrence.

"Holy smoke!" He yelled, loud enough for Bernice to lift up one earphone in surprise.

"What did you say, Lewis?"

"Bernice, where's the Chief? I've got to talk to him."

"He's gone out. I think Conroy and Puchalski are around, though. Do you want me to ring them?"

"Nah, but thanks. I'll go down there myself." He printed out the truck's picture and the plate information and went down the hall.

"Hey, Puchalski! You won't believe what I've got," he called as he went into the detectives' workroom.

"Keep it down, Lewis," Puchalski said with a scowl. Conroy's on the phone."

"Check this out," Lewis said as he handed over the picture and printout. "Your man Chuck was right here on the night of Lilly Lawrence's death. He was on the North-South Highway around the approximate time of her drowning."

Puchalski looked at the printout. "Holy shit! Maybe we've got our murderer. I'd love to nail that guy. Let's call the Chief."

The last time Chief Barnett was at the Lawrence's home, Jan Lawrence had broken down. Now, as then, Tom rang the bell and waited in front of the screen door, looking into the darkened foyer. After a long wait, Bob Lawrence finally came to the door.

"You again? Shouldn't you be out looking for the killer instead of harassing us?" He looked at Tom with unconcealed disdain. Then, shaking his head, he opened the door and led Tom into the family room with its high ceilings and French provincial furnishings.

Jan Lawrence was seated rigidly in a flowered chintz armchair, gazing blindly out the window. She wore a stained white terry bathrobe. Her stringy hair hung down her cheeks. She had lost weight and her long, thin fingers played with the fringe on the terrycloth belt. A cup of tea was on the table beside her.

Across the room next to a matching armchair stood a table bearing a tall glass of what looked like a gin and tonic with lime. From the stale smell that clung to Bob Lawrence, Tom guessed this wasn't his first drink of the evening.

"My wife is losing it! Look at her! And you're here to pester us again," Bob snapped.

Tom ignored him and went into the room, addressing Jan. "Hello, Mrs. Lawrence. May I sit down and talk with both of you for a moment?"

She nodded. He moved over to the deep-cushioned sofa and sat down, sinking into the puffy pillows. He felt at a disadvantage imprisoned in its soft depths. He took out his notebook and opened it on his knees. "I just wanted to discuss your brother's visit. Could you please run through it again? When Charles came, what you did and why he left so abruptly Saturday morning?"

He looked at each of them. Jan blanched. Bob looked away.

"Why are you torturing us?" Jan cried. "Why do you keep coming here with your questions? We didn't kill our own daughter. What's wrong with you? Bob's brother wouldn't want to hurt Lilly. Why don't you hunt for the real killer?" She began to sob.

Bob looked at his wife with disdain "You want to know why Chuck didn't stay? It's because I kicked him out. You think she's crying for Lilly? She's crying because she feels like a shit. She's crying because I found her in bed with my brother! Is that what you want to know? That's why she's crying." He gulped down his drink and looked at his wife with revulsion. "Now, tell me, Chief Barnett. Now that you've dug up our dirty laundry, is that going to help you find my daughter's murderer?"

Yari was exhausted. It had been a very long day. She parked the car on the street in front of her house. She could hear her boys' laughter coming from the backyard. They must be playing that beanbag toss game. Luis had made the game board with some pieces of wood Mr. Smith had given him. The whole family had been having knock-down, drag-out games lately. The boys were amazingly adept, even better than their dad.

She sat in the car, looking out the window at nothing. What was all this work for? They never seemed to get ahead. She was exhausted. Luis was exhausted. They barely saw each other these days and when they did it wasn't always so great. They'd had their first real fight last night; about who would do the laundry and when. It was such a stupid thing to argue about. She knew they had blown things way out of proportion because they were both so tired; maybe also because they were both disappointed that they wouldn't be able to send the boys to baseball camp. The kids were really looking forward to it. Yari hadn't told them the bad news yet.

She got out of the car and grabbed the pizza Hero had given her when she left the market. He said he wouldn't be selling it since he was shutting the store early and going with Vicky to Ravinia to see the Gypsy Kings. She had a feeling he'd probably made the pizza for her in the first place. He was so nice, but she felt uncomfortable. It was like taking charity.

She walked over to the mailbox and looked inside. There was an advertisement from Kohl's for a super summer sale with a 20 percent coupon. Like she could ever buy a new bathing suit or a pair of shorts. Then there was the bill from the loan company for the car and an ad for a deal on new Andersen windows plus installation. At the back lay a plain white envelope with no return address. Some bill she had forgotten? The phone bill? The electric bill? Some reminder? It made her sick just looking at it.

She stuffed the mail into her purse and opened the front gate. As she went around the house, she replaced her worried frown with a happy smile. "Hola, chicos. I'm home! Come give me a hug."

Both boys ran over to hug her and started to tell her about their day. "Mama, we had a picnic at the park today. Mrs. Smith took us there for the afternoon. There were a lot of kids to play with. It was so fun."

"Hey, is that pizza for us? Can we have that for dinner?"

She raised her eyebrows in mock surprise. "Who do you think it's for?"

Mrs. Smith came out on the back stoop. "Both boys were angels. Henry and I had a great time with them at the park." She looked at Yari with concern. "Are you all right? You look a little peaked. Do you want the boys to stay down here for a while?"

"No, no, Señora, you have done more than enough. You need some peace. We'll go upstairs and I'll keep the boys quiet."

Mrs. Smith smiled. "Don't worry about us. We love hearing you upstairs. We don't like it when it's too quiet!"

Yari and the boys said goodbye and trudged up the back stairs to their second-floor apartment. The breakfast dishes were still in the sink. Milk glass rings and toast crumbs marred the kitchen table. Sofa pillows and newspapers were strewn across the living room floor. The picture of Catalina Island was askew on the wall over the sofa. It seemed as though everyone's shoes were scattered throughout the apartment. What a mess!

Luis wouldn't be back until late tonight. Yari turned on the oven to heat up the pizza and sent the boys to pick up their room. She would make a pile of laundry. Later, after the kids were in bed, she could take it downstairs. She picked up the living room and began to clean up the kitchen. Once things were in order she would feel better.

By eight-thirty the boys were bathed and in bed. Yari went down to the basement with a basket of laundry. She put in a load of whites and went back upstairs. *Dios mío*, she was tired. She took a Coke out of the fridge. In the living room, she flopped onto the sofa and turned on the TV. She flipped through the channels. Nothing caught her interest.

Her gaze fell on her purse, lying on the front hall table. She took a long drink of Coke and then went over to retrieve it. She might as well look at that letter now. It had been eating at her all evening. The envelope was made of heavy, high-quality paper. The name and address were carefully printed in blue ink: *Mr. and Mrs. Luis Gonzales, - 124 East Walnut, Apt. B, Banner Bluff, IL.*

Maybe it wasn't a bill. Maybe it was an invitation of some sort. That thought made her smile. Maybe she and Luis were invited to a ball with the mayor at the Oak Hills Club. Yeah, right! She slit open the envelope. Inside was a folded piece of white paper, the same kind as the envelope. She unfolded the sheet. A check fell into her lap, a cashier's check made out to her and Luis for fifteen hundred dollars.

She couldn't believe it. Her hands shook as she read the letter:

Please accept this small check. We want Raul and Roberto to have a fun-filled summer. This amount will provide 3 weeks of baseball camp for each boy. In addition, I hope the entire family will enjoy a day at Six Flags Great America. Take time to relax and enjoy each other's company. Life is short and good memories sustain the soul.

Wishing You Well.

Yari put her face in her hands and began to cry. She sobbed from happiness, from sadness, from fatigue and from gratitude. There must be a God, because she had just received a miracle.

Against her better judgment, Francesca had agreed to go to Ravinia tonight with Susan, Marcus and Brad. She didn't know if she could stomach Brad for all those hours. The Ravinia Festival was an outdoor concert venue, with a vast green lawn under leafy trees and a covered pavilion and stage where the music was performed. People came early to picnic on the grass before the concert began. Then they could either enjoy the concert seated on the lawn or buy a ticket and sit inside the pavilion. Tonight's concert was the Gypsy Kings. She had heard Hero say that he and Vicki were attending. The Gypsy Kings were a favorite of young and old alike.

Francesca had been given tickets for the pavilion after agreeing to do a couple of articles about the Ravinia season. This was the first non-classical concert of the summer. Ravinia had also contracted with the *Banner Bee* for advertising space during the summer, a nice chunk of change for the three-month season.

She'd offered to bring the picnic and had spent much of the day shopping and cooking. At five o'clock she was busy filling the rolling cooler and her willow basket with the picnic fare. There was a wedge of brie and a round of goat cheese with water crackers, plus a small jar of fig jam that was to-die-for with the brie. Next came an antipasto salad and spicy lemon-mustard chicken with a green salad, and she had also made a decadent chocolate caramel cake. Finally, she tucked in a bag of cherries and a box of raspberries. They definitely would not starve.

Marcus and Brad were bringing wine, Susan the silverware, plates, tablecloth, napkins and so on. The Weather Channel promised a perfect evening. The best thing about an outdoor picnic in June was that there were practically no bugs. Francesca was not a lover of creepy, crawly creatures.

With the cooler packed, she ran upstairs to take a quick shower and get dressed. What to wear? She decided on jeans and a pale pink ruched scoop tee. She caught her hair in a high ponytail and put on some dangly pink and pearl earrings. A little blush and a little mascara was her usual makeup routine. She applied some pinkish lipstick, grabbed a cardigan and she was ready to go.

They had to park some distance from the entrance to Ravinia. Marcus took the picnic basket and a blanket, and Francesca pulled the rolling cooler with a small, collapsible wooden table balanced on top. They joined the throngs of people heading for the entrance. Francesca stopped at the ticket booth and received an envelope containing two complimentary tickets for the pavilion. Susan and Brad would remain on the lawn and guard the picnic paraphernalia during the concert.

Francesca took out her phone and called Susan. "Where are you?" she asked when Susan picked up.

"We aren't there yet. Brad had some business to finish. Why don't you pick a spot and I'll call you when I get there. Okay?"

"Okay, see you soon. Bye!"

160

Francesca and Marcus looked around for a grassy spot that was under the trees and away from large, noisy groups. The park was crowded already. It was amazing, the set-ups some parties had: large tables with linen tablecloths, candles, flowers in vases and crystal goblets for wine.

They settled in a shady spot and spread out the blankets, set up the table and unfolded some lawn chairs. Then they sat down together on the blanket to wait for the others. Marcus put his arm around her shoulders and leaned over to give her a quick kiss on the cheek.

"I like being here with you," he said.

Francesca turned and kissed him on the cheek. "Likewise," she said, smiling into his eyes.

As usual, Marcus was dressed impeccably in jeans and a blue and white plaid shirt with the sleeves rolled up. "So what has been going on in your life this week?" he asked.

"I've been super busy. That is the upside and the downside of running the *Banner Bee*. The upside is that I love writing, I love learning about people and issues and I do love being busy. But the downside is that I don't ever have a day off."

"I know what you mean. I love my job and although I do have days off, I feel as though I'm always on call. When I'm at home I always feel I should be reading my medical journals or reading online to keep up with the latest research." He thought for a minute. "I suppose that if you love your job and you try to do it well, it occupies most of your time." He reached for her hand and caressed it gently.

"Yes, it becomes all-consuming." Her voice trailed off. She had this terrific urge to pull her hand away. What was it with her? Marcus looked up, searching her eyes.

Her cell phone rang. She pulled her hand away to answer the phone. It was Susan. Francesca described their picnic site and then looked up to see Brad and Susan threading their way among the blankets and tables. She stood up and waved.

Brad looked irritated as he approached them. "The traffic was horrendous. We had to park a million miles away."

Marcus stood up and shook hands. Francesca was about to introduce them, but they seemed to know each other already.

Susan looked lovely in pale blue, with silver earrings and a multi-strand silver necklace. She even had on silver sandals. From her bag, she pulled out a tablecloth and matching napkins with a Southwestern geometric motif. She set the table and Francesca unpacked the cheese and crackers. Brad unfolded two lawn chairs and they all sat down. He reached into a bag and brought out a bottle of Caymus cabernet. He opened it and poured them all a glass.

"Wow," Marcus said. "This is a treat."

"How's that?" Francesca asked.

"Caymus cabernet 2008 is a highly prized, and highly priced, wine." Marcus chuckled. "But it would be vulgar to talk about that."

Brad looked pleased that Marcus knew what he was serving them. Francesca wondered if he was a wine connoisseur or if he just went for the expensive stuff.

They talked about the upcoming concert. "I think the Gypsy Kings come from southern France," Francesca said.

"Yeah, but they mainly sing in Spanish. It's kind of flamenco pop music. We're going to want to get up and dance when they start," Susan said, looking at Brad. "It's a great beat."

"I don't think so," Brad said. "I am not a dancer, but I'm a great listener."

"Hey, if you girls want to dance the flamenco, I'll be glad to watch," Marcus said. They all laughed.

"So what's new in the medical field?" Susan inquired.

"Well, there are rumblings that the hospital might be bought out by the Crandon Hospital group. No one knows if this is a good thing or not. And no one on the board is revealing what's going on. So people are feeling a little nervous," Marcus said.

"What do you think?" Susan asked.

"I guess I'm worried that if we're part of a big group of hospitals, we're going to lose some of our independence. We'll just be a cog in the wheel."

"Well, maybe some of you doctors will be paid a more reasonable salary," Brad said. "I mean, look at the cost of health care.

We need to cut costs, and you've got to admit that you doctors are a big part of the problem. You're way overpaid."

There was a moment of uncomfortable silence. Francesca felt her ire rising. Marcus looked nonplussed. "You're certainly entitled to your opinion. I'm not going to argue with you."

"Well, I will," Francesca said. "I think you work damn hard, and you paid a high price to get through medical school. You ought to be well-paid." She glared at Brad, who started to laugh.

"Hey, calm down! Don't fly off the handle. We're just having a little discussion here." He grinned at her and then looked across the lawn. His eyes lit up and he got up quickly. "I'll be back in a minute. I see a guy I need to talk to over there."

Francesca was still fuming. "Come on, calm down," Marcus said, smiling at Francesca, "but thank you for coming to my defense!" He reached for the bottle of cabernet and poured them all a little more.

Susan helped herself to some brie and fig jam on a cracker. "Yum, this is so good. I've never had fig jam before."

Marcus reached over and prepared a cracker for himself. "How do the two of you know each other?"

"Francesca and I went to UCLA and were in the same sorority. She's a California girl, but I come from out East."

"You do? So do I! I grew up in Connecticut," Marcus said as he munched on a cracker loaded with Brie.

"I actually come from Maine, from Bar Harbor," Susan said.

"You're kidding! We used to spend all summer on Mount Desert Island. Heck, I spent a lot of time in Bar Harbor, but we had a house in Northeast Harbor."

"What a coincidence! My parents, actually my grandparents, owned a hotel, so I spent the whole year there."

Francesca sat back as the two of them compared memories. She had never been out East, let alone to Maine. As they talked, she let her mind wander. Brad really got to her. There he was across the lawn chatting up some senior citizens. Exuding charm, he had their full attention. They were like adoring puppies. How did he do that?

She must be impervious to his charisma. And what was he talking to those people about, anyway? He'd sure high-tailed it over there when he spotted them.

Chapter 15
Monday afternoon, June 21st

Tom and Puchalski arrived at the local police station a few minutes early. It was a free-standing wooden building with a porch across the front like in a western movie. They knocked on the screen door. A pretty young officer greeted them and ushered them into an interview room at the back of the small building. "Officer Harland will be back with Mr. Lawrence right soon. He went to fetch him, 'cause Chuck's truck conked-out. Would you fellas like some coffee or a Coke?"

They both declined a drink and sat down to wait. Pent-up adrenalin coursed through Tom's veins and he wanted to get up and pace the room, but he reined in the feeling. Knowing now that Charles Lawrence had not left town on Saturday, coupled with Bob Lawrence's revelations, made Chuck a prime suspect in the kidnapping and drowning of his niece.

When the young officer had left, Tom cocked his head. "These recruits seem to be getting younger and younger. Could it be that I'm getting older?"

Puchalski chuckled. "Nah."

They heard angry shouting in the hall, and then Chuck Lawrence appeared, shaking off the hand of a grey-haired officer who was ushering him into the interview room. He was unshaven and unwashed, judging by the acrid body odor that filled the room.

"Thank you Officer Harland," Tom said.

Seeing Tom and Puchalski, Chuck barked, "What in the hell do you want now? I've already told you everything I know."

"We have some additional questions," Tom said calmly. "Detective Sergeant Puchalski, will you please read Mr. Lawrence his Miranda rights?"

"I didn't do nothin' wrong. Gimme a break! I don't need any Miranda rights, or a lawyer."

"Please sit down, Mr. Lawrence." Tom indicated one of the four plastic chairs around a square metal table. "Some information has come to light since we were up here a week ago. Maybe you could enlighten us."

Chuck sat down, as did Tom and Puchalski. They offered to get him a cup of coffee, but he refused. Puchalski read him his Miranda rights. Chuck didn't flinch and signed the document attesting that they'd been read to him. When that was completed, Tom turned on a recorder and they got down to business. He let Puchalski lead off, while he sat back and watched.

"As I remember," Puchalski said, "you said you left Banner Bluff on Saturday morning, May fifteenth. Is that right?"

"Yeah, I came home. I told you that." He looked at Puchalski through a tangle of long, unwashed hair.

"So why was your truck in Banner Bluff at three-fifteen AM on May sixteenth? Did you go home and come back?" Puchalski's voice was ripe with sarcasm.

Chuck looked down at his hands, which were balled into fists. "I don't know what you're talking about."

"We've got your truck on videotape taken from the security camera on the corner of Longview and the North-South Highway. Can't miss that vanity plate, POWER8. It was either you or your phantom," Puchalski said.

Chuck eyed them warily.

Puchalski continued. "You probably got a ticket in the mail for going through the red light, so you know exactly what we're talking about."

Chuck looked surprised. "I don't look at my mail these days. It's just a bunch of damn collection notices and bills."

"Tell us where you were on Sunday, May sixteenth," Tom said quietly. "Lilly was drowned about three AM. You were seen leaving town fifteen minutes later. We need to know what you were doing there."

There was a long silence. Chuck Lawrence sniffled. He wiped his nose on his arm and then wiped his eyes with his palms. He was blubbering, and Puchalski got up and went into the outer room to get

166

some Kleenex. When he came back in, Chuck started talking. "After I left Saturday morning, I just drove around. Man, I was bummed. I'd really messed things up with Jan. Then I went to a motel in Zion. I got a bottle of Johnny Walker and I spent the day drinking and sleeping." He took a deep breath. "Sometime in the afternoon I called Jan. I kept calling, but she didn't pick up." He looked at Tom. "I wanted to tell her I loved her and that I was sorry about what happened."

"Which was?" Puchalski asked. He knew already—Tom had filled him in—but they needed to hear Chuck's version.

Chuck cleared his throat. "Well, Friday night after Bob went to bed, Jan and I kept drinking and talking. We really are on the same wavelength, you know. I understand her and she understands me. My brother puts her through hell. Well, uh, one thing led to another. Somehow we ended up in the guest bedroom." He swallowed and looked at them sheepishly. "Bob woke up early and found us together. He kicked me out."

That fit with Bob Lawrence's story, Tom thought.

"Okay, so you drank and slept during the day. You need to give us the name of this motel and where it is. Now, where were you Saturday night?" Puchalski continued.

"I drove by my brother's house a bunch of times. I wanted to see Jan. I could see the police cars parked out front, but I didn't know what had happened. I mean, I didn't know about Lilly." He gulped. "I wondered if Bob had beat Jan up or something. I went over to that bar, the Hog's Head, for a couple of hours and then they closed down. I finally decided I'd better go home. That must have been about three o'clock."

"We'll need a sworn statement recounting what you just told us," Tom said. "You better hope someone at the motel or the Hog's Head remembers you."

"Oh, the waitress will remember me. Blonde and stacked. She was coming on to me pretty strong until they closed." He smiled, managing to look smug despite his blotchy, tear-stained face.

Bradley Harrison was in his office. It was five PM and he could hear muffled voices as the staff left for the day. He rarely required anyone to work late. As a matter of fact, he enjoyed being alone in the office. He would open his door and wander around the large front room. He would look through his employees' desks and sometimes he'd switch on their computers and see what they'd been up to during the day. Knowledge is power, and Brad thrived on power.

He'd installed Websense on all the office computers, which enabled him to track every keystroke his employees made. He liked to know they were devoted to Harrison Financials when they were at work. There was also the issue of security since the company was responsible for investing large sums of money.

He had just poured himself an inch of Glenfiddich when the phone rang. He hesitated as he eyed the caller ID. He didn't recognize the number and he didn't know if he felt like dealing with a disgruntled or needy client. Mollifying ruffled feathers was not his forte. He took a sip and felt the smooth brown liquid slide down his throat. What the hell, he might as well answer it. It could be a new AUIC member. "Good evening, Harrison Financials, Bradley Harrison speaking."

"Good evening, Mr. Harrison. How fortuitous to find you in your office and answering the phone." There was a pause. "This is Calvin Juniper."

Calvin Juniper? Calvin Juniper? Where had he heard that name before? "Hello, Mr. Juniper, or shall I say Calvin?"

"*Mr.* Juniper," the voice said flatly.

"Yes, sir." Brad bit back annoyance and answered smoothly instead. "Where have I had the pleasure of meeting you? I can't recall."

"You have never met me. I would like you to invite me for lunch at the Oak Hills Club this Wednesday at one PM. Please order a secluded table for four."

"Wait a minute," Brad said. "Are you a member of Oak Hills?"

"No, I am not. Please call your friends, Royce Canfield and Harry Silverman, and tell them to be there at one o'clock as well."

Brad felt anger rising. He took another swig of Glenfiddich. "Listen, I don't know who the hell you are, but you're not going to order me around. Plan your own little luncheon and leave me out of it." Then he started to think fast. What did this Juniper guy mean by his friends, Royce and Harry?

"Mr. Harrison. You will do as I say. I represent Rocco Ciliegie. Mr. Ciliegie and his colleagues have taken an interest in the American United Investment Club. He has noted some discrepancies in the reported financial figures. It would be in your best interest to meet with me."

Shivers ran down Brad's spine. Shit! He'd read about the Ciliegie Mob. They had interests in Chicago and in Las Vegas. What was going on?

"Okay, Mr. Juniper. I'll try to set up the lunch for this week. But I don't know about the other gentlemen." Brad's voice wavered.

"They *will* be there to meet with me. If they aren't, then you have a problem. Do you understand?" The phone went dead.

Brad sat back and drained his glass. For the first time in his life, he was scared.

Chapter 16
Wednesday afternoon, June 23rd

Susan was looking through the day's scheduled events. The Women's League was having their annual Fiesta Fun outing. The day included eighteen holes of golf followed by a Mexican-inspired brunch in the Sandhurst Room. It would be a noisy affair with all the giggling, gossipy ladies. Other than that, things looked pretty quiet. There was only one reservation in the main dining room: *Wednesday, June 23, 1 p.m. Scheduled luncheon: Bradley Harrison, table for four. Quiet, secluded table requested.*

Susan went into the dining room and through the swinging doors to the kitchen. She caught Chef Jeremy's eye. He glared at her. "What are you doing in here?" he grumbled.

"Just checking if things are all set for the Fiesta Fun brunch. Any problems?"

"If there were problems, I would have come to you!" He banged a pot on the stove.

"What delicious dishes have you got planned?" Susan continued cheerfully. She was not going to let him beat her down.

"Shrimp fajitas, chicken enchiladas, taco salads, churros…everything the ladies requested and more."

Susan knew that they were serving margaritas and sangria. The women would be a rollicking bunch by two o'clock. "Sounds great! I see Mr. Harrison has a private lunch planned. They'll be in the East Alcove. He wanted a quiet spot."

"I know all about that," Jeremy growled. "It won't matter what I serve him after he has a couple of drinks."

At twelve forty-five PM, Brad, Royce and Harry were sitting nervously at their table in the East Alcove. No other diners were seated near them. It was ideal for an intimate conversation.

"I don't know what your problem is," Royce grumbled. "I had to cancel two appointments to come here."

"I'm telling you, this guy was adamant. I couldn't say no. He seemed to know all about the AUIC," Brad said defensively.

"How would he know about our investment figures? I don't buy it. We better watch what we say and not divulge any unnecessary information," Harry advised.

Just as he finished his sentence, a man came striding toward their table, accompanied by Susan Simpson. The new arrival was dressed impeccably in a Valentino black suit with a dapper yellow bow tie and matching pocket kerchief. Although he wasn't a large man, he projected an air of authority and purpose. His black hair was parted in the middle, 1920s-style. Black eyebrows formed wings over his deep-set dark eyes. Thin lips were set in a perfunctory smile. He carried a briefcase in his right hand.

"Good afternoon, gentlemen. How nice to meet you." He shook hands with each of them in turn. Then he sat down.

Susan hovered in the background. "Will this table be acceptable, Mr. Harrison?" she asked, with her most gracious smile.

Brad winked at her. Anything to keep up the pretense that Calvin Juniper didn't make him nervous as hell. "Everything is perfect, Susan. Perhaps you could ask Pierre to bring over the wine list and menus. Then we would like to be left undisturbed."

"Certainly, Mr. Harrison. Enjoy your lunch." She moved off.

After Pierre brought their drink order—a double scotch for Brad, iced tea for Royce, a Coke for Harry and a glass of sherry for Calvin Juniper—there was a moment of silence. Brad glanced around the table at the others. They looked like recalcitrant school boys standing before the headmaster.

"I have come with a proposal from Mr. Ciliegie," Juniper said, with no hesitation. "Some acquaintances of his would like to buy the Smithfield property. I have the proposal in my briefcase."

Royce looked shocked. Harry let out a low whistle. Brad knew they recognized the name Ciliegie and weren't happy about it.

"What does that have to do with us?" Royce asked aggressively.

Harry put a hand on his arm. "Let's listen to what Mr. Juniper has to say."

Juniper continued. "Mr. Canfield, you are on the Village Council. Mr. Harrison is on the City Development Advisory Board. Mr. Silverman has a respected real estate firm. Mr. Ciliegie finds you to be in ideal positions to help us carry through our project."

"I don't get it," Royce said. "We can't ramrod something through the Banner Bluff Council."

"Oh, but I think you can. You have established a web of power within the village establishment. Each of you is well placed to present our project in its best light. You have proved yourselves to be excellent," he paused, as if considering, "wheeler-dealers, shall we say?"

"And what is this 'little project?' Brad asked.

The waiter appeared, and they ordered: grilled chicken Caesar salad for Royce, a Reuben sandwich for Brad and a hamburger with onion rings for Harry. Calvin Juniper asked a multitude of questions about each dish. He inquired about the provenance of the fish, if the beef was grass-fed and if the vegetables were organic. Finally, he chose filet of sole Veronique with parsley potatoes and lightly sautéed spinach. Then he requested a glass of Fiegl Pinot Grigio.

Brad eyed him in disbelief. This guy was something else; a fastidious asshole who liked to make people dance to his tune. Harry looked deep in thought about this business deal, and Brad hoped his quick mind was figuring out the best-case scenario for the AUIC.

The waiter left, and Calvin Juniper smiled. "Now, let us get back to business. Mr. Ciliegie's associates would like to buy the Smithfield mansion and the surrounding land. They will be turning the property into a private club."

"What kind of club?" Brad asked.

"A private supper club, shall we say."

Royce scowled. "Why would we want to push that?"

"This club will be a good solution to the ongoing arguments about the development of the property. People are worried about increased traffic, more children in the schools, if a residential developer gets hold of it. Our proposal avoids both. You'll barely know we're there. We'll build a guard house at the entrance to the property to control the flow of members. We'll enlarge and improve the Smithfield mansion and add outdoor porches and terraces. We'll landscape the gardens and lawns, and enclose the property with an attractive wrought-iron fence. This project will be a jewel for Banner Bluff."

It sounded good, but... "Who'll be coming to the club? Who are the members?" Brad asked.

"A select clientele," Juniper responded.

"Okay, so this sounds like a great plan. But you represent Ciliegie and we all know he's a mobster. I'm not sure we want him in town." Brad had an edge to his voice.

"Dear Mr. Harrison, you will put through our deal." Juniper paused and looked directly at each of them. "No one else will know whom I represent. As you will see in the documents, a California developer of sports complexes will officially buy the Smithfield property. You've heard of the Sanders Family Sports Company?" He raised his eyebrows.

"But it won't be a sports complex, right?" Royce said, thinking out loud.

"No. It will be a gentlemen's club."

"What in the hell does that mean?" Brad's voice shook with anger. He hated being manipulated.

Their lunch arrived and there was a lull in the conversation as they each busied themselves with their chosen dish. Juniper took a bite of sole, and then wiped his lips carefully "Delicious! As I was saying, a gentleman's club. There will be dancers, geishas, female attendants—call them what you will."

Brad spat out a mouthful of his hamburger that luckily landed back on his plate. "A strip club?"

"No, no. Let's call it a club with superb food, expensive wines and," Juniper paused, "artistic dancers."

At that moment, Susan Simpson, who had been hovering in the background, approached their table. "Is everything to your liking, gentlemen? Is there anything we can get for you?"

Brad was fuming, but he managed a smile. "Everything is great, Susan. Thank you."

She went back across the room. Brad and the others sat there in disbelief. Was this guy for real?

"Let's get back to where we stand in all this," Harry said.

"Let me say that you will be generously rewarded for your help." Juniper raised his wine glass and then looked up. "Especially considering that you have no choice. We have in our possession a complete accounting of your shenanigans with the AUIC. At any moment, I can reveal to the appropriate authorities what you have been up to. You gentlemen are running a Ponzi scheme that has become transparent to our accountants. We are willing to look the other way, since you *will* be fostering the approval of our plans."

Frank Penfield was having lunch with a former colleague from his days at the *Chicago Tribune*. They had not gotten together for over a year and were reminiscing over old times. As they were enjoying coffee and peach pie à la mode, Frank looked around for the waiter. He needed some cream for his coffee. Across the room in a small alcove he saw Royce Canfield, Bradley Harrison and someone else with a fourth man he recognized… or at least, he thought he did.

"Joe," he said to his friend. "Isn't that Calvin Juniper over there, Ciliegie's lawyer? You know the one that got him off on that murder charge?"

Joe glanced over. "My gosh, I think you're right. What's a Mob lawyer doing in Banner Bluff?"

Frank frowned. "Nothing good, I would say."

The County Homicide Task Force met on Wednesday afternoon in the conference room at City Hall. The general feeling was frustration and disappointment. They had practically nothing to go on in the investigation of Lilly Lawrence's kidnapping and drowning. Officers had gone back to interview friends, acquaintances and church members. No one had seen anything. No one had heard anything. No one knew anything.

The team had combed the church building and the St. Francis garden for evidence. Nothing. According to Ramirez, the evidence technician, they'd covered the beach with a fine-toothed comb and found all sorts of trash and trinkets; everything from condoms to a diamond ring. It didn't help that the incident happened on the first warm weekend in May; all sorts of people had headed down to the beach that afternoon.

Ron Puchalski had tried to trace the pink princess dress Lilly was wearing. It could be bought online at Target, Wal-Mart or any number of stores. There was no way to know where it came from and who bought it.

As for Chuck Lawrence, his alibi had checked out. The motel owner confirmed that Chuck was in his room all day. His truck was visible from the office, and a maid had walked in on him in the late afternoon and found him zonked out in bed.

"We went over to the Hog's Head yesterday," Tom reported. "The waitress and bartender remembered Lawrence because he was pretty liquored up when he came in. He sat in a back booth by himself and didn't leave until the bar closed."

"Yep, the waitress sure remembered him. Thought he was cute!" Puchalski shook his head. "She swore he looked like Elvis Presley. Give me a break!"

Tom snorted. "There's no accounting for tastes."

Chapter 17
Sunday morning, July 4th

He wanted her. He needed her. She was perfect: pretty, blonde, blue-eyed and saucy. She was ideal. He had observed her these last few weekends. One day, he had sat under an umbrella outside the pool area watching her play with her little friends. He'd brought a newspaper and worn sunglasses and a plain beige baseball cap. Dressed in khaki shorts and a dull grey tee-shirt, he was nondescript. He'd sat in the shade and read the paper. If he looked up and someone looked his way, he smiled. He had a nice smile. He was unremarkable except for his height. He was too tall. It was always better to sit down, and move when no one was looking his way.

He'd watched her at Gillmore playground. She was a little monkey, swinging on the jungle gym and climbing up the ropes. He had sat inside his van and thought about how delicious it would be to bring her home, bring her to his basement. He had waited so long. Today was the day. She would be his. After the parade was over, during all the commotion, he would make his move.

Rosie was excited. It was the Fourth of July. She was going to be in the children's parade. Yesterday, Mommy had helped her weave red, white and blue crepe paper streamers through the spokes of her bicycle. She didn't ride her tricycle anymore. It was in the back of the garage. But her bicycle did have training wheels. Daddy said he would help her learn to ride without them when she was ready. She didn't know if she was ready, though.

In the children's parade, she was going to wear her white shirt with red and blue stars and her red shorts. Mommy had made her hair into handle-bar ponytails and tied red ribbon bows on them. After the parade, they would go to the carnival and then they were having a barbeque at Mrs. Boucher's house. Rosie knew that there would be hotdogs and homemade ice cream and a special cake with an American flag on top. Mrs. Boucher always had Jell-O salad, too. Rosie loved that. It wasn't like the green leafy stuff she had to eat at home. It was like a dessert salad with marshmallows in it. Mommy didn't care what she ate on the Fourth of July.

She was sitting on the porch with Jack. He was chewing a big white chewy bone. They were waiting for her parents. Daddy was taking special care of Mommy. She didn't feel good in the mornings and she didn't like coffee anymore. Daddy told Mommy to go lie down and he would do the breakfast dishes before they left for the parade. They were taking a long time. Maybe she would go next door and help Mrs. Boucher get ready for the party.

Emma had made the sheet cake last week and frozen it. She pulled it out of the freezer and removed the plastic wrap, then placed the cake on a royal blue plastic platter. This morning, she'd made the buttercream frosting and she began spreading it generously over the cake. She was thinking about the meeting she'd had with Royce Canfield. He had handled things when her husband Todd died and she respected him as a lawyer. He seemed to feel that this American United Investment Club was a wise way to invest some money.

Todd had invested money with Bradley Harrison's father. Her husband had great respect for the senior Harrison. As far as she knew, Brad had continued to handle things in her best interest. But somehow, she felt unsure about the investment they were suggesting. This afternoon she might have a chat with Frank Penfield. He might be able to give her some good advice. Maybe he could do a little investigating into the AUIC. Frank and Todd had been good friends, and she valued his opinion.

Actually, everyone who was coming this afternoon had been a friend of Todd. Warm and outgoing, he'd collected friends wherever he went. For today's barbeque, Emma had encouraged Frank to bring along Francesca Antonelli from the *Banner Bee*. She was a gem.

177

Emma heard the back door open. In came Rosie and Jack. Jack eyed the cake with appreciation and started drooling. Emma pushed it further back on the counter just in case Jack wanted to take a lick. Rosie asked if she could help.

"Why, sure you can, honeybun. Pull a chair over here and you can help me decorate the cake."

Rosie pushed a chair over and climbed up on it. She looked longingly at the cake and the bowl of frosting. "Can I lick the bowl when we're finished?"

Emma considered this. She looked at Rosie's clean shirt and shorts. Then she reached down for an apron and covered Rosie from head to toe.

Emma had washed and dried blueberries and raspberries. Together they put rows of raspberries for stripes and blueberries for stars on the flag cake. It wasn't as perfect as it would have been without Rosie's help, but Emma much preferred companionship to perfection.

Francesca, Frank and David met for breakfast at Churchill's. Francesca was dressed in a French blue drape-neck knit shirt and slim black cropped pants. She wore her hair in a low ponytail and a pair of silver hoop earrings dangled from her ears. She was ready for a busy but fun day.

They each ordered large coffees and cinnamon rolls covered with gooey white frosting. Definitely not the most nutritious breakfast around, but oh so good! As they munched and licked their fingers, they discussed the day. David would rove around throughout the morning taking pictures and "capturing the moment." They agreed that some candid photos of parade watchers were a must. Banner Bluffers loved to see themselves and be seen. Francesca had been invited to sit in the stands with the judges and she would interview the parade organizers. She had already done some phone interviews earlier in the week.

Frank was going to talk to the people in the parade itself. There were high school bands here from Indiana and Wisconsin, as well as bagpipers from Chicago, gymnast groups, the Shriners on their little motorcycles, clowns on stilts, Boy Scouts, church groups and drivers of antique cars. Every local club would have a float. This year the theme was "Stand up for Liberty" and there was a preponderance of Statues of Liberty and freedom fighters.

"Why don't you post your story for tomorrow? Won't it be a description of the event?" Frank asked.

"Right, I'll cover the winning floats and give the judges' perspective."

"Good! I'll post on Monday. I want to tell the stories of the people who traveled here to be in the parade and the work that went into making the floats, that kind of thing. It will be a human interest slant. If we include a bunch of pictures each day, the *Banner Bee* should have quite a following."

"Sounds good," Francesca agreed. She turned to David, who was leaning back in his chair and sipping his coffee. "Hey, David, what are you doing after the parade?"

He shrugged. He had a tendency to take life as it came. As he'd told Francesca, "I like getting up in the morning and knowing there's nothing I have to do that day." Maybe that's why he'd never married, Francesca thought.

"Why don't you come with us over to Emma Boucher's? She knows you and I know you'd be welcome," Francesca said.

David smiled his slow smile. "Thanks, but no thanks, I've got something to do...but I will post those pictures tonight. Okay?"

"Deal! Now we better get going! The children's parade will be starting."

Tom Barnett was in the conference room with the entire police staff verifying the plans for the day. They would need to close off streets and redirect traffic. People poured in from all over the area to attend the Banner Bluff parade. It was one of the highlights of the summer on the north shore.

Deputy Chief John Conroy displayed a map of the village and pointed out parking areas and blocked streets along the parade route.

He had assigned each officer to an area and a specific task. Everyone would be working that day. As police chief, Barnett would spend the first hour riding in the parade in Bradley Harrison's vintage Mercedes. Apparently, this car had been in the family for years and was rarely taken out of the garage, so it was in amazing shape.

When Brad called to say he would be chauffeuring Tom, it was the first time they had spoken in a while. Their Friday golf game had been suspended since Lilly Lawrence's drowning and Colman's difficulties. Royce Canfield had not wanted to participate, claiming overwhelming business commitments. He avoided Tom whenever they met in town. Once, when Barnett was waiting in line at Churchill's at lunch time, Royce had walked in, seen him, turned right around and walked out. Although Colman had not been arrested, the embarrassment of his son's behavior was more than Royce could stand. He was a proud man and his ego had been bruised. But there was something pitiful about his complete withdrawal from Banner Bluff society.

He stood across the street as the parade went by. He could watch her. She jumped up and down, laughing. Many of the participants in the parade were tossing out candy and she grabbed at the Tootsie Rolls, the mini bags of Skittles and the Starburst chews. She turned to smile at her mommy as she stuffed her loot in a blue canvas bag. She was dressed in red, white and blue for the parade and she looked perfect. She was in awe of the teenage cheerleaders when they stopped to do a routine; bored by all the antique cars; fascinated by the giant men walking on stilts.

For an hour, he watched her. When there was a break in the parade, he moved across the street with a group of people. Then he stood behind her family, waiting for the parade to end. Waiting for his moment! It would be after the parade or at the carnival.

When the parade broke up, he moved into the street. She went to get her bike, leaning against a tree, while her parents picked up chairs and the blanket they had brought to sit on. She took off down the street, as independent as always. People poured into the street, heading for the carnival grounds or to return to their cars. It was hard to see a small child on a bike. He spotted her and moved in directly behind her, holding a folded lawn chair at her height. No one could see her from behind. People were talking loudly; the cars began to stream across the intersection behind them. When she stopped to look around, he spoke to her.

"Hi! Are you lost? I think I saw your daddy go down the side street." He smiled in a friendly way at her bewildered face. "I know your mommy and daddy. They'll be looking for you over there. Come on! We'll find them."

She looked at him uncertainly and then smiled. She wasn't supposed to talk to strangers. But she knew he was safe. She turned around to look behind her, but couldn't see around his folded beach chair.

"Wasn't that a great parade?" He said, smiling. "Did you get a lot of candy?"

Her face lit up. "Look!" She showed him the blue bag full of candy that was stowed in her bicycle basket.

"Wow, you're a lucky girl!"

"You can have one if you want!"

"No thanks, honey. Come on! Let's go find your mommy before she worries about you."

She got off her bike and walked beside him. They went down the alley, unseen by the crowd.

Chapter 18
Sunday afternoon, July 4th

The Caseys had told Corinne to wait while they folded up the blankets and chairs after the parade. But she had pedaled off towards the carnival.

"John, I told you to watch her," Laura Casey said. She was carrying a blanket and baby Jason on her hip. Jason was hot and grumpy. The parade had been too long for him and he was ready for a nap.

"Right! Like it's my fault! You're the one who gives her way too much freedom," John Casey replied.

Ignoring her husband's response, Laura said, "Listen, I'll take Jason home for his nap. Let's pile this stuff on the stroller and you can go after Corinne. She'll be at the carnival. Okay?" Laura sounded annoyed.

"How am I going to find her?"

"She'll probably be over by the ice cream stand. Caroline Wright is in charge of that booth. Corinne'll probably be with Jennifer Wright. They always play together at the park." Jason started to cry. She reached down and put him in the stroller. "Jennifer's the little girl with all those dark curls and big brown eyes. You know her, right?"

John Casey strode off without answering. Sometimes Laura drove him nuts. When he got home from work she would be on the phone, a pot boiling over and every toy in the house littering the floor from the front door to the kitchen. Nothing seemed to bother her. She would just laugh and tell him to relax. He knew that her nonchalance was what drew him to her initially. He had grown up in a strict home and led a regimented life until he met Laura. Now, it was a free-for-all!

He approached the village green. It was bustling with children and parents. He was trying to locate the ice cream booth when his neighbor Mike Weaver came up to him. "Hey John, long time no see! How are you?"

They settled into easy conversation, and Mike suggested a cold beer in the nearby beer tent. John glanced over toward the ice-cream booth, a pink and blue tent with an ice cream cone on top. He thought he saw Corinne's blonde head and red and white tee-shirt. She was over there with her friend. What the heck, why not have one beer with Mike? Corinne couldn't get into any trouble here with all the people around. He should stop worrying so much. The uneasy thought of Lilly Lawrence crossed his mind, but he dismissed it. That kind of thing was a fluke, surely. And he wouldn't stay here for long.

They sat with their beers, talking politics and sports. After a while Mike looked at his watch. "Oh my god, it's almost one-thirty. We've been talking for over an hour. Listen, I better go."

"Me, too. It was great talking, Mike. Let's get the families together soon. Okay?"

"Okay. Give me a buzz." Mike left the tent and so did John.

As he strode across the grass, he looked at his phone. There was a text message from Laura wondering where he was. She was on her way over. Then his cell phone rang.

"John, where have you been? I've been trying to reach you. Where's Corinne?"

"I'm just going over to the ice cream booth to get her."

"What! You haven't been with her all this time? And you tell me I'm not an attentive mother?"

"Calm down. I'm almost there. I'll meet you here and we'll get Jason a vanilla cone."

But Corinne wasn't there. Caroline Wright and her daughter Jennifer had not seen Corinne at all. John began to panic. Where could she be? When Laura arrived, she yelled at him and then began to cry.

Tom Barnett arrived back at the office after a very long morning. On the whole, the parade had gone well. One majorette had been stung by a wasp and there was a fender-bender on the corner of Lake and

Ash. Other than that, no major incidents had occurred. He gave a sigh of relief and turned to his paperwork. He'd get some of this done before heading off to the barbeque at Emma Boucher's later this afternoon. He usually refused party invitations, but he liked Emma and he'd had a great deal of respect for her husband. Why not take some time off?

He worked steadily on reports until the Caseys showed up around two-thirty with Officer Lewis. Their six year-old daughter had been missing for two and a half hours. According to Officer Lewis, Mrs. Casey had gone home with the baby and Mr. Casey had decided to have a beer with a friend. They had let their little girl wander around the carnival all alone.

Tom called all his officers together. He had a bad feeling. Corinne Casey's disappearance was eerily similar to Lilly Lawrence's. Both girls had simply vanished during a public event. He recorded a message for the Code Red system and had it sent out to all Banner Bluff homes.

As before, he put Officer Johnson in charge of responding to phoned-in tips and email messages. Again he asked Lieutenant Rodriguez to organize the volunteer search party. He knew they would get fewer volunteers. People were busy with family events on the Fourth of July. They would also get less help from surrounding towns this afternoon and evening, since those police officers would be involved with town celebrations and fireworks displays. Again Banner Bluff was divided into quadrants and a search was begun.

Deputy Chief Conroy assigned two officers to search the Casey home from top to bottom. Two more officers were to interview the Casey family's friends and neighbors, in case Corinne had gone over to one of their homes after the parade or during the carnival.

After an extensive interview with the parents, Ron Puchalski came in to see Tom. "I feel sorry for these people," he said. "John Casey really thought his little girl was busy with a friend and her mother. I don't know that he's such a bad guy. But the interview wasn't pleasant. They blame each other. After I finished questioning them, they sat there in angry silence. Of course, they're thinking about Lilly Lawrence and what happened to her."

"That's what we're all thinking, isn't it? Along with the search parties in town, we've got to patrol the beach, especially after dark," Tom said somberly.

"People will be down there to watch the fireworks," Puchalski said. Banner Bluff did not have fireworks on the Fourth of July, but Lake Woods did, and people could view them from the Banner Bluff shoreline.

"We're going to have to close the beach. I don't want anyone down there except police officers."

After checking out the carnival and interviewing several children and their parents, Francesca went over to Hero's Market and her office. The shop had done a brisk business before and after the parade. Now things had calmed down. Hero was cleaning up with the help of his two teenage employees. Vicky and Colman seemed to be great friends now.

"Hi, you guys," Francesca said. "I bet this place was a madhouse today."

Vicky giggled. "You should have seen Colman working the coffee machine before the parade! He was a madman!"

"Yeah," Colman said. "We were bumping into each other trying to fill all these orders. It was a zoo, right, Mr. Papadopoulos?"

"Yes, my two young people work very hard. But today we are overwhelmed, as you say. We needed Mrs. Gonzales to come work this morning. But she wanted to take her boys to the parade."

"It was a great parade and it's too bad you missed it," Francesca said.

"Oh, we didn't." Vicky smiled shyly. "We could see a lot just standing at the door, and we went upstairs and looked out of your windows!" She blushed.

"Oh you did, did you? Well, that's fine by me." Francesca smiled. "I've got to get up there and write my parade story. Are you closing up now, Hero?"

"Yes! We're taking the rest of the afternoon off. Vicky and Colman are going to cook an American dinner for me tonight!"

185

"What are you guys going to make?"

"Hamburgers, baked beans, coleslaw and Vicki is going to try making a cherry pie!" Colman said.

"Wow! A real spread! Have fun!" Francesca hurried up the stairs. She couldn't get over how much Colman had changed. It seemed like a miracle.

Chapter 19
Sunday evening, July 4th

Tom Barnett was alone in the police station except for Arlyne, the evening-shift dispatcher, and Officer Johnson, who was fielding calls about Corinne Casey. Tom had been out earlier, showing Corinne's picture door to door and asking if anyone had seen her. So far, no one remembered seeing her after the parade ended. People had called in about her presence in the children's bicycle parade. Others had seen her with her parents watching the main parade on Oak Street, but no one saw her afterward or at the carnival.

They were using a white board in the Investigation Room to record information about Corinne. At this point, they had neither clues nor evidence. No one had found her bike. They had searched all the streets, front yards, backyards and garages. Corinne Casey had vanished.

Tom was at his desk studying a map of Banner Bluff. He was analyzing the layout of the streets, trying to imagine where Corinne could have been kidnapped right after the parade. How could anyone grab her on Oak Street? It had been crawling with people. But maybe that was the answer. Everyone was heading for their cars or the village green. All the kids were hyper, some laughing, some crying. Who would even notice one more noisy kid? Someone could have dragged her to a car and people would just have thought she was spoiled, undisciplined, or high on candy.

A knock came at his door. "Come in," he said distractedly.

"It's Francesca Antonelli. I've got dinner for you." She pushed open the door with her hip and came in balancing two plates. She placed them on his conference table, since his desk was piled with files and the map was spread over most of its surface. "I'll bet you're hungry," she said with an uncertain smile. "Emma asked me to bring over your dinner since you missed the party." She gestured towards the plates. "You definitely will not starve."

There was a moment of uncomfortable silence. He looked up at her. Her eyebrows were raised over her deep brown eyes. "Have you got time to eat?" she said. "Why don't you come over here?" She sounded like she was ordering him around, and hesitated as if she'd just realized it. Then she softened her tone. "You're going to love the potato salad."

Tom gave her a wry smile. Why did they always rub each other the wrong way? She had come all the way over here to bring him something to eat. He ought to be grateful. "I forgot all about the party at Emma's. I never even called." He shook his head. "I'll have to call her and apologize."

"I wouldn't worry about that. We're all concerned about Corinne Casey. Everyone knows your place is here. Actually, the party was a bust. Several people left to help in the search and I stayed on to help Emma clean up."

Tom got up and came around the desk to the conference table. He looked down at the two plates piled with food. There was a cheeseburger, potato salad, pasta salad, Jell-O salad, baked beans, a pickle and chips. "Wow," he said. "This looks great."

Francesca handed him a napkin and a fork. "I'm going to run out to the car. I've got your dessert and a plastic travel cup filled with iced tea. I'll be right back."

Tom sat down and took the plastic wrap off of the plates. He hadn't realized how hungry he was. By the time Francesca came back, he had finished half of the cheeseburger and most of the potato salad. He wiped his mouth and smiled at her. "Thank you for doing this." He gestured with his hand. "Would you like to sit down? I've got enough here to share."

Francesca eyed him questioningly. "Are you sure? As I remember, I'm your enemy, the yellow journalist."

He considered her for a moment. "That's right! But you brought me dinner, so I'll have to fraternize with the enemy."

They both laughed. He patted a chair. "Come on, sit down. I'll try to be civil."

"How is the investigation going?" Francesca asked tentatively as she sat down.

"We're hopeful that someone will find her tonight. But so far we have no leads and no clues. It's like she vanished right after the parade. I have to admit, I have a bad feeling about this."

"You're thinking about Lilly Lawrence."

"Yes. I've got several officers down on the beach... I hope we can avoid a replay." They looked at each other. Unspoken fear hung heavy between them.

"So, off the record," Francesca said. "Lilly was not physically harmed in any way. Right?"

He nodded as he took a forkful of beans.

"So why was she kidnapped and drowned? Do you think she saw or heard something she shouldn't have? Maybe at the fair?"

"We never came up with a lead. We questioned everyone multiple times. No one heard or saw anything suspicious. But that's precisely why I'm worried about Corinne. There doesn't seem to be any rhyme or reason for her disappearance either!"

A knock at the door announced Officer Johnson "Chief, I just got a call from a man over on Lincoln Street. He found a bag of candy in the alley behind his house. His alley runs between Oak Street and Beech. It's right near the parade route. I told him we'd come over and check it out. Should I go and leave Arlyne here to take calls?"

Tom thought for a minute. "No, you stay here. I'll drive over there and talk to this man. What's his name?"

Johnson handed him a piece of paper. "Harold Hobson. Here's the address."

Francesca busied herself with the paper plates. Then she looked up and said tentatively, "Could I go with you? I could follow you over in my car."

Tom frowned. "That's not quite police protocol." Then he smiled. "But you did bring me dinner. Let's go."

Harold Hobson was a grouchy seventy-five year-old man. He was sitting on the porch in a rocking chair and holding a blue recycled bag printed with the U.S.A.P. Foods logo. He was painfully thin and his hands were gnarled with arthritis.

"It's about time. I called over a half hour ago. Where have you been?" he groused.

"Good evening, Mr. Hobson. Sorry to keep you waiting," Tom said as he came up the steps. "I'm Chief Barnett and this is Francesca Antonelli from the *Banner Bee*."

"I know you. You don't have to tell me. But what in the hell is the *Banner Bee*?"

Francesca smiled, stretching out her hand. "It's an online newspaper."

"Oh, you mean on the Internet. I don't waste time with the Internet. I've been getting the *Chicago Tribune* for fifty years." He held her hand, challenging her with his eyes.

"So tell us what you called about," Tom said.

Mr. Hobson raised the blue bag. "This here. I found it by the trash can in the alley. It looked like it had been thrown there and it made me think about this little girl everybody's looking for. Maybe it was her candy?"

"When did you go out in the alley?" Tom asked.

"About four o'clock. I decided to have a beer. My daughter doesn't think I should drink beer in case I get drunk and fall over. But you know, it's the Fourth of July and I decided I should have one. So after I finished, I took the bottle out to the garbage and hid it under some trash so she wouldn't find it. She'll be over here sooner or later." Mr. Hobson was clearly enjoying their undivided attention.

"Can you tell us what you remember around the time of the parade?" Tom asked.

Mr. Hobson thought for a moment. "Somebody parked their van right there in the alley just down from my garage. If I wanted to get my car out, it would have been nearly impossible. But this happens every year when there's the parade. People park everywhere and anywhere and you policemen don't give a damn."

Tom let this slide. "Do you remember the color or make of the van?"

"Give me a break. I didn't go out there and look at it. What was the point? It was dark-colored, maybe green or blue."

"Did you go to the parade?"

"You've got to be kidding. I can barely walk down to the corner. Besides, I've seen that fool parade plenty of times." He rocked back and forth. "The best parade was in 1945 when I was a kid and the war was over. Now that was a fine parade."

Tom nodded. "I'll bet it was. That was a great moment in history."

Hobson looked over at him. "What do you know? You weren't even born!"

Tom nodded. "Did you hear anything when the parade was over? Did you hear the van start up, or any voices?"

"No sir-ree," Hobson said. "I was sitting right here on the front porch. I like to watch the people walk by. Most days there aren't that many, but on the Fourth of July, it's a regular parade." His eyes twinkled.

Tom had brought an evidence kit. He pulled out a large evidence bag and asked Mr. Hobson to drop the U.S.A.P. Foods bag into it. "We'd like to look out back. Can we get around on the side of the house?"

"Oh, you can go right through the house. It's fine by me." Hobson stood up slowly and hobbled over to open the screen door for them. Inside, the living room was old and tired, but spotless. Hobson pointed towards the kitchen. "You can go right out that way."

Up until this point, Francesca hadn't said a thing. "Mr. Hobson, why did you think the bag of candy might be Corinne Casey's?"

"Just that kids love candy and they're not going to lose a whole bag of it, right? I'm thinking she was grabbed like that other little girl. Don't tell me you didn't think about the other little girl that got kidnapped and drowned back in May?" He looked up at Francesca, his gaze sharp under bushy eyebrows.

"I think everyone is making that connection," Francesca murmured. "That's why they need to find Corinne as soon as possible."

"What's the name of your computer newspaper again, the one competing with the *Tribune*?"

"It's called the *Banner Bee*."

191

"Humph! I'm going to ask my daughter about it."

Tom and Francesca went out the back door and through the small yard to a gate next to the garage. It was getting dark. Behind them in the house, Harold Hobson turned on the outdoor floodlights. They lit up the yard and the alley.

"You stand right there," Tom said to Francesca, pointing to a spot inside the wooden gate. "We don't want to destroy any evidence. I'm going to get a team over here when we're finished." He dug booties and a pair of latex gloves out of the evidence kit and put them on, then pulled a flashlight off his belt. He moved into the alley and shone the flashlight beam around the area. A few feet from the garbage bin, he saw a mini Tootsie Roll and a Jolly Rancher.

"These must have fallen out." Tom placed them in an evidence bag.

"What's that over there?" Francesca pointed to a small, glittering piece of metal by the neighbor's fence. Tom walked over and picked it up. He came and showed it to Francesca. It was a small triangular pin with a circle in the middle, maybe a globe. It had the letters ALPA on it.

"What does that stand for?" she asked. "Do you know?"

Tom shook his head. "No. I'll have to look it up back at the office."

"Wait," she said. "I'll look it up right now." She pulled out her iPhone, accessed the Internet and typed in the letters. "Just a sec. Here it is. ALPA: Airline Pilots Association, international." She looked at Tom. "What do you think? Could this pin just be lying here randomly? There's not much debris in this alley. I'll bet it's been cleaned recently. So how did this pin get here?"

Tom dropped the pin in another evidence bag. "I don't know." He turned to look at her, holding up the bag of candy. "You know, Corinne's father works for U.S.A.P. Foods."

She was asleep now. She would never wake up. It had been easy to get her in the van. He'd just told her he was taking her to her mommy and daddy. After she got in, he quickly picked up the bike, which had fallen over, and threw it in the rear. No one had seen him, but his adrenalin had been pumping. Once he was in the van, he pulled on a beige cap and sunglasses.

After they drove away, she scrambled to the back to get her candy out of her bicycle basket. It wasn't there. It must have fallen out when he threw the bike in the back. She'd started to scream. But no one could hear her.

Chapter 20
Monday morning, July 5th

Corinne Casey's body was found in the water at the beach below Hollyhock Farm. A young couple was canoeing along the shoreline from Somerset down to Lake Woods. It was a peaceful morning and the lake was as smooth as glass. They were enjoying the early morning quiet. When they came around a rocky promontory to the north of Hollyhock Farm, they noticed a pink blob floating in close to the shore. They paddled towards it and were horrified when they realized it was the body of a small child.

Tom Barnett and the Homicide Task Force were on the scene before eight AM. Edmund Hollister, the ME, had given a proximate time of death as three that morning; the body had been removed a short time ago.

"I don't like what this looks like," Hollister said. "Have we got a serial killer or is this some copycat murder? It's the same MO down to the pink dress. This is some sick dude."

Tom shook his head. "I don't know what we've got… or rather; I know we've got nothing. There've only been two murders in Banner Bluff in the last twenty years, and now this summer we've doubled the record."

Hollister picked up his bag. "I'll contact you with the lab results ASAP; I'll be available when you need me." He turned and trudged up the sandy path.

The Homicide Task force was combing the beach and the bluff looking for evidence. As before, the scene provided few clues. The sand had been trampled the night before and there were no distinct footprints indicating where someone had entered the water. It looked as though a bunch of kids had been down here partying and watching the fireworks up and down the lake shore. They found beer cans, marijuana roaches and cigarette butts. Tom saw remnants of a fire; the kids must have sat around it and gotten high. The police would have to talk to some of the kids in town to find out who was down here and when they left. Usually someone would spill the beans after a little prodding.

Tom and Ron Puchalski looked across the sand. Puchalski said, "Whoever abducted Corinne would have had to come down here after the kids cleared out. The fireworks were going off around ten. But I'll bet the kids were down here until well after midnight."

"Yeah, so our guy would have been taking a chance. We had men covering the public beaches, so he was forced to go north," Tom said.

"You know, if it was dark enough and the kids were drunk enough, he could have come right down here and they wouldn't have noticed."

Tom frowned. "That sounds too risky to me. And how did he get down here? It would have been quite a walk from Eastern Avenue."

"Maybe he came down through one of the ravines south of the farmlands. Or did he come down through Hollyhock Farm? And where did he park his car? He wouldn't have wandered around Banner Bluff carrying a child." Puchalski scratched his head. These were all questions that neither one of them could answer.

They drove up to the farmhouse to interview the Meriwether family, who owned Hollyhock Farm. They took the rutted dirt road that ran adjacent to the gently rolling green fields separated by white fences. Tom could see horses under a giant live oak and the glistening surface of a small pond in the distance.

"This place is gorgeous," Puchalski said. "It's like another world, and yet so close to downtown Banner Bluff."

"Yeah, it feels like old Kentucky." Tom glanced at Puchalski. "Do you know the Meriwethers? They keep a low profile. You don't see them much in town."

"Not really. I know they've been pretty vocal about the Smithfield business. As I remember, they're opposed to building anything on that land. Aren't there some equestrian paths in those woods behind the Smithfield Mansion?"

"Yeah, they probably take riding classes along those paths. They could access the woods along Eastern Avenue." He pulled up to the parking area beside the farmhouse. Both men got out and surveyed the residence. Straight ahead was a driveway leading to a large paddock, surrounded on three sides by stables and a barn. The buildings were freshly painted red, with white trim. The fourth side was open to a training arena and open fields. Hollyhock was a thoroughbred training and breeding farm, and boarded horses as well. Mrs. Meriwether and her daughter provided riding lessons for local kids bitten by the equestrian bug.

To the right of the driveway was the family home, a sprawling two-story affair with a long porch across the front. The house was painted white with bright red shutters and a red front door. Hanging from the porch beams were baskets of red geraniums. A white pebble walkway, lined with red, orange and fuchsia impatiens, led to the door.

They heard voices coming from the back, so they continued down the driveway. Daphne Meriwether was working with a horse in the arena. A dark-haired man was leaning on the fence, gesticulating and yelling. She shouted something back and he banged the fence with his fist. Tom couldn't hear what they were saying; but when the man looked over at the approaching policemen, he turned abruptly and headed for the stables.

Daphne seemed shaken by the conversation. She looked over as they approached, waved and trotted over to the fence. She dismounted, tied up the horse, came around to the gate and let herself out. Daphne was a tall, elegant woman of sixty or so. She had the bearing of a queen, straight back and chin held high. Her blonde hair, nestled in a neat bun at the nape of her neck, showed strands of white and grey. Small lines fanned out from her kind grey eyes and deepened as she smiled at the officers. She was dressed in jodhpurs, riding boots and a tailored, short-sleeved white shirt.

"You're here about the little girl, aren't you? I told the fellow this morning that they could use our side road to get down to the beach." She put out her hand, and Tom shook it.

"Good morning, Mrs. Meriwether." Tom introduced himself and Puchalski. "Is there somewhere we could sit down and talk?"

"Why don't we go over to the house? I could offer you a cup of coffee. I bet you've got a long day ahead of you and could do with some caffeine." She led the way down a pebble path to a back porch graced by comfortable wicker furniture with striped chintz pillows. "Please sit down. I'll be back in a jiffy."

Tom sat down. Puchalski stood looking across the fields towards Lake Michigan. "Man, this place is heaven on earth. What a spread!"

Tom looked towards the stables. He saw the dark-haired man crossing the paddock leading a sleek brown horse. He didn't know much about horses, but this one must be a thoroughbred, he thought. It was beautiful.

Mrs. Meriwether returned with a tray of steaming mugs bearing the red Hollyhock Farm crest, along with cream, sugar and a plate of warm blueberry muffins. She smiled as both men's eyes lit up. "Ina makes the best muffins on Sunday morning. They're a treat we always look forward to. Please help yourself."

After they had their coffee and muffins in hand, Mrs. Meriwether said, "We all feel terrible about what happened. Somehow it's more frightening, since this little girl was killed on our land." She paused and looked down. "I almost feel responsible. Do you know what I mean?" She swallowed and continued, looking up with deep concern. "Is it like that other little girl? Was she drowned?"

"There may be some similarities," Tom said. He looked over at Puchalski, who took out a pencil and notebook. "Could you answer some questions for us?"

"Certainly. I want to help all I can."

"Did you hear anything last night, a car, voices?"

"Well, I heard a lot of noise early on with all the fireworks last night. I went to bed about ten-thirty when all the racket was over. I take a sleeping pill most nights, so I don't hear anything once I'm asleep."

"Is there only that one road down to the beach?" Puchalski asked.

"Yes. Anyone trying to get there some other way would have to ride a horse through the fields and jump some fences." Daphne smiled over the rim of her mug.

"Who else lives here?" Tom asked. "As I recall, you have a daughter who helps out with the horses?"

"Yes, Carina lives here with me. My husband died of a heart attack several years ago. " She paused, looking towards the paddock. "Her fiancé, Randal Jansen, lives in an apartment over the stables. I was talking to him as you drove up. Well, actually, arguing with him. We have very different ideas about running this farm."

"Would it be possible to talk to both of them while we're here?" Tom asked.

"Certainly. Let me call them." She pulled a cell phone from her pocket and called her daughter.

A few minutes later they saw the pair walking towards them from the stables. Jansen had his arm around Carina's waist and she was laughing up at him. They looked like a loving couple. Tom turned to look at Mrs. Meriwether, who wore an expression of worry and distaste.

"Here we are!" Carina's voice was ebullient. The two police officers rose as Carina Meriwether and Randal Jansen came up the steps. Carina was a younger version of her mother, with long honey-blonde hair and the same regal bearing. Her face was a perfect oval with deep blue eyes and a wide mouth. She wore jeans, a pressed light blue cotton blouse and brown riding boots.

Randal Jansen was a powerfully built man with wide shoulders and a muscular torso. He wore jeans and a white tee-shirt, along with a disdainful expression. A lock of jet black hair hung over his sharp, dark eyes.

"This is Chief Barnett and Detective Puchalski. They've come to interview us about what went on here last night when the little girl was drowned." Mrs. Meriwether turned to the officers. "What is the little girl's name?"

"Corinne Casey." Tom turned to Carina and Randal. "We just have a few questions."

Carina smiled. "Please, sit down. Randal, honey, do you want some coffee?"

"Yeah, that would be great. Thanks, darling." He patted her on the rear as she walked past him and into the house. Her mother watched her go, looking irritated and anxious.

Tom turned to Randal. "We need to know what you might have seen or heard last night, or in the early morning hours."

"I went to bed about midnight, right after Carina left my place. We rode in the parade yesterday dressed as cowboys. It was a hoot. Then we were at a party all afternoon and into the evening. We were both bushed by the time we got back here." He looked up as Carina returned with two bright yellow mugs of steaming coffee. "Isn't that right, honey?"

Carina sat close to him on the wicker sofa and handed him a mug. "Yes. I went over to Randal's apartment and, uh, we had a glass of wine and, uh, then we just fell asleep on the sofa." She blushed as she looked at her mother. "I probably came home to bed about midnight."

"Did you see or hear anything out of the ordinary during the evening?" Puchalski asked.

"After the fireworks, things quieted down, though I thought there might have been some kids down on the beach," Randal said. He looked at Mrs. Meriwether. "That's happened a couple of times this summer. These kids are trying to get away from you guys, so they come down to our beach through the ravine south of Banner Bluff and over the boulders."

Tom let this jibe slide by. "Did either of you hear a car going down the road to the beach in the early morning?"

Carina cocked her head in thought. "Actually, I think I did. I got up to shut the window about two-thirty AM and I heard a car or maybe a truck, but I didn't see any lights on the road." She looked over at Randal. "You must have heard it too! I saw your light was on."

Randal gave her leg a sharp squeeze and smiled. "You must have been dreaming, baby. I was fast asleep."

Carina looked at him searchingly, but she didn't contradict him.

Later, back in the car on Eastern Avenue, Puchalski looked at Tom. "Something fishy is going on," he said. "That Jansen is a slimy dude. I wouldn't like him as a son-in-law, let alone an employee."

Tom agreed. "I wouldn't trust him as far as I could throw him. And I don't think Mrs. Meriwether is thrilled about this engagement."

"Did you see the look he gave Carina when she said she saw his light on? I think he was lying through his teeth."

"Let's do some research on Randal Jansen. I'd like to know who he is and where he came from."

Francesca's dreams were a jumble of candy raining from the sky and smashing all around her amid painful, frightened cries. In her mind the intruder of her childhood had morphed into this lakeside kidnapper. Several times she dreamed she was a child again. She awoke trembling and drenched in sweat. Was he there in the room, ready to carry her off?

At six o'clock after only a few hours of sleep, she dragged herself awake. The night before, she'd left Mr. Hobson's house and driven home lost in thought. She'd arrived at her door with hardly any memory of how she got there. The security lights switched on as she pulled into the driveway, and as the garage door went up the whole place lit up like a Wal-Mart parking lot. Her neighbors probably thought she was nuts.

Only after she'd gone into her condo, shut the curtains and typed in the numbers on the security system could she begin to relax. Granted, she had Bailey and Benjy. Initially, they might bark ferociously at an intruder but then they would probably cover him with kisses.

She'd poured herself a glass of pinot noir and carried it up to her office. Her mind was in high gear. Why not do some research on ALPA, the Air Line Pilots Association? From the Internet, she learned it was the largest airline pilot union in the world and represented more than 53,000 pilots working for 39 U.S. and Canadian airlines. Delta, United, FedEx, Continental; all the big airlines and a whole slew of smaller ones she'd never heard of before were listed.

Francesca felt sure the ALPA pin was a clue to their kidnapper and murderer. Was he a pilot? How could she find out the names of all the pilots living in the area? She wondered if the police could obtain that information. She glanced at the clock. Was it too late to call Tom Barnett? She knew he had gone back to the station and probably wouldn't be going home that night. But when she called the station, they told her he was out of the office. He was probably assisting the evidence team at Henry Hobson's house. She left a message that she would call him in the morning.

She'd spent some more time on the Internet researching kidnappings and the psychological background of kidnappers. The litany of their predatory practices, the sexual abuse and the horrific torture they inflicted on their prey left her sickened. After delving into multiple kidnappings of young girls, she'd had enough. It was time to turn off her computer and go to bed.

This morning, she felt as though she'd been run over by a steamroller. After a couple of cups of coffee, she would go for a run at Liberty Grove. That ought to clear her head.

She arrived at Hero's Market at eight AM and found the side door open. Hero usually spent Sunday morning doing a thorough cleaning of the shop, followed by a big Sunday dinner and a long afternoon nap.

"Hello," Francesca called. "It's me."

Vicki and Hero, as well as Colman, were working this morning. They had buckets of water, scrub brushes and rags. Every surface of the small shop was getting a scrubbing, it seemed.

"Can I make you a latte?" Colman asked. "We're all having one before I clean out the machine."

"Sure, that would be great." Francesca picked her way across the damp floor. "I'll go upstairs and get out of your way."

"I'll bring it up to you," Vicki said. Her expression was grim, in contrast to her cheerfulness yesterday. "Francesca, do you know anything more about the little girl who disappeared?"

"I haven't heard anything this morning. Have you?" She decided not to mention her visit to Hobson's house.

"The police came and asked us what we heard and saw yesterday afternoon, but we were just too busy to notice anybody."

"I think they wanted to know where I was all day yesterday," Colman said. "I don't think they trust me." He looked gratefully at Hero. "Anyway, Mr. Papadopoulos could vouch for me from sunup to sunset."

Francesca went up the stairs to her office thinking about Colman. He would probably be on Tom Barnett's radar every time there was an incident. It didn't seem fair. She sat down at her computer and booted it up. There were still no pictures from David. Why hadn't he posted them yet? He was usually on the ball. She saw an email from Frank and opened it. He wanted to meet this afternoon and shoot his article by her. He also asked after the missing Casey girl. She wrote back: I'll be at the office all day. I'm working on some advertising spots. I've got a new client and the Cool Cow wants to change the design of their ad. You would provide a happy respite. Let's have tea! P.S. I'm feeling very apprehensive about Corinne Casey. I guess no news is good news?

Vicki arrived shortly with her latte and an invitation. "Pappou wanted me to ask you if you would like to come for dinner at one o'clock. We're having roasted lamb that is already in the oven, garlic roasted potatoes and briam."

"Mmm, I can smell the lamb. What's briam?"

"Baked summer vegetables in tomato sauce. You'll like it."

"I know I'll like it. Tell your grandfather I would be delighted to have dinner with you."

"Colman is staying for lunch too. It will be a party."

Francesca smiled as Vicki left. She was sure Vicki was the prime reason that Colman would be joining them for lunch. Just then her cell phone rang. She didn't recognize the number. "Hello, Francesca Antonelli speaking."

"Francesca, it's Tom Barnett." He hesitated, then continued in a low voice devoid of inflection. "I have bad news. We found Corinne Casey's body. She was drowned at the beach below Hollyhock Farm."

"Oh my God. How terrible! Is it just like Lilly Lawrence?"

"It seems so. I'd prefer not to discuss the details yet."

"I understand, but can I ask you one question? Was she wearing a pink princess dress?"

He sighed. "Yes. Yes, she was. But keep that under your hat."

Francesca gripped her latte cup and took a deep breath, "That's Sleeping Beauty's outfit. I think he's putting these little girls to sleep, literally. This guy is a monster."

He didn't respond to what she'd said. "Why did you call last night?"

"I wanted to tell you I researched that pin. The ALPA union includes thousands of pilots from just about every airline in the country except American Airlines. Can you find out the names of any pilots living in Banner Bluff or nearby?"

"We'll look into it. Listen, I've got to go. We have a meeting in a few minutes."

"I'll write up a short piece about Corinne's death and shoot it over to you for your approval."

"That would be good. Thank you, Francesca. Goodbye."

"Bye," she said, but he'd already hung up.

She sat for a few minutes feeling sadness and anger. How could these two little girls disappear in a quiet and safe community like Banner Bluff? If she were the mother of a little girl, she wouldn't sleep at night.

She went downstairs and shared the bad news with Hero, Vicki and Colman. Vicki rubbed her upper arms as though she were cold. "Do they have any idea who this guy could be? It must be someone living in this area. Maybe someone we see every day!"

"They think he drives a dark van," Francesca said, sitting down on the last step of the staircase.

"That could be anybody around here," Colman said. "Half the contractors in town drive vans."

"What kind of person could he be?" Vicki's voice shook.

"I was reading online last night about kidnappers of little kids. They're usually loners and keep themselves aloof," Francesca said. "They might seem quite unremarkable if you met them."

"Man, this guy must be driving around stalking his prey. He must know who he's going to grab and how." Colman tossed his rag in a bucket. "If I were a parent, I wouldn't trust anyone."

In spite of her fatigue and a low-grade headache, Francesca managed to design a new ad for a shoe store down on the North-South Highway. It was a coup to have landed that new subscriber, and her design was pretty zippy. She emailed it to the store owner just as she heard the call for lunch. As she got up from her desk, she looked out the window. Through the tree branches, she thought she saw Marcus and Susan. It looked like they were heading over to Sorrel's. She felt a sudden, unexpected pang of jealousy. Why shouldn't her two friends enjoy brunch together? She wasn't attached to Marcus... or was she? She felt disgruntled and a little ashamed of herself. This was turning out to be one hell of a day.

Chapter 21
Monday afternoon, July 5th

In spite of the depressing news, lunch was enjoyable. The young people were fun to be around. They laughed at everything and Francesca felt her spirits lift. Hero served her a generous slice of tender lamb. The potatoes were crispy and garlicky. The briam vegetable dish was perfect. After enjoying some espresso and baklava, Colman and Vicki did the dishes. They sang Beatles songs at the top of their lungs while they worked. Francesca wondered at the longevity of the Beatles. These kids weren't even born when the Beatles were the rage.

Francesca smiled at Hero. "You've performed a miracle, you know?"

He leaned back in his chair. "What do you mean?"

"You've given a whole new life to Colman. Because of your generosity, he's a changed person."

Hero nodded. "Colman works very hard. He is the one who has brought joy to his own life. Actually, he is a very good boy who just lost his way. Growing up is a very complicated affair. You know, my friend, I was not always a perfect citizen when I was young…"

Vicki and Colman came out of the kitchen. "Pappou, we're going to go down to the beach for the afternoon," Vicki said. Colman knows a special little beach."

"I'm surprised you want to go down there after the drowning," Francesca said shivering in spite of the warm afternoon.

"We'll be on the other side of the rocks. There's this path behind that big mansion, the one that's been under construction for years," Colman said. "Not many people know about the path. It's camouflaged by bushes. It leads down to the ravine and this little beach. It's really cool."

"Is this a safe place to be?" Hero asked.

"It'll be safe, Pappou. We're not going swimming. Colman is going to teach me how to play chess."

"Chess? Chess on the beach, that is something new."

"Colman says it's cool and shady there and we can concentrate."

"Well, okay." Hero rolled his eyes at Francesca. "Take something to drink out of the cooler in the store and record it on that paper beside the cash register."

Vicky bent over and gave her grandfather a kiss on the cheek.

Detective Sergeant Puchalski went home for a shower and lunch. As he arrived, Bonnie was heading out with the kids in tow.

"I didn't think you'd be back today, so I called Mom. We're going over there for lunch and to play in the pool. Sorry!" She turned to the boys who were playing tag and tromping around in the flower beds. "Will you two just stop it? Go get in the car. *Now.*"

"Don't worry about it," he said. "I'm just going to take a shower, eat something and go back to the station." He took the baby from her arms and helped her corral the boys into the minivan. He settled his daughter into her car seat and kissed Bonnie goodbye. As he watched them drive off, he thanked his lucky stars that his children were safe.

After a long, hot shower, he put on a fresh uniform: white short-sleeved shirt and blue summer weight slacks. In the kitchen, there didn't seem to be much for lunch. He made himself a couple of peanut butter and jelly sandwiches and poured a big glass of milk. *Thank God for peanut butter*, he thought as he munched. What would Americans do without PB and J? When he had finished, he put his dishes in the dishwasher, grabbed an apple and went back out to the car.

He'd made up his mind to do a little research on Randal Jansen. He didn't like the guy, but more importantly, he didn't trust the guy. When he got to the station, he went right to his desk and went online. Jansen didn't pop up anywhere in the NCIC database.

Then he googled Jansen's name and got a hit. Randal Jansen, complete with picture, advertised himself as a horse trainer and breeder. Apparently he had worked with several breeders in northwestern Kentucky and southern Illinois. Puchalski wondered in what capacity Jansen had been hired at Hollyhock Farm. Certainly getting engaged to the owner's daughter was a coup. Maybe that had been his plan all along.

An article in an equestrian magazine referred to Jansen as a trainer at Conway Farm. The article discussed some of his controversial training methods and included a short bio. The bio said Randal Jansen was also a pilot, and came from a small town in Wyoming. Puchalski looked up the number for the farm and reached for the phone.

"'Hello, Conway Farm, Dolly speaking," a cheerful, female voice said.

"Hello. May I please speak to Kenneth Conway?"

"Well, now, I don't know. Who are you?"

"Detective Sergeant Puchalski. I'm with the Banner Bluff Police Department. We're located in northern Illinois. I have a few questions for Mr. Conway about a former employee."

"Mr. Puchalski, this is the Fourth of July weekend and we've got the whole family here for a picnic. Could you call back tomorrow?"

Puchalski swallowed his impatience. "Is this Mrs. Conway?"

"It certainly is."

"Maybe you can help me, then. Though it might be easier if you'd just get your husband. It won't take long."

"Okay, but Ken won't like it."

The wait was nearly five minutes. When Kenneth Conway finally answered, he sounded out of breath and ticked off. "This had better be important. Now, who are you?"

Puchalski identified himself and where he was calling from. "Could you answer a couple of questions?"

"How do I know you're for real?"

Puchalski suppressed a sharp sigh. "Call back to the Banner Bluff police station and verify my identification."

"Forget that. Let's just get it over with. What's going on?"

"I need to know about Randal Jansen."

"Jansen? He's been gone from here for a couple of years. Is he up there in your neck of the woods? What is it again, Banner Bluff?

"Yes, sir. Mr. Jansen lives in Banner Bluff. His name came up in connection with an investigation. How long did Jansen work for you, and when and why did he leave?"

"Did he commit a crime?"

"Not that I know of, sir. This is just a preliminary request for information. So how long was he at Conway Farm?"

"He was here for about two years. He sure knew how to work with horses, but he was an arrogant son-of-a-bitch."

"Why did he leave your employment?"

"Because I fired him, that's why. He questioned all my decisions. Sometimes, he blatantly went against my wishes. One day we had a shouting match and that was the last straw. I told him to get packing."

"Can you tell me anything else about Mr. Jansen?"

"What do you mean?"

Puchalski thought a moment. He was fishing, but there had to be something. "His likes and dislikes, his family, friends, acquaintances…"

"I don't know anything about his personal life. He didn't have any friends that I know of. He kept pretty much to himself." Conway paused. "I will tell you that I didn't like his relationship with my daughter. She was always traipsing around after him. I think he led her on. Dolly was glad when I kicked him out."

That piqued Puchalski's interest. "How old is your daughter?"

"She's fourteen now. She cried her heart out when he left. Anyway, I say good riddance. Now, if you don't mind, I've got to go. I'm supposed to be manning the grill."

"Thank you for your time," Puchalski said as Kenneth Conway banged down the phone.

He went down the hall to talk to Chief Barnett. The Chief was in the investigation room with Johnson, Lewis and Conroy.

"I just did a little research on Randal Jansen," Puchalski said. "He worked downstate for a couple of years with an outfit called Conway Farms. I called up and talked to the owner, Kenneth Conway. He said Jansen is great with horses, but he fired him for insubordination. It sounds like Jansen didn't take to being told what to do. And get this. Jansen had some kind of relationship with Conway's daughter, and Conway didn't like it. I guess it was a little too cozy. She was only ten or twelve at the time. I know that's older than our victims, but..."

Barnett looked thoughtful. "Interesting. Anything else?"

"The bio in an article about him said Jansen is a pilot. At some point he flew for some little Western outfit."

"I'd like to know more about where he was yesterday," Barnett said. "Why don't you give Carina Meriwether a call? Tell her we're coming over for another little chit chat."

"Are you thinking he's our guy?"

"At this point, I just think he's keeping secrets." Barnett turned to Lewis. "See if you can get a list of pilots living in the area. Check with O'Hare and Midway airports and then ALPA—the Air Line Pilots Association. Find out if Jansen is a member while you're at it."

"Yes, sir. I'll get right on it." Lewis said as he left the room.

Chapter 22
Thursday afternoon, July 8th

Francesca had been working all morning. She needed to get out of the office and walk around to clear her head. After saving the piece she was working on, she got up and stretched her arms up towards the ceiling, yawning mightily. Then she bent over and stretched down to touch her toes. She felt as though her body had been molded into her chair. It felt good to move. That was the problem with modern employment. So much of it meant sitting for hours in front of a computer screen until your eyes went buggy and your body became a congealed mass. *Time to get out of here,* she thought.

She grabbed her bag and headed down the stairs. She made a miniature salute to Vicki and Colman and walked out into the hot summer sunshine. Before grabbing a sandwich at Churchill's, she decided to walk once around the village green and breathe in some whopping hot, humid air. You could complain about the heat, she thought, but if you had to endure a Chicago winter, you should be grateful for every single tropical day Chicago had to offer.

There weren't too many kids on the playground. They probably had opted for the beach or the swimming pool. Or, more likely, their parents had chosen to keep them safe at home. Banner Bluff was a town living in fear. If a stranger ambled down the sidewalk, people immediately picked up their cell phones and called the police. Parents eyed gas meter-readers suspiciously. Dads glared at the overly friendly postman. Mothers yanked their children out of the grocery store if the checkout man smiled at their little girl.

At the Recreation Center, the kids in summer camp were having lunch at big picnic tables. Each age group wore a different colored tee-shirt and their camp counselors were sporting yellow. The cacophony of children's voices carried through the air. Overseeing the group were two uniformed police officers. Francesca walked under the giant oak that spread its generous branches over the footpath and provided shade for the picnickers. At the corner of Elm and Washington, she turned down towards the Post Office and Churchill's restaurant.

Street parking was full, as were the outdoor tables along the sidewalk. Francesca decided she would just get her sandwich and take it back to eat in the office. Then she spotted the Marshalls, who were seated by the door. "Hi, you guys," she said. "What's for lunch?"

"I'm having a hotdog with catsup and Mommy said I could have chips," Rosie said. "Right, Mommy?" Next to her, Kate nodded in agreement.

"That sounds yummy, "Francesca said.

"Would you like to join us?" Kate asked.

"Sure. That would be nice. Let me get a sandwich and I'll be right back."

Inside, the small restaurant was bustling. There was quite a line of customers waiting to order. Francesca took her place in line and looked up at the list of sandwiches posted on the wall. Everything sounded good. Decisions, decisions! Maybe she would have the chicken salad on multigrain and an iced tea with lemon; hmm, or maybe the turkey BLT. She checked out the other people in line. They were from every walk of life: construction workers, postmen, office workers, nattily dressed executive types and mothers with children.

Next to her on the counter was the digital picture frame, a favorite of local residents. It was displaying a slideshow of pictures from the Fourth of July. She recognized a lot of people. There were candids of people in the parade and pictures of those watching along the parade route. She spotted a photo of herself in the judge's grandstand. They'd caught her with her mouth wide open; not her most flattering pose.

Gosh! There was a picture of Corinne Casey and her family. All kinds of thoughts raced through her mind. Why had Churchill's decided to display that picture? It seemed kind of morbid. Behind the Casey family was a guy she recognized from somewhere. Where had she seen him before? Francesca struggled to remember. The guy was looking at Corinne, not at the parade. He wore a baseball cap and it was hard to see his face in the shadow of the brim.

The picture was gone in ten seconds. She wanted to see it again. "Please go ahead," she said to the woman behind her. She continued to wave people around her as she examined the photographs. A few minutes later, the judges' stand reappeared and then Corinne's picture. She scrutinized the guy again. Yes, she had seen him somewhere, but where?

She bought her sandwich and went back outside. The Marshalls had almost finished their lunch. "Sorry to keep you waiting," Francesca said. "Listen, I'm not going to sit down. I've got way too much to do back at the office and you're already done."

Rosie was pulling Kate's skirt. "Mommy, let's go," she whined. "I'm too hot. I want to go to the pool."

"We'll get together next time," Martin said as he rose from the table.

Puchalski and Johnson drove over to Hollyhock Farm to have another conversation with Carina Meriwether and Randal Jansen. They spotted Carina near the arena, talking with a very thin woman and a young girl. A silky brown quarter horse was tethered to the fence and the girl was stroking its muzzle.

Johnson parked the car and they walked over. Carina was dressed in jodhpurs and a lemon yellow sleeveless shirt. She had on a straw cowboy hat that curled up on the sides.

"Hello, Detective Puchalski. Welcome. May I introduce you to Mrs. Robertson and her daughter Suzanne?"

The officers smiled and nodded at the leggy ten-year old and her mother. Puchalski thought the mother looked painfully thin, maybe anorexic. He introduced Johnson and then got down to business. "We'd like another little discussion with you. We can wait in the car until you're free."

"No problem," Carina said. "We've just finished our lesson for today." She smiled at the girl.

"Come on, Suzanne," her mother cajoled. "We have to leave now." She turned to the policemen. "Suzanne would like to spend the entire day here; but she needs to get to her piano lesson."

Carina watched them go. "Poor kid," she said. "She's way over-scheduled. There's no time for her to just play and have fun. Mrs. Robertson is a helicopter parent par excellence."

"I suppose parents want to give their kids every opportunity and it gets out of hand," Puchalski said.

"You're probably right. But I know Suzanne would like to stay here and just hang out." Carina turned to the officers. "Let's go sit in the shade. That sun is brutal today." She led them over to some lawn chairs under a tree, collapsed into one and fanned herself with her straw hat.

Once seated, Puchalski took out his notebook. "Tell me about what you did on July Fourth."

"All day long? Whatever for?" Carina raised her eyebrows and shook her head in apparent exasperation. "Didn't we already go over that?"

"I'm hoping you'll remember something else that occurred that would help us out, something you didn't think of before. I don't know, maybe you observed someone around here who didn't belong." He smiled disarmingly.

Carina sighed. "Okay. In the morning Randal and I got dressed up in our cowboy outfits, saddled the horses, put them in the horse trailer and took them over to Banner Boulevard to line up for the parade. Jose Jimenez, our caretaker, was here all day. You could talk to him. I don't think anything happened while we were gone. He would have told me or Mother."

"Was your mother here all day?" Johnson asked, wiping his forehead. His fair skin was flushed in the heat.

"No, she came to watch the parade and then she went over to a friend's house to a party. I know she didn't get back until about four."

"What about you and Randal? What exactly did you do after the parade?"

"We were at the beginning of the parade, so by eleven o'clock we were finished. We got back to the trailer, Randal loaded up the horses and brought them back here. You could ask him if he saw anyone around." She wiped her forehead with her arm.

"What did you do?"

"I ran into an old friend. We went over to the carnival and had a drink."

Puchalski leaned forward. "When did you and Randal get back together?"

"Well, Randal was gone forever. He didn't answer his cell phone so I got my friend to drive me home, because I wanted to change clothes before we went to the barbeque." A look of irritation flitted across her face. "He had been up in the barn loft, looking for some old equipment, while I was waiting and waiting." She twirled her hat around on her finger and then laughed good-naturedly. "He just forgets what time it is."

"So when did you get back here?"

"Oh, I don't know, probably about one-thirty. I showered and changed and we left for the party. I didn't see anybody or anything strange. I mean, no one was lurking around."

"Where was the barbeque?"

"At Bradley Harrison's place. It was a blast. He had a great band and a fun crowd. We got back at about ten." She looked away. "But I already told you about that."

Ron flipped pages in his note book. "Yes, I have it right here. How long did you stay at Mr. Jansen's apartment after you got back?"

"Oh, I had a glass of wine, you know, probably came home about midnight," She studied her nails. "It was quiet around here after the fireworks."

Puchalski nodded. "You said you woke up about two-thirty and thought you heard a car, but saw no headlights. Right?"

"Yes."

"You said Mr. Jansen's light was on?"

"Oh…" Her voice wavered. "I was wrong about that. I didn't see any light that night, it was the night before."

"How can you be sure?" Puchalski asked. "You originally said you saw lights on in his apartment, and that was the very next morning."

Carina plucked the edges of her hat. "Maybe I did, maybe I didn't. Whatever!"

Puchalski looked her in the eyes. "Ms. Meriwether, this is a murder investigation. I would ask that you think carefully whether you saw a light on in Mr. Jansen's apartment or not."

"All right, I probably did. But you can't possibly think Randal has anything to do with all that. It's ridiculous!" She rose from her chair in one fluid movement. "Why don't you ask Randal? He's in the stables. I've got another riding lesson in fifteen minutes." She strode off towards the house.

He certainly would ask Randal Jansen, but on police terms. Puchalski turned to Johnson. "Let's have Mr. Jansen come into the station. Go on over to the barn and tell him we want to talk to him." His voice dripped sarcasm. "At his convenience." He looked over toward the barn. "I'd like to get into that barn and check it out, but we'll need a warrant and no judge is going to issue one at this point."

As Johnson headed toward the stables, Puchalski walked over to the patrol car and started the engine. It was an inferno inside. He turned up the air conditioning. Then he got back out to wait for Johnson in the slightly cooler outside air.

From her desk chair, where she sat staring out the window, Francesca heard Frank Penfield trudging up the stairs. She'd been staring out the window off and on all afternoon. She couldn't remember where she'd seen the guy with the baseball cap before. After an hour back at the office, she'd returned to Churchill's and watched all the pictures on the digital frame two more times. The guy was wearing a white shirt and he had a grey sweatshirt or sweater hanging over his shoulders. There was a peculiar set to his shoulders, as though he were favoring his left arm. He looked tall. His eyes were shaded by his cap, but his mouth was visible and was set in a hard line. He gave Francesca the heebie-jeebies.

"Hey, Frank. I'm glad you're here," she said as he entered the office. "I've been going nuts." She turned her chair to look at him. "Whoa, Frank, nice legs."

"It's so damned hot that I succumbed and put on shorts." He was wearing old plaid shorts, a Hawaiian shirt, brown loafers and dark socks.

She gave him a once-over. "No loafers with socks when wearing shorts. It is definitely not cool."

He chuckled. "What are you, the fashion police? I'll jolly well wear what I choose. Now, are we going to have tea?"

"Sure. You really want hot tea, though? The air conditioning is not at its best up here."

"Oh, I always drink hot tea when it's hot. It makes you sweat and then you cool off." He wiped his forehead with a handkerchief and collapsed in a chair.

"Hmm, I've never heard that logic, but I could go for a cup!"

As she disappeared behind the screen and plugged in the electric kettle, she heard Frank walking over to look out the windows. "You do have a great view of the village green from here. You could play spy and watch everyone's comings and goings."

"Even without playing spy, I do see a lot. On market day, I can check out Louisa Gorton attacking one passerby after another. What a busybody."

"Louisa is a lonely lady. Who does she have to talk to at home? No husband. No kids. No family. She's out and about gathering her tidbits of information. Poor soul," Frank said.

"She could probably work for the *Banner Bee*. We could have a gossip column. People would love that." Francesca brought in the teapot, cups, milk, sugar and cookies. Today it was white chocolate chip and macadamia nut.

Frank leaned back in his chair studying her face, "How are you sleeping these days? I've been worrying about you."

"I've had some restless nights and I do dream about that walk to the beach. Usually, I get up and read for a while and then I can fall back asleep." She looked up. "I'll be all right, Frank."

216

Frank helped himself to a large cookie and munched thoughtfully. "I've actually come to discuss some issues with you."

Francesca frowned. "Issues? Problems here at the *Bee*?"

"No, no. I want to discuss what I've seen and heard recently. I think we should put our heads together and think through what is going on around here."

Francesca poured water into the teapot, replaced the kettle and came to sit down. "Does this have to do with the murders?"

Frank raised his eyebrows. "No. It's about some financial hanky-panky. Where shall I start? I had a discussion with Emma on the Fourth of July after all of you left. She told me Bradley Harrison approached her about this so-called investment club, the American United Investment Club. Her late husband had great respect for Brad's father, who handled their finances. But Emma is uncertain about investing in this club, so she asked me to look into it for her."

Francesca poured him some tea and added milk and sugar, then served herself and took a cookie. "Is that what Brad is up to? I've seen him chatting up a couple of people." She thought back to the concert, when she had watched him schmoozing a well-heeled elderly couple.

"I asked Emma to get all the printed information she could and give it to me. Then I thought I'd do a little research. That's where I am right now." He opened his bag and pulled out some glossy brochures. "There are a lot of figures and information here, but nothing substantial. I'm going to get a buddy of mine to look into it."

Francesca perused the brochure. "Impressive. Look at the graphics and the layout. Who cares what it says? It's beautiful."

"Slick is more like it," Frank retorted. "There's another twist to all this. Bradley Harrison, Royce Canfield and Harry Silverman had lunch a month ago with Calvin Juniper at the Oak Hills Club."

Francesca gave him a questioning look. "So who is Calvin Juniper? Great name, by the way."

"Calvin Juniper is the head counsel for the Ciliegie Mob. He is a powerful individual."

She raised her eyebrows. "Well, well. What could that possibly be about?"

"I don't know, but I'd like to find out. Something is definitely afoot."

"Maybe I could ask Susan Simpson if she knows anything. Maybe there was a reason for the meeting? Maybe this Calvin Juniper represents someone else as well?"

"Nah." Frank rubbed his chin. "Somehow, I don't think so."

Francesca reached for a cookie. "Okay, I'll talk to Susan and do some detective work on my own."

"Meanwhile, I'm going to do my financial research." He paused and met her gaze. "I'm glad to share this with you, Francesca. I've been feeling a bit down of late." His kind eyes, usually a lively blue, looked dulled with worry. "I feel like things are going very wrong in Banner Bluff. We've had two horrendous murders, and some of our citizens seem intent on stirring up trouble."

"We'll get to the bottom of it, Frank." Francesca smiled and reached over to give his hand a squeeze.

Chapter 23
Thursday night, July 8th

Royce Canfield was alone at home. Amanda had taken Samantha and left for Grand Haven, Michigan. She was staying with her mother. Initially, she had planned to spend just a few days; but two weeks had gone by and she still wasn't back. Before her departure, things were rough. They had barely been talking. When they did address one another, it became a shouting match. Often they fought about Colman. Amanda accused him of being a lousy, uninterested father. He retorted that she was too indecisive and a bad disciplinarian.

They fought about money and Amanda's spending habits. They fought about Royce's frequent evenings out.

"You don't understand that I have to support you and the kids. This means I've got to work all day and all night," he'd shouted.

"Working? I don't think so; not when you're out with Brad and that scummy Silverman. Give me a break!"

He knew she had only vague knowledge about the AUIC and she certainly didn't know about their involvement with Ciliegie and the Smithfield real estate deal. She wouldn't understand the situation. But she had never liked Brad or Harry, and she was suspicious of their relationship with him.

Royce walked into the family room and over to the bar. He made himself a pitcher of martinis and poured the first chilled drink. He took a sip and felt the icy liquid burn down his throat. He had never been a big drinker, but lately he had started imbibing on a regular basis. The martinis took the edge off; he might be able to sleep.

The house was dark and silent. The only light was the lamp over his chair. It was nearing ten o'clock. Colman would be back soon to meet his curfew. This summer, the boy had been a model child. He was up and out every morning before his parents stirred. He worked at the Greek's shop during the day and attended therapy sessions in the late afternoons. Afterward, he went back to the shop to help close up. Royce rarely saw him or spoke to him. This boy, his son, was someone he didn't know anymore.

Royce considered his role in the Ciliegie affair. He had worked diligently to sway the City Council towards the Sanders Sports proposal. Initially, Brad Harrison had presented the plans to the City Development Advisory Board. He had detailed the capital improvements planned for the mansion and displayed the elegant landscaping design for the dilapidated gardens. Once the Advisory Board was sold on the concept, it was not hard to convince the City Council. Royce and Brad were careful to present their views independently so there would be no apparent collusion. Harry Silverman appeared, representing the Sanders Sports Group, and answered questions as to the use of the property as a private club. The Council was pleased to learn that in contrast to the condominium proposal, Banner Bluff would not suffer an increase in school-age children or a major increase in vehicle traffic.

Proponents for a community center on the Smithfield property grew disgruntled, but it became abundantly clear that there were no public funds in the current economy for the village to develop the property. Royce himself had pointed out that the taxes collected from the club would be a boon to the town.

The vote would take place in two weeks. Once the decision was made, Royce wanted to forget all about this despicable business. There was no reason for people in town to think he was involved with the Mob. When they discovered the actual use of the club, it would be too late and he would act as surprised and horrified as everyone else.

Yet he was filled with unease. Every time the phone rang, he worried that it would be Calvin Juniper. His heart banged in his chest and he perspired heavily. The few times Juniper called, he had been icily cordial and explicit in his directives. Royce had responded like a well-trained puppy and had done as he was told.

He sighed heavily and took another sip of his martini. Things were spinning out of control. What was he working for? What did he really want out of life? He didn't know anymore. In his mind, he saw a long, straight road stretching across an empty field. He could see nothing on the horizon. Yet, he had to keep trudging along. It was a painfully lonely endeavor. He bent over, put his head in his hands and closed his eyes. God, he was exhausted.

"Dad, are you all right?" It was Colman. Ten o'clock. Right on time.

Royce looked up and saw his son in the doorway. He stood there tall and lean. This summer he had grown and filled out. Gone was the disinterested sneer and indolence. He radiated strength and assurance. Royce didn't know this clear-eyed young man.

"Hello, son. I'm just exhausted is all. You must be tired, too."

"Yeah, it's been a long day." Colman turned to go up the stairs. He was dressed in running shorts and a sweat-stained tee-shirt.

"Are you jogging these days?"

"Yeah, without the car I've taken to running everywhere."

Royce took this comment as a plea. "Well, maybe we should talk about getting you a car next fall."

"Maybe, but I don't need a car now, Dad. I'm fine." He cocked his head. "I actually like running." He turned again to go.

"Come sit and talk, Colman," Royce said plaintively. "Tell me what you're doing every day. Tell me what you're thinking about your future."

Colman leaned against the doorframe. "I'm living for today. I'm surviving. I am not thinking about the future." He scratched his head and grinned. "It's called carpe diem." With that he turned and jogged up the stairs. A few minutes later, Royce heard the muffled throb of music coming from his son's room and the bang of the shower door.

Royce envied Colman and his newfound life. He wished he could be eighteen again and start over.

Francesca went home early. The heat was oppressive and there was barely a breeze. She shifted the grocery bag she carried enough to grab her mail from the mailbox and went up the steps to her front door. All of the condos looked pretty much alike except for the front doors. Francesca had had hers painted a bright spring green. With two stone pots of pink and orange Gerbera daisies flanking the door, her entrance was a knockout. Balancing the groceries on her hip, she opened the door and went into the cool interior. It was wonderful to come home at the end of the day. She sighed with pleasure. Benjy and Bailey came bounding over to greet her.

Tonight she would make a French-inspired dinner. In the refrigerator, she had crepe batter she'd made for breakfast on Sunday. From her brown grocery bag, she took out a container of mushrooms, a small bunch of asparagus, a carton of mascarpone and a chunk of gruyère cheese. In a short time, she had prepared mushroom and asparagus crepes with a creamy, cheesy sauce. She popped them into the oven and made a small grapefruit and avocado salad on crisp greens. In the refrigerator was a bottle of sauvignon blanc that would be just right to complement her meal. Would she qualify as a bona fide "foodie"?

On the way upstairs to change into her UCLA tee-shirt and a pair of ancient boxer shorts, she heard her cellphone ring. She turned and raced downstairs to the kitchen. It was Susan.

"*Bonjour, mon amie, Comment ça va?*" Susan said in her best French.

"*Très bien, merci,*" Francesca replied. "Long time no talk. How are you?"

"Good, but tonight I'm hot and tired. I left early so I'm on my way home."

"What are you doing for dinner?" Francesca asked. "I've got crepes in the oven and there are enough to share."

"Dinner? Are you for real? I would love to come over. Should I bring anything?"

"No, just bring an appetite!"

"Sounds good. I'll be there in twenty minutes."

By the time Susan pulled up, Francesca had made another salad and set the table in the dining area. When she opened the front door, Susan came in carrying a mini box of Belgian chocolates and a single salmon-pink rose.

"This is dessert," she said, handing Francesca the chocolates. "And this is a rose of friendship."

Francesca gave her a brief hug and they went into the living room. "Let me put this perfect rose in a vase and would you like a glass of wine?"

"That would be heavenly!" Susan collapsed on the sofa. "Ouf, what a day!" She laid her head back against the pillows and kicked off her shoes. She was still dressed in her club "uniform": a well-cut suit, tailored shirt, heels and understated jewelry.

"I was actually going to call you this evening," Francesca said as she brought in two glasses of wine. "We haven't talked in a while and I wondered what was going on in your life."

"It's been a frenetic summer with parties, weddings and golf outings daily. Managing the busy calendar, planning with members and handling employees have kept me hopping." Susan sipped her wine. "How about you, what have you been up to?"

"Work, work, work. I've been covering a variety of stories: everything including ruse burglaries, the Presbyterian Church's rummage sale, summer programs for teens, road construction, and beach closings. We even had a story about a wayward turkey inhabiting the corner of Lakeland and Green Bay." Francesca paused. "Should I go on?"

Susan was laughing. "Oh, I've read your stories. Not every day, I have to admit. But you're doing a great job, Francesca, performing a service, really. I hear people talking about what they've read."

Francesca blushed with pleasure. "Now, let's get down to the nitty-gritty. Are you still dating Brad?"

"I don't know that I was ever dating him. Actually, I've barely seen him lately. He used to be at the club a couple of times a week schmoozing clients."

"What do you mean by schmoozing?"

"Whenever there was a golf outing, he would show up during the cocktail hour even if he wasn't invited. He'd have a drink and make the rounds talking to everyone. I didn't think it was quite right; but he is a member of the club and he paid for his own drinks."

"What did he want to talk to people about?"

"It sounded like he was discussing investments, you know, mutual funds and stuff."

Francesca thought of the conversation she'd had with Frank earlier that day. "Did you ever hear him talk about the American United Investment Club... the AUIC? Remember we joked about that once."

"Oh yeah, now that you mention it, I remember hearing that name recently. In the foyer of Oak Hills. Some older guy was irate, talking about the insufficient yield on his investment. Brad was trying to calm the guy down. I suggested they use a private room for their discussion. They went into the Walnut Room together. Members definitely do not like to hear loud arguments, especially not in the lobby."

"He's been approaching lots of people in town, primarily senior citizens. I guess they have the bucks to invest."

"I think he does business with Royce Canfield and Harry Silverman. They're as thick as thieves."

Francesca took a sip of wine. "That was the other thing I wanted to ask you about. Were you there the day they had a gentleman guest for lunch? It was at the end of June, I think."

"Oh, for sure I remember that date. There was a women's league luncheon, a big affair with a Mexican theme. But the dining room was practically empty. Brad, Mr. Canfield and Mr. Silverman had invited a guest; a real character from the city. I remember because they wanted a quiet corner to talk."

Francesca's ears perked up. "Did you hear what they were talking about?"

"Well, the atmosphere was tense and the guest seemed to be running the show." She took another sip of wine. "I do remember something I heard. I came around to see if everything was to their liking, and guess what they were talking about?"

Francesca cocked her head. "I give up, what?"

Susan giggled. "Strip clubs!"

Francesca looked at her in surprise.

Susan nodded. "Yes, strip clubs. I remember that because the three guys looked like they'd swallowed a canary. You would think Brad had seen plenty of strip clubs, right?"

"Right." Francesca's mind was racing. What could they be up to? She needed to think all of this through, but she would do that later on. "Let's have dinner. Everything should be ready to go."

After enjoying the crepes and salad, Francesca made two espressos and they settled back on the sofa with their coffee and one of the delectable chocolates.

Susan was quiet. She took a small sip of the espresso, glanced at Francesca and then down at her cup. "I haven't been dating Brad, but I did go out with Marcus a couple of times." She looked up at Francesca again, a guilty expression flitting across her face. "I feel like a rotten friend." She hurried to explain, looking helplessly at Francesca. "It all started when I offered to help with a fundraiser at the hospital and he invited me for lunch to talk about it, and then we had such a good time that he asked me again... I guess I should have said something earlier..."Her voice trailed off.

Francesca realized that she hadn't heard from Marcus for several weeks. She should have seen this coming. Nonetheless, she felt a wave of disappointment. For her friend's sake, she kept her voice casual. "Don't feel so bad. I certainly don't own Marcus. I'm actually glad that you two are hitting it off."

"Really?"

"Yes, really! I like you both and I'm glad you've found each other. Remember when we talked about the 'zing zing' thing! Well, it was never there!" She smiled slyly at Susan. "So?"

"Yeah, I feel all giggly when I'm around him. Is that nuts or what?"

"No, honey, that's zing zing!"

After Susan left; Francesca cleaned up the kitchen and then poured herself another glass of wine. She truly was happy for Susan and Marcus; they probably belonged together. But she couldn't help feeling a vague sense of failure. Another botched romance. She liked

Marcus, but the relationship had remained superficial. In a way, she'd been playing the role of girlfriend like an actress on the stage; going through the motions without opening her heart.

She shook her head. Enough self-analysis; better to move on and get working. She marched up the stairs and into her office. Once seated at the computer she googled the Banner Bluff Municipal Code. It seemed to cover every contingency from school bus pick-up areas, alcohol permits, and junk dealing, to filming and videotaping within the city limits. There wasn't anything concerning strip clubs, but she did find an ordinance that forbade solicitation and prostitution.

She thought about everything she had learned recently and decided to make a list.

1. Brad, Royce and Harry are involved in an investment club: the AUIC.

2. Brad and Royce are seeking new members for the AUIC.

3. Brad, Royce and Harry are meeting with a lawyer for the Ciliegie Mob.

4. Brad had a confrontation recently with a disgruntled investor.

5. Emma Boucher and Frank are suspicious of the AUIC.

What else did she know about them? Ah, yes. *Bradley Harrison is a member of the City Development Advisory Board and Royce Canfield is a member of the City Council.*

What was the city council dealing with right now? The Smithfield estate. Ah-ha! *The Smithfield estate vote is imminent.*

But what did the Smithfield estate and the AUIC have in common? She would talk with Frank tomorrow about the current proposal, since he had attended most of the meetings.

Francesca yawned mightily and headed for bed. She lay awake for a long time thinking about what she had learned, while at the back of her mind churned the picture of the unidentified man at the parade.

Sally had just spent an hour in the bathroom removing her make-up, taking a long herb scented bath, smearing on night cream and body lotion and brushing her hair one hundred strokes. She came out of the bathroom dressed in only a cloud of perfume. Harry realized that this would not be a "snuggle night". Sally was all about her beauty rest and maintaining elastic skin and fighting wrinkles. She would be too slippery for a hug. He rolled over and turned off his light. "Night, hon'," he said, his voice muffled by the pillow.

"Harry?" Sally said.

"Yes?" he said, instantly alert.

"Are you sure we're safe, with this vote coming up next week? No one is going to come after us when they figure out what kind of club is being established in town?"

"No problem." He sat up in bed, fully awake now. "I'm representing the Sanders Sports Group. I can always claim to be as much in the dark as anyone else. They told me it would be a private club. I assumed it would be a sports facility, like everyone else. No one knows the Sanders Group has anything to do with Ciliegie."

"I don't know, Harry. It all makes me nervous."

"You're forgetting something. We don't have a choice. They've got us by the balls."

She grabbed her robe from a chair. "I'm going downstairs for some chamomile tea." She bent over and licked his lips, then kissed him deeply.

Harry could never figure out what made Sally tick, particularly her attraction to him. It was a total mystery.

Chapter 24
Tuesday morning, July 13th

Frank Penfield had been talking to people in town. He'd been on the links at Oak Hills, hanging around for lunch or having a drink in the bar. He'd been to Starbucks, spending an hour in the morning and another in the late afternoon. Sitting at a table, sipping coffee and reading the paper, he would chat with friends and acquaintances that came in.

"Hey, Frank. Mind if I sit down?"

"No, it would be a pleasure. How are you, Matt?"

Matthew Byrne, a retired army colonel, sat down and stretched his legs out in front of him. He rubbed his knees and groaned. "These legs are not what they used to be. Some days my knees hurt and the next week it's my hip. I don't get it! I've always taken good care of myself. I used to be in perfect physical condition."

"It's called old age and it creeps up on you," Frank said, smiling wryly. He folded up his paper and gave his friend his full attention.

"Well, I don't like it but I guess it's part of the territory; along with hearing loss, hair loss... and all of the other losses."

Frank leaned forward, his arms crossed on the table. "I've just been reading the business section. Things don't look good. How do you see our financial future with the current government?"

Matt took the top off of his large no-foam latte, poured in a packet of sugar and stirred briskly before replacing the cover. Frank watched this, patiently waiting for his friend's response.

"I don't see any improvement in the foreseeable future. Congress doesn't know what to do about unemployment and we've got to get people back to work."

"Yes, I agree. I guess I'm just worrying about my own investments in this economy." Frank paused to let the slight change of topic take root. He sipped his coffee, glancing up at his friend.

"You are so right." Matt paused. "All I can say is, don't get mixed up with the American United Investment Club."

Frank feigned ignorance. "What's that?"

"The American United Investment Club, the AUIC," Matt repeated, his voice full of sarcasm. "I invested a nice sum of money a year ago, but I'm not seeing the return I was expecting. As a matter of fact, I feel like I've been royally screwed." He looked down at his latte as he turned it around and around in his gnarled hands. "You know what, Frank? I haven't told a soul about this. I feel kind of stupid."

"Who did you deal with?" Frank asked.

"Bradley Harrison! His dad was a great guy, but I don't know about Brad. I almost get the feeling there's something fishy going on."

"What do you mean?"

"Well, I'm wondering if he really bought real estate with my money. Is this one of those Ponzi schemes like that guy Madoff? I confronted him at the club the other day and he assured me I would see an improvement next month. But I just don't know." His voice trailed off.

Frank commiserated and asked a few more questions. When Matt left, he pulled out a small notebook and jotted down everything he had learned. His buddy at the *Tribune* was an investigative reporter and had the necessary connections in the financial world to uncover investment irregularities. He'd assured Frank he'd be in touch when he had something definitive. Meanwhile, Frank decided to continue his own investigation. Matt Byrne wasn't the only one who smelled something fishy.

The Homicide Task Force was meeting in the conference room. The white board was the center attraction. They all sat in silence, looking at the evidence that was printed in Officer Johnson's neat hand. Tom liked to have the facts visible for all to see. Who knew if someone would make an unanticipated connection? No one had yet, though. The atmosphere was heavy with frustration.

On the left side of the board was the evidence collected on Lilly Lawrence; on the right, the known facts about Corinne Casey. The two lists were almost identical.

Corinne Casey had received the same cocktail of drugs as Lilly and had a puncture wound on her left arm. Unlike Lilly, her upper right arm bore bruises that indicated she had been roughly grabbed by someone. An investigation into the provenance of the drugs had yielded no leads. Both girls were wearing identical princess dresses and had undoubtedly been unconscious when drowned.

Officer Rodriguez reported that the blue canvas bag with the U.S.A.P. Foods logo found in the alley bore Corinne's fingerprints, as did the two pieces of candy Tom had found nearby. It seemed certain that she had been abducted in that alley.

Johnson had made calls and received a short list of pilots flying into and out of O'Hare and Midway airports. There were eight pilots living in and around Banner Bluff. All of them had alibis for the nights of the drownings. They were either out of town, on a flight or had families that could vouch for their presence at home.

Puchalski reported that Randal Jansen would be arriving shortly. He gave the group an update on his conversations with Carina Meriwether and Kenneth Conway. He added that Jansen was a pilot as well. "Maybe he's our man. Hopefully we'll learn something this afternoon."

There was another long moment of silence. Then Johnson spoke up, his words slow and precise. "I don't know how you all feel, but I think our murderer is still out there. I think he needs to kill again. I don't think he'll stop unless we stop him."

Francesca had been digging through the financial reports of the Sanders Sports Group. Information about the company had been made public since the group's offer to purchase the Smithfield estate. She'd emailed a former sorority sister from UCLA whose husband, Hank Russell, worked in the California Department of Consumer Affairs and he agreed to check out the group. Francesca provided the information she had gleaned and suggested that Rocco Ciliegie might have an interest in the company. A few days later, Hank called back.

They spent a few minutes chatting about Hank and Karen's two young children, and Francesca felt a familiar squeeze in her heart— here she was in her thirties; still no kids, let alone a husband. Then Hank got down to business. "I was able to track down a definitive connection between the Sanders Sports Group and Ciliegie's known financial interests."

"Wow! Really?" Francesca was stunned.

"I've got an FBI acquaintance that gave me a tip. He said that once the Sanders Group buys the land, they can pretty much do what they like. A similar situation occurred with the purchase of a property outside of Houston last year. It was in an upscale community. Sanders was the front. But the Mob established a private men's club, kind of a la-di-da strip joint and maybe more, if you know what I mean. There's a court battle brewing as we speak."

"Hank, can you email me any documentation you've got? I need to act on this immediately. The vote on the Smithfield estate is a week away. We're cutting it close here."

"Will do... and Francesca, come out to visit soon. Remember you *are* a California girl!"

Francesca laughed. "Thanks a million, Hank!!" She hung up feeling elated.

As she laid the phone on her desk, it rang again. Another California call. She recognized the number and sighed as she answered. "Hello, Mom. Isn't this pretty early for you to be up?"

"Listen, sweetie, I just had to call."

"Why? What is it?" She felt apprehensive. "Is something wrong with Dad?" She knew he'd had some heart palpitations recently...

"Your dad is fine. He's meeting some of his buddies for breakfast at the Sunshine Grill."

Relief flooded through her. "I'm glad to hear that. So what's the big news?"

"Well, I just thought you should know. Janice called me yesterday. She told me that Dan and Jessica are having some marital problems and..."

Francesca felt her good mood melt away. Her mother always managed to burst her balloon.

"Francesca, are you there?"

"Yes, Mom, I heard you."

"I was just thinking that maybe you could, you know, call Dan up and show some sympathy. Maybe he would like to get together or something."

She gritted her teeth. "Mother, you don't get it, do you? I do *not* want to see or talk to Dan. It's *over*."

Oblivious, her mother charged on. "Honey, you should give him a chance."

"Sorry to disappoint you, Mom. I have absolutely no desire to speak to Dan. I'm going to hang up now. Bye!" She tapped the red phone icon harder than necessary and tossed her phone onto the desk. She stood up and walked back and forth across the room, stretching her arms towards the ceiling and taking deep breaths. The picture of Capri caught her eye. Maybe she should just escape to Italy. She could take cooking lessons and lead a bohemian life. And she could throw her phone in the Tyrrhenian Sea.

Randal Jansen strode into the Village Hall. He didn't answer Gloria's friendly hello, but continued down the corridor to the Police Department. He walked into the reception area and addressed the receptionist. "I'm here to see Officer Puchalski. He better be ready for me. I don't want to waste my time."

"You mean Detective Sergeant Puchalski. And your name is?"

"Randal Jansen. J-A-N-S-E-N. Got it?"

The receptionist dialed Ron Puchalski's extension and told him a Mr. Jansen, J-A-N-S-E-N, was there to see him. Coolly, she maintained eye contact as she spelled the name.

A few minutes later Puchalski came through the security door. He greeted Randal and led him through to an interview room, where Officer Johnson joined them. Arms braced on the table between them, his body language hostile, Randal refused coffee or water. "I'm not here for a nice friendly chat, so let's get down to business. Why do you want to see me? What do you want to know?"

Puchalski held up a hand. "Hey, we just need to go over what happened on the Fourth of July." He indicated a chair. "Please sit down."

Jansen dropped into a chair and leaned back, crossing his arms.

"I found out you're a pilot," Puchalski said. "Do you fly now?"

Jansen shrugged. "Sometimes I rent out at Palwaukee airport. I like to fly and I want to keep up my skills. What does that have to do with anything?"

"How often do you go out there?"

"Maybe once a month. I'm busy at Hollyhock and Mrs. Meriwether really needs me whether she realizes it or not." He grimaced. "She can be a real bitch."

"Isn't she soon to be your mother-in-law?"

"Yeah, so she ought to listen to me. I'm good at my job. I have a great track record."

"You had some trouble down at Conway Farms, though, didn't you? I've spoken to Kenneth Conway."

"You've been busy, Officer Puchalski," Jansen sneered. "Sorry, I mean *Detective Sergeant* Puchalski."

Puchalski remained stone-faced. Jansen, oblivious, went on. "Conway was a jerk. I got fed up with him and he got fed up with me. So what?"

"So what about Conway's daughter?"

Jansen smirked. "She liked me a lot better than he did. I bet she's a real looker now. I don't go for them that young, though."

Puchalski fought the urge to punch the smirk off Jansen's face and continued. "So let's hear again about your day on the Fourth of July."

Jansen talked about the morning parade and bringing the horses home in the horse trailer while Carina remained at the carnival. The details matched what Carina had said. "Why didn't you return to pick her up as planned?" Puchalski asked.

233

Jansen eyes burned with scorn. "I had to brush down the horses; water and feed them... all that takes time. You wouldn't have a clue." He leaned back in his chair, hands behind his head, legs crossed at the ankles.

His casual arrogance irritated Puchalski. Was it a performance, calculated to make him think Jansen had nothing to hide? There wasn't much to link Jansen to the murders, except that he was a pilot and he'd lied about his light being off at two in the morning. And they weren't sure their perp was a pilot, anyway. He decided to push a little harder. "You were busy a long time. Carina said you were looking at old equipment up in the hayloft when she got home. I don't get it. Your fiancée's calling you repeatedly and you're rummaging around in the hay." Puchalski leaned forward across the table. "Are you sure you weren't busy with a little girl up there?"

Jansen dropped his casual pose. Raising his voice he said, "I'm not into little girls, and I had nothing to do with that drowning. Is that what you're suggesting? That's some nutcase."

"Kenneth Conway said you seemed overly interested in his daughter. What was she, eleven? Twelve?"

"You're crazy. I flirted with her 'cause she was always following me around. She was pretty and she worshiped me. What do you think?"

Puchalski half-rose from his seat, leaning on the table. "I think we're going to take a look in that hayloft." He turned to Officer Johnson. "Call Hollyhock Farm and tell Mrs. Meriwether we'd like her permission to send a forensics team to go through her barn and stables."

Jansen shot to his feet. "You guys are crazy. I had nothing to do with that kidnapping. You can't pin that on me."

"Then sit down and explain where you were at two AM, July fifth. Why was your light on and why did you lie about it? Why did you want your fiancée to lie for you?"

Jansen sat, scowling. "I was busy."

"Busy with what?"

"Busy with a very nice piece of ass. Come on, you're a man. You understand. This girl comes over at all hours. She's hot for me."

"Who is she?"

"A riding student. She's home from college. She's over eighteen. She can't get enough of me. And..." He broke off, face flushed.

"And?" Puchalski's voice was hard.

"So we had a roll in the hay, isn't that what haylofts are for?"

"Give us her name."

Jansen hesitated, then said, "Fine. But keep Carina out of it. Okay?"

That afternoon, Francesca decided to do some sleuthing. She went over to Churchill's for a late lunch. She was going to chat with people and see what she could uncover.

The digital picture frame on the counter had changed from the parade to pictures of homes and gardens from the recent Garden Walk of Banner Bluff. She saw photos of Garden Club members wearing wide-brimmed straw hats and pastel summer dresses. They looked like English aristocrats visiting lovely formal gardens. As she was ordering a tuna sandwich on multigrain and a diet Coke, someone poked her in the back. She turned to find Louisa Gorton beaming at her. *This is definitely my lucky day*, Francesca thought. She could learn a monumental amount of info if she played it right.

"Louisa, how are you? Won't you come and sit down with me?" Francesca gushed. "I haven't seen you in ages."

"I've already eaten," Louisa said. She sounded uncertain, as if she wasn't used to people greeting her with such overt good will. "I need to be over at the museum in a half hour. I work there one afternoon a week."

"Come sit with me for a few minutes, just while I eat my sandwich." Francesca smiled and then turned back to the young woman who had taken her order. She paid for her lunch and was given a plastic number to display on her table.

She picked a quiet table in the corner and pulled out a chair for Louisa. "What have you been up to these days?" she asked. *Come on, Louisa. Tell me all the gossip around town.*

"You know, Francesca, I keep pretty much to myself in the summer. I don't do well with the heat. I like to stay in the house. Now, I don't really like air conditioning so I open the windows at night to cool things down and then I close up during the day and keep the fans going. I've read that air conditioning really just circulates the same dirty air around and it's filled with germs and..."

She droned on for a while, as if the topic was inexhaustible. The sandwich arrived; Francesca thanked the teenager who delivered it and then leaned forward, lowering her voice to a conspiratorial murmur. "Tell me, what do you think of Bradley Harrison? I just wonder why he never married."

Louisa's eyes gleamed. "Well, he was married, you know, to a beautiful young woman, but it didn't last. I don't know for sure, but I think she had questionable morals." Her expression reflected distaste. "Brad is just so sweet and he comes from a very good Banner Bluff family. He has excellent manners."

Yeah, right, Francesca thought. She took a bite of her sandwich and a sip of Coke. She cocked her head and looked at Louisa. "What does he do exactly? Does he work with his dad?"

"Oh, no, Mr. Harrison senior is retired. It's really rather sad. He has Alzheimer's, and Brad took over the company. He's on his own, poor boy..."

Francesca listened, nodded her head and munched her sandwich. Between bites, she dabbed at her mouth and then asked carefully, "Doesn't Brad have some other business in the works?"

"You mean the AUIC." Louisa lowered her voice and moved her chair closer to Francesca's. "It's an exclusive investment club. I was fortunate enough to be invited to join by Brad and by Mr. Royce Canfield."

As Louisa told the whole story, Francesca was able to finish her sandwich and her Coke, including every piece of ice. She was amazed at the amount of money Louisa had invested and the fact that she had yet to receive any return on her investment. When she said as much, Louisa waved her remarks away. "Oh, Brad explained that it takes quite a while to get the paperwork completed and entered into the system. A lot of security issues need to be in place. You know, they do it with an electronic system. They have firewalls. It's all very complicated. You wouldn't understand."

Francesca had heard enough. She looked at her watch. "Oh, my goodness, it's two o'clock. I better get back to work."

"Two o'clock! I'm late! I've got to get over to the museum. Now Francesca, dear, I told you this information in strict confidence. Don't tell a soul!"

Don't tell a soul, Francesca thought. *Give me a break.*

Chapter 25
Sunday morning, August 1st

At nine AM, Francesca and Frank pulled up in front of the Canfield residence. It was going to be another hot day, but at this hour there was a cool breeze coming off the lake. They stepped out of the car. Francesca was wearing her one and only black business suit, a pink and white striped shirt and classic black heels. Her unruly dark hair was rolled into a shiny bun at the nape of her neck. Frank was similarly attired in a dark grey suit with a blue striped dress shirt and tie.

Francesca had shared with Frank the information Hank Russell sent her. He had sent everything on to his pal at the *Tribune*, Anders Petersen. Anders and his partner in investigative reporting, Kaleigh Corrigan, had pulled out all the stops. They had finagled the help of a couple of junior financial reporters and were hot on the story.

On Friday morning, July 30th, Frank emailed Francesca:

Good and bad news. Anders and Kaleigh's story is coming out Monday morning in the *Tribune*. That's the good news. The bad news is that Royce Canfield, Bradley Harrison and Harry Silverman will undoubtedly be indicted for fraud in a real estate Ponzi scheme perpetrated against the citizens of Banner Bluff.

We need verification that they are also involved in the purchase of the Smithfield estate by the Ciliegie Mob. This should be included in the story. I suggest we meet with Chief Barnett to apprise him of our information and see how best to proceed. I will try to set up a meeting this morning.

Francesca felt elated. She dearly wanted to see Bradley Harrison get his comeuppance.

She hadn't seen Tom Barnett for a couple of weeks, not since the night of the Fourth. Despite the grim circumstances, they had hit it off. She'd liked his quiet ways and honesty. Since that night she'd thought of him many times. Had he thought about her? Probably not. He seemed to be a confirmed bachelor and likely saw her as a feisty female. Maybe he was just being nice that night since she'd brought him dinner.

She and Frank had spent Friday afternoon with Tom and Detective Puchalski, outlining the case against Royce Canfield, Bradley Harrison and Harry Silverman. They had offered all the details of the Ponzi scheme, along with their suspicions that the three men were also involved in Ciliegie's purchase of the Smithfield estate. Barnett called Anders and Corrigan and was apprised of their investigation. Time was short, Francesca knew; the City Council was set to vote on the Smithfield estate purchase Monday night.

Now, they waited on the sidewalk as Chief Barnett pulled up behind them and got out of the car. He took a long, appreciative look at Francesca, smiling slightly. Then, with a heavy sigh, he said, "Let's get this over with," and led the way up the curving brick sidewalk to the Canfields' front door.

Barnett rang the doorbell. A musical chime sounded inside. A few moments later, Colman Canfield opened the door. His hair was wet as if from a recent shower. He was dressed in a striped red and blue polo shirt and navy blue shorts. He looked surprised at the sight of them, then apprehensive. There was a brief moment of silence.

"We're not here to see you, Colman. We're here to see your dad," Barnett said. "Is he home?"

Colman smiled with relief and said, "I think he's in the kitchen having coffee. Come on in. I'll go get him." He left the three of them in the foyer and went down the hall.

Royce had been sitting at the kitchen table for some time. He was on his third cup of strong coffee preceded by two aspirin and he still didn't feel alive. His head felt foggy, his mouth dry and his throat scratchy. He looked across the kitchen at the stack of dishes in the sink. The counter was littered with a pizza box, white Chinese take-out containers and a half-eaten plate of tortellini. The cocktail shaker and two empty bottles of gin were on the wet bar. When had the cleaning service been here? Monday? But that was nearly a week ago. Had he accumulated this mess since then?

Friday, he'd played golf in the morning with Brad and Harry. Afterwards, he'd bowed out of the ritual breakfast and headed home. Being with them and talking about the AUIC and Monday's vote was the last thing he wanted to do. On the way home he'd called Silvia at the office and told her he would not be coming in.

"What about the meeting with Mr. Cole at ten AM.? We already rescheduled once," she said.

"God damn it, Silvia. I said I was not coming in. You call Cole and handle it. That's what I pay you for."

There was silence on the other end. Then Silvia said, very precisely, "Yes sir, Mr. Canfield." There was none of the usual warmth in her voice. Then she hung up.

He had gone home and put on the shorts and shirt he was wearing now and he'd fixed himself a martini at nine AM. Now, it was Sunday morning. He had pretty much drunk martinis for two days and nights. Periodically, he'd called Amanda in Michigan but she never answered the phone or called back. He had been alone all weekend. Colman was always gone at the damn Greek's store. He only came home to sleep and change his clothes.

He looked across at Amanda's little pots of herbs and the African violets above the kitchen sink. They were all dried up and brown. He had never thought to water them. Just then the kitchen door swung open and Colman came in. "Dad, Chief Barnett is here with Mr. Penfield and Francesca, I mean, Ms. Antonelli."

Royce shook his head in disbelief. "God damn it, Colman. What did you do now?" He banged his fist on the table, looking at his son with rising anger.

Colman looked blandly at his father's red-rimmed eyes and unshaven face. "I didn't do anything, Dad. They're here to see you." He left the kitchen, the door swinging behind him.

Royce got up and walked heavily out of the kitchen and down the hall. By the front door, he saw Tom, Francesca Antonelli and Frank Penfield illuminated by the light pouring in from the stained glass transom. They were speckled with blue, red and gold. Dressed in black, Penfield and the Antonelli woman looked as though they had come to a funeral. He felt a sense of foreboding.

Colman came charging down the front stairs. "I'm going downtown with Vicki to Millennium Park, Dad. See you later." He waved to them all as he ran out the door. The house was quiet after his departure.

"So to what do I owe the pleasure of your company?" Royce said, his voice raw with sarcasm.

"We've come to have a little talk with you." Tom nodded toward Royce's attire. "It looks as though you aren't heading out the door to church. Where can we sit down and talk?"

Royce led them into the dim formal living room to the left of the front door. A room befitting a queen, Francesca thought as she looked around. Beside a white marble fireplace were two fauteuil armchairs covered with pale floral motifs. An ornate gold mirror hung over the mantel. Two rose silk bergère-style armchairs flanked a marble-topped table. Between two French windows swathed in rose-pink silk curtains stood an elegant settee covered in yellow and cream striped satin. Reproductions of Watteau and Boucher hung in gold frames on the walls and the marquetry tables were covered with porcelain figurines and Chinese lamps.

Francesca sat gingerly on one of the delicate armchairs. Tom and Frank each sat in a more comfortable bergère and Royce sat in the middle of the settee. His wrinkled shorts and tee-shirt, bare feet and slovenly appearance were in sharp contrast to the décor. Francesca had to swallow a giggle that bubbled up in her throat. *Here we've got a pig in a china shop.*

"So what's all this about? Why are you disturbing my Sunday morning?" Royce said.

Tom spoke. "I'll get right to the point, Royce. Mr. Penfield and Ms. Antonelli have been researching the American United Investment Club, and they're here to share what they have learned."

Royce stared at Tom and swallowed hard. Francesca could almost see his mind racing. "Okay. Right. I'll listen to them…if I have to," he said, his voice throbbing with anger. He crossed his outstretched legs at the ankle and folded his arms across his chest. If body language meant anything, he was definitely on the defensive.

Frank began to talk. He explained that he and Francesca had spoken to several people in town and that many were unhappy about their investments with the AUIC. He talked about the investigative reporters for the Tribune and their research into the purported purchases of foreclosed homes that were far fewer than claimed. The Trib reporters were investigating Trustworthy Real Estate and Escrow Services, and the FBI would be looking into a possible wire fraud indictment. He made his case clearly and precisely.

Little by little Royce seemed to shrink before Francesca's eyes. His face was drawn, his thin lips ashen, his eyes unfocused. When Frank finally stopped bombarding him with the facts, he bent over and covered his face with his hands.

Eventually, Royce spoke. His voice was low and gravelly. "I'm glad it's over. I'm so glad it's over. I couldn't stand it anymore." And then he began to sob.

Frank looked at Tom. Tom looked at Francesca. They had witnessed the undoing of Royce Canfield.

Francesca got up and went in search of some Kleenex. She walked into the messy kitchen and found a clean glass that she filled with water and ice. She brought the water and some tissues to Royce. He looked up and thanked her, taking the Kleenex and blowing his nose noisily and then sipping the cold water. He looked into the glass and swirled the ice around.

"How long have you known?" he asked in a dull voice.

"We've been working on this for the last couple of weeks," Francesca replied. "We felt that the truth had to come out before Monday."

Royce frowned at her.

"We're not finished," Tom said. We need to know what all this has to do with the Ciliegie Mob. We have a good idea, but we need you to fill in the blanks."

The French antique clock ticked away the seconds. They waited. Finally Royce sighed and began to speak. He told them about the call from Calvin Juniper, the luncheon, the threats, the money. He told them about the Sanders Sports Group and the plan for the Smithfield estate as a gentleman's club. Frank and Francesca had pieced most of this together, but now they had his confirmation.

Finally, Royce looked up. "I'm sorry, Tom. I've made a mess of my life and I've lost the respect of my family and friends." Bewildered, he said, "What will become of me?"

Francesca was thinking of all the people he had cheated and robbed. They would probably never recover the money they had invested with the AUIC. She looked over at Royce, a community leader gone wrong. What was the saying again? "Pride goeth before a fall."

Banner Bee
Banner Bluff Ponzi Scheme Uncovered

A federal grand jury has returned indictments in a real estate Ponzi scheme, resulting in the arrest of three Banner Bluff men. The indictments were returned August 1st, but were sealed until the defendants were arrested.

Royce Canfield, 45; Bradley Harrison, 45; and Harry Silverman, 40, of Banner Bluff were arrested Tuesday on charges of wire fraud in an investment fraud scheme and are to be arraigned Friday.

According to the five-count indictment, from January 20-- to July 20--, Canfield, Harrison and Silverman were operating an investment scheme that solicited people to invest in purported purchases of real estate. They promised

243

investors to take care of purchasing the property for them in exchange for a small fee or percentage of the purchase price. The AUIC promised a 14 percent annual rate of return on their money.

To make the investment opportunity appear more legitimate, Canfield and Harrison told investors they were using an escrow account at Trustworthy Real Estate and Escrow Services. In fact, officials said, Trustworthy was run by co-schemer Harry Silverman.

The indictment alleges that Canfield and Harrison took in hundreds of thousands of dollars of retirement funds from investors, but instead of purchasing real estate, they used the investors' money to pay for purported returns to earlier investors as part of a Ponzi scheme. Of the approximately $10 million in deposits received by the American United Investment Club, only about $2 million was invested in real estate. The threesome also allegedly used a significant amount of the victims' money for their personal benefit.

The days were long but the nights were impossible. Aching pain radiated from his inner core. Stringent exercise and a strict diet didn't relieve his angst. He was unfulfilled. No longer did he dare drive his van around. They knew about it. He drove the other car but sometimes he walked. At night he would merge into the shadows and approach Her through the ravines. He knew his way down through all the hidden paths. As he got to the beach he would strip out of his clothes and enter the water pure and unfettered.

Chapter 26
Wednesday afternoon, August 11th

A ladies' luncheon! It seemed so retro to Francesca. No one had luncheons anymore. Everyone was so busy; taking time in the middle of the day seemed an indulgence. Work, work, work; that was the essence of American life. But she had accepted Emma's invitation with pleasure. Emma's niece was coming out from Chicago and Emma had invited Francesca and Kate Marshall for an informal party.

Francesca had dressed in a "ladies-go-to-luncheon" frock. It had small flowers on a white background, cap sleeves, a butterfly collar and mother-of-pearl buttons up the front. It felt so very 1940s. She had pulled up the sides of her hair and styled it in a soft pompadour in front, long in the back. Definitely a 1940s hairdo.

They had a wonderful, relaxed luncheon with crispy Asian chicken salad, fragrant warm popovers and a peach crumble with cinnamon ice cream for dessert. Emma was a cook par excellence and everything was delicious. Because it was a perfect summer's day, they ate on the back screened-in porch. The sun was shining; the bees were buzzing; the flowers were blooming. Heavenly!

Emma's niece, Claudia, worked in Chicago in an advertising agency. She had been thrilled the preceding week because a client hawking a mocha-flavored sports drink had chosen her proposed national advertising campaign. She was glad for the recognition but also because her job would be stable for another six months. During the past year, fifty percent of the firm's workforce had been fired. With this economy, she felt fortunate to still be employed.

As they were sipping coffee, they could hear Rosie and a friend giggling and screeching next door. "Martin's put on the sprinklers," Kate said, cocking her head. "I'll bet the girls are running through the water and jumping in the plastic pool."

"They're having a wonderful time," Emma said, smiling. "I love to hear their happy voices."

"We don't go to the beach or the pool anymore." Kate sighed and looked over at Francesca. "The lake seems threatening to me and the pool is so crowded; I worry that I might lose Rosie from sight. So we just stay close to home these days."

"What's the latest?" Claudia asked sympathetically. "Have they got any leads on the Lake Monster?"

"I think they had a couple of guys in for questioning, but they had alibis for either St. Luke's Fair or for the Fourth of July. The police are pretty tight-lipped about their investigation," Francesca said grimly. "Meanwhile, Banner Bluff is living in a state of suspended fear."

The four women sat quietly, their unease almost palpable as the little girls next door screamed ecstatically.

After the luncheon, Francesca started home. She took a different route than the one she'd taken over. She felt slightly guilty about taking the afternoon off, like she was playing hooky. She was deep in thought when she looked up to see Tom Barnett standing in shorts and a tee-shirt watering some thirsty-looking roses. He didn't see her and didn't respond when she yelled hello.

"Hey, Tom," she called again. "Over here!"

He waved and put down the hose. "What are you doing in this neck of the woods?" he asked, frowning slightly. "I've never seen you walk by before."

"I just had a long lunch at Emma Boucher's and I'm on my way home. I'm taking the scenic route. I sort of took the afternoon off."

He nodded. "So did I. I haven't been home except to sleep and change clothes these last weeks and I needed to get some chores done, bills paid and laundry washed." He looked at the droopy flowers. "I haven't had time to think about the yard or the roses."

"They're beautiful; so many different colors and types."

"They were my wife's," Tom said quietly. "She was the gardener. I've been thinking I should pull them all out or hire somebody to take care of this garden. It's too much work for me. I've got a kid cutting the grass…." He seemed to be pondering something, and then he gestured to the gate. Almost shyly he said, "Why don't you come in and have a beer with me? I was just going to get one myself."

"A beer? Thanks anyway. I've just had a gallon of iced tea this afternoon; but I'll come in and talk if you're going to take a break." She pushed open the white picket gate. It screeched on its hinges.

Tom grinned at her, "There's one more thing I should take care of someday."

They walked around the perimeter of the yard and Francesca admired the roses and perennials that grew in profusion. She bent to smell the flowers and yanked out a couple of weeds. Her hair fell over her shoulders, and she could sense his gaze on her.

"Hey, don't do any more gardening in that dress," he said. "You can come back tomorrow in your overalls if you're hell bent on pulling weeds."

Francesca looked up. "I'd have to come back and spend a week."

He stretched out his hand. Francesca took it and he pulled her to her feet.

"Let's sit down over here." He gestured to two green-and-white striped lawn chairs and a matching hassock. "I'll get a beer and how about if I bring you a small glass of ruby port."

"Ruby port?"

"Yeah, my wife used to love a small glass of port to sip on."

"Okay, I'll try it."

Francesca brushed some leaves from one of the lawn chairs and sat down. She slipped off her sandals and put her feet up on the hassock. Leaning back, she could stare up into the branches of the trees. She sighed deeply and closed her eyes. This was heaven. A few minutes later, she heard the back door slam shut and she looked up as Tom came across the lawn carrying a bottle of beer and a lovely cut-glass goblet filled with a rich crimson liquid. He handed her the glass and sat down in the other chair.

"Cheers," he said, raising his bottle. Francesca raised her glass. Tom took a long drink and she took a short sip. The port was delicious, sweet and fruity.

"I've only had port with melon. But I've never actually had a glassful. This is a treat. Thank you."

Tom nodded. He leaned back in his chair and took a deep breath. "I don't think I've relaxed for two months and I don't know that I can really relax now. We're under terrific pressure to solve these murders and every tip we've received has turned out to be a dead end. We're at a standstill and yet we're living in fear that this monster is just biding his time."

Francesca nodded and told him about the Marshalls' little girl, who was being kept under virtual house arrest. "That's how scared her parents are that this guy is out there, ready to grab her."

He pushed his hand through his hair in frustration. "I wish we knew his next move. We had an army of officers covering the rummage sale at the Presbyterian Church and the summer camps are under constant watch. None of us are sleeping well." He looked over at her. "How are you doing?"

"Not so well, I have nightmares…"

A cloud moved across the sun, as if Nature shared their mood. They sat without speaking, looking out at the floral border that was covered in shadow and then sunshine again.

"Tom," she said tentatively.

"Yes."

"Tell me about your wife?"

He was silent for a long minute and then spoke in measured sentences. "She died of cancer three years ago. She was expecting our first child." He paused. "We were both so happy. Then during some routine blood tests, they discovered she had acute lymphocytic leukemia." He fell silent briefly. "She died only a few weeks later."

"How terrible for you, "she said quietly. "What was her name?"

"Candace. Candy. We met in college. I was studying art history and she was studying botany and psychology."

"Art history?" She turned to look at him, astonished. "How in the world did you ever become a cop?"

"Well, we got married and Candy found a job at the Chicago Botanic Gardens working as a therapist with autistic children. You know, she would use flowers and plants to help them communicate. They would plant seeds and grow stuff. Her greatest attribute was that she could connect with anybody. People always felt comfortable around her."

"She sounds like a wonderful person."

"Yes, she was." He gazed over at the roses. "Anyway, I was looking around trying to find something in my field—which was almost impossible—when one of my buddies was murdered in his apartment by a druggie who was looking for cash. It was horrendous and I wanted to help solve the crime. Out of the blue, I got this idea that I could make a difference if I became a cop. I really thought I could change things and be a force. It sounds ridiculous when I say that now. Anyway, Candy encouraged me to go ahead and do what I wanted. So I went to the Law Enforcement Academy and ended up here."

He glanced over at her. She smiled. "From art history to chasing robbers; it does seem a reach."

"May I?" he said as he slipped off his loafers and propped his feet on the hassock next to hers. His were solid, nails neatly clipped; hers slim and high-arched, with rosy pink nails.

She laughed. "Be my guest!" She felt suspended in time, here with him in the quiet enclosed garden; both facing the rear wall of flowers with only a peripheral view of each other. It made for a strange kind of intimacy.

"So what about you? What's your story?" Tom inquired.

"I grew up in California and met my ex-husband, Dan, in high school…" She told him about her marriage and her divorce, her career in journalism and starting the *Banner Bee*.

He turned to look at her. "I admire you, finding your niche in electronic journalism. You're right on the cusp of this revolution. It's like a gigantic wave and you're riding on the crest."

"Let's hope I don't get smashed in the process. I never was a very good surfer!" She took a last sip of the port and then a little lick. "That was delicious!" She handed him the glass and reached down for her sandals. "All this talk makes me think that I'd better go and check out my stories for tomorrow. It's getting late. And I'm keeping you from all your chores."

They both stood up and walked towards the squeaky gate. Francesca turned and held out her hand. "Thank you again. This was a nice respite from the daily grind."

Tom took her hand and looked into her eyes. "You're welcome... any time...when I'm here... which is not often." They both laughed.

The shadows were lengthening and Francesca wanted to get home. She walked briskly down the street, her mood buoyant in the soft afternoon light.

Three AM. Francesca woke suddenly and sat up. The light beside her bed glowed softly. She had a weird sense of panic. She'd been dreaming of the looming, dark intruder. As always she'd been unable to move or scream. Then the dark form morphed into the guy in the photographs.

Nearly a month had passed since she'd seen the Fourth of July pictures at Churchill's. Something yesterday had triggered a sense of déjà vu. What was it? Her brain had been sifting through images all night long as she slept. It had come to her all of a sudden. She had seen the same guy in the pictures from St. Luke's Spring Fair. She was sure of it. He had worn the same hat or something like it.

She got out of bed, went into her office and woke up her sleeping computer. She found the file with the spring fair pictures and started to scroll through them. It was funny how they were still so familiar. An image really stuck in your mind. She continued to scroll through pictures of kids and parents.

Ah-ha! There he was, the same guy. In one photo, he was turned away, but she recognized him. He was looking off to the right and was wearing a cap down low over his forehead. The other photo had caught him in full view. His calculating expression was similar to the one in the photo displayed on the digital frame at Churchill's. What was he looking at?

He wore a white shirt with a dark sweatshirt tied over his shoulders and dark pants; the same outfit he wore to the parade. It seemed out of place at these two events where everyone was dressed in shorts and tee-shirts. Chills went down her spine. Who was this strange man?

She went back to bed and lay in the soft light, thinking. Something else was niggling in her brain. She'd seen this guy somewhere else, not just at the spring fair. She turned over on her side and tried to clear her mind.

It had been fun getting dressed up and going to a luncheon party. She really like Emma and Kate, and Emma's niece was full of great ideas. They had discussed the *Banner Bee*'s home page. Claudia had suggested some layouts and color schemes to make it snap and pop. After five years, the *Banner Bee* was ready for a makeover, and Claudia had gotten her thinking.

Another lovely part of the day was the time spent with Tom Barnett. It had been a very special afternoon. When she thought back to the comfortable atmosphere and their lazy conversation, it felt almost dreamlike. Together they had escaped to a peaceful netherworld. Calmed by these musings, she drifted off.

Tom lay awake. His mind was churning. Mentally he sifted through the evidence they had concerning the Lake Monster. It was precious little. Hard to believe that no one had seen anything suspicious at either St. Luke's fair or on the Fourth of July. This wasn't a big town and people basically knew or recognized each other. How was it that this man could slip through town unnoticed? Tom felt inadequate and ineffective. He hadn't talked to the right people and he hadn't asked the right questions. All the leads he'd pursued had led nowhere. Maybe he shouldn't be leading this investigation. He felt way over his head with no solution in sight.

He turned his thoughts to his afternoon with Francesca. It had been a special interlude in his current feverish life. He pictured her tall willowy figure, her smooth gentle curves and her luxurious wavy hair. They had talked easily, sharing each other's lives. Yes, he would like to see more of her. She had that essential quality that drew him to a woman. She had charm. A woman could be beautiful, clever and funny; but charm gave a woman depth.

Maybe they could have more interludes like today's, if this damned investigation ever sorted itself out.

Puchalski had agreed to work the graveyard shift. Johnson's father was ill and he needed to go to Indianapolis for a couple of days. Since the baby was born, Puchalski had learned to function with very little sleep; so taking over Johnson's shift for a few days wouldn't be so bad.

He was able to sleep a few hours before the alarm rang at 11:30. Bonnie was slumbering on her back, snoring softly. He got dressed quietly and crept downstairs. In the kitchen he made a cup of coffee and poured it into a travel mug.

At the station, he met with Lewis briefly. The officer apprised him of the evening's activities. The only significant movement had been at 10:30 when the summer theater performance of *Oklahoma* ended at the recreation center and the audience headed for their cars. Since then, Banner Bluff had been quiet.

"Everyone is tucked in bed. Things have been pretty dull," Lewis said.

Puchalski grinned. "I think I like it better that way. Anything else I need to know?"

"I filled up the tank."

"Thanks, pal. I owe you one." Puchalski walked around the patrol car to check for nicks or scratches and peered inside. "Everything looks fine. I'm outta here." He opened the door and stepped into the cruiser.

"See you tomorrow." Lewis yawned as he headed for his own car.

Puchalski was patrolling the east side of town. Another officer, Cliff Williamson, was covering the west side. After about two hours, they met up in the parking lot behind Appleby's and kibitzed about sports and Williamson's allergies. Then they went back on their beats.

Puchalski drove slowly along Lake Avenue and pulled up in a parking spot by the service road that led down to the beach. Since the murders, a beach curfew had been established, which began at sundown. He got out of the car and walked down the service road to check out the beach. The air was still. He could hear the gentle lapping of the water below him. About halfway down he could see someone was at the water's edge. He began to jog and was quickly down on the tarmac between the north and south beaches.

He looked north. The man stood at the water's edge, his arms raised above his head. He seemed to be exercising. Puchalski headed towards the shoreline. "Hello, sir," he called as he trudged through the sand. The man turned slowly, lowering his arms as though in a trance.

"Sir, there's a curfew in place. You can't come down here after sundown."

The man took off running in bare feet, leaving his shoes behind. He headed up the beach towards the steps beside the stone shelter.

Puchalski took off after him. "Hey, stop. I'd like to talk to you."

The guy was at the stairs and running up them two at a time. Puchalski was some distance behind. As he arrived at the first set of stairs, he could hear the man pounding up the second flight that led to the top of the service road. Puchalski took the stairs two at a time, then raced up the path. As he approached the second flight of stairs, he heard no footsteps above him. He was huffing and puffing when he got to the service road. He looked both ways, seeing nothing. Then he heard the roar of an engine. From the darkness of the construction site, a van emerged onto Lake Avenue. It turned down Elm, heading west away from the lake.

Puchalski radioed Williamson and the dispatcher. Williamson radioed back when he arrived at the other end of Elm Street. The van had disappeared, swallowed up by the night.

Puchalski was sure that the man he'd seen was the Lake Monster. Why hadn't he approached him quietly? Why had he shouted at him? If he hadn't screwed up, the guy would be on his way to jail now. He banged his hand on the dashboard in anger.

He was trembling and breathing hard. Sweat poured down his face; his hands were slippery on the steering wheel. The cop had almost caught him. He turned off Elm, clicked his headlights on low and took a circuitous route home through a back alley behind the golf course. When he pulled into his garage and the door was shut behind him, he was still trembling. He got out of the van and began to dry heave. He could taste the bile in his mouth. That had been a close call. Why had he taken out the van? Stupid idiot! He would need to be very careful now.

Chapter 27
Saturday afternoon, August 14th

There had been much discussion in town about whether or not to hold Banner Bluff Sports Day. Traditionally, the Rotary Club organized the events. Local restaurants provided a variety of tasty international dishes, including favorites like pizza and tacos, but also spanakopita, Chinese egg rolls, Thai curries and falafel patties topped with salads and pickled vegetables. The Cool Cow provided ice cream and the Bonnie Bakery displayed a wide range of delicious cookies and mini-desserts.

On the village green there were races for every age group. Summer Little League teams played their championship game and the local tennis league played the final matches of the season. In the late afternoon there was a band concert and an award ceremony for all the events, with red, white and gold ribbons and trophies for the baseball and tennis championships.

Everyone looked forward to Sports Day, but the recent kidnappings and drownings had paralyzed the city council as well as the town. Families with children kept them on a close rein; the police were called every time someone saw a stranger walking down the street. The council decided to go ahead with the event, but with increased police presence. Certain areas would be fenced off, and Chief Barnett arranged to borrow law enforcement from nearby towns. Younger children and especially little girls would be closely watched.

August 14th dawned hot and muggy, with storms predicted by late evening. After much discussion, Martin and Kate Marshall decided to go to the village green; they would keep an extra-sharp eye on Rosie and make sure she never was out of sight.

They spent the morning enjoying the opening ceremonies and the high school band's spirited rendition of several Sousa marches, and even entered some events. Rosie joined in several kiddie races. She and Martin participated in the three-legged race. It was a true Mutt-and-Jeff routine; it was practically impossible for a three-foot girl and a six-foot-plus man to coordinate their stride sharing a burlap bag. Afterward, they'd eaten soft tacos and ice cream for lunch. Now, Rosie sat with Kate on the sidelines, watching the big kids lining up for the sixteen- to eighteen-year olds' races.

Kate felt nauseated most mornings, and today was no exception. Her doctor had confirmed her pregnancy and had told her to take it easy and rest. Right now she wanted to lie back on the grass and close her eyes, but Rosie was a bundle of energy. She was balancing on one foot with her arms spread out. "Mommy, can I go over and talk to Lucy, she's right over there."

"No, sweetie, I want you to sit here with me. Let's watch the four hundred meter race. Look, there's Daddy in charge of it. Come sit down."

"Do I look like a flamingo, Mommy? Look, I'm balancing on one foot." Rosie was tottering back and forth. Just as she was about to fall over, someone grabbed her hand and steadied her. It was Vicki Papadopoulos.

Rosie giggled. "Hi, Vicki. Mommy, it's Vicki, my babysitter."

Kate smiled at Vicki and patted the blanket she'd spread out under a shade tree. "Why don't you sit down with us and watch the race. We haven't talked in a long time." Kate had been Vicki's French teacher for two years. Often after school, Vicki would come to Kate's room for a talk and they had become friends. Kate had a feeling that sometimes Vicki missed having a female presence at home, though she loved her grandfather dearly.

Vicki sat down next to Kate. "I do want to watch this race. Colman Canfield is running. You know Colman, right?"

"Yes, I do. Mr. Marshall told me Colman is working at your grandpa's store. Have you made friends?" Kate stretched out her legs and leaned back on her elbows.

Vicki nodded. "He's really nice. We have a lot of fun together while we're working," she said shyly. "He taught me how to play chess." She crossed her legs Indian style and bent over to pick a yellow dandelion. She studied it intently.

"That sounds fun," Kate said encouragingly. "I've learned to play a bunch of times but I always forget the moves."

"Colman is really a good teacher and he's very patient."

"That is definitely a good characteristic for a teacher." Kate smiled to herself. "Is he a good runner?"

"Oh, he's really fast. Colman never, like, ran on the team or anything at school, but he's been running back and forth to the store this summer and down to the beach. Everywhere! I bet he'll win." Vicki smiled at Kate. Then she turned to Rosie, who was doing somersaults back and forth. "Rosie, let's see If you like butter." The little girl rolled over to Vicki and held up her chin. Vicki held the dandelion under it. "Yes, you love butter, don't you?" She started to tickle Rosie, who wriggled and giggled.

"Let me see if *you* like butter," Rosie said, and she reached for the dandelion to put under Vicki's chin. "Yes, you do!" She giggled and tried to tickle Vicki's neck.

"Hey, girls," Kate said, "the race is about to start."

Vicki sat up and looked up the field. She spotted Colman, who waved at her. She waved back and did a thumbs-up. He smiled at her and got down in starting position.

Kate had never seen Colman like that, with a real smile on his face. It brought tears to her eyes to see the change.

Someone shouted, "Go!" The runners shot forward as the race began. Kate and Vicki were on their feet, yelling at the top of their voices. The boys came racing by; Colman had taken the lead. His face was strained in concentration. Kate and Vicki shouted encouragement. Almost before they realized it, the race was over. Vicki hurried to congratulate him. "You did it, you beat them all!"

Colman was beaming, sweat streaming down his face; his heart beating with the thrill of success. He grinned at Vicki and Kate.

Martin walked over to congratulate Colman as well before he started the next heat. "Great job, Colman. Too bad you didn't run in high school! You would have beaten all the records." He reached out and shook Colman's hand.

Rosie stayed behind her mother and pulled on Kate's wrist. "Mommy, I need to go potty," she whispered.

Kate bent down. "Just a minute, honey. I'll take you over to the restrooms in a moment." She straightened up and spoke to Colman. "Vicki said you've been running all summer. It sure paid off."

Hero arrived to congratulate Colman as well. "Good job, my boy! You ran as though chased by Kerberos."

Vicki laughed. "Pappou, no one knows what you're talking about." She turned to the others. "Kerberos was a fifty-headed dog that guarded the gate of Hades in Greek mythology."

Colman grinned. "Your Pappou is right. That sure would make me run from Hell."

As Martin walked back to the starting line across the grass, Kate looked up at the sky. Big black rain clouds were rolling in from the west, crowding out the blue. The breeze had picked up; it whisked Martin's red baseball cap off his head as he jogged across the lawn. She looked around for Rosie, but her daughter wasn't there. She must have gone off to the restroom by herself. Kate fought down a jolt of fear, swiftly followed by anger. Rosie couldn't have been gone more than a minute or two. How many times had she told Rosie to ask permission before running off?

She picked up their blanket and headed for the park building that housed the restrooms. As she looked across the grass, she saw Rosie standing by the water fountain, talking to one of the policemen who were supervising the event. She recognized Rosie's turquoise-flowered shirt and matching skort, her current favorite outfit. Reassured, she started across the grass. By then, Rosie had disappeared around the corner of the building.

Francesca Antonelli came up and said hello. "I can't believe this change in weather, can you?" The temperature had dropped at least ten degrees. "You know what they say about Chicago: if you don't like the weather, just wait a minute."

Kate kept moving toward the park building. "Yeah, I thought we were supposed to have great weather all day. This is going to ruin the rest of the events. It looks like it's going to just pour! Listen, I've

258

got to get to the Rec Center. Rosie just ran off to the bathroom by herself. I don't know what to do with her. She won't listen!"

"I'll go with you. I have to make a pit stop."

They walked quickly towards the building. The sky had turned a churning dark grey. One ray of sun came through the clouds and illuminated the large oak tree in front of the Rec Center. Its green leaves glowed, set off by the leaden sky. Kate walked faster as the wind propelled her forward.

"Isn't it amazing how Colman has changed?" Francesca said over the noise of the wind "I know you had him as a student."

"You know, I think the best thing that ever happened to him was stealing that money and facing the consequences. Who knows what would have happened if he hadn't been caught."

They went around the corner of the building to the entrance to the ladies' restroom. No one was around. A lone car turned out of the circular drive in front of the Rec Center and headed down Eastern Avenue. "I don't get it," Kate said. The fear came back, a creeping sensation in her stomach. "I just saw her right here talking to a policeman. Now, they're both gone. That's impossible."

They walked through the restroom door. "Rose Marie Marshall! Where are you?" Kate called. The brown metal doors of the four stalls were open. Kate went to each stall and looked in. "Rosie, are you hiding? Come out right now!" Her voice was strident, her face ashen. "She has to be here. I just saw her, a couple of minutes ago." She looked at Francesca, panic in her eyes.

"Let's go out and go around the building. You go one way and I'll go the other. I'm sure we'll find her," Francesca said.

Kate walked around the building, yelling Rosie's name. She could hear Francesca doing the same. When they met up on the west side of the building, Kate was trembling. "Where is my little girl? Where is Rosie?"

Francesca put an arm around her. "Maybe she went back over to her father when she saw the storm coming. Or the policeman took her to the station. Let's go check with Martin and then we can head to the police station."

The bright afternoon had turned as dark as night. The wind was howling and people were running for their cars. Kate saw Martin rolling up banners on the far side of the green. "There's Martin, but I don't see Rosie." In her haste she dropped the blanket and then tripped over it.

Francesca steadied her, then picked up the blanket and opened it. "Let's walk under it," she said as the rain began pelting down.

They made their way slowly across the green. Through a blinding downpour, they could see Martin heading for the car with a pile of boxes.

Kate screamed his name over the din. They walked faster, nearly running. They finally caught up with Martin near the Marshalls' car. "Martin, I've lost Rosie," Kate yelled.

He looked at her and around her, water streaming down his face. His hair was plastered against his head and his clothes were stuck to his body. "What do you mean? Lost her? Where is she?"

Kate fell into his arms, crying. "I don't know where she is." Just then there was a crack of thunder and a flash of lightning. Across the green, the large oak was split in two, as if by a giant ax falling from the sky. One side toppled onto the grass. Francesca screamed in horror over the deafening noise of the storm.

Martin and Kate clung together as the rain pounded down. Martin looked at Francesca, his eyes wide and frightened. "Come on," she said. "We've got to go to the police right now!" He nodded, pulling Kate towards the passenger door and opening it. With Francesca's help he got her into the front seat.

"I'll come with you," Francesca yelled as she pulled open the rear door and climbed into the back seat. It was raining horizontally and the wind seemed to be increasing in intensity. Kate looked back at her, then over at Rosie's car seat beside her. It was unbearably empty.

The storm caught the meteorologists by surprise. No one had predicted its intensity or the speed of the wind. Gusts of over eighty miles an hour downed trees and tore off branches that went sailing through the air. They flattened parked cars and downed hundreds of electrical wires. In Banner Bluff, downed trees and large broken branches blocked many streets. Porch furniture and bicycles were thrown through windows. Debris covered the roads and lawns. Power lines writhed like snakes across the roads, snapping and crackling. The fire and police departments and the Department of Public Works were on high alert. Phone lines were down and it was difficult to communicate except by cell phone.

The power grid went down just as Martin, Kate and Francesca walked into the Banner Bluff Police Department. Standing in darkness, they could hear people yelling up and down the hallway. After a few minutes, the lights came back on. They heard the computers and air conditioner whirring back into life. *Generators*, Francesca thought. Of course the Police Department would have their own.

The dispatcher was frantically answering calls. Martin tried to get the receptionist's attention, but she was on the phone and only nodded in his direction. The phones kept ringing.

"Follow me," Francesca said, and strode down the hall to Tom Barnett's office. Martin and Kate reminded her of two lost children, clinging to each other, their faces wet with rain and tears.

She pulled open Tom's door and walked over to his desk, heedless of her sodden hair and clothes. Absently, he looked up and then gestured for her to wait out in the hall. Francesca gestured to Martin and Kate. "Chief, we need your help."

Tom covered the mouthpiece of the phone. "What's the matter?" He was irritated.

"Rosie Marshall has disappeared. We need to find her."

She was deeply asleep. There had been no problem with the lemonade. She was very thirsty and drank two cups. She had gotten in the car with no problem when he told her the storm was coming and he would drive her over to her parents. She had been so trusting.

Now she lay on the princess canopy bed. Swags of pink satin with lace trim hung around it. He had dressed her as Sleeping

261

Beauty, then combed her hair and spread it around her. The candles were lit around the room. It was quiet down here. He could not hear the storm raging. Strains of Tchaikovsky's Sleeping Beauty *filled the basement room. He'd outfitted it with the best acoustics and sound-proofed it from the world outside.*

This was the part he loved, when he possessed his own princess. She was his sacrificial lamb. Religions for centuries had made sacrifices to their gods. He knew his Queen was yearning for her own princess. Sleeping Beauty was pure. She was the chosen one. He lay down next to her on the bed and stroked her cheek. Now he possessed her.

Chapter 28
Saturday night, August 14th

Tom's face reflected disbelief and then shock. He got up, went to the office door and yelled down the hall. "Where's Puchalski?"

"He's out on a call, Chief," someone answered.

"Get him back here, quick."

He came back into the room and asked the Marshalls and Francesca to sit down. Francesca remained leaning against the wall by the door, a pool of water at her feet. Tom turned his focus on the Marshalls. "What happened?"

"We were sitting on the green watching the races. Rosie was with me," Kate said shakily.

"I was running the high school races," Martin added.

"Colman, you know Colman Canfield?" Kate said. Tom nodded. "He had just won a race and we were congratulating him. Rosie wanted to go to the restroom and I told her to wait. Why did I do that? Why didn't I just take her then?" She began to cry uncontrollably, shivering from wet clothes and shock. They waited while she regained enough composure to continue. "She went over there by herself. When I couldn't find her, I looked across the green and I saw her. She has on her favorite turquoise outfit. She was by the water fountain. So I started over there."

Kate began to cry again. Francesca took over. "We went through the restrooms and around the building. She was nowhere to be seen."

Kate choked back a sob. "She should be here! She was talking to a policeman when I saw her. Maybe she's stuck in a police car somewhere, you know, with the storm."

"You saw her with a police officer?"

"Yes, he was by the water fountain." Kate's face had regained some color.

Tom stood abruptly and went down the hall. When he reached Arlyne, the dispatcher, he asked her to send out a call to all police officers. "See if someone picked up a little girl, Rose Marie Marshall, by the Rec Center. It would have been about the time the storm struck," he added.

"Yes, sir." Arlyne wrote down the information and made the announcement into her headset mike.

Tom went back to his office. "I've put out an all-call on Rosie. We'll hear back shortly. You understand that right now we're getting calls from all over town. We're in a state of emergency, so all staff is on alert. People are reporting downed electric wires, broken windows, and smashed cars. Half the streets in town are impassable and the storm hasn't blown through yet."

"Maybe Rosie and the policeman are stuck somewhere and can't get back here," Martin said hopefully.

A few minutes later, Puchalski came in. "I just got back from 122 East Elm. An elderly man was pinned under an enormous branch..." He looked from Tom to the Marshalls. "What's going on here?"

"Rose Marie Marshall has disappeared." Tom's voice reflected the fear and pain they were all feeling.

Arlyne walked into the office. "All officers have reported back, Chief. No one saw Rose Marie. No one picked her up." She looked around the room. "I'm sorry," she said quietly.

Martin's shoulders sagged; Kate covered her face with her hands. Puchalski's eyes met Tom's in a silent question. They still didn't have a clue who this monster was.

"That's *it*," Francesca said, nearly shouting. "That's how he does it. He looks like a policeman. The kids think he is one! That's why they go off with him."

"What do you mean?" Tom said.

Francesca looked Puchalski up and down. "He's dressed in a white uniform shirt and blue pants, just like you." Images swirled through her mind. "I know what he looks like. I've seen his picture. He wears a sweatshirt around his shoulders to obscure his uniform;

then he whips it off to entice these kids." She looked both jubilant and horrified.

"Where are these pictures?" Tom asked.

"They're on my laptop. Let me go home and get it. I probably don't have any power, so I'll bring it back here." She got up to leave. "And Tom, there was a picture of the guy on the digital frame at Churchill's from the Fourth of July. Could you get hold of it?"

He nodded. "We'll send somebody over there."

Martin stood unsteadily, placed his hands on Tom's desk and leaned over. His face was distorted in anguish. "We've got to find him. We don't have much time."

"You're right. We know he'll probably head down to the beach tonight. We need to cover every possible access. The problem is we're severely understaffed. I've got officers out dealing with all kinds of storm-related problems. Everybody else around is suffering through the same disaster. We can't get help from any other towns tonight."

"Surely we can get volunteers?" Martin pleaded.

"I'll send out a Code Red," Tom said as he rose from his desk. "You need to go home and find a picture of Rose Marie that we can print off. I'd send you in a police car, but I don't have one available."

They all stood up to leave. Tom accompanied the Marshalls to the front door. He said with more assurance than he felt, "We'll do everything we can. We're going to find your daughter." He was remembering the little girl he had interviewed not long ago. He tried to tell himself otherwise, but he felt personally responsible for this third kidnapping.

Outside the wind roared and the rain was coming down in sheets. Huddled together, the Marshalls fled to their car. Francesca headed down the middle of the street towards her condo. She figured she was less likely to be hit by a falling branch there. She jogged most of the way, shivering with cold.

She fumbled with her key and finally let herself in, then felt her way down the hall to the kitchen. In the dark she could feel the warm muzzles of the dogs on her knee. They had been frightened by the storm and stuck close. Her heart was beating against her chest and she felt slightly dizzy. She needed to keep calm. Nothing could hurt her in the darkness. Where was the flashlight? She rummaged around in the pantry, using the face of her cellphone to light up the shelves. There it was; her trusty Black Fire flashlight. She switched it on, fought down the frantic fear that pulsed through her body and willed herself to the stairway.

Upstairs in the drawer of her bedside table she found another flashlight and turned it on. She changed into some jeans and a clean white tee-shirt and grabbed a dark blue hoodie. Finally, she donned dry socks and running shoes.

Both flashlights in hand, Francesca headed downstairs. She let out the dogs, who dashed back in after just a few minutes. The rain seemed to be tapering off, but she put her laptop in a plastic bag just to be safe. Her computer would be protected from the elements. At the back of her closet she found an old poncho and slipped it over her head. She set out again on foot, her flashlight in hand.

The sky was clearing in the west as Francesca headed down the street. Above her there were still thick clouds and she felt a few sprinkles on her cheeks. Gusts of wind ripped at her poncho and pushed her down the street. She turned on to Eastern Avenue and then made her way across the green that was strewn with branches and debris. Banner Bluff would have a lot of cleaning up to do.

The town hall was buzzing when Francesca arrived. Phones were ringing and lights were on in the Department of Public Works as well as the Police Department. The storm had abated and cleanup crews were already at work. The first priority was to make roads passable for fire engines, ambulances and police cars.

Gloria, the receptionist, was lacking her usual cheery smile and friendly hello. She looked worried and distracted. Perhaps she had a little girl at home, Francesca thought.

She went down the hall to the communal break room. There was a large table surrounded by ten chairs. On the long wall across from the door were a fridge and a counter with a microwave and a functioning coffee pot. She helped herself to coffee and realized how hungry she was. There hadn't been time to get something to eat when she was at home. They had to find this maniac before something happened to Rosie.

Francesca set her laptop on the table, opened it and plugged it in. She quickly found the picture file from the church fair and began scrolling through its contents. After a few moments she had the guy on the screen. She could feel her heart thumping. They had to get to him somehow.

Tom Barnett appeared at the door. He looked frazzled. "There you are. I'm sorry I was so short earlier. I didn't realize what you wanted."

She gave him a small, reassuring smile. "No problem, Chief, we're under a lot of stress. This is a nightmare we're living through." Then she turned serious. "Come here and look at the picture of our monster."

He came around behind her and leaned over her shoulder for a long look. "I've never seen this guy before."

"This is at the church fair. See, he's got that sweatshirt draped over his shoulders, but underneath, he's wearing a police uniform."

"That's not our Banner Bluff uniform. Can you blow that picture up?"

Francesca zoomed in on the image. Tom bent to look at the screen more closely. His face was inches from hers. He turned to look at her. "Do you see what I see?"

She nodded. On the left-hand pocket of the white shirt, peeking out from under the sweatshirt sleeve, was a small pin. It was the ALPA pin they had found in the alley. "He's a pilot," Francesca whispered.

"Yeah. If he whips off the sweatshirt, any little girl would think he was a policeman; somebody to trust."

"Let's print these two pictures and we'll ask Gloria to make copies."

Tom went down the hall to get Ron Puchalski, who was meeting with Officer Johnson and the volunteers. They returned to the break room just as Officer Lewis arrived with the digital frame from Churchill's restaurant. "We had a terrible time getting to Mr. Churchill. He'd gone home and the road to his house is impassable.

We climbed over a downed telephone pole and all sorts of branches. There was even someone's wooden picnic table in the middle of the road. Who knows where it came from? Anyway, Churchill came back with us so we could get into the restaurant."

He placed the digital frame on the table. Francesca reached over to plug it in and it began to flash through the pictures from the Fourth of July. She paused it when they came to the picture of the guy behind Corinne Casey.

"Here he is again…and see how his eyes are glued on her. He's got the sweatshirt on and something in his left hand. What is that?"

They all looked. "It looks like the metal tube of a folded lawn chair," Lewis said.

"I think you're right," Francesca murmured.

As they stared at the images, Luis Gonzales came into the break room and helped himself to coffee, then opened the fridge and took out a wrapped sandwich. "What are you looking at?" he asked as he came around to see the computer screen and the digital frame. He took a bite of his sandwich, chewed and swallowed. "I know that guy," he said.

Francesca and the officers turned around. "You do? Who is he?" Tom's voice was sharp.

"I don't know his name, but he comes down and parks at the north end of the beach, you know, by the abandoned mansion." Luis sipped coffee. "What's the big deal, anyway?"

"We think he's the Lake Monster," Puchalski said. "Please tell us everything you can."

Chapter 29
Saturday night, August 14th

Dusk had fallen as Francesca left the police station. In her purse were pictures of Rosie Marshall and the Lake Monster. Thanks to Luis, and to Kate, they knew a lot more about the Monster than they had half an hour ago. Unfortunately, they still didn't know the Monster's name or where he lived. Or where he might be keeping Rosie before heading down to the beach.

This guy often drove to the lakeshore, Luis had said. "He's got a blue van and another car, maybe a Honda. Grey. I've walked right past it when he's parked in the street. He's got a blue sticker from Mitchell Airport. My brother-in-law works maintenance there. He's got the same kind of sticker on his car, but a different color."

"Chief," Francesca had said. "Kate Marshall and I saw a car pulling away from the Recreation Center. I think it was a grey Honda."

Tom looked grim as he spoke to Detective Puchalski. "Get copies of the perp's picture to the volunteers, so they can go door to door and see if anyone knows him. How many volunteers do we have?"

"Not as many as we'd like. People are afraid to go out, with no street lights and electric wires down. We've actually been telling everyone to stay inside."

"Get everyone we can. That'll free us up to cover the beach. He's going to want to get down to the water."

It was unseasonably cool and eerily quiet now, except for the sounds of sirens in the distance. The rain had stopped and the wind had died down. Francesca swallowed a couple of times, then switched on her flashlight and plunged across the village green towards Hero's Market and her office. Inside the market, she saw dim lights and movement.

Hero must have a generator. She concentrated on the light and didn't give in to her mounting fear. When she arrived at the market, she tapped on the door.

Vicki came to open up. The girl's eyes searched her face. "Francesca, are you all right?"

"No, I'm not. Rosie Marshall has been kidnapped." The words came tumbling out. "I was with Kate after the race, and Rosie disappeared. She wandered off to the Rec Center by herself. We think the Lake Monster took her."

Vicki stood still, her hands shaking. "Oh, my God. I can't believe it. Mrs. Marshall must be frantic."

Francesca fumbled in her purse and took out the Monster's picture. "This is the guy. We don't know his name or where he lives. Does he look familiar to you?"

While Vicki studied the picture, Colman and Hero emerged from the basement. Francesca beckoned them over and told them what had happened. Hero looked stricken. "Not another one! We just saw her a few hours ago. "

"I've seen that guy down at the beach before," Colman said. "He'd come down at night when I was sitting in the shelter getting high. He's kind of weird."

Vicki stared at him. "Why didn't you say something?"

"I've been trying to forget the time I wasted down at that beach. I mean, most of the time I was too drunk or too high to register what was going on around me anyway."

"What do you mean, he was weird?" Francesca asked.

Colman shrugged. "He kind of worshipped the lake. I mean, I love Lake Michigan. It's beautiful. But this guy came down and talked to it. A couple times, I saw him spread out his arms and chant something at it. And he'd throw things into the water, too."

"Like what?"

"I don't know. I couldn't tell."

"Do you remember what he looked like?" Francesca gestured to the picture Vicki held. "I mean, more than that. How was he dressed? Did you ever see his face?"

"No. He always had on a baseball cap. He'd wear jeans and stuff, or khaki shorts in the summer." Colman looked regretful. "I'm sorry. I wish I could help more."

"You and Vicki can help me now, showing these pictures around. I've got one of Rosie, too. We can find out if anyone saw Rosie this afternoon and if they've seen this man. Right now, the police need all the help they can get."

"Shouldn't we go down to the beach and help patrol it? Isn't that the most important thing?" Colman said.

Francesca shook her head. "Chances are he won't try to make it down there until later. He drowned the other girls in the early morning hours. By that time, the police will have the area covered. We're hoping we can find him before then."

"Pappou, will you be all right here?" Vicki asked.

Hero looked uneasy. "Vicki, I don't think it is safe for you to go outside."

"Pappou, we need to help save Rosie. I can't sit here and do nothing."

He nodded in agreement, but his tired eyes shone with worry.

The leafy trees that provided welcome shade on a hot afternoon blotted out all light from the starry sky. Francesca's hands were clammy but she willed herself to control her fear. She *would not* hyperventilate. She *would* find Rosie. They turned left towards Lake Michigan, walking in the middle of the road since there was no traffic. The storefronts were dark and no one was out. Colman took Vicki's hand and they walked in step beside Francesca. Despite her anxiety, she smiled to herself. There was nothing as wonderful as first love.

They turned down Elm Street and split up when they arrived at the first block of houses. Francesca took the right side of the street, Vicki and Colman the left. Candles flickered through the windows of the houses. When Francesca knocked on the first door, a woman peered suspiciously out of the window. "What do you want?" she yelled.

271

"I'm Francesca Antonelli. I'm canvassing Elm Street for the police department. Another little girl has been kidnapped. We have a picture of her, and of the suspect. Could you please take a look?"

There was a moment's pause and then the sound of a turning lock. The woman who opened the door was a pretty redhead with frightened green eyes. She was dressed in a pink bathrobe and her feet were bare. Behind her in the hall was a teenaged girl with long red hair, dressed in blue plaid boxer shorts and a blue tee. She moved forward and said, "We know about Rosie Marshall. We got the phone call from the police. Mrs. Marshall was my French teacher last year. I feel just terrible." The girl's green eyes filled with tears and her mother put a comforting arm around her shoulders.

Francesca shone the flashlight on the pictures. "Did you see Rosie today after the races?"

"We weren't there today," the woman said as she and her daughter studied the pictures. "I took Beth downtown to the Art Institute to see the Renoir exhibit. It was a nightmare getting home. All the traffic lights were out and we just got back an hour ago."

"I recognize Rosie because Mrs. Marshall had that picture on her desk," Beth said, sniffling. "But I've never seen that man."

"It's hard to see what he looks like with that hat pulled down over his eyes," the woman added. "I don't think I've ever seen him before." She shook her head. "No, I don't have a clue who he is. Sorry."

Francesca continued down the street, with similar results. Colman and Vicki did no better. A man in one house didn't recognize Rosie or the suspect. In the next house, the people wouldn't open the door. "Let's keep moving," Francesca said. But they had no luck. Of the people who came to the door, no one recognized the suspect and no one had seen Rosie Marshall during or after the races.

In the next block, Francesca strode up a brick sidewalk to an imposing front door. She knocked and waited, tapping her foot. She had a nagging feeling that she was wasting precious time. At last, the door was opened by a scruffy guy in shorts, bare chest and bare feet. He was carrying a massive silver candelabrum that was dripping wax. He scowled at her. "What do you want?"

She shoved the pictures under his nose, illuminating them with her flashlight. "I'm canvassing for the police department. Have you seen this man or this little girl anywhere today?"

He spent some time checking the pictures. "This little girl, I've never seen before. We don't have children, so I don't know any kids." He looked again at the Monster, taking his time. "I met this guy at the gas station down on the highway. I remember because we were talking about gas prices and how they've gone through the roof. He told me airline tickets are going to go up because of the price of fuel." His eyes narrowed. "I remember he had a great smile, but he looks pretty grim in these pictures." He looked back up at Francesca. "Who is he, anyway?"

"We think he's the Lake Monster. This little girl went missing at the Banner Bluff Sports Day this afternoon."

His face drained of color. "Oh, my God, not another one? And this is the guy? I can't believe I actually talked to him."

Francesca wanted to move on. "Listen, I've got to keep going. Go over to the police station and tell them what you know. You might remember something useful." She pointed at the dripping candles. "You better bring a flashlight."

She left the house and continued down the street, feeling anxious and moving quickly. Luis, Colman, Kate and now this guy all recognized the Monster. But they still didn't know who he was and where he lived, or where Rosie might be.

Detective Sergeant Puchalski had hovered by the phone for the last half hour. He kept looking at the clock. He was waiting for a call back from the Vice President of UPR Airlines. Finding someone to research flights from May would have been difficult on any Saturday night, but had been damned near impossible with phone lines down all the way to Milwaukee.

Kate Marshall had given them the first ID on the criminal they sought, when she and Martin came into the station with a copy of Rosie's school picture. Kate looked terrible, ashen-faced, her eyes smudged with dark circles. She and her husband both still wore the same wet clothes. Her attention was caught by the computer screen. Kate had asked what they were looking at. They almost hadn't let her see the pictures; she was already under enough strain. She'd insisted, though, her voice raw and her hands in tight fists. She came over and bent down to see, then slowly raised her head and looked at them all.

"I know him," she said in a low voice. "He was the pilot on my flight to Paris in May. I showed his picture to all my classes. I even looked at it recently." She collapsed into a chair; her face reflecting shock and disbelief.

Once she'd regained some composure, she told them the airline and the date she'd flown to Paris. That was enough to start tracing the guy. Puchalski had finally reached someone of authority in New York, scanned the pictures they had of the Monster and emailed them. Now the airline's vice president was checking the pilots on Kate's flight and matching their ID photos to the company's ERP. Arlyne had promised to shoot the call through as soon as the airline called back. Puchalski only prayed they weren't putting things together too late.

"Call's in!" Arlyne shouted.

Puchalski picked up. "Detective Puchalski here. Any luck?"

"We've found him. The pictures match. The other pilot on that flight was a woman. Your man is Vern Schuler."

"Vern Schuler? Can you spell the last name, please?"

"S-C-H-U-L-E-R, Schuler." The airline guy's voice turned hesitant. "He's been an excellent employee and a first-class pilot. I can't believe he's involved in your murders."

Puchalski felt rushed. He didn't have time to discuss Schuler's culpability with this man. "Have you got an address?"

"Yeah, 1435 Hennessey in Banner Bluff. I just can't believe...."

Puchalski cut him off. "Thank you so much for your help, sir. I've got to get moving." He banged down the receiver and yelled down the hall. "Chief, I've got him. His name is Vern Schuler and he lives at 1435 Hennessey."

Tom came running down the hall. "Hennessey? That's the major east-west street in the Campbell condo development. Let's go!" He spotted Lewis, who had just come in from a 911. All the other officers were out on calls. "Lewis, follow us in your car," Tom shouted down the hallway. "We're heading to 1435 Hennessey. That's where our Lake Monster lives."

Several trees on Eastern and Lakeview were down. Tom cursed at the delay as they worked their way through side streets. Near the Campbell development, they turned their sirens off and went silently down Kavanagh Street to Hennessey. Number 1435 was the last house on the right. They parked in front of 1431. The streets were pitch black, though flickering lights shone fitfully in some of the homes. They got out of the squad cars and stepped behind Puchalski's vehicle, guns drawn.

"Puchalski, go around back, while Lewis and I take the front. If no one answers the door, we're going in. Be ready if he tries to escape through the back. Don't shoot unless absolutely necessary and remember that he has Rosie Marshall in there. Proceed with extreme caution."

Quietly, they moved forward.

Chapter 30
Saturday night, August 14th

At the end of Elm Street, Francesca could see the moon rising over the lake. As she turned the corner, a car came slowly down Elm towards the lake. Its headlights on low beam barely illuminated the street. What a dangerous thing to do with all the branches down, she thought. As the car drew parallel with her, she raised her flashlight and got a quick look at the occupant as he drove by. He glanced over at her, looking surprised to see someone on the sidewalk. Then he looked away.

She froze, stunned. It was him. She was sure of it. She had caught a glimpse of his face through the car window. After all the time she had spent studying his picture, she'd recognize him anywhere.

Would he break his usual pattern and go down to the beach now? It was only ten o'clock or so. Then again, maybe he thought he wouldn't get caught. Her flashlight picked up the Honda logo on the back of the car. It was impossible to tell the color in the dark.

Her mind raced as she thought about what Colman had said. This freak was irresistibly drawn to the lake. He probably had to get down there no matter what. Francesca spotted Colman and Vicky coming out of a house and called out to them, her voice raised in alarm. "I think I just saw him… the Monster… in that car." Her voice shook as she gestured toward the receding Honda. "We've got to stop him," she said as they reached her. "They won't have the beach covered yet. Come on!"

They began to run. The car had sped up and was far ahead. Then it was swallowed up in the darkness. Vicki fell behind, unable to keep up, but Francesca and Colman matched strides and ran down the street. "Call 911," Francesca yelled over her shoulder as they moved ahead. "Get them down to the beach now."

Francesca's heart was beating rhythmically. Thank God she was wearing her running shoes. She was running faster than she normally did, but Colman was pulling ahead of her. "Go ahead, you'll get there before me," she panted. "Save Rosie." She slowed a little and watched Colman sprint down the street. Maybe they should stick together. How could either of them confront this maniac alone?

She was still two blocks from the beach when she felt the laces loosen on her right shoe. She stopped and bent over to re-tie them, placing her flashlight on the ground. Moonlight bathed the street. She heard a slight sound to her left. She turned off the flashlight and listened intently; a car door shutting quietly. She heard heavy footsteps moving away, then the crunch of pebbles.

She picked up her flashlight and stood very slowly. To her left was a short street that abutted the northern ravine. A footbridge spanned it, leading to Beech Street. To the right of the bridge was a path leading down to the bottom of the chasm and eventually to a small beach. A creek ran along the bottom of the ravine and emptied into Lake Michigan.

She should probably follow Colman down to the beach, but her intuition told her to turn left towards the muffled sounds she'd heard. She followed her instincts and headed toward the ravine. Soon she reached the tall trees that cast deep shadows. She felt the darkness closing in, grabbing at her and pulling her into its depths. Her hands felt clammy and sweat ran down her back. She felt the irrational fear swelling up, filling her mind but she knew she had to keep going.

There were only three houses on this tiny street, all masked in darkness. Francesca walked quietly towards the footbridge, keeping the beam of her flashlight pointed at the ground. Ahead, behind some bushes, she saw a flash of metal. As she got closer, a car was visible. She crept closer and listened; then approached the car from the rear. She could just make out the Honda logo. Her foot hit a pebble that went sailing into the darkness and hit the pavement. Damn! She listened again and then moved slowly to the side of the car. She beamed her flashlight into the interior, half afraid of she what she might see. The car was empty.

Francesca knew the Monster was there. She could feel his presence. He was going down into the ravine. Listening, she heard footsteps below her on the pebbled pathway. She flicked off the flashlight and stood for a few seconds while her eyes adjusted to the darkness.   The moon lit the silhouettes of the swaying trees and made the winding path visible. The ravine had been spared the mini-tornadoes that had ripped through the rest of Banner Bluff, but the rain had drenched its steep walls and the path was muddy and slippery. Heart in her throat, Francesca started down.

Tom pounded again on the door of 1435 as he yelled, "Open up! Police! We're doing a neighborhood check to make sure that people are all right." He waited a moment then nodded to Lewis. Together, they rammed their shoulders into the heavy oak door. It held as if reinforced.

Tom radioed Puchalski. He spoke softly, "No one's answering here and we can't force our way in. Can you get in back there?"

"Yeah," Puchalski answered. "There are French doors. I can't see inside because he's got heavy drapes, but I'll break the glass."

A few minutes later, Tom and Lewis heard Puchalski inside, fumbling with several locks. He finally opened the front door and greeted them with his flashlight illuminating his face. "I don't think there's anyone here."

"Let's check," Tom said. "I'll head upstairs; Puchalski, you check this floor; Lewis, find your way down to the garage and the basement."

On the landing upstairs, Tom found doors leading to three bedrooms. He opened the door to his right. It was a small room that held a twin bed, carefully made up with a teddy bear sitting on the pillow. In the closet, Tom found neatly organized clothes: pilot uniforms including shirts, pants and jackets. The dresser drawers contained underwear, shorts, jeans and t-shirts. Everything was carefully folded and in neat piles. It felt like a monastic cell. The second bedroom was empty. The master bedroom contained a treadmill, a weight bench and a stack of weights. In every room the walls were white and bare. Both bathrooms were spotless and neither held a mirror.

Tom went back downstairs and met up with Puchalski. The dining room was bare of furniture; the living room had only two arm chairs and a small coffee table. There was nothing on the walls and no TV. "I checked the closets and cupboards," Puchalski said. "I found a UPR airline trench coat and a battered briefcase. There're a couple of flight manuals and a headset in the bag. The kitchen looks sterile, like nobody ever uses it. I found milk, eggs, lemonade, vitamin bottles and packets of bodybuilding supplements in the fridge. And these." He showed Tom evidence bags containing pharmaceutical bottles that bore French labels. "And get this; the bathroom has no mirror. Weird, huh?"

Lewis went through the kitchen and found the door to the garage. He walked in and saw a dark blue Dodge van. No Honda. He illuminated the interior of the van with his flashlight. The driver's section was separated from the back with a wire-mesh divider. The back section was padded with pink carpeting. A child-size pink armchair stood in the middle. He looked underneath and circled around the vehicle, then went back inside the condo and opened the door directly across the hall. Behind it was a staircase going down to the basement. For a moment he stood and listened. His nostrils filled with the faint smell of burning candles and the heavy scent of roses. Flashlight in one hand and gun in the other, he started down the stairs, hugging the wall as he made his descent. He could hear classical music; something he recognized but couldn't place. A door at the foot of the stairs was partially open. He moved slowly towards it, then kicked it open all the way. Inside, it looked like a set for a Hollywood film. He stood there and gaped.

Barnett's voice came from above. "Hey! Lewis! Is anyone down there?"

"No, but it's unbelievable, you've got to see this, Chief," Lewis shouted back.

"Get up here, now. I just got a call from Arlyne. Francesca Antonelli spotted the Monster heading for the beach."

Lewis hurried up the stairs. "Stay here and secure this place," Barnett said. Then he and Puchalski disappeared out the front door and headed for their patrol car.

Francesca breathed in the earthy smell of wet leaves and mold. As she moved forward, she reached out and grabbed branches to steady her descent. She couldn't see the man she pursued, but when she stopped she could hear his footfalls. In the distance she heard sirens careening through the streets. *Hurry*, she thought.

She slipped and slid down the path. As she tried to hurry, she skidded on mud-slick leaves. Her feet shot out in front of her and she fell down on her rump. As she scrambled up, she could hear the hoot of an owl and the sound of scurrying little feet among the bushes.

At the bottom of the ravine, the rivulet had become a rushing creek. The path was under six inches of water. The sides of the ravine were too steep to maneuver, so she stepped into the current and continued downhill towards the lake. The darkness contained its demons, but she shook off her fear and kept going.

There he was, ahead of her. She could see his back silhouetted by the full moon that hung like a crystal ball over the lake. He walked like a zombie, moving irresistibly forward. Tall and powerfully built, his long legs plunged ahead through the rushing water towards Lake Michigan. His shoulders were oddly uneven, the right shoulder dipping slightly. He carried a limp bundle. Rosie, she feared, though at this distance she couldn't be sure. Rosie, being borne like a gift to the gods.

She tried to run but tripped on a branch and fell forward into the fast-moving creek. Her right knee smashed onto a sharp stone; her left hand struck a jagged, protruding rock. She pushed herself up, water dripping from her sweatshirt and jeans. Warm blood oozed from the cut on her hand and her knee throbbed painfully, but she kept on going. She was angry, and the pain made her angrier. This man had controlled an entire town through his maniacal cravings. People had lived in fear and distrust as he slithered through their midst like a malevolent serpent. White heat pulsed through her veins.

She had to get down to the lake. Rage crowded out her primal fear of the darkness, shattering the heavy weight of her childhood terror. She felt strangely liberated by this fulminating fury.

Ahead, the Monster seemed oblivious of her as she ran and splashed through the water. When she fell, she struggled up again and kept running. She was getting closer; but he never turned to look back. He had reached the mouth of the creek where a small pool formed as the water flowed into Lake Michigan.

Terrified, furious and exhilarated, Francesca rushed forward.

He had arrived. Walking down through the creek in the ravine brought him close to his Beloved. His feet and legs were wet with the seminal liquid that the earth brought to Her; this water from the Heavens that pooled before merging into her vaginal depths. Once a month, she was full and ripe like the moon above. He carried his sacrificial lamb; the Sleeping Beauty that would bring Her full circle.

He walked through the pool and stepped into the lake, raising the drugged child towards the sky in a gesture of adoration.

Someone screamed behind him, breaking the aura. This was his *moment. He roared with anger.*

"Stop!" Francesca screamed as she sloshed through the widening creek. The Monster made an inhuman sound, like the roar of an injured animal. She ran the last few feet through the pool and into the lake as he bent forward to place Rosie in the water.

Francesca leaped forward and grabbed him around the shoulders, pulling on his arms and kicking. He dropped Rosie in the shallows and turned to knock Francesca off his back, swinging his arms and slamming her into the lake. She got up unsteadily, water dripping down her face. Her head was spinning and her legs were shaking. She darted forward, dodging his swinging arms, trying to reach Rosie. She felt hands around her neck, pressing her throat and shoving her down into the shallow water. She pushed upward against the sand as the Monster's heavy body came forcefully down on top of her.

Another loud crash came, another voice shouted. The Monster rolled off of her. Francesca got up on all fours and looked around. Another figure grappled with the Monster. She stood unsteadily and flailed through the water toward the little girl. Behind her, she heard the violent sounds of thrashing bodies. She reached down and pulled Rosie from the lake. She wasn't sure that the child was breathing. Francesca pounded her on the back and then threw the child head down over her shoulder. Rosie began to cough, spitting up water.

Francesca was reliving the morning in May that haunted her dreams. Rosie was dead weight in her arms. She didn't wake up or respond to Francesca's shouts, but she seemed to be breathing as she vomited up water. Francesca turned back towards the shore, struggling under the burden.

Ahead of her, two bodies wrestled in the shallow water. The Monster was holding his adversary under the surface, hands around his neck. Then the Monster screamed and toppled backwards.

Colman rose unsteadily from the water. He plunged forward and grabbed the Monster's arm, twisting it and then leaping forward to cover the man with his body.

Light caught her eye, cutting through the blackness. Coming over the boulders from the public beach and racing across the sand, she saw policemen with flashlights and guns raised. Several officers splashed into the lake and pulled the wrestlers apart. There was a mad scramble and a cacophony of shouts. Francesca kept going toward the shore, Rosie over her shoulder. Finally, she reached the beach and looked back. Four officers were wrestling with the Monster. As she watched, they managed to subdue him and handcuff him. He fought them all the way as they dragged him to shore. He was crying and thrashing. "I won't go down there. You will not take me down there!"

Detective Puchalski waded into the lake towards Colman, who was seated in the water fighting for breath. Puchalski bent down and helped him stand. He wrapped an arm around Colman's waist, leaned in and led him to shore. Colman, clearly in shock, was still trembling from the struggle. "Are you all right?" Puchalski asked. Colman nodded, unable to respond. "You did a fine thing tonight, you saved a little girl's life."

Francesca kept pounding Rosie's back as the little girl coughed and gasped for breath. Tears of relief streamed down Francesca's face. Rosie would be all right. Rosie would live. She felt a hand on her arm, turned to find Tom Barnett beside her. He took her elbow, led her over to a large boulder and helped her sit down. Then he lifted Rosie from her shoulder and placed her in Francesca's arms. She held the little girl tightly against her chest.

"The paramedics will be here soon. Are you all right? Is Rose Marie all right?"

"We're going to be fine, Tom. Everything is going to be fine."

He looked down at the sleeping child cradled in Francesca's arms. Rosie's breathing was even, but she was shivering in the sopping pink princess gown. Francesca pulled her closer. "You know what the best thing is?" she murmured.

"What?" Tom said softly.

"She's not going to remember any of this."

He nodded. "Hopefully we'll all be able to put it behind us someday."

Francesca looked out across the lake. The water was calm. In the distance were massive cloud banks, the remnants of the storm that had moved east across Lake Michigan.

Epilogue

Phone Conversation: September 8th, 20__

"Now, Emma, I heard he swallowed a bunch of Prozac pills and washed it down with a bottle of gin. You know, his wife and daughter have left him and his son has got his own place in town. He's lost everything: his house, those fancy cars and that showy boat. But I think he should pay for his crimes. I want him to suffer. Suicide is too easy. Don't you think?"

(silence ... click)

"Hello? Emma? Emma? Are you there?"

Email message: November 17th, 20__

Tom—Thank you for the invitation. I would love to have Thanksgiving dinner at your house and meet your sister. Tell me what I can bring!

See you Friday!

Francesca

The Banner Bee
December 8th, 20___

Last night the North Shore Art Consortium agreed to buy the Smithfield estate. The interior will be used to foster the arts. There will be classes in everything from painting to pottery to glass blowing. The ballroom will be used as an art gallery and the intimate theatre will house the Thackeray Thespians. Outside, the terraced gardens will be cultivated by the Garden League. A variety of flower and vegetable gardens will serve as a learning environment for adults and children alike.

The Banner Bee
January 5th, 20___

The Well-wisher has struck again. Yesterday morning, Colman Canfield, 19, of Banner Bluff received a smooth white envelope printed with his name. Inside were a letter and a check for $8,000! In the letter, our kindly local benefactor expressed his wish to support Colman's plan to enroll in the County Community College this semester.

Colman is a hard-working young man who supports himself with a job at Hero's Market and volunteers at the West Haven Behavioral Clinic. He lives in a room above Churchill's restaurant. Dr. Hanson, director of the clinic, says that Colman has been invaluable working with young people afflicted by alcohol and drug addictions: "Colman is an admirable young man who understands our patients and serves as a role model and friend."

Mr. Canfield is also an assistant coach with the Fun Run After-school Club, which seeks to encourage self-confidence in young teenagers. Coach Jordan says, "Colman is a dependable young man and the kids love him."

The staff of the *Banner Bee* is thrilled that Colman will be able to attend college this spring. Mr. Canfield would like to pursue a career in sports medicine. He wants his benefactor to know that he is grateful for the money and that he will work hard to be deserving of the Well-wisher's trust and support.

The Banner Bee
February 1st, 20__

Vern Schuler, the alleged killer of Lilly Lawrence and Corinne Casey, has been ruled mentally unfit to stand trial and has been sent to a high-security mental hospital in Sedona, Illinois. According to Lake County District Attorney Ben Johnson, "The psychiatrist's assessment of Schuler's mental state provided convincing evidence that he did not have a rational and factual understanding of the charges. It also indicated he would be unable to communicate with his attorney. He remains prone to hallucinations, barking, growling and other nonsensical noises, making him mentally unfit to stand trial."

Schuler was charged in the kidnapping and drowning of Lilly and Corinne on August, 16th, 20__.